MW01004661

─────────── legend ───────────
1 Dollarwise   5 Library   9 Marcie's House
2 Riis Beach   6 White Ship   10 Time Tunnel
3 House of ? ? ?   7 Northwood   11 Gig's Lover
4 Apt. on Franklin   8 Kellogg's

A/S/L

ALSO BY THE AUTHOR

The Dream of Doctor Bantam

The Black Emerald

We're Still Here: An All-Trans Comics Anthology

Summer Fun

A/S/L

Jeanne Thornton

SOHO

Published by Soho Press, Inc.
227 W 17th Street
New York, NY 10011
www.sohopress.com

Library of Congress Cataloging-in-Publication Data

Names: Thornton, Jeanne, author.
Title: A/S/L / Jeanne Thornton.
Description: New York, NY : Soho, 2025.
Identifiers: LCCN 2024049018

ISBN 978-1-64129-604-5
eISBN 978-1-64129-605-2

Subjects: LCSH: Video games—Fiction. | LCGFT: Queer fiction. | Novels.
Classification: LCC PS3620.H7837 A85 2025 | DDC 813/.6—dc23/
eng/20241022
LC record available at https://lccn.loc.gov/2024049018

Interior design by Janine Agro

Printed in the United States of America

10 9 8 7 6 5 4 3 2 1

EU Responsible Person (for authorities only)
eucomply OÜ
Pärnu mnt 139b-14
11317 Tallinn, Estonia
hello@eucompliancepartner.com
www.eucompliancepartner.com

To draco and flimsy, and also to vin.
Wherever you are, I hope this meets your approval just a little;
I hope you think this is just a little cool.

Out of the One comes Two, out of Two comes Three, and from the Third comes the One as the Fourth.

—Marie-Louise von Franz

But there are worlds we can travel to lovingly, and traveling to them is part of loving at least some of their inhabitants . . . by traveling to their "world" we can understand what it is to be them and what it is to be ourselves in their eyes.

—María Lugones

It's like this train. It can only go where its tracks take it.

—Cloud Strife

A/S/L

readme.1st

```
     0123456789ABCDEF          0123456789ABCDEF
00   ☺☻♥♦♣♠•◘○◙♂♀♪♫☼  01    ►◄↕‼¶§▬↨↑↓→←∟↔▲▼
02    !"#$%&'()*+,-./  03    0123456789:;<=>?
04   @ABCDEFGHIJKLMNO  05    PQRSTUVWXYZ[\]^_
06   `abcdefghijklmno  07    pqrstuvwxyz{|}~⌂
08   ÇüéâäàåçêëèïîìÄÅ  09    ÉæÆôöòûùÿÖÜ¢£¥₧ƒ
10   áíóúñÑªº¿⌐¬½¼¡«»  11    ░▒▓│┤╡╢╖╕╣║╗╝╜╛┐
12   └┴┬├─┼╞╟╚╔╩╦╠═╬╧  13    ╨╤╥╙╘╒╓╫╪┘┌█▄▌▐▀
14   αβΓπΣσµτΦΘΩδ∞φε∩  15    ≡±≥≤⌠⌡÷≈°∙·√ⁿ²■
```

DIRECTIONS:
Multiply the row number by 16.
Add it to the column number.
Type #char [result] into the editor
   to become that character.

USEFUL RESULTS
1, 2, 3-6, 32, 65, 97, 176-178, 219.

Three teenagers—Abraxa, Sash, Lilith—and one of them dreams of computers. In the dream the teenager is typing, the sky dark and a candle burning on the desk: blue light, red light, sandy brown hair concealed in a green hoodie with the name of a surf shop. Beside the teenager is a mug of soda, black and ninetiesish and advertising a radio station over whose frequency the teenager has painted a pentagram in red nail polish, a mug that's long gone flat, but from which the teenager sips. The candle is the holder for a tea light, which in the dream seems to burn forever. Dreaming, the teenager programs while the candle burns forever.

The teenager is using the computer to make a mosaic. The keyboard chooses colors, and each click places a tile. Click: cyan, click: green, click coral, click violet. The teenager is drawing an ocean. How did they not realize this before? They are drawing an ocean and a shore. They are drawing a woman standing on the shore in a black dress: click gray, click silver, click black. Black on a computer is no tiles at all: no pixels, just dark, at rest.

The woman in the mosaic is looking into the screen. If the teenager continues to click, the woman will become more and more real. She will become so real that she can move—she

will turn around—the teenager will see her face. The teenager
yearns for this. And yet in the moment the teenager sees her
face, something will come to a stop.

The teenager gets up; they don't want to finish the mosaic
yet. They want to see the ocean, for real. With the speed of
dreams, they are in their father's car, driving to the ocean. (Did
they steal it? Yes, they probably stole it: they've done it before;
their shitty school friends came over to watch horror movies
and play Super Nintendo games and drink punch made from
powder, sugar, stolen vodka; the father puts his earplugs in;
everything's allowed.) The teenager is driving a stolen car, the
candle burning on the dashboard. Travis Dark is playing on cassette. The houses of Venice, California, are bright.

The teenager parks the car on the sand. When they step out
of the car, the tide has already risen: sand covers their bare feet,
seawater washes it away. They walk, step by squishing step.
All the colors of the mosaic are in the ocean, bright as noon,
except the sky is void, erased. No one else is on this beach.

The teenager thinks about Lilith and Sash, whom the teenager has never met, except online, except in dreams.

Then the teenager places the candle in the sand, and the surf
comes up to meet it, and water starts to flow between candle
and sand. It'll drown—or no, the wind will blow it out. But
then the tide rises—the surf comes in stronger—and the candle,
rather than drowning, floats.

The teenager on the sand watches the candle float away. The
earth is curved, so certainly the fire will disappear soon behind
the horizon. But it doesn't. Instead, as it grows distant, it rises,
rises until it joins the stars, which are just now waking up.

1. Querent

The following is an FAQ for *Saga of the Sorceress*, forthcoming from the video game corporation Invocation LLC in 1998. You are a teenage girl, and you will always believe in your dreams, and that is why your video game will be released in 1998. Everything depends on this.

Here are some technical notes on the world of *Saga of the Sorceress*. The game is constructed in the CraftQ adventure game editor, available as shareware from Capitol Computer Programmers and widely distributed on Internet networks such as America Online. (This is where you—Sash—and your friends, the other two stakeholders of Invocation LLC, all independently downloaded it. You found it while searching for fan art from the Mystic Knights video game series; you changed your life.)

All the objects in a CraftQ game like *Saga of the Sorceress* are constructed from fixed-width text. Think of a typewriter, the letter *I* taking up the same horizontal space as the *W*. CraftQ uses the widely adopted fixed-width text standard ASCII, which contains 256 total characters. The first thirty-two ASCII values are normally invisible, reserved for program instructions, but

CraftQ displays them as symbols. On many computers, char no. 2 is how a program represents the start of a text file. In a CraftQ game, however, char 2 renders as a smiley face. Char 2 is the CraftQ convention for representing a human being.

Each of the 256 ASCII text characters can appear in one of sixteen basic colors: white, cyan, violet, green, red, blue, and so on. A game designer can combine two colors, one in the foreground and one in the background, to produce subtle, even painterly effects. (The player is traditionally shown as a char 2 smiley face, white text, blue background.) A CraftQ game is divided into screens called ROOMs, and each ROOM is arranged in eighty columns and twenty-five rows of characters.

A typical CraftQ room looks like this:

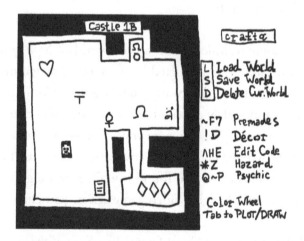

A typical CraftQ room looks horrible. It doesn't look like a game. Text mode is for the DOS prompt, for the point-of-sale computers you once saw at your father's postal station while waiting for him to finish work. (Your parents have only recently begun to trust you to walk home alone: *Anything might*

happen, your mother tells you. *The last thing I need is you getting killed*.) Text mode is for banks, cash register displays, video store customer account systems. It's absurd to make a game in text mode. Text mode was never meant for games. Text mode graphics were out of date even when CraftQ was first released, around the same time as Microsoft Windows 3.1. The people who programmed CraftQ used text mode because they had no other choice. They wanted to make games, and text mode was the tool at hand for that.

To a pioneer, a tool is anything you already own. To a pioneer, a tool is always beautiful. You understand that. When you see text mode now, you don't see a cash register. You see color—you see frescoes, mosaics—you see your future, all mapped out.

When you're making a CraftQ game, you are a body at a computer. Teenage body—gravity heavier on you now than before—squinting in the Brooklyn streetlight that comes through your living room window, once your mother's asleep and you've moved aside the heavy curtains she uses to seal in the space: *prying eyes, we don't need them to see our business.* Your cup of water with ice, which you keep on the floor so as not to spill on the keyboard. A notebook at your wrist for observations, lists of instructions. Good posture, wrists and fingers curved as if at a piano. Clarity of mind comes from good form. A body is a filter, the one you sadly need in order to make a CraftQ game. Keep the filter clear. Try to forget its presence.

Yet when you play a CraftQ game, you're not a body anymore—you're not Sash—you're not anyone. You're whatever the game says you are. You're ASCII text, information: a smiley face, char 2, white on navy. And when you step in any of four directions, using the arrow keys on the keyboard of your aging PC—150 MHz burning at 166 overclock, fan blades whipping the air to cool the electric fire—the PC sound card renders a whispery tick tick tick.

I'm talking about *you* here, and after, because you are the player in a game. A game is an experience that happens to you.

A typical CraftQ game can contain anywhere from one to almost ninety ROOMs full of friends, treasures, puzzles, or enemies. There are four default enemies, which the in-game documentation describes thus:

♥ WITCHES: They fire magic seduction spells at you, but don't be fooled!
♣ PYROS: They try to use their burning bodies to damage you. Who do they work for?
♦ GOLDMEN: Their golden armor is so tough, it takes multiple attacks to bring them down!
♠ KILLERS: The most dangerous of all. Are they even human?

There are other default objects, according to the in-game documentation: BLOCKS, TNTS, PYRAMID CIRCUITS, PARALYZERS, CLOCK SPINNERS, COUNTERCLOCK SPINNERS, GREENTEETHS, ZAPS, RAYS, COLLEC-TORS, GENDERSWAPS, ICE SLIDES, HYPNOSPIRALS, ILLUSION ZONES. All of these are useless to you. The CraftQ online community, in the seven long years since the initial release of CraftQ in 1991, has long since evolved beyond using the default objects and enemies. Seven years of teenagers just like you, all releasing games, playing games, writing games that respond to games: themes have evolved, fads, practices. One teenager released a whole game of dos and don'ts when programming in CraftQ: don't use the default objects near the top of the list. It's social death to use the default objects.

The themes of the games evolved, too: early games about solving puzzles in ancient pyramids and spooky islands giving way to games with real diversity of genre. The top CraftQ games of 1998, were you to really sit down and make a list (you've done this, but not recently; a flaw in your practice?) satirize banal TV shows, contain scenes of shocking and boundary-pushing graphic violence, explore modern sexuality. Sometimes, when you are lying in your bed unable to sleep, you think about analogies for the CraftQ scene in the larger tradition of human culture. Popular music: once the measure of a great performer was their ability to cover existing folk standards, yet sometime in the 1960s, individual songwriting became the norm. Visual art: once subject matter was determined by the church, later by the soul. Movies in the 1950s used to be boring studio productions, antiseptic and geared to the lowest common denominator; now, in the 1990s, they explore morally complex themes. There is sex in the movies—there is sometimes queerness.

No, *Saga of the Sorceress* will not use the default objects. You've explained this to your friends and coworkers. It will be programmed and designed from scratch, written with the skill of a morally complex film, illustrated in painterly ASCII textmode. It will be the greatest CraftQ game anyone has ever seen, the top of every list. When you can't sleep, you can always think about just how great it is going to be.

Here's the promotional flyer for *Saga of the Sorceress* you wrote and posted to the Invocation LLC website on GeoCities, so all the other teenagers who make CraftQ games (or really anyone in the world!) can see it:

- a truly massive craftq world (three fully stocked 32K .qek files, connected by a unique password system)
- over 120+ intricate cutscenes of hi-definition ASCII art
- over twenty distinct and "living" dungeons to explore
- full rpg combat with *true* random battle
- robust magic system with 512 different spell effects, each based on well-researched occult principles
- a 55-#song soundtrack
- dynamic "town building" minigame: construct the rebel city of northwood abbey as you desire (whether that's helping the unfortunate or developing your mining and mana resources to unleash devastating attacks)

It's easy to write bullet points like these; lots of teenage CraftQ corporations do it. It's easy to promise, harder to deliver: something your mother likes to say about her students, something she used to say about you. But you learned to deliver: got your grades up, stopped hyperventilating before tests, stopped asking questions and making excuses, stopped being a problem. And this is the difference between you and these other corporations, the quality that sets you apart. You've worked it all out, in your sleepless nights: schedules, divisions of labor, approvals rounds and sign-offs. Reasonable delivery dates—high goals—a solid plan—and friends, real friends, to help you with all of it.

■ ■ ■

Tonight, your schedule has you reviewing a series of ROOMs your level designer made. Your goal is to find the flaws and correct them.

The ROOMs form a level from the early part of the game, a dungeon-in-progress called the Bell Prix Sewers. Reflect on this moment in the story of the game: the sorceress of the title—the player's character, represented by ASCII char 2, white on blue—still a teenager, has been exiled from her village by the wizards of the malevolent "System D." (System D is the system that controls everything.) The player must lead the sorceress through the sewers to their academy, which is where she can steal a magic lantern of protection. The dungeon represents a restriction, a challenge, before the player receives her reward. Gathering the magic lantern is the first stage in the work of founding the rebel city of Northwood Abbey, which will dominate the rest of the plot. If this dungeon fails to come together, everything else fails with it. You must not allow your level designer to fail.

Load the ROOMs from your friend in the CraftQ editor's debug mode to begin your review. Find yourself in a narrow lime tunnelway. The artwork, though right now a crude yellow for-placement-only blockout, you know will one day be gorgeous when your artist completes it: gradient blends of brown, yellow, and green, ASCII chars 219 plus 176 through 178, inclusive. Savvy CraftQ artists know how to blend the ASCII extended characters into a bright mosaic, one that suggests far more colors than the underlying code permits. A skillful blend sparks the player's imagination. Yuck, she will say to herself. Is that sewer water trickling past my feet? Is there air to breathe in this place? Have I been trapped in here my whole life?

Continue to test the blocked-out dungeon: there are flaws here, and you must find them. Travel east, down the tunnel, toward the wizard academy. The tunnel is tight: your level designer has done a very good job implementing the principle of Ecology by using the visual limitations of the CraftQ engine to create a sense of claustrophobia and tension. You'll have to do some tricky maneuvering to get through here. (Remember, tap up, down, left, right on the keyboard to move; hold SHIFT + direction to attack.) There are no enemies here yet, but the tightness of the tunnel is a kind of enemy, too. Add a note to your to-do list: *tell a: simple enemies here only once l revises blockout.* And another, to yourself: *add treasure box: health restorative—principle of interactivity.* Pacing is key in dungeon design: do not give your player more than they can bear.

Once through the tunnel, descend the mossy staircase (char 240) to floor 2B. The staircase is another smart choice your level designer has made in line with the principle of Ecology. You're using a sewer system to break into a secret enclave of genocidal wizards: it is both logical and thematically appropriate to travel down first, into the heart of the earth, before you go up. So far, the level designer hasn't made any mistakes that you can see. But remain vigilant: there are many dungeon floors ahead.

Sometimes it's hard to sleep, thinking of how good your game is going to be. Sometimes you can't believe how lucky you are to have been born when you were, to be a teenager right now in the year 1998, to have found your way to CraftQ: a tool that allows anyone, even teenagers in the late 1990s, to make interactive video games. You are here, present at the adolescence of what you know will be the dominant art form of the twenty-first century. You and your friends have already taken the first step: you've created a successful video game corporation, just like The Critical Hit in Tokyo, the publisher and developer of the Mystic Knights games, your inspiration and model.

All the information you have about The Critical Hit comes from two sources. One is the credits at the end of each Mystic Knights game, which, no matter how many dozens of employees come and go, always contain the classic five names:

Char & Battle GFX   *R. Omori*
Sound Design   *T. Sato*
Dungeon Planning   *S. Suisha*
Scenario + Direction *Oshiro99*

Programmed by MELKIOR

The other source of information is an interview in a video game magazine you convinced a friend at school to show you over lunch and never actually returned. The interview, celebrating the upcoming release of the new *Mystic Knights V*, the first in the series on the brand-new Sony PlayStation, was short and you suspect poorly translated. But it gave some context, at least a whiff of the early days of RPG design. The story has the contours of legend, including a visionary hero: Oshiro99, inveterate gambler, sometime actor, political radical expelled from Tokyo University who spent his formative years living with a band in some kind of intentional community before being hired, through nepotism, by a dying video game studio called The Critical Hit. The company's products have been failing; bankruptcy and closure are imminent. Oshiro99, a Dungeons & Dragons fan, took his chance: gathered and trained his staff of novices to make a new kind of RPG, one about a team who'd become greater than any one hero might. The game would have state-of-the-art graphics and RPG combat design that blended the best of *Dragon Quest, Wizardry, Ultima,* all the genre standards. *All for one:* this would be The Critical Hit's motto and standard. The first brutally hard Mystic Knights game was the result. The sales were the proof.

For many sleepless nights you've imagined what it must have been like in The Critical Hit's office in those early days. The programmer, a Filipino exchange student and evangelical Christian convert operating under the alias MELKIOR, programming more by passion than attention (resulting in the infamous bugs of the early games, but also ambitious combinatorial effects no other studio dared attempt). The artist R. Omori, older than the rest at forty and with a complicated sadness in his past—you imagine an exile, a family lost—that led to his having answered the unknown Oshiro99's employment ad, frowning over his watercolors and lightbox as he transferred sensitive illustrations of bridges, castles, eerie crystalline caverns to his graph paper in preparation to convert the art into assembly-ready code. The musician T. Sato, then a high-strung teenage refugee from the piano conservatory, starving and haunted as he fused melodic invention and ambience. The level designer, S. Suisha, (SuFish, per the credits of the first two games), industry newcomer and cipher, an oddity not merely due to her gender in the misogynist corporate culture of 1980s computer entertainment, her designs organic, recondite, thoughtful, considerate, and often startling, considered by many (certainly by you) to be the secret heart of the games. (It's from SuFish's levels that you generalized the principles of Thereness, which will set the game you and your friends design apart from your teenage peers.) And of course the leader, Oshiro99: perched at his desk, smoking and rolling a d20 for relaxation as he studied the tomes of occult lore, political theory, and obscure religious symbolism that informed his narratives, sometimes strolling the room to adjust the others' work toward a common vision. A quiet trust, a partnership in silence.

You can imagine people objecting to your taking inspiration from this. But you're teenagers, people might say. Those people were professionals with capital financing, neither of which describes you and your friends. You don't have time for small-minded doubters. There's no logical reason you should fail. You have CraftQ, for one: teenagers are already using it to make video games, perhaps rough in execution, but pure in spirit. All right then, people allow, but The Critical Hit had five people on staff to perform the only jobs you need to make a video game. There was a writer: someone to posit what the game will be and mean. A level designer: someone to use the principles of Thereness to create the receptacle of space through which you, the player, will walk. And of course, artists, musicians, programmers: the ones who make it beautiful, emotionally affecting, and playable without errors on a modern electronic system.

Your company, Invocation LLC, has only three people to cover these five jobs. But you've thought of this. One of your friends—Abraxa—is brilliant and can do three jobs at once. And then there is your other friend. You are working closely with your other friend. Your other friend has potential, and part of being a good leader is learning not to turn potential away. A good leader learns how to cultivate it, to shape it.

Floor 2B starts less promisingly: right away your level designer has put you into a crude switchback maze. It alternates, north, south, north, south, with some alcoves where treasure boxes are probably meant to go. You suppose you're expected to write flavor text for this. A maze is not good design: it violates Ecology (why would someone build it?), Interactivity (the interaction is annoying), Enticement (you're not enticed.) Add it to your notes: *2B—inappropriate maze.* The first flaw you've discovered tonight. There will be more; you're certain of it. Mistakes are the dungeons of reality: treasures wait at the end for those brave enough to confront.

For now, continue through the inappropriate maze, tick tick tick-ing north and south, imagining what it must feel like to be the sorceress: the main character of this video game, the character your smiley face represents. Imagine the reek and slosh of sewer waste around your knees as it seeps into the hem of your violet skirts. You have been exiled from your cursed village—you are the inheritor of overwhelming magic you are only beginning to learn to control. You do not deserve to be in this sewer, and so you'll push through it.

This is how you realized that your dream had to take the form of a video game. You were playing *Super Mystic Knights 3*, the first in the Mystic Knights series to appear on the Super Nintendo. It was old even when you played it, years stale; you coveted a Super Nintendo for so long before your father bought it for you, very much over your mother's objections. He found it at one of the secondhand electronics stores where he probably still picks up his music equipment; it was a deal he couldn't refuse. The secondhand store owner even threw in a sampling of games, most of which are not relevant, one of which was *Super Mystic Knights 3*.

Super Mystic Knights 3, unlike the game you are now making with your friends, had actual pixel graphics: brilliant 320 × 240 resolution, 16.7 million possible colors. You were holding a controller in your hand; you were looking through the window of the ancient Trinitron at a castle room, your vantage point high above it, as if looking down on the game's characters from a tall building: their world reduced to two dimensions. The paladin Philippe, at the direction of his liege lord—later revealed to be acting at the direction of duplicitous wizards—has just attacked an innocent village, slain their defenders, stolen an enchanted scepter on which the fate of the world may depend. Innovatively for its time, Oshiro99 here made the choice to cast the player in the role of the paladin for this opening: in other words, it's you who, as if sleepwalking, are forced to commit these atrocities. You, the paladin, attack the village. You slay the defenders. You lay hands on the scepter. But then, as you're walking out of the room with your prize, the elder of the village steps forward. *Why are you doing this?* He asks you that. And you bow your head.

You can still see the little pixel sprite now, bowing his head. In that bow, you realized something deep and mysterious: the little character you were controlling, the you in the screen, this character is thinking. This character is evaluating his actions. This character is regretting them, in ways that will lead to change. And this means the character is a real person, as real and alive as you.

Someone had scripted this scene. Someone had to draw those pixels; someone had to write the code that made the paladin bow his head. Someone built that whole interactive world, one that contained a soul that hid its face, yet revealed itself in the act of hiding. And if someone did it, you could do it, too.

At last, you and your char 2 sorceress turn the corner out of the maze to find that the passage splits into three. To proceed, you will have to choose one route, leaving the others behind. A game is a dance between player and level designer: What cues has the level designer given you here? The level designer has given you nothing. There's no way to know which path is right.

Is this good level design or bad level design? The player, faced with this level, will feel anxiety over not having enough information. That anxiety causes the player to become invested: the design begins to work. This is not a flaw, you decide. This is Enticement—this is still good work.

For now, ignore the fork north, ignore the fork south. Continue east, which is the logical direction: the path directly through the sewers to the wizard academy, your goal. That's what the sorceress *would* do, so as the player, that's what you'll do, too.

CraftQ is full of teenagers making games like the one you're testing now. Dozens of teenagers just like the three of you gather to chat on IRC every night to brag about the astonishing games they're making, most of which you already know will never be released. So why are you and your friends different? Why are you and your friends different. This is why you're different. The reasons are obvious. Because you're thorough: that's one of the reasons. And because you have a vision that will see you through. Your vision is about shame, and learning not to be ashamed, about being stronger than wizards, about—you can't describe what it's about. But you know that it's big, as big as all your feelings about it. You can't describe it because the game will be the description. Finish the game and the statement is made.

You're so fortunate to have a vision and friends to help you carry it out. There is a purity to the connection between you and your friends. The video game corporation the three of you comprise is not about money. It would be absurd to release a CraftQ game for money: some have tried, and are quickly laughed off the forums. CraftQ is about bigger things than money. If a friendship is going to last, it needs to have a common purpose, and your corporation is that. You're pretty sure you understand the truth of friendship better than other people: this is why it's so hard for you to make friends. You've thought a lot about your dream, which means it will happen exactly as you've thought.

The path east quickly becomes another up-and-down maze. What is your level designer doing here? Write it in your notebook: *2B—second inappropriate maze. Why?* The path east, the direct road, is the most logical, and therefore the one most players will take. If your level designer was good, the east path would terminate quickly, either in a dead end or a treasure chest. That way the player can cross it off her list and continue traversing the decision tree, pursuing her sense of Enticement. Maybe she will go north, or maybe she will go south. It's up to her, the energy built up from her frustrated choice driving engagement. This will, in turn, create a feeling of accomplishment once the level is cleared. That's what a good designer would do. But your designer just sends you into a maze. No, worse than a maze: because the yellow walls that surround you, framing your movement, suddenly stop. You're no longer in a maze at all: you're in nothing. There's no char 240 staircase down to floor 3B, just black screen, the absence of text altogether.

You're outside of the level. There is no Thereness—there is no design at all. The ROOMs your level designer sent you are incomplete. This, and you haven't heard from them now in over a week. And this game has to be released in 1998, and 1998 is halfway over, and here you are, outside the level, in the dark.

In the first page of your notebook, you drew the design that will carry your two friends with you into the future. It looks like this:

This is your corporate logo: a candle you'll light, and the three of you gathered around it. Believe in that. Don't think about the homework you didn't do. *I'll take the zero, Mr. Papazian*, you'll say to your teacher when he asks for the homework you didn't do tonight. He'll be angry; let him be. One day, after you're discovered—after the work you and your friends have been doing here silently is rewarded, as all good work will be, after you're in charge of a studio of your own, after you've met SuFish and Oshiro99 and the rest of The Critical Hit and they've told you how proud they are of you, and you have a house on a mountain with a spire and stained glass and plants and clouds, a place where you can think, where you can work—none of this is going to matter. This small room, this TV laughing through the wall, this tiredness. One day, false things will fall away.

Believe in that as you creep, sleepless, out of the window unit's cool inverse umbra and enter the summer heat spaces, in transit to the bathroom, hoping no one hears you. Resist thoughts, intruding, from the day: the test at school you don't need to study for, questions of the lunch table, the forging of a permission slip. Resist turning on the light, which is also wired to a loud fan; pee in silence. Resist looking in the mirror as you wash your hands, spiral of bulk yellow soap on your palm. But you catch a glimpse of your body. Blur out. Forget it.

Don't think about how great the work will be when it's done. Don't think about the last time you talked to your friend. The time that you know, because you know you live in a rational world where dreams are real and where you will always believe in them, is not the last time you will ever speak to your friend. Don't think of that now. Instead: sneak back to your room, sneak back to the computer your father brought home from work at the post office and never brought back. Its fans grind—and as you sign onto your ISP, the scream of a 28.8 modem comes—and you feel your body disappear. False things fall away, and you know where your soul will go. And you know you will find what you need.

2. The Abyss

<irc.austnet.net, channel #teengoetia, 2212 PDT 1998 21 Jun>

* sash joined #teengoetia

* azimuth set topic at 0342 PDT 1998 5 Jun to <AbRaXaS>
how glorious it is and yet how painful to be an exceptio-
asdfnnsddn lmfao

<BarthesWasWrong> I mean I guess the song is good!
The distorted microphone is just not my thing?

<RyanThomp-san> sash!!!

<NecroPizza> okay so like, a, YOU'RE AN ASSHOLE, and
b, your friend is WRONG

<NecroPizza> Smashing Pumpkins was kinda always a
weird studio band?

<NecroPizza> SASH

<BarthesWasWrong> Sash!!!!!1

<PhilippeDark> Sash! Always a pleasure ^_^

<MazeRyder> Hail, m'lady, and merry meetings to you!

* MazeRyder tips his tall hat

<sash> hello.

<useless_x> whoa, like, it's sash, hyuck hyuck

<reficul> hi sash

* apollyon nods gravely

<azimuth> hi sash! you're just in time for the next round of
. . . PORNO PASSWORD

<sash> has anyone seen lilith. i need to talk to him.

<reficul> no

<sash> or abraxas.

<RyanThomp-san> They haven't been here that I've seen?

<MazeRyder> I saw them! Those hideous visages! In the
mirror! They're . . . they're . . . me!!!

<azimuth> okay everyone ready for the CLUEZ
:DDDDDDD ????

<NecroPizza> NO

<NecroPizza> NO ONE LIKES THIS GAME

<RyanThomp-san> Ha ha ha, I like it!

<NecroPizza> EVERYONE HATES IT, AND YOU

<NecroPizza> EVERYONE ALSO HATES YOU, RYAN

<reficul> lol

<BarthesWasWrong> lol

<apollyon> i don't think there's anything wrong with the
game.

<RyanThomp-san> Ha ha

<NecroPizza> YOU WOULDN'T

<sash> so no one has seen lilith or abraxas is what i'm
hearing?

<useless_x> hahaha, welps, *i'm* definitely into porno
password, i like 'em titties n'stuff! B-O

<apollyon> it's sexuality. it's healthy. are you a prude?

<NecroPizza> uh no i'm not a prude. i just think this game
is for idiots.

<NecroPizza> ARE YOU AN IDIOT

* RyanThomp-san rolls his eyes at useless_x

<azimuth> okay TOO BAD HATERZ here comes the clue!
<PhilippeDark> Sash, I hope it's okay we're playing this
    game. ^_^
<apollyon> i'm not an idiot. are you? there are tests.
<sash> PhilippeDark: why would you ask that?
<sash> because i'm a girl, and girls supposedly don't
    appreciate sexuality?
<NecroPizza> uh, i guess i haven't been tested for being
    an idiot, no. why would you ask me that.
<NecroPizza> i get fs in class a lot for not turning shit in.
<NecroPizza> does that meet your standards for idiot y/n
<PhilippeDark> sash: Most girls don't, no! ^_^
<useless_x> mmmmkay sash! what's it like to look at tits
    when you HAVE tits? like, inquiring minds want to know! :o
<BarthesWasWrong> Perhaps *no one* is an idiot!
<sash> useless_x: it isn't different.
<NecroPizza> SHUT UP BARTHES YOU'RE THE TRUE
    IDIOT HERE METHINKS
<NecroPizza> EXCEPT APOLLYON WHO IS ALSO A
    DUMBASS
<reficul> lol whats the difference between an idiot and a
    dumbass
<NecroPizza> YOU'LL HAVE TO ASK APOLLYON ABOUT
    THAT, GIVEN HIS LIVED EXPERIENCE WITH BOTH
    THESE DIVERSE IDENTITIES
* apollyon 's hands gesture. a slow trickle of a grin creeps
    up apollyon 's features as the eldritch syllables form.
    "ph'nglui mglw'nafh Cthulhu R'lyeh wgah'nagl fhtagn . . ."
<NecroPizza> um, what are you even typing
<PhilippeDark> useless: That's a pretty rude question, no?
    ^_^

<apollyon> clearly you're not familiar with the cthulu
   mythos.

<apollyon> that's perhaps for the best.

<sash> philippedark: please don't help

* apollyon was kicked from #teengoetia by NecroPizza
   (CLEARLY NOT)

* apollyon joined #teengoetia

<apollyon> i'm done.

* apollyon left #teengoetia

<NecroPizza> GOOD RIDDANCE TO BAD RUBBISH, I SAY

<reficul> lol

<NecroPizza> um, philippe, stop trying to hit on sash,
   she's like . . . gay?

<NecroPizza> gay = not you

<PhilippeDark> We're just talking. ^_^

<sash> boys are practice.

<sash> but what i'd prefer to talk about is lilith. lilith's
   whereabouts, whether any of you have seen lilith.

<sash> can anyone help me with this in a practical
   way.

<sash> lilith and i have to talk about our game.

<sash> we have to talk about saga of the sorceress.

* MazeRyder is now known as xLilithx

<reficul> lol

<BarthesWasWrong> Oh whoa, eerie

<xLilithx> uh, hi! it's me, lilith! :/

<sash> changing nicknames. pretending to be other
   people. extremely mature.

<xLilithx> sorry about whatever i did! :/

<NecroPizza> lol

<reficul> lol

<azimuth> hi lilith! maybe you're more interested in PLAYING THE fv(#!n6 GAME than these other yokels, hmm?

<PhilippeDark> sash: Happy to be the subject of practice any time! ^_^ Again, if you ever need help with SotS, i'm happy to oblige ^_^ Did you know I worked on the ROM hack of MK 2: Mammon's Counterattack? ^_^

<BarthesWasWrong> PhilippeDark: is that one good? I've played 1, 3, and 4, plus the sidescroller one for like five seconds?

<PhilippeDark> so there's that ^_^

<NecroPizza> lol PD stop trying to get in her panties

<NecroPizza> just stop

<reficul> lol

<NecroPizza> stoooooppppppp

<sash> it's fine. my panties are inviolate (also in purple)

<RyanThomp-san> purple panties? nice

* useless_x jerks off imagining sash in her purple panties

<azimuth> um . . . pics?

<xLilithx> oh my god, i'm so sorry :/ i didn't know :/

<reficul> maze this is so mean, lol

<sash> useless_x: i imagine you've become . . . skilled at it.

<useless_x> hahahahahaahshaahaa yes trkk me more abuot e=ats wrong with mre

<xLilithx> please don't kick me out of your company :/ who will be mean to me in front of my friends then :/

* useless_x was kicked from #teengoetia by NecroPizza (YOU'RE DISGUSTING)

<PhilippeDark> So I mean, I'm not saying I want to *join* invocation llc or anything. But if you guys (*and* gal ^_^) need any kind of advice or help or anything from a really

experienced semiprofessional translator, well, you know who to call, ne? ^_^

<azimuth> omg you kicked him lol

<RyanThomp-san> Doesn't xLilithx live in Texas with diLute?

<reficul> i think they both live in texas, yeah, lol

<reficul> i mean, dilute lives there, lol

<reficul> i guess i don't know where your friend lilith lives, lol

<RyanThomp-san> Does anyone know what's going on with diLute, also?

<azimuth> what do you mean?

<RyanThomp-san> All the stuff about like not wanting to be called Dennis?

* BarthesWasWrong whistles the X-files theme

<reficul> i dunno, dilute likes that anime stuff or whatever, lol

<NecroPizza> SINNERS ALL

<NecroPizza> PERVERTS

<sash> this conversation is not helping me talk to lilith.

* useless_x has joined #teengoetia

<useless_x> Hey, why you gotta kick a brother-man?

<NecroPizza> AGHHHGHHH

* useless_x was kicked from #teengoetia by NecroPizza (FAG YOU'RE NOT BLACK)

* useless_x was banned from #teengoetia by NecroPizza (FOR FAGGOTRY)

<BarthesWasWrong> whoa

<reficul> lol

<BarthesWasWrong> Tough but fair!

<PhilippeDark> *Thank you*, NecroPizza. I'm sorry you had to see that, sash

<azimuth> so what name is diLute using instead?
* xLilithx is now known as MazeRyder
<BarthesWasWrong> Just D; mononym
<azimuth> di? like princess di?
<BarthesWasWrong> lol / also, rip
<reficul> lol
<NecroPizza> TOO SOON
<NecroPizza> i dunno. isn't di like . . . a girl's name?
<NecroPizza> is dilute gonna turn into a girl or something?
<BarthesWasWrong> Great Shades of Jerry Springer!
<RyanThomp-san> I'm sure diLute wouldn't do that!
<reficul> why wouldn't dilute turn into a girl if he wants
<BarthesWasWrong> Ha! Ha! Staying out of this one!
<reficul> it's a free country, lol
<RyanThomp-san> Come on, you guys, diLute's a *Christian*
<NecroPizza> aren't you also all xtian and shit
<NecroPizza> all up in jesus domain
<BarthesWasWrong> jesus > jesus' </grammarnazi>
* BarthesWasWrong was kicked from #teengoetia by
   NecroPizza (SHUT UP BARTHES)
* BarthesWasWrong joined #teengoetia
<reficul> can christians not become transsexual or some-
   thing
<PhilippeDark> Well, this IRC evening has certainly taken
   a sordid turn . . . ^_^
<RyanThomp-san> NecroPizza: I believe that He is the
   life, and the way, and the door, yes, and I stand by that
   against the world
* RyanThomp-san was kicked from #teengoetia by
   NecroPizza (THEN TO THE LIONS, ASSHOLE)
* RyanThomp-san joined #teengoetia

<RyanThomp-san> Ha ha, nice
<RyanThomp-san> Got it, no preaching
<NecroPizza> THAT'S RIGHT
<NecroPizza> THIS IS SATAN'S IRC CHANNEL
<NecroPizza> HAIL TO OUR DARK RULER
<reficul> wooo
<RyanThomp-san> Ha ha ha
<sash> i'm done with this.
<sash> if lilith shows up, tell him i need to talk to him about saga of the sorceress, and that it's urgent. he'll know what it's about.
<sash> i hope you all enjoy your infantile jerk circle.
<MazeRyder> wait, wait, no, DON'T LEAVE, I know where Lilith is
* MazeRyder is now known as xLilithx
<xLilithx> hey, sorry :/ i'm here! :/ i'm really sorry! :/ :/
<xLilithx> me and dilute were just trying on frilly skirts :/ but i'm here now :/ sorry :/
<xLilithx> here to work on this vaporware game :/ sorry :/
<NecroPizza> STEERS AND QUEERS
<sash> changing nicknames and pretending to be other people is pathetic. goodbye.
<xLilithx> no, wait, don't go!
* xLilithx is now known as MazeRyder
* MazeRyder is now known as AbRaXaS
<AbRaXaS> hahahahahahahahahahdfjdfjhahajjhajskjkkl;; whats up youll talk to me rite
<reficul> lol
<AbRaXaS> sorry i couldnt be here i was makin seven more games and lost track of time lol, so who wants to talk about dicks

* wtf_its_abraxas_whos_using_my_nickname joined
  #teengoetia
<AbRaXaS> big meaty ohahahahahahajfjjkal !!!!!!1
<wtf_its_abraxas_whos_using_my_nickname> lol is
  everyone impersonating everyone again
<wtf_its_abraxas_whos_using_my_nickname> THERE
  CAN BE ONLY ONE BRAX
<NecroPizza> LMAO REAL ABRAXAS
<wtf_its_abraxas_whos_using_my_nickname> that's-a me!
<reficul> lol hi brax
<RyanThomp-san> Hi AbRaXaS! LOL, perfect timing.
<PhilippeDark> Brax! What's up, my friend ^_^
<sash> abraxas, have you seen lilith
<AbRaXaS> Crikey, the jig's up! *foof*
* AbRaXaS is now known as MazeRyder
* MazeRyder bows at the real abraxas's feet
* wtf_its_abraxas_whos_using_my_nickname is now
  known as abraxas
* abraxas pouts. 'who me????' strikes a sick marilyn
  monroe poes
* abraxas strikes a sick marilyn manson pose
* abraxas strikes a sick charlie manson pose
<abraxas> charlie dont surf lol
<abraxas> hahahaha you guys im so fucked up
<abraxas> i havent seen lilth no
<abraxas> you guys im haunted
* BarthesWasWrong laughs nervously at the grim fetishiza-
  tion of serial murder
<abraxas> hahaha no like, charlie didnt kill anyone
<sash> so, lilith: no?
<abraxas> thats what made it WORSE

<abraxas> did u know charlie knew eddie from the get
    haps
<RyanThomp-san> Ha ha, nice, Apocalypse Now
<abraxas> im just in space tonight guys
<azimuth> i hate to even ask this, but brax:
<azimuth> the PORNO PASSWORD is HAMMER WITH
    BOW
<abraxas> oh, easy: chixx w dixx
<NecroPizza> LMAO
<MazeRyder> !!! Delectable synchronicities! Four thumbs
    way, way up!
<reficul> lol
<BarthesWasWrong> lol, whoa
<NecroPizza> I CAN'T EVEN
<PhilippeDark> Wow. "Chicks with dicks." How . . . exactly
    were we supposed to guess that, again?
<azimuth> LOL, DING DING DING
<azimuth> (nmiaow)
<NecroPizza> I CAN'T BREATHE
<sash> has lilith emailed you? have you two talked on aim?
<NecroPizza> wait, brax, like
<sash> has he logged on? you can tell if he's logged on by
    checking his profile. it'll show the last login date.
<NecroPizza> explain how that answer came to you so
    READILY
<reficul> lol
<abraxas> hahahaha oh its cause i was just reading a
    bunch of he-she porn stuff
<NecroPizza> WHAT THE FUCK BRAX
<abraxas> its like a main interest of mine lol
<reficul> hahahahahahah lol hahah

<abraxas> LIKE U NEVER

<PhilippeDark> Um, no, I haven't. -_-

<RyanThomp-san> Just another night in #teengoetia! LOL

* azimuth sets topic: <abraxas> he-she porn stuff, its like a main interest of mine lol

<abraxas> theres nothing wrong with being turned on by trannies

<abraxas> oh also sash i never talk on AIM, GET THA MEMO

<NecroPizza> wait brax are you like gay or something?

<abraxas> i dunno maybe, lol! i just like chixwdix

<NecroPizza> but dicks = gay

<abraxas> actually its mostly text porn files hahahahaha

<abraxas> with like ascii dicks lol

<reficul> lol

<abraxas> TEXT PORN CRAFTQ, why hasnt this been done omg

<abraxas> i mean i guess INVOCATION LLC, we're doing it, lol

<abraxas> lol hahaha we're so great, KISS OUR FARTERS EVERYONE ELSE, lolll

<abraxas> but yeah text is better

<abraxas> i mean not always but

<MazeRyder> The cerebrum cerebellum, truly the world's largest erogenous zone!

<abraxas> they can do stuff reg porn cant do

<abraxas> even with MOVIE MAGICKS

<abraxas> CGI ELEMENTALS

<NecroPizza> lol wait explain this to me, you read WORD PORN?

<NecroPizza> THAT'S STUPID

<RyanThomp-san> I've never even heard of this! Where do you even get stuff like this, brax? Is there a website?

<NecroPizza> (lol ryan is interested)

<azimuth> *i'm* kinda interested!

<NecroPizza> wait so what can WORD PORN do that like, a movie can't do?

<BarthesWasWrong> Erotica in literature is a pretty classic tradition I guess?

<NecroPizza> (shut up barthes, like you read books instead of pron)

<BarthesWasWrong> I don't like much pron?

<BarthesWasWrong> The women in it always seem sad and hard to identify with

* BarthesWasWrong was kicked from #teengoetia by NecroPizza (FAGGOTRY SQUARED)

<abraxas> it's just better lol

* BarthesWasWrong joined #teengoetia

<BarthesWasWrong> IT'S TRUE! JEEZ SORRY

<abraxas> you got your stories with magic rings

<abraxas> that turn dudeliest dudes into femmeliest females

<abraxas> where theres like an all girls school and a jock kid

<abraxas> has to go to it and they make

<PhilippeDark> Um, no thanks?

<abraxas> him be like a girl lol

<abraxas> hahaha i wish i wnet to a school like that instead of my school

<abraxas> I'D BE THE COMELIEST GIRL IN SCHOOL

<reficul> lol

<azimuth> *whoa* . . . would you wear like, a brassiere and stuff?

&><

<abraxas> lol obv havent yall ever tried that
<NecroPizza> THIS ISN'T HAPPENING
<reficul> not really lol
<abraxas> panties are surprisingly comfortable also, u just
  gotta tuck ur stuff
<abraxas> all mr fantastic
<RyanThomp-san> Ha ha ha
<abraxas> oh shit y'all
<BarthesWasWrong> We're through the looking glass,
  here, people
<abraxas> whats this weird magic ring next to my keyboard
<MazeRyder> where? Where????
<abraxas> better put it on to find out hahahaha
<abraxas> AH OH SHIT
<abraxas> PINK LIGHTNING
<reficul> ive read stuff like that, its interesting sometimes lol
<abraxas> MESSIN UP MY MIND
<abraxas> MELTING
<sash> i really need to talk to lilith
<abraxas> CHANGING
* abraxas is now known as aBrAxA
<BarthesWasWrong> lol
<NecroPizza> DOCTOR, MY EYES
<reficul> lol omg
* aBrAxA is now known as abraxa
<abraxa> hi everyone~!
<MazeRyder> by hermes trismegistus!
<abraxa> i'm so much happier now~!
<abraxa> better, stronger, more energy efficient~! lol
* abraxa puts on fishnets and a boa made of starlight as
  miss world plays

* abraxa shopwers of confetti and bats and shit around everything

\<azimuth\> hahaha, sash has competition now!

\<abraxa\> i wish i really had this ring lol id never take it off

\<abraxa\> shit is better as a girl

\<abraxa\> like the air is better

\<NecroPizza\> um, no?

\<abraxa\> i'd buy a plane and fly everywhere in it

\<abraxa\> invisible plane cruise lines to fuckin space lol

\<PhilippeDark\> Perhaps you haven't considered some of the, ahem, monthly disadvantages . . . ^_^

\<abraxa\> the moon is now a girl planet

\<abraxa\> every future poet will know that

\<sash\> philippedark: as ever, you're garbage.

\<abraxa\> fuck earth hahahaha

\<abraxa\> fuck everyone on it

\<RyanThomp-san\> Ha ha, Sailor Moon, nice

\<NecroPizza\> FAGGOTRY

\<NecroPizza\> FAGGOTRY OVERWHELMING

\<BarthesWasWrong\> ~bye june, going to the moon~

* abraxa tosses magic moon rings over the side of her invisible plane to everyone

\<NecroPizza\> NO ONE IS GOING TO THE MOON TODAY

\<PhilippeDark\> Sash: Aw, you don't mean that ^_^ But I'm curious.

\<PhilippeDark\> As a feminist, what's your take on all of this?

\<abraxa\> here assholes~! moon rings for everyone! lady rings

\<sash\> describe "all this" for me, please?

<abraxa> averyone get yr lady on

<PhilippeDark> i mean, this is a man pretending to be a
woman.

<PhilippeDark> doesn't that offend you?

<abraxa> put em on quick

<sash> no, it doesn't offend me.

<abraxa> join me in heaven

<sash> i don't have feelings about transsexuality one way
or another

<sash> what i do have feelings about: finishing our game.
finding lilith.

<sash> these are the things that i have, repeatedly,
expressed emotional interest in.

* abraxa taps her high-heeled boot

<azimuth> oh my god wait: so sash you're a lez right

<sash> can you help me with these actual problems i have.

<sash> do you know where lilith is.

<sash> i am a lesbian woman, yes.

<abraxa> no one is putting on my rings wtf~

<azimuth> so as a lez, would you do it with brax

<azimuth> or NOT do it with brax?

<abraxa> whats wrong yall

<abraxa> dont u want 2 be PERFECT

<reficul> oh wow lol

* RyanThomp-san plays an mp3 file of pornography music

<abraxa> dont u want 2 live with me in PERFECT
FREEDOM

<BarthesWasWrong> lol

<NecroPizza> YOU'RE ALL A DISGRACE TO THIS FAMILY

<abraxa> perfect lunar bliss on the
mooooo000o0o000o0o0o0o0o0o0o0()))()0oooon

<MazeRyder> An official orgiastic display of all Invocation LLC members! I'd pay to see that?

<sash> now?

<sash> mazeryder: you couldn't afford us

<NecroPizza> lol, oh snap

<PhilippeDark> Hmm. Interesting. I thought you ladies were upset about, shall we say, men of the feminine persuasion. Apologies if i've offended ^_^

<sash> philippedark: i think i've made it clear that i despise you.

■

* abraxa sent you a private query

<abraxa> lol uh

<abraxa> soooooo~

<sash> yes?

<abraxa> you didn't really answer but

<abraxa> I mean lol

<abraxa> pecifically vis a vis getting

<abraxa> it on

<abraxa> like cybersexxing I mean

<abraxa> lol

<abraxa> oh wait you kinda answered lol

<abraxa> sorry, just read it over again

<abraxa> but like

<abraxa> were you

<abraxa> lol, DRUMROLL

<abraxa> serious?

<abraxa> hello

<sash> are you?

<abraxa> lol

\<abraxa\> I
* abraxa left the conversation

■

\<azimuth\> omg, illc orgy, perfection
\<BarthesWasWrong\> I . . . I confess I'm interested in this, good lord help me
\<RyanThomp-san\> Ha ha ha
\<NecroPizza\> WELL DON'T JUST STAND THERE
\<NecroPizza\> IF YOU'RE GOING TO BONE, BONE
\<NecroPizza\> NO SKIN OFF MY NOSE
\<azimuth\> If only lilith were here also \<perfectstorm\>
\<reficul\> lol
\<BarthesWasWrong\> One male, one female, one "swirl!"
\<NecroPizza\> lol, like neapolitan ice cream
\<MazeRyder\> Except . . . suppose . . . *Lilith* puts on one of the rings! Presto-change-o!
\<NecroPizza\> lol
\<BarthesWasWrong\> Whoa, paradigm shift!
\<azimuth\> that . . . makes a twisted amount of sense?
\<reficul\> lol
* MazeRyder looks longingly at one of the rings
\<NecroPizza\> PUT THAT RING DOWN
* abraxa is now known as AbRaXaS
\<AbRaXaS\> show's over
\<AbRaXaS\> moon crashed into the earth
\<AbRaXaS\> everyones dead now
\<NecroPizza\> okay so, like, here's why i think shemales are bullshit

<AbRaXaS> all the magic rings melted and no one is girls anymore

<NecroPizza> it's because there's no magic rings

<NecroPizza> i mean there's operations or whatever. but that doesn't like, magically make you not male.

<NecroPizza> i mean obviously it's better to be female. but trying to make yourself one just makes you into a joke.

<NecroPizza> like, why try at something you can never succeed in?

<NecroPizza> better to just, like, let other people leave you alone

<NecroPizza> WHILE YOU WAIT FOR THE GRAVE

<reficul> lol

<BarthesWasWrong> Dark!

<BarthesWasWrong> Seriously, though, I don't think there's no hope?

* BarthesWasWrong was kicked from #teengoetia by NecroPizza (SHUT UP)

<PhilippeDark> Necro, I think that's a pretty reasonable position.

<AbRaXaS> fuffffck

<PhilippeDark> I must admit . . . never thought you'd have me feeling sorry for a "female impersonator," NecroPizza ^_^

* BarthesWasWrong joined #teengoetia

<BarthesWasWrong> omfg NP what is even your problem

<AbRaXaS> yo sash

<BarthesWasWrong> DO YOU STAND AGAINST HOPE, SIR

<NecroPizza> YES

<AbRaXaS> what is it u need lil for
<reficul> lol
<AbRaXaS> lets have a fuckin business meeting
<AbRaXaS> lets talk business
<AbRaXaS> stocks and bonds and shit
<azimuth> let's return to a happier subject: pr0n
* AbRaXaS puts on a green visor and pinstripe suit sitting
   among piles and piles of money
<sash> all i need, maybe in this life, is to speak to lilith.
<AbRaXaS> cum on lets talk qbout revenues an shit
<AbRaXaS> why tho?? I mean lil will be back eventually prolyl
<sash> it's for a legitimate reason.
<azimuth> so like what kinds of pron do people like? (other
   than brax, l0l)
<AbRaXaS> hahaha oh okay, sounds real legitimate!
<sash> it's specifically to get the .qek file from lil
<sash> the schedule says we need to have the objects for
   the wizard academy scripted soon.
<MazeRyder> A good intercourse with Donne or the Bard
   trumps any carnal corruptions!
<BarthesWasWrong> I've said my piece on this matter
   looks warily at NecroPizza
<NecroPizza> THE ABYSS STARES ALSO
<sash> the object code needs to be done by end of june
   latest in order to meet our release targets
<reficul> uh i dunno lol
<RyanThomp-san> Nice, I don't look at porn either
<NecroPizza> lol, you probably look at Narnia porn
<sash> and i need the room layouts from lilith to be done
   so that i can finish the detail work on time to hand off to
   you for art and coding.

<AbRaXaS> lol we shoulnt be talking about this in an open
    channel
<sash> and right now they're not done. also they're not good.
<sash> there are mazes.
<sash> and lilith hasn't spoken to me in days. and i'm
    concerned.
<BarthesWasWrong> lol
<AbRaXaS> they gonna steal our corporate seeeeeekrets
<BarthesWasWrong> STROKIN' ASLAN'S MANE
<RyanThomp-san> Ha ha ha
<AbRaXaS> i dunno.
<sash> ryan: i like the narnia books
<AbRaXaS> why don't i just do the rooms in a new .qek
    file and you can do scripts on that
<AbRaXaS> like, I can do them faster???? Lol prolly
    anyway???
<AbRaXaS> easy peasy come on sleazy. That'd work
    though right???
<AbRaXaS> we don't need no steenkin lilitshss
<RyanThomp-san> sash, nice! Which is your favorite?
    Mine's the Dawn Treader
<sash> no, lilith is the level designer. he has to be the one
    to design the levels.
<azimuth> brax, you're feeling pretty share-y tonight!
* azimuth shoves a mic in brax's face, paparazzi flash
<AbRaXaS> um yeah but lil isn't designing anything!
<sash> ryan: why?
<sash> ryan: i like that one also, yes
<sash> well, lilith needs to. this is my point. it's lilith's job.
<AbRaXaS> i unno, you and lil talk all the time and shit,
    ask him why

\<sash\> that's the whole point of this. i do the writing. you do the code, art, and music. lilith does the layouts.

* MazeRyder takes a bow, twirls his mustaches. "The horror! The horror! C'est moi! Et apres, le deluge!"

\<sash\> the harmony comes from us doing it like that.

\<AbRaXaS\> lol if level design was lil's real job he'd be fired though

\<sash\> we're not that kind of company

\<AbRaXaS\> i mean he's never released a game

\<AbRaXaS\> lol we're not any kind of company

\<NecroPizza\> you're not a company. you aren't like, paid.

\<sash\> we're a collective.

\<RyanThomp-san\> This incredible voyage into the unknown to meet the Lord

\<sash\> ryan: my favorite is the last battle

\<MazeRyder\> Collective? Sounds like COMMIE talk! And commies don't fire people . . . they PURGE them! Dosvidanya, tovarischchch!

\<sash\> ryan: there's a part where this crypto-arab character encounters aslan and he's worshipped a false god called tash all his life

* MazeRyder has been kicked from #teengoetia by NecroPizza (DOSVIDANYA YOURSELF DOUCHEBAG)

\<sash\> i mean the books say tash is a false god that i guess is allah, like how aslan is jesus

\<RyanThomp-san\> Nice, The Last Battle, got it

\<sash\> which is uhhhhhhh, but whatever

\<NecroPizza\> ASLAN IS BORING

\<sash\> anyway, aslan tells him that all the service he's done to tash is really service to aslan

<sash> because it was done with true faith

<sash> this idea that devotion is its own justification

<BarthesWasWrong> ~every time i see you caaaaaaalling~

<sash> i don't know. i liked it.

<NecroPizza> it's HEAR you calling, DUMBASS

<RyanThomp-san> Oh wow

<NecroPizza> YOU CAN'T SEE SOMEONE CALLING

<PhilippeDark> By the by, sash . . . I shouldn't tell you this maybe, but I slew your favorite death priestess last night ^_^

<RyanThomp-san> So in the end, everyone is really doing service to Christ

<sash> ryan: yeah, no?

<reficul> lol i think maze is gone for real

<PhilippeDark> Or I should say, I slew "KARMLA," as CritHit's USA localization team decided to make it back in 1990 ^_^ She was pretty rough!

<sash> i mean, i should say i like the narnia books in spite of all the racism, misogyny, spiritual arrogance

<sash> fucked up geopolitics and latent fascism that runs through every line of them

<sash> and through all xtianity, really

<PhilippeDark> It's intriguing how they used the same sprites for her in Mystic Knights 2: MC, even after she was on the same side as them ^_^

<RyanThomp-san> Guys I have to go to bed

<RyanThomp-san> good night

* RyanThomp-san has left #teengoetia

<PhilippeDark> *Extra* interesting when you consider how far they tweaked Philippe's normal paladin design for

MK5 on PSX, even *before* he becomes a blackguard.
It's subtle. ^_^

<reficul> lol

<PhilippeDark> I'd love to send you a copy of the working
build of our IPS translation patch for MK2

<PhilippeDark> Are you there? ^_^

<sash> philippedark: so like

<PhilippeDark> I think you'd enjoy it, and maybe have
some interesting things to say about it ^_^

<PhilippeDark> Yes? ^_^

<sash> when you landed the killing blow on karmla in
mystic knights 1

<sash> did you ejaculate?

<reficul> lol

<PhilippeDark> Um, no, but thanks for asking? ^_^

<NecroPizza> THAT'S IT

* PhilippeDark was kicked from #teengoetia by NecroPizza
(SHE DOESNT WANT TO FUCK YOU, ASSHOLE)

<azimuth> lol necro are you gonna kick out evvvvveryone

* azimuth was kicked from #teengoetia by NecroPizza
(YES)

<BarthesWasWrong> lol

<reficul> lol

* BarthesWasWrong was kicked from #teengoetia by
NecroPizza (LOL YOURSELF I NEVER LIKED YOU)

* AbRaXaS was kicked from #teengoetia by NecroPizza
(YOURE WEIRD)

* NecroPizza sets topic: ALL HAVE SINNED

<NecroPizza> GARBAGE

<NecroPizza> YOU'RE ALL GARBAGE

* AbRaXaS joined #teengoetia

* reficul was kicked from #teengoetia by NecroPizza
  (SORRY REF YOU'RE COOL BUT I GOTTA)
<AbRaXaS> lol u cant keep a good dog down
<NecroPizza> EVERYONE'S GARBAGE
* AbRaXaS was kicked from #teengoetia by NecroPizza
  (YES I CAN)
* You were kicked from #teengoetia by NecroPizza (WHAM
  BAM NO THANK U MAAM)

■
/query abraxas
<sash> hey
<sash> sorry if i'm intruding
<sash> i just wanted to say sorry about earlier
<sash> i got the sense you were maybe offended?
<sash> and i really, really didn't intend that
<sash> i mean, you know how #teengoetia can be. ugh.
<sash> and anyway, i just wanted to say that, i don't
  know.
<sash> like, listen, if you do identify as transgender, i
  really, really get that?
<sash> like, i really do.
<sash> so, yes
<sash> i'm also really worried about lilith
<sash> i mean not just bceause of the file
<sash> bceause > because
<sash> sorry, it's hard to type this
<sash> anyway a thing happened with lilith, i guess?
<sash> and i wasn't worried about it, but now i am?
<sash> and lilith was supposed to meet me tonight, but
  isn't here

\<sash\> and i'm worried that lilith never wants to talk to me again

\<sash\> um

\<sash\> anyway, that's why i was worried.

\<sash\> although yes we do need the file to make our release date

\<sash\> i mean that's also true.

\<sash\> i guess was just hoping lilith would be here tonight

\<sash\> tonight, on porno password night (god help us)

\<sash\> anyway, um, and please don't take this the wrong way

\<sash\> like i really hope you don't.

\<sash\> because maybe i'm misinterpreting or maybe it was a joke or something.

\<sash\> i mean i never know with you?

\<sash\> but um, if you ever want to talk about that stuff, i'm around?

\<sash\> like, the magic ring stuff?

\<sash\> or about anything?

\<sash\> are you there?

\<sash\> are you still in #teengoetia or something? i got kicked out, and i really don't want to go back? so i can't check if you're there?

\<sash\> brax?

■

/ping AbRaXaS

* The username AbRaXaS could not be found.

/quit

3. Crossing

It happened far from her computer, in the back seat of the car on the drive up to Camp Weathering, ten hours from Texas with the Scoutmasters taking the wheel in shifts, fast food and nuclear green Game Boy in the backseats, her Tenderfoot uniform so snug around her chest she could feel her rank pins scratch. The lanky ginger quartermaster in the passenger seat had radio control: *so in love.* She got lost in the song, viney trees flanking the car as it wound up the road, bound for the campground that would teach the secrets of knotcraft and woodlore that made boys into men. I could become a man: that was what Lilith thought.

The nice weather lasted through the afternoon's loadout and hike to the campsite. A small group of Scouts had started to explore the trails that led away from the big firepit at the center of camp; Lilith tagged along with them, sticking close enough to laugh softly at their jokes. The land felt alien, overripe: Texas, her piece of it, was parched and flat, but Tennessee was vertical, and the leaf-crusted path climbed and fell so that she had to pant to crest it. The soil was steeped with water, a dirt meringue across which black ants crawled.

Lilith had echoed the boys' steps all the way to a place where a steep fallen log provided a path to the other side of the ravine. They took a hard left turn down the slippery ladder, continuing their conversation about A-wing fighters and merit badges. The ladder looked scary, and if she climbed down it would be too obvious that she was following them. So she continued past the log, ravine over her left shoulder and high dirt wall over her right. I could turn back, she told herself. At any point, I can turn back, and be back at camp, and nothing will change. She felt good, thinking this as she moved deeper into the woods.

Soon the path bent at a semicircle of stones, a kind of couch dug into the mountain to her right. The thick ritual granite look of it: like Stonehenge, the Siege Perilous, the table to which Aslan got tied. She stopped walking, her wrists goose-pimpling. She imagined touching it: the stone would ripple at her touch, like a gate opening. Quickly she turned back to the green nylon tents, the smell of cherry cobbler warming in an iron skillet.

They all made it through dinner before the clouds burst over the meandering troops and masters. The rain continued into the morning, and in melancholy, Lilith watched it from the tarp by the cooking tables, five feet of space between her and her fellow Scouts: the *blood circle*, as they called it in her Wood Carving merit badge class. Every tree caught water in a different way, depending on the shape of its leaves: bowled, piney, flat, drooping, wide, weird. Lilith couldn't identify trees; the only page of the *Boy Scout Handbook* she'd seriously studied was the one with photos of the slow and awful progression of a brown recluse bite drilling an acid spit hole into a human hand.

The other Scouts under the tarp were roasting foil potatoes on the iron grill, playing aggressive chess, talking about music videos or mutual friends from the school most of the troop attended. The campout was a time to make closer connections with friends, but how did you do that? How did they all know what to talk about with one another?

She imagined her friends from #teengoetia were here: they could all play Porno Password under the trees. They could find sticks and practice sword fighting. They could talk about music, and Lilith could listen. They could—her mind hit a wall. How would it be different? She was sure it would be. She imagined the other Scouts looking at her and her friends having a conversation, how much she would laugh, how interested everyone would be.

She didn't have to sit here, staring at her peers from the far side of the tarp. There were other places she could go. For example, there was the Scoutmasters' tarp: old men smoking and arranging tackle boxes while they talked about home renovations. There was the outhouse, its reek, its maggots. There were the camp showers in the rain. She'd already pledged not to take a shower for the entire five-day duration of the campout, not to show her body to the nervous, giggling boys who showed theirs.

She could go to the woods, she thought. She went back into the tent instead.

She'd animated rain before. She'd needed a rain scene in her CraftQ game, *Dragon Gaiden*; she'd spent a whole week working on it back at home in Texas between geometry assignments, nightly chapters of the fantasy novel she was reading, and silent suppers in the eat-in kitchen, her and her parents' attention turned to the Sci-Fi Channel on the TV propped on the counter. It was the most complicated thing she'd tried in CraftQ yet, and it felt dangerous to attempt. Sash and Abraxa were both preternaturally good at CraftQ: they could do graphics, programming, even music, which no one was good at. Lilith wasn't preternaturally good at anything, but for some reason Sash had invited her to join their company, Invocation LLC, the company everyone secretly wanted to join. Lilith had no idea why she'd been chosen, but she knew she was on thin ice: any day now, her business partners might find out she was only pretending to be a competent and reliable person. If she could make a beautiful rain animation, it would buy her some time.

But she'd fucked up the rain animation. She knew the basic algorithm from studying other people's CraftQ object code:

- create and display individual raindrops using appropriate text characters (/, !, i, |, ,)
- distribute the raindrops evenly along the vertical axis, one per horizontal grid space
- program the raindrops to move south on the screen (i.e., from the top of the screen to the bottom)
- once they reach the bottom, turn them invisible and send them back to the top to restart the cycle, moving in secret like black-clad puppeteers

When other people did it, this technique produced an even, splashy-looking rainfall that seemed randomly distributed. Lilith's rain all fell at once, like someone had cut open a water balloon, like a tray of dropped water glasses. How did she fail to understand water? She'd watched the animation she'd coded over and over, trying to breathe—it wouldn't be that hard, maybe just slow that drop down, maybe speed that one up?—and then she deleted the scene. The story would just have to get along without it.

Sash would know how to program rain, Lilith knew, how to shelter and guide it as it fell.

The boy she'd share her tent with for the next ninety-six hours—Scott Buckworth—was in his sleeping bag when she got back. He lay on his stomach, thick yellow-edged SF paperback propped open on his thin pillow and his mean red lip hanging open as his eyes scanned its lines.

Sorry, she said. —Sorry, I'm wet, I'm sorry.

That's what she said, Scott murmured, wiping a raindrop from his page. Lilith, balancing on one muddy foot, knew to laugh. Grit and endurance, she told herself, determine the character of a man. If you want to become one, endure proximity to your tentmate. Be a man. Don't do what you want.

Why did the rest of the troop dislike Scott Buckworth? He was smart, clearly, mean when he spoke, attractive in a strange way: compact, white-blond, upper lip seemingly permanently curled upward by a short nose. One morning on a previous campout, the troop had assembled for the mess hall and breakfast, and Buckworth hadn't yet left his tent, so everyone else stood in formation—khakis and epaulets, troop patches messily sewed or hot-glued to uniform sleeves, socks and packs on shoulders or fanny the only markers that distinguished one Scout from the next—until finally the head Scoutmaster directed the whole troop to surround Buckworth's tent, still in formation, all chanting in time with the Scoutmasters who led them:

> *Eat our breakfast too darn late*
> *If we don't get to the mess by eight*
> *Mess hall, mess hall, feed me please*
> *Get up or you'll go on your knees*

Over and over they all chanted, Lilith mumbling along—
Buckworth, Buckworth *clap* *Get Up!*—until at last, slowly,
the zipper drew up and Scott got out, shirtless. He pulled his
Class A on slowly over his shoulders as he walked leisurely
around the ranks and got into his assigned place, where he
buttoned the shirt, his expression a weary squint. The Scoutmaster told him he'd just volunteered for latrine cleanup that
afternoon, and Buckworth said that he guessed that was reasonable, and the Scoutmaster told him he'd better tuck his
shirt in, and Buckworth snapped his fingers theatrically—*guess
what I forgot!*—before he did it. Lilith imagined Buckworth in
a video game, how his little pixel sprite would snap its fingers
as his jaunty theme played.

There were rumors about Buckworth. Someone at high
school had called Buckworth a faggot, and Buckworth had
beaten them up. Or no: Buckworth had accused a boy of
being a faggot, and the boy had beaten Buckworth up. Or had
a group of boys beaten Buckworth up for being an accused
faggot? None of the rumors agreed, and the Scoutmasters shut
down any discussion of them as soon as they arose. (A Scout is
friendly; a Scout is reverent; a Scout is clean.)

Despite the rumors, Buckworth was a patrol leader. His dad
was a Scoutmaster too, and Lilith guessed he pulled strings. (Her
own father didn't like the woods, had some allergy.) Despite
that, none of the Scoutmasters seemed to trust Buckworth, and
none of Lilith's peers seemed to like him. Lilith tried to ignore
the rumors, even to forget she knew them. So far, Buckworth
had been civil to her, diplomatic, probably more than any of
the other Scouts would've been. She knew this would end the
moment he guessed what she'd heard. (A Scout is loyal; a Scout
is also discreet.)

■ ■ ■

Careful to avoid any contact, she scooted to face away from Buckworth, took her spiral notebook from her hiking-frame backpack, an unchewed ballpoint still clipped to its binding, and got to work on her game maps for the first time in weeks. She should start with Sash's feedback on her last submitted batch. Blocking the page with her body, she unfolded the email she'd printed on her father's inkjet and read it again, and then again.

TO: AParker01983@aol.com
FROM: sashiel@yahoo.com
DATE: August 15, 1998
SUBJ: (no subject)

hello. i won't waste our time. your work is not where it needs to be. i started to leave itemized feedback on specific points, but in the end i decided it'd be easier just to remind you of what we're attempting to do here. okay?

so, remember the principles of Thereness underlying good level design:

- interactivity. each logical area of a ROOM should contain at least 2-3 affordances for player interaction. example: painter's tower in super mystic knights 4 (sufish, 1996.) a whole gallery of paintings by the mad artist daster, all of which give insight into his character and the slow progression of his curse, and all of which unlock further dungeon corridors. you've drawn whole rooms without any affordances. why?

- ecology. everything in a ROOM should be a logical consequence of the dungeon's narrative meaning, which should be a logical consequence of the story as a whole. example: the slime canals in mystic knights 2 (sufish, 1990), a risible gross-out theme made sublime by rendering plausible the waste disposal needs of the small wild-magical communities of the lost continent. what is the theme of the rooms you submitted?

- enticement. i'm not enticed. players should be drawn in by meaningful choices and possibilities. example: the cursed trade in super mystic knights 3 (oshiro99, 1994): a half mana accessory that you can exchange for the life of one player character. do you spare the life, but then pay full cost for spells in the final encounters, potentially resulting in game over? there isn't anything like that in what you sent.

- involution. do we even need to discuss this again?

i've included what i assembled of my room-by-room notes. but what i really want is more understanding of the underlying principles we're working toward here. the details are a means of arriving at the general vision. please look at the examples i laid out, maybe study and try some variations on them as exercises, and take what you learn from that into the next draft of the work. i know you can do this, lilith. let's discuss next week.

s.

ps: i hope our last chat was okay.

She read the postscript again, the words blurring and the tent canvas staining the printout green. Then, head hot, she put the letter aside and took out her notebook.

Sash had given her the list of maps to produce for the completed game, of course, along with indexes of all the dialogue, combat interactions, treasure flowcharts, and other information Sash would need to write and Abraxa would need to draw, program, and musicalize. Sash had arranged everything, laid out the whole game file with blank ROOMs: *wizard academy courtyard, wizard academy secret passage to stairs, wizard academy B1, wizard academy B2, wizard academy B3 (north), wizard academy B3 (northeast),* etc. It was a massive amount of work, and to complete it—which would constitute proof that she belonged in the company—she'd need to sacrifice. She skipped TV evenings with her parents, didn't study for tests (she could afford some Bs and Cs), lost track of shows she'd followed. Yet somehow she still fell behind.

She rotated the blank page—sometimes this could help—and she tried to focus. Next was the bottom floor of the Wizard Academy sewer systems, B3, the one she'd left incomplete in her latest scheduled email submission to Sash. All she had to do was outline it, think through the player's chain of interactions, give Sash's story a surface on which to adhere and grow, like a dandelion spore implanting. All she had to do was think of what might be on the bottom floor of a wizard academy's sewer system. A pool of sewage? (No, there were no affordances for Interactivity.) A puzzle of levers and switches? (No, this would violate Ecology.) A long, straight corridor so that Lilith could just be done already? (Be patient—a Scout is patient—a Scout is cheerful.) She could just copy a map from some other professional game from GameFAQs. She'd done it before: Sash hadn't noticed, had even praised her for it. At the time, this had been Lilith's only betrayal.

Sash was so good at games. She had made very few short CraftQ games, yet somehow all of them felt like her, short, taut, and rich in all her theories: enticing. Lilith had a save file just before a scene in one of Sash's games, in which a novitiate and a Mother Superior take off one another's clothes and have rich, Eucharistic sex in the chapel of a monastery with lushly described stained glass windows. *here is the space where we can be most open, naked and without defense. here, sister, we can be ourselves at last.* Lilith sat at the den computer with her skin washed in cathode rays for a long time after she first read those words, and just outside the window the brown summer grass lay still in suburban streetlight. She never let herself replay this scene more than once a month. She thought about it alone under her blankets, falling asleep thinking of Sash's words braided with another word: *safe, safe, safe.*

Sash always insisted that there had been gay stuff in the official Mystic Knights games. The content had been censored, never made it out of Japan: lovers demoted to cousins or friends, nude pixel sprites clad, a crossdressing supporting character quietly bowdlerized. The Japanese game magazine article Sash had found and translated told the whole story. *and this is one of our goals,* Sash told her coworkers. *we're not just making a fan game. it's a restoration.* Lilith could believe in it a little when Sash spoke about it. She could believe in lots of things.

Now she was thinking of the last time she and Sash spoke. Thinking, she drew a tiny box on the corner of her layout page, and she filled it in with tight hash marks first in one direction and then the next, blackening and blackening the space without ever violating its boundaries, tearing the paper but leaving the rest of the page clean.

Are you drawing a map or something, asked Buckworth.

She flushed: Why had Buckworth spoken just then? Did he somehow read her thoughts, did he somehow know about—? On instinct, she twisted the paper away so he couldn't see it anymore. But no, that was a crazy thing to do. She breathed, tried to remember the lessons she'd gleaned from her father's copy of *The Tao of Pooh*: you are not in control; this moment is nothing, passing away as soon as it's born.

It's for a video game, she said, as if this could possibly help anything.

Buckworth kept his face still. He extended his hand, as a movie Jedi might, and beckoned with his fingers. He was a patrol leader now; he could order her to give it to him if he wanted, she thought. She handed over the maps.

He looked at her notebook, frowned, and started to fold the pages back toward the other maps.

Bell Prix Wizard Academy, he read. And then, more softly: —Is this a Mystic Knights thing?

She turned toward him. —You know about Mystic Knights? Just the new game, or the older ones?

Definitely the older ones, Scott said, his eyes fixed on her. —There's none where they actually go to the wizard school, though. In the new one there's a level where you go to its ruins after it's destroyed.

No, I know, Lilith said, trying not to sound too eager. —They don't ever go to the academy in the games; you're right; it was always *really frustrating* actually because if you look at the *design documents* they, you know, the designers, Oshiro99 and SuFish, they actually *planned to* in a couple of different games during the SNES era, but you know, like, cartridge memory limitations? So they *couldn't*, which is why the plot of *Mystic Knights GAIDEN* is that way? Since it had to be set up by this whole part where you study and get new powers at the academy, but you never go to the academy, so instead it doesn't make sense, like you just meet that singing frog in the swamp who teaches you *suspiciously powerful* magic techniques for a frog?

Scott stared at her; *shut up*, Lilith told herself, and she managed to do it.

So this is a map of a level they didn't make, Scott Buckworth said.

Yes, exactly, Lilith said. —Based on the design document? And they did *sort of* make it finally in *Mystic Knights X*, or anyway they made the ruins? And so this map is based on what the ruins would be like, you know, if it wasn't ruins? —She forced casualness into her laugh. —Sorry, I get *way* too excited about this stuff.

Don't apologize, Scott said.

She watched him as he ran his finger over her map, as if his skin was playtesting it.

You said this was for a video game? he asked. —How are you making a video game?

It's a game-making program, she said. —A program where you and your friends can make games. Not like professional games, except we want them to be as good as that. But it's dumb. I'm sorry. It's really dumb.

This time he didn't tell her not to apologize. —Can I play your game?

No, she said immediately. —No, I don't think you'd like it.

Scott raised his eyebrows. —I might, he said. —I like games. Why don't you want me to play it?

Nothing, no reason, Lilith yelped. Scott winced, made a little hand motion like he was turning down the volume on her; she found her voice obeying the motion. —It's just, I don't know. It's just this dumb game-making program I downloaded on AOL. It's just this thing I do.

He was watching her. He was still holding her book of map layouts; she wanted it back from him, but she knew she had no power to ask for it. Whenever you asked someone who had power over you to give up that power, it only made them want to hold it more tightly. The right thing to do was to wait patiently for them to give up their interest in the power they held, maybe to feel guilty about having held it. Eventually they would grow bored and yield the power back to you, and that was like winning. So she waited, and she let stomach acid dissolve any feelings within her that might trouble her waiting. He was still maybe a friend, she thought. A friend like she had online, only real. He knew about Mystic Knights.

For me, the first game is the best, he finally said. —The NES one. No question.

She wanted to ask him which NES one; there were two, one released only in Japan. But maybe it would be better not to seem to know too much about the series, so they would feel more equal. —I thought everyone hated that game, she said.

Why would they make all the other games if no one liked the first one? he asked. —People only make games if there's money in it. It's a business.

I think games can be art, also, maybe? Lilith ventured. —I mean, my company—I mean my friends and I—I mean, we make games without there being any money involved.

Games aren't art, he said, ignoring the fact that she had friends. —That's stupid. They're just something to do, like practice.

She bit her lip. —What do you practice? she asked.

Go jogging, he said. —Weight training. Real things.

She was surprised: Scott looked sickly as a rule, as if soaked in laudanum and milk. She imagined herself weight training: her body becoming muscular, strong, the flesh of her chest solidifying into pecs, from which hair would soon sprout. She felt tired at the thought. She realized she'd been sitting back on her heels for a while, and she slumped onto her sleeping bag, its sour miasma rising around her like flour dust.

What's wrong? Scott asked. —You don't exercise, that's why you get tired.

Nothing's wrong, Lilith said. —What was your favorite part of *Mystic Knights* for NES?

All of it, Scott said. —Probably the big final battle with the Elder Serpent, where he keeps casting full heal spells on himself? Or Northwood Abbey, in that part where you fight giants every step. Makes leveling up a joke. It doesn't waste your time. Have you beaten it?

I usually don't beat games, Lilith said.

You should, Scott said, as if winning were a choice. —This one's good, and it isn't that hard. So I don't know what the problem would be. —He got to his knees and tossed her maps neatly onto her pile of clothes. —I've got to see a man about a dog, he said. —Thanks for showing me your game.

He went into the rain then, zipping the tent flap behind him; she could hear him walk around the tent to a space in the woods a few feet away, imagined she could separate the sound of his spatter from the still falling rain. She imagined how his urination might look in CraftQ—how to code it, inscribed within the weather, the little yellow drops creeping down the screen and then invisibly back to the top.

She lay on her sleeping bag, head on the hard ground beneath the pillow she'd forgotten to bring. She did feel tired, she thought: she always had. Would exercise fix that? The old SF paperback he had been reading lay, spine cracked open, on his pillow. She never treated books like that. Should she? And should she beat the first *Mystic Knights*, that is, as soon as she was home indoors, not surrounded by boys in uniform, connected again to her computer and TV and all the systems she understood herself through? Was that what was wrong with her, that she'd never taken the time to win any of these games? A good person would beat those games. Sash and Abraxa had beaten them.

She imagined Scott Buckworth talking to Sash, the two of them facing one another on opposite sides of a great crystal bridge over a roiling cloudscape. Sash with long silver hair—she'd never seen a picture of Sash or anything, pictures on the Internet were not safe, but she imagined Sash had silver hair like the moon—a flowing black cloak, a crystal staff. Buckworth, his uniform untucked, his slow, confident walk. She imagined the two sprites approaching one another, imagined the chip-tune music starting to swell.

In the woods, time drifted. At school, home in Texas, she could look up at the clock halfway through a World History lecture and guess exactly which slice of the hour the minute hand would be resting on; here, her watch hands floated free, like a Ouija planchette. That evening, sun setting and the rain over, she sat on the wet crest of a blackhead in the earth, pretending to gaze at the trees with the *Boy Scout Handbook* open and unread across her thighs, and she watched the other Scouts. Everyone had already returned from the dinner hall with guts full of chipped beef (or peanut butter sandwich, for the troop vegetarian.) So strange the way they moved, ricocheting around the clearing and the pavilion—careful to keep distance from the Scoutmasters, who were known to draft idlers to pick up real or invented litter around the campsite—and forming clusters of two, three, five, to talk, to laugh, to break apart and retreat alone to tents or to travel in groups to the bug juice cooler or the pavilion and chessboard or the cooktables or places unknown, to talk, to trust. She wondered what they talked about. The earlier conversation with Scott was her only insight into what normal people's talk might be like.

She wondered what everyone was talking about on #teen-goetia tonight, and then the thought floated away, a baby spiderweb with nothing attached.

In the clearing, a group was scrabbling to build a fire. No one was quite clear on how to do it: Do you start by lighting easy things, grass and weeds, then work up to whole logs? How many matches does it take to light a log? Do you need gasoline? Do you rub sticks? The boys worked, built, laughed and called one another dumbass, douchebag, pussy (occasional barks of Scoutmasters interrupting, exhorting to be respectful) as they stuffed shredded newspaper beneath roasting logs. No one could see Lilith here alone in the dark. She felt a strange pride growing through her like a sapling. Slowly, she extended her hand and waved to the circle. Scott Buckworth didn't see her; no one did. She suddenly felt very powerful.

She remained invisible, she was certain, as she stood and walked into the woods, her *Boy Scout Handbook* clutched tightly against her hip.

The best thing about video games was that they gave you a whole big world to explore that had nothing to do with you at all. Her teenage world in Texas was nothing like that; there she felt uncomfortably visible, clumsy, awkward, inadequate. But in the world of the Mystic Knights, she could be nothing but a pair of eyes, floating over an imaginary space. You couldn't be clumsy or awkward in a game, and a game would always tell you what it needed from you. Expectations were transparent, fair, safe.

This walk, alone in the forest, felt a little like *Mystic Knights*. She imagined herself surrounded by the classic party lineup: the brilliant paladin Philippe on his destrier Senator, the criminal warrior Ern bringing up the rear with his electro-axe hungry for blood, the mysterious mages Susuru and Arden lost in a murmured conversation about Probabilities, the silent druid Wren contemplating the bugs he might be crushing beneath his boots, the rogue Brecca mentally inventorying his treasures as he absently finger-combed his mane, the ranger Katoki whistling as she picked a trail through the branches that now surrounded Lilith on all sides. And of course, the sorceress: a gothic death priestess, radiating chilly cheer as she walked with her whip coiled at the side of her fur jacket.

Sash told her, in one of their private query sessions on IRC, that she'd played at being the sorceress as a little girl, around the time the first NES game came out. She'd organized other kids from her block into an undead army under her control, and they'd gone on kid adventures together. (Sash lived in a big city somewhere, Lilith was pretty sure, someplace with *blocks*, not like Richardson with its long lawns, its strip mall grills, the howl of faraway traffic on Highway 75.) One time they had stopped a mugging, Sash had said; one time they had brought food to a hungry man sitting on a bench. Lilith had never pretended to be any of the characters; she had never played games like that with other kids. Even now, alone in the woods with fantasy misting into her perceptions, she could imagine herself only as the person at the front entrance to towns who tells the player the name of the town. She tried to imagine this town greeter really loved his job, had an inner life as rich and complex as she imagined her own must somehow be.

She kept her bulky flashlight low, focused it on the roots that broke up the packed dirt path. She had never before understood stories in which people became lost in the woods and couldn't find their way back home; by day, it seemed impossible that you could become so turned around that you couldn't remember which way meant *retreat*. Somewhere just out of sight in the dark, she knew, was a ravine, its bank steep with loose stones; she kept her long stride as short as she could. She imagined something leaping out of it—kobolds, skeletons, rakshasas, *worse*—something to challenge her, accompanied by a musical sting. If she had to, could she kill a skeleton with her Swiss Army knife (would slashing damage be enough?) What level was she? What class, what strength, how many hit points? She wished something from the woods would spring out at her so she could learn. Or maybe this was one of those story battles you couldn't win: the kobolds beating her with their fists, Scott Buckworth leaping from the woods with his own more powerful knife to take them down in a series of aspirational strikes. He'd give her his knife. *It's dangerous to go alone*, he'd say.

She wished she could be attacked by something she could name, quantify, or understand.

Imagining herself inside a video game—a comfort, as if wrapped in gauzy blankets in a forest bower—was way easier here than it ever had been in Richardson, the streets of her neighborhood sidewalks too wide and glittering, bright cicadas and tungsten phone lines making it hard to dream that this house might sell her health potions, that one stronger weapons, yet another a secret entrance to a ciphered tomb that hid the power she needed to advance. Every true first level in an RPG was either the woods or a cave; it was not a suburb in Texas. Maybe that was why she was still in the Boy Scouts in the first place: Scouts meant camping which meant forests, a vector toward clearly delineated adventures. Here maybe the veil was thinner; the possibility of slipping through it more close.

Tonight, as the sun was setting on her and she drew deeper and deeper into the woods, she knew Sash was waiting for her, online. She'd asked Lilith to meet her in their private query window again; *we should talk about what happened.* Lilith had agreed, and then she'd stepped into the car with her Scoutmaster and patrol leader, knowing that it was taking her into the mountains, a place where the Internet could not reach. She would have to pretend that she had forgotten all about the appointment. There was no way Sash could blame her for that. She would apologize, and the company would let her keep her job.

Two years ago, Lilith's mom had brought home a PC for work, freshly loaded with Windows 95 and its many sound schemes (Jungle was Lilith's preference), along with AOL and its file archives. The first file Lilith downloaded was a Lisa Simpson animated cursor; the second thing was a copyright-flouting CraftQ game about *Calvin and Hobbes.* She soon found more CraftQ games, and then the CraftQ forums, and then all the people she would think of as friends. She found she could think of herself as a person with friends.

The first step one took on discovering CraftQ was to establish a corporation; she called hers ChallengeSoft, and she announced that she was making a game called *Dragon Gaiden* on the ChallengeSoft website, which was a members.aol.com page with an animated *under construction* gif and an email address for job applications. Within two weeks she'd allowed herself to be acquired. Her new owner, Endless Destiny Productions, was a corporation run by an older Mormon teenager and three of his friends from church, none of whom Lilith ever met. No one at Endless Destiny seemed to work on games, and the company mostly posted aspirational release schedules to its official AOL forum. She and her CEO would chat over IM about his games and how excited he was about his girlfriend in Utah. Lilith liked to imagine her CEO and the girlfriend going on dates, imagined him buying her gifts and surprise desserts, the two of them talking quietly in the seat of the car he probably owned while VistaVision sunsets bled over the mountains.

Over time, following forum hints, she grew out of AOL and migrated to IRC, a place where your creativity was unrestricted. On IRC you could share illegal music downloads and say *fuck*, and worse things. IRC patched her into a network of other teens, other places—disembodied teens, safe teens. And the teens she talked to connected her to even more dangerous websites in turn: webcomics about alternative sexualities, interviews with evil music by evil bands, Smashing Pumpkins, Donna Black Zero, Erasure. Descriptions of dreams, weblogs, pornographic text files, even gifs, even clips. She abandoned the Mormon company; she never looked back.

Abraxa was one of the people she met on IRC. Abraxa unnerved her a little: funny people always did, because she wasn't funny enough, and that said something bad about her. Abraxa was also senselessly talented, the way Sash was, but somehow totally different. Everyone knew Abraxa was a great CraftQer, releasing more games than anyone had probably taken time to play. Lilith wanted to become a better CraftQer too, so she dug through Abraxa's game code. Abraxa's code was thrillingly deft and chaotic: most of the objects were named things like @ dewp and @d00dz and @jfjffdkd and @lol, and they were full of surreal comments about salvia, school crushes, band lyrics, ghost writing that the program would ignore when it compiled and executed object code. Had anyone but Lilith seen these comments, lodged deep in the guts of these files hosted on unmoored download servers? Did Abraxa herself remember them? Her indifference, her profligacy, these were the secrets to her power.

Once, burning and sleepless, Lilith started a new CraftQ file and made a room, populating it with two smiley face people. This was how Abraxa did it: find some characters, figure out what they have to say to one another. She stared at them for some time, and then she opened the code editor for one of the smiley faces, where she typed dialogue: *I want to kiss you.* As soon as she'd typed it, her brain fired: unsafe, delete. Her fingers didn't listen, saved the game, dragged the .qek file to a hidden folder where her family would never look. Sometimes she thought about this tiny game on her hard drive, a little light burning like a candle, clearing space from wax.

IRC is also where she met Sash: the lone girl in the CraftQ scene, far too cool to interact with, a locus of attention. There was a line of gender that could not easily be crossed, and Lilith, though of course curious about Sash—the idea of a Girl Who Programmed Games was almost too compelling—never dared approach.

At school, she had no idea what to say, or even what the protocols were for saying it; the feedback she'd received from her peers—fortunately, as a tall girl, there hadn't been many physical components to that feedback, but the message was the same—had convinced her to stop making the attempt. With the boys, the safest bet to avoid mean comments and physical harm was always something silence-adjacent: not so silent as to be noticed as a silent person, but neutral, laughing at jokes, offering sincere homework help, venturing that she had seen a movie other boys had seen and agreeing with their opinions of it. The girls in her school always seemed as if they'd be better to talk to than the boys; she retained fond memories of the time before everyone turned seven, discovered gender, and segregated themselves. There was no reason to dread puberty so much, she thought, if puberty meant that she got to be friends with girls again at last: bodily trauma as reunion. But she also had no idea how to talk to the girls she went to school with. She had little idea of how to talk to anyone.

But online, things were different. There were rhythms to fall into, secret languages, and unlike in the so-called real world, you had enough time to study them. Everything moved so fast in the real world. In a classroom she had zero friends, but in the world of text, when she had time to think before speaking—she did.

She had tried many times, then and now, to work out why Sash had sent her the email inviting her to join Invocation LLC. There was something in her Sash must have seen, some goodness or diligence or other quality that the only girl in the CraftQ online scene had perceived and judged worthy of friendship. And if this were true, it meant that a good life wasn't closed to her. All she had to do was see herself as Sash saw her, through Sash's eyes, and do more of the things Sash had loved, and so become worth it.

■　■　■

Her friendships often took the form of company meetings. Company meetings happened in a three-way private query, a pocket dimension outside the main channels like #teengoetia. Lilith tried to be early, but somehow she was never earlier than Sash, who responded to her *Hi?* immediately, always with: *hello*. Whenever Abraxa rolled in, Sash would begin the meeting with a story about The Critical Hit, often germane to their own challenges: the time SuFish drew a hallway with ten exits, the disappearing NPC and how it revolutionized the narrative, the week when everyone rotated jobs to learn how the others saw the world. (Sash sourced these stories from her translated interview in the Japanese gaming magazine, which Lilith guessed must have been really long, given how many stories from it Sash had to tell.) From there, Sash would ask each of them for *updates*, after first giving her own: *this week i reworked the chapter 8 outlines, this week i polished merchant barks on the promenade level of the great tree outpost.* She randomly picked either Lilith or Abraxa to give updates first. Lilith prayed never to be picked, because her updates were often the same—*I'm still working on it, I haven't finished*—and Sash would follow them with demands for explanations, strategies for moving past the blocker—*what's going on? is something in your life making you upset?* And the team would brainstorm ways to fix it. She wanted to lie, but lying was wrong, and there was no real way to lie about whether you'd finished something or not, though she guessed *working on it* could be a kind of lie.

Abraxa's updates were also repetitive—finished it, drew it, already did it—but at the same time, they were expansive—*and I was thinking, what if this battle had this? What if you could recruit like, a bear to your town? What if the bear could do human jobs, like serving drinks, and if you talked to him he'd be all like*

GRONNNNK? Lilith's favorite part of these updates was when Sash liked Abraxa's ideas, which would make the whole meeting derail so that the two of them could talk about them, and Lilith might never have to give her update at all.

Sometimes the three of them would shift into a kind of free play with the Mystic Knights characters. *Well, if a bear was in the tavern, maybe the sorceress would go there with all her skeleton soldiers and buy them drinks, lol yeah and beer would run down their spiiiiiines.* Sometimes they would start to pretend to be the characters, wearing them like disguises, saying what they would say. Once—and had this been Abraxa's idea?—the three of them held a kind of seance. *repeat after me,* Sash had typed, and then she had typed a series of actions that she was performing, and that Lilith, in repeating, would mirror: *i turn, i walk ninety degrees deosil, i turn again.* Lilith never copied and pasted, always retyped—part of the magic of the seance must be in the physical work of this—and she closed her eyes as she did, imagining what it would be like for the words to really turn into matter, their two figures tracing a circle about Abraxa. Sash kept typing—*you find your consciousness begins to dim, you find your eyelids failing, falling, you find a strange violet mist flowing from the spaces in your keyboard*—and Abraxa typed back—*lol oh shit violet mist, aaaaaa*—until something shifted, and Sash announced:

<sash> the summoning is complete.
<sash> the borders of the ego have dissolved.
<sash> the sorceress is here. she is riding you.

And Abraxa would really become the sorceress, or at least she would type more like her. Really Lilith could tell it was still Abraxa, pretending. But she never minded; it was fun to pretend. It was fun to see the world the way Sash saw it—enchanted, urgent, alive. And the two of them mostly ignored Lilith, which let her stay quiet at her keyboard, smiling at her coworkers' interactions scrolling by in the blue static light of her screen, as if at a Christmastime fire. She was lucky that they included her. She was lucky not to have to give her update.

Company meetings usually lasted three to four hours, or until everyone fell asleep. At least this was the case on nights when Abraxa showed up. And then there were the other nights, when it was just Lilith, and it was just Sash.

When they were alone, there were no inspirational parables or company updates. Instead, Sash asked how she was doing. That helped; she knew how to answer that. She talked, and Sash, like a *Breakout* paddle, impelled her one way or another, and Lilith could relax and enjoy herself, as if she were in an inner tube floating on the surface of a still, clear pool; she could get as wet as she wanted, no more. And of course Lilith loved Sash's work, and if she talked to Sash she had some connection to that work: in a way, the work could love her back. Sash was nice to talk to, also. She wondered what it would be like to meet Sash for real one day. If she were in Sash's house, what would they do? Would Sash invite her up to her bedroom? Would they sit on her bed? Would Sash comb her silver hair, and let Lilith watch? Part of her felt sick and part of her felt relieved that they would never meet. She knew they wouldn't: it was like a law, what you wanted you would never get.

The logs of their final chat were on the computer, there for just anyone to discover and read. She'd read them over what must have been ten times in the four days before leaving for camp. She should have deleted them, she thought—someone might find them. She wouldn't.

Here is how Sash had once explained to her the principle of Involution. In the original NES *Mystic Knights* game (the one that if Scott Buckworth loved so much, why didn't he marry it), the first city sits directly next to the final dungeon, Mammon's Sky Palace, a stone castle that floats above a gloomy mountain peak. The story of the game is about constructing the Jumping Boots that allow the party to leap into the clouds to face the final challenge. In other words, *in your beginning is your end.* You will see that which you desire; in seeking to achieve it, you will part from it; you will try, for the long duration of the game, to find it again. The other principles of Thereness operate on the level of the ROOM; Involution operates on the level of the life of a game. Involution is the heart of Thereness.

A dungeon without Involution might look like this:

But with Involution, like this:

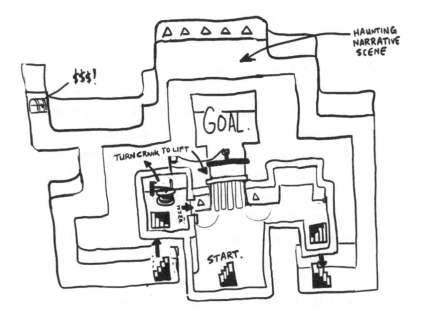

It was Sash, not Lilith, who that night had lifted the gate.

Lilith had seen cybering before, late one night in an AOL cha-troom where you had to be eighteen, or to say you were. *A/s/l*, someone typed—age, sex, location—and Lilith typed what she had to.

A woman was in the chat, describing actions she was taking vis-à-vis someone else's penis, the way her own body reacted to those actions. There was a waiting list; the woman was working her way through it, taking requests. A crowd of other screen names (people like SemperFi1949, BeachBUM, DivisionBell) typed while it was happening: *Getting hot in here, whew!* and *You're a dirty little slut, aren't you?* and *Do his balls next.* The woman was efficient, tossed off one-liners and sideways smileys. Lilith—terrified that the family computer was somehow recording her actions, that tomorrow morning there would be a printout waiting at her place at the breakfast table—kept typing and erasing the same words: *Me next.*

What she and Sash did in their final chat hadn't been like that. It hadn't been cybering, really. It hadn't. It had been something else. It had been a story they were telling together. That was all: she kept telling herself that, long after Sash had dispelled the magic circle of text that had held her mind separate from her body, had restored her to herself and said goodnight— long after Lilith had shut out her light and come carefully into her underwear, which she then folded and hid.

She imagined, for a moment, that the story was still here, following her like a cloud over her head. It was a thought balloon, full of words. It was silly: years ago she had, for a time, been obsessed by the fear that her thoughts were visible in word balloons over her head, that other children might read them and know there was something wrong with her. But that was ridiculous: no one could read your thoughts, and there was nothing words could do to you. Words could not affect her body, not really. There was no way—she was certain, then, at fifteen—to turn words into something as solid as this trail she was walking on, its trees becoming thin as she approached a clearing. She thought about a seed carried on the wind, the knife of its taproot as it slowly extends, divides, implants.

She had come again to the stone seat along the forest trail.

She'd known before arriving what this place would look like by her flashlight: a dark stone sofa, nearly black, that curved around the snaking cliff wall with olive stains of creeping ivy, dust of russet leaves, citrine sparkles of stone against the beam.

Her stomach felt sick, and her blood felt somehow light at the sight of the stone, as if she'd been injected with helium. If she were in a Mystic Knights game, she knew, this was a place where a haunting narrative scene would happen. Something would change.

She wished she had candles. Instead she set her flashlight down on its wide base and let its light extend in a halogen column straight above her at the center of the circle. It was spooky, its light casting no heat on her face, and she thought about the story of Jacob's ladder, one of the few Bible stories she'd internalized from that one month when her mom had decided the family ought to be more religious: the ladder where angels moved.

She drew closer to the stone seat, faced the beam, and told herself: sit down. Sit down, she told herself. It's a seat, which is for sitting. But there might be dirt on the seat; there might be spiders—a brown recluse!—animals that might eat her body away. Suppose a brown recluse bit her on the dick—massive damage, no possibility of salvation, *we have no choice but to give you a sex change so you can lead a normal life, everyone at the hospital is so deeply sorry.* She laughed aloud, as lunatics must, and she kept standing, looking down at the flashlight beam that tied together the earth and the stars, and she wondered how long the battery would hold out.

Her mind moved, strange weeds growing. So was Sash like her girlfriend now? Did the nature of what they had done online matter? How bad was what they had done, how unnatural? Would Sash still be her girlfriend if she didn't finish her maps? And was she going to hell? And if the Scouts knew what she had done, would they kill her quickly, or would they make it slow?

She flipped the blade of her Scout knife open and shut.

Around her, the woods creaked, chirped; woodpeckers rattled; distant things growled. Against the night, she said the words of the Scout Oath—*I will keep myself physically strong, mentally awake, and morally straight*—again and again until the words faded away, and the night was closer around her, and somehow she still felt safe.

After some time, she let her hand come up to the buttons of her uniform shirt. She was careful; she let it fall into one hand, held her knife in the other. She stood there, chest exposed, wind over her nipples with a shudder. She waited as patiently as she could for whatever was going to happen, for some tear in the veil. Sash had done magic to her, had woken up something impossible to name. So come on: so let the magic finish its work. So let the doorway open. So let the pit to the underworld crack open below her feet.

She waited for a long time: her Class A uniform clean, her knife unstained in her hand. The stars, visible here far from the phone lines, were either getting brighter or her flashlight was dimming out. That broke the spell: hurriedly she bent down, closed her knife, and turned it off.

Traversing a dungeon is different than designing one. When you experience a dungeon as a player, you do not know how long it will take to reach the end, whether your end is visible in your beginning. Your hit points and magic must sustain you for that entire unknown distance. To successfully traverse a dungeon, you need to keep something back. You must not use everything inside of you. If you do, you throw away your chance of returning safely home.

She stopped to pee against a tree on the way back to join the others at camp.

■ ■ ■

The next morning, everyone hiked: a snake of Scouts following the five-mile trail that looped through a series of
spectacular summits—farther and farther from the tents, her
blankets, her notebook. In a break between the trees, Lilith
could just make out the outer rim of the stone seat: an insignificant thing, next to the mountain the Scoutmasters had
set for them to climb.

Everyone else seemed able to go faster than her, not to feel the
ache she felt in her knees and ribs, the stab of stone through
the thinning soles of her sneakers. They must feel the same ache
she did: How did they teach themselves to ignore it? She must
have missed the lesson. She had to pay more attention: the
lesson might come again. She would be ready next time.

The trail led to a tall boulder that tapered to point, like the
awning of a roof. The trail resumed just above and beyond it.
One by one, the Scouts all pulled themselves atop it as if doing
chin-ups. Soon it was Lilith's turn. She stood at the boulder
and put her hands at the top of it, pressed with her shoulders.
She was taller than most of the others had been, could even
peer over the rock to the bootlaces of the boys who waited for
her. So why was this so difficult? Another secret lesson she had
missed? Her palms slipped with sweat against the rock, and
she pulled back her hands and breathed hard. The whole troop
was waiting. Her mind crackled like Pop Rocks; her hands slid:
How could she solve this problem? Maybe someone had dry
gloves? No one else had needed gloves.

After some time, a Scoutmaster screamed: *Come on, Parker,
quit being a pussy and get up there!* They all began to clap. *Let's
go, Par-ker, let's go,* clap, clap. She took her hands back, started
swallowing at the back of her throat: a proven technique to stop
vomit, or tears.

It's okay, she said. —I don't want to make anyone wait; I'll just go back to camp—

But that only made them angrier, and they kept chanting, until finally a Star Scout almost as tall as Lilith dropped down the side of the boulder. He braced his hands into a step for her. She put her boot into his hands: how much her weight must be hurting him. But he lifted her up enough to let her pull herself the rest of the way, then shimmied up easily behind her. *FINALLY*, shouted the others, and she nearly lost her balance on top of the boulder. It would have served them right if she had died, she thought, blinking very fast. (No, don't think that: a Scout is kind.)

One of the Scoutmasters dropped back to walk with her for a while. He said it was a hard part of the trail; he gave her credit for sticking to it. *Leave*, she willed, and she avoided eye contact and answered in monosyllables until he slunk away, slapping her hard on the shoulder: a signal of comfort.

Other lives all spread out on the top of the mountain, some of them eating bag sandwiches and chips and carrots and dip, talking as they sat or paced or tossed stones over the edge to see where they'd land, heedless of avalanche. No one offered to share food with her—she should have brought some from the tent, she guessed—so she went to the edge to look out at the valley. It looked like the cut scene in *Super Mystic Knights 3* when the party looked out over leagues of tilemapped trees, the camera programmed to zoom over them in glorious Mode 7 as the music swelled and came to rest on the spire of Skyveil Keep. But there was no spire here: nothing but trees, lakes, bad country trails and sheds without power lines and stupid boulders that she wouldn't be able to climb. She felt very small and very alone, and she imagined the others watching her. Maybe they were imagining shoving her off so they wouldn't have to wait for her anymore. What would it feel like to fall?

Rocks crunched, and she stiffened—was it about to happen?—but it was just Scott Buckworth.

Whatcha looking at, he asked.

Nothing, she said, too tired to pretend.

I don't know what anyone's looking at either, he said. —Fuck nature. Everything always respirating.

He sat down on the dirt beside her, so she sat down too. He opened his backpack, which contained a private hoard of powdered donuts, the throat-desiccating gas station kind.

You don't look like you've eaten, he said, shaking the backpack at her.

Normally she avoided powdered donuts—they were brutal and graceless relative to the pillowy tunnels of a good glazed—but she liked that he could get in trouble for having them. She turned, trying not to look suspicious: everyone else was closer to the center of the summit, in safety. She took a donut.

Ank oo, she said, mouth full.

He passed her his canteen; she drank from it after hesitating for a second to touch her lips to boy spit. —You've gotta keep hydrated also, he said. —You sweat out most of the good stuff in your body each time you exercise. That's the first thing I learned; now I'm teaching it to you.

She stared out over the cliff edge. —How much exercise would I get if I rolled over the side back to camp, she muttered.

I can't hear you, Scott said.

She repeated the joke like a boring assigned reading: —How-much-ex-er-cise-would-I-get-if-I-rolled-over-the-side-back-to-camp.

Do it, he said, deadpan. —Attempted suicide merit badge.

She felt a glow. —I don't understand what we're even *doing* up here, she continued, emboldened. —Everyone's acting like it's this big spectacular thing we've done, and it isn't.

Correct, Scott said. —It's nothing. Everyone knows it's nothing, too. They're pretending to feel things. People do it all the time.

Lilith watched him—he sliced off a piece of donut with his rat's teeth; how was it possible to eat a powdered donut so slowly?—and she imagined how his words would look in an IRC window. She wondered which of her feelings were real and which were pretend. It was a gnarly question. Part of her liked the idea that all her feelings might, in the end, be pretend, clothes you could put on and take off, and just you would be left underneath.

Listen, he said. —Have you ever thought about training?

Training how, she said. —Like, training to feel things?

He looked at her strangely. —Physical training, he said. —Lifting weights. Cardio. Have you ever considered it? Hiking might be easier if you did.

I'm not good at gym class, she said quickly.

Gym class isn't real either, he said. —But training is real. You can feel it in your body. —He held his arm out to her, flexed a muscle. —Feel it, he ordered.

She didn't want to touch him. —I'm not good at a lot of things, she warned.

People wouldn't hurt you so much if you weren't so weak, he said, withdrawing his arm to a safe distance. —Did that occur to you?

This hurt, and on instinct, she smiled. People called her weak all the time, of course—the whole camp had just shouted it at her—but this felt different. He was trying to help her, she told herself: really help her, not like the Scoutmaster before. He was teaching her something real.

I don't know that I'm weak, she said, weakly. —I think maybe there are powers besides physical strength? Don't you think? I mean, like, remember *Super Mystic Knights 4,* where Katoki spares the vampire teen? Maybe there's also mercy.

Maybe there's also mercy, Scott repeated in her voice. Did her voice really sound like that? She sounded like a girl. When he saw her, a girl was what he saw.

And then another voice interrupted: *BUCKWORTH!* It was Scott's father. Lilith put her hand behind her back, fast, so there was no possibility Scott's father would think she had touched him. Scott didn't startle. He closed his eyes and breathed in very slowly, once. And then, still holding his donut half, he got up, brushed powdered sugar off his shorts, and went to the center of the hill as all the other Scouts and masters grew silent and turned to watch. Lilith licked sugar off her lips. Scott ate the remaining donut in front of his father. And then Mr. Buckworth pointed to Scott's bag, had him open it, pulled out the remaining powdered donuts, showed them to the assembly— *this is not how a leader behaves*—and crushed them with his cowboy boots, white sugar into red dirt, a valentine smear. Mr. Buckworth's boots looked just-purchased, black and pointed and inlaid with studs and a stitchwork skull; they seemed not useful for hiking at all.

Scott didn't look at her, didn't get upset. He closed his bag, and he gathered his patrol as usual, speaking softly to them; softly, they gathered for him. She followed at some distance as they descended, watching him: the way his patrol hung close to him, the way they whispered jokes to him, tried to make him laugh. She kept thinking of his voice as he'd spoken to her: *maybe there's also mercy.*

Inevitably they came to another horrible set of rocks: two wide, flat stones spaced five feet apart, a maybe bottomless pit between them. A third thin rock balanced on top of the far stone. To cross the gap, everyone would have to jump, stepping onto the third rock and off again quickly so as not to dislodge it and be forced to surf the rock down into earthy hell, much like the sled crash sequence in the little-loved *Mystic Knights GAIDEN*. She stared into the ravine, where spurs of rock pierced up like teeth through the earth. That one would smash her knee, she thought, and that one would crack her skull, yolk of her brains and dreams disappearing into the valley soil.

The Scouts quickly made the leap over the ravine and gathered on the far side, and soon Lilith was once more alone. She braced herself for them to turn against her. But no, she wasn't alone: Scott hadn't yet made the jump. Here he was, standing close.

The trick is to commit, he said. —If you step just at the edge of the rock, it'll start to slide. So jump to the middle, and it'll equalize the friction.

From across the pit someone called her a pussy.

Ignore him, Scott commanded. —Jump. You won't be a pussy if you jump.

She looked at the stones again, powdered sugar churning in her stomach. But there was no way to back out of this: on the other side of the gap were the others, and here he was with her, his stare drilling into the flag patch on her shoulders.

Jump, he growled, and she suddenly knew how much he hated her.

■ ■ ■

When she thought about this jump in later years, she could never remember her exact thoughts, only sensations: the feeling of his eyes hating the sight of her, the feeling of cool air coming into her nose. The way she pushed off the ground, the way her legs split out and a fist punched up, like she was trying to break an imaginary block above herself. And the way her outstretched foot caught the rock, pitched her forward, slammed her against the stone knee first—she screamed in pain—and she scrambled down in an adrenaline fugue to join the rest of the troop, her knee wet with blood, hyperventilating as everyone cheered. The way she found her face smiling through the blood and lack of air. Then the way Scott made the leap easily, accepting their applause. He had done it, she thought, and she was proud.

On the rest of the hike down, as she limped, people kept coming up to her with compliments. She'd done great; her knee would be fine soon. The other Scouts were talking to Scott as well; his father watched at a distance. Everyone saw it. He'd led her over the gap, and therefore proved himself a leader. They'd both benefited from her taking the risk.

She tried to see all of it through Scott's eyes. You won't be a pussy if you jump—you won't be a girl if you jump—and she had jumped, and so she wasn't. This was the possibility he had seen, and she hadn't. The world has rules for you, standards you can meet. But if you work very hard, you will meet them, and the world will leave you alone. You will be worthy of invisibility.

Sash didn't know everything, she now realized. No kobolds were going to attack her, either. But experience points were real, and this is how you earned them. You met real challenges the world set for you, and the Boy Scouts were the whole of the world.

What were other lives? What did it mean that they could reach out to you, the way Scott had? The way Sash had, too: but Sash felt different, a wind whispering in your head, text on a screen, a choose-your-own-adventure. It was safe to trust your secrets to a screen: you could turn a screen off. You could go to the woods, where reality was, and your secrets would be gone forever. But Scott was not a role-playing game. Scott was here, and Sash was not. Scott's rules were not some abstract philosophy of level design; Scott's rules were real rules. When she obeyed them, the world started to like her.

What were your ethical obligations if there were other people like you in the world? She closed her eyes, there on the grass back at camp, and she pictured the souls of the other Scouts across the field: the little green candles, marsh lights drifting and blowing about the space.

It was dusk, and Scott was trying to get them to build a fire again. He directed them enthusiastically: gather cardboard, newspapers, anything that burns fast. Keep burning. But he was giving them exactly the wrong advice. Burning fast would be just like the fire they'd built before, a quick heap of ashes. And she intuited, with a small shock of pride, that she knew what they needed. They needed a structure that could endure burning.

Again she stood, invisible, and again she slipped away down the path and into the forest to gather sticks. At first, every stick she found looked wrong, wet, twisted. But then she found one good one, and then another, and there on the living tree, a third that she might cut free with her knife if she stretched. In this game, you had to find solid wood, wood that could let air and fire pass through it without collapsing. A fire is also a dungeon. A fire also has *Thereness*.

Later in life, when Lilith reflected on Camp Weathering and what she had learned there, she would think: *the main ethical choice in life is who to betray*. At the time, she didn't formulate this in words: the knowledge instead came as a feeling of happy purpose, earning XP at the job no one had asked her to do. So she worked, her arms filling with heavy, scratching sticks, and she imagined how proud Scott would be. And this helped her work faster, mind the scratches less.

4. Severance

<Post to CraftQ.warpmonkey.net's official CraftQ News and Company Announcements forum, 26 Aug 1998>

hello. owing to the apparent departure of one of our founding members, invocation llc is disbanding as a corporation effective immediately. all its projects are placed under immediate and indefinite hiatus. no questions will be taken. it's not your business.

sash

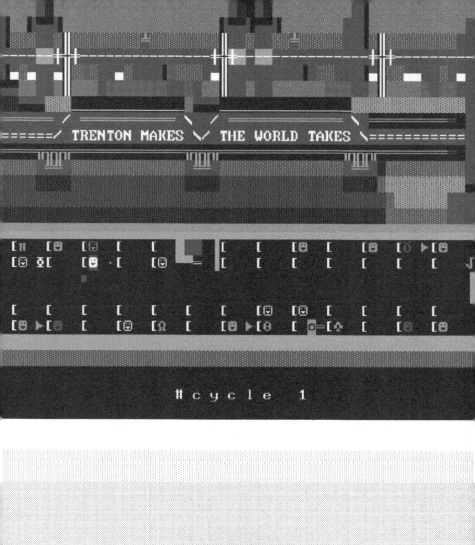

TRENTON MAKES ∨ THE WORLD TAKES

cycle 1

1. The Arrival

Fire will never destroy me; only in water will be my end. This is what someone's saying in her dream when Abraxa wakes up on the Amtrak. She twists in her seat, thigh still aching from the Mystery Wound she received when she was last in the ocean (surely shark bite), her legs crushed under her from the bulk of her duffel (which, *con*, now carried everything in the world she owned, but which, *pro*, was getting lighter all the time). For a minute, she believes she's still a teenager in Los Angeles, making weird video games with her online friends. But then she feels the chronic ache in her thigh, her lower back. The year is 2016—she's thirty-three—she's going to Marcie's house, which is the only safe place she can think of to go. She'll think of something else after that.

She offers the man sitting next to her some of her crackers and homemade nutritional spread: tuna, valerian, acorns, star anise, lox oil, cardamom. He pretends not to hear: Why? After days on this train she guesses she smells bad; maybe it's also the usual reason, maybe because she's trans. She can feel the fear gusting off him: *What if the tranny falls asleep on my shoulder?* What would it feel like to fall asleep on his shoulder? What if she does, and he falls in love with her? She imagines herself in an apron in his kitchen, roasting meat for him while whistling cartoon birds do their dishes.

Comfort is being comfortable with the people around you. If you do what makes you comfortable, and if other people take their cue on how to feel regarding a situation from you, then comfort should logically radiate from you to them, and everyone should become 100 percent comfortable in any situation. She tries to transmit comfort to him, imagines a cloud of hormonal sweat sublimating out of her sweat glands, encircling his head until it begins to circle with little cartoon hearts. She laughs aloud, and he looks at her, and she tries to look back at him in a friendly way. There is no reason he should not become her friend.

For the moment, she trusts her friend with her bag and goes to the café car, smiling at the sleeping passengers along the aisle as she imagines a vampire might, allowing them either to be afraid of her or in awe. She perches spread-eagled in a café car booth, alone at this hour, and she stares out at passing New Jersey, its vast TRENTON MAKES THE WORLD TAKES bridge. She repeats the words to herself, and they jumble and swim around her brain until she's just thinking *TAKES TAKES TAKES*, and she doesn't want to freak out now; her thigh hurts and she doesn't want to freak out now. She wants to keep calm and safe until she can get back to Marcie. Against *TAKES TAKES TAKES*, she repeats: *MARCIE MARCIE MARCIE*. She watches her reflection—legs half shaved half not, big jaw, ocean-freckled cleavage and hair burned sun-white, holes in her boots where fishnet toes waggle—and she repeats her mantra, louder and louder, so anyone who gets near her can hear it. Marcie is good, therefore if someone hears Abraxa's mantra about Marcie, that person will become better. Everything will get better, in time.

The man beside her is asleep as the train pulls into Newark, her bag tucked in next to him, his cheek resting on nothing. His iPhone sits face up on his thigh; she should lick its face and place it back where it was. She's tired, she needs to get off this train. She doesn't need to lick someone's phone. Self-care, maturity: she congratulates herself on these things. Being in her thirties has brought her these things; she is sobered, grateful at the thought as she waits for Marcie in the Newark station, bouncing on her duffel like a horse. She is back in New Jersey: its houses and buildings the thin cheese layered over a noodle of concrete, wet dirt and roots trapped beneath.

Through the canvas bag, through her fishnets, she can feel the floppy disk press against her: stiff plastic, 3.5 inches in length, poke of the metal shutter sharp.

The 2016 edition of Marcie no longer matches Abraxa's mental picture. Abraxa remembered T-shirts, hyperfemme with slogans, big black platforms, ribbon skirts with chains. Instead Marcie gets out of her weird old station wagon wearing sneakers, running shorts, and an ancient hoodie, her great kelp-clouds of hair frizzed from the city summer sweat that hangs thickly over her skinny skull and pointy chin. She smiles dippily, either very relaxed or stoned, when she catches sight of Abraxa bouncing on her duffel, and Abraxa leaves her bags and rushes across the station foyer to pounce, and Marcie lets her. She knew Marcie would let her. She swoops the skinny girl's body into the air, and Marcie laughs down at her. And every rando and retiree and rogue who rides Amtrak is staring at them: the two-headed trans woman colossus around whom the whole world now turns.

■ ■ ■

The back of the wood-panel station wagon Marcie's driving tonight is full of yellowing mail and packages and at least one transparent sack of cans for recycling, some from sodas no longer made, all of it crushed beneath Abraxa's massive duffel bag.

Sorry, says Marcie. —It's my grandma's car; we haven't cleaned it for kinda a while. —She eyes Abraxa; Abraxa feels her doing it. —You have to be quiet around my grandma, she says.

Quiet? shouts Abraxa. —What? Quiet? What? —She laughs.

Marcie nods slowly, keeps her eyes on the road. —She's really old, she says. —She gets confused sometimes when too much is happening.

One of the first things Abraxa's friend decided to say to her was *Don't hurt my grandmother*. Abraxa slumps against the passenger door, lets her head rest on the closed window, feeling its cool.

I'll be quiet, she says.

I think she's really going to like you, Marcie replies.

A pang of strange loss mixes with Abraxa's elation at being with her friend again. Marcie has lost the nervous, baby-chick quality she once had, the way she palpably found Abraxa exciting to follow. And if Marcie no longer looks up to Abraxa, what will keep the friendship viable? Bouncing her teeth against her lip, she focuses on the names of businesses along the road.

Medical supplies, she reads. —Does your grandmother have medical supplies at her house? Can we stop and get some?

We maybe have medical supplies? Marcie says. —It would help if I knew what kind you needed?

This kind, Abraxa says, and she thunks her boot on the

dashboard and hikes her skirt to present the Mystery Wound in her thigh. The gash is no longer hot around the edges, but the AC tickle around its perimeter still feels nice. —I got bit by a shark probably. So I need whatever kind of medical supplies treat that. Bandages, maybe, or some cloth for a tourniquet?

We have bandages, Marcie says. —And Neosporin? So it doesn't get infected. How long ago was this? There are probably a lot of really old bacteria in shark teeth, is why I'm worried.

Abraxa looks at Marcie and loves her. —I love you, she says.

I love you toooo, Marcie says. —So, did you do anything to keep it from getting infected?

It was the ocean, so I didn't have to, Abraxa says. —The ocean is full of salt. The water there is balanced.

At the next light, Marcie leans over to look at the wound. —There aren't teeth marks, she says. —It looks like it's just maybe a cut from a rock?

Maybe it just had one big tooth, like an axe blade, Abraxa suggests. —An axe shark. That's a kind of shark that exists. The Pacific is full of crazy things. Its name—is a *mis*nomer.

Axe sharks sound awful, Marcie says nervously.

They *are*, Abraxa insists.

I be*lieve* you, Marcie says, and Abraxa gets quiet.

She tries, quietly, to jog her memory of the day she got injured for any other supporting details that might advance her theory of the axe shark attack or of the existence of axe sharks more generally as a species, because it's extremely important that Marcie not just want to believe in axe sharks out of personal affection. She wants Marcie to truly believe in axe sharks as a real phenomenon that Abraxa has discovered, maybe that she alone *could* discover.

Nothing about the day itself was strange until the fight. It was just another day on the boat, island-hopping up the US Pacific coast from Carmel-by-the-Sea toward Oregon, British Columbia, Juneau. In Abraxa's mind, their course would lead them back across the Bering Strait, down the outer orbit of Kamchatka to Korea, Japan, the South China Sea, Vietnam, beyond. She pictured sunsets for herself, squatting naked at the summit of Angkor Wat and staring over red solar jungles, undeniably alive, her shipmates at her side.

Initially her shipmates—Elias, the captain, whose father's Morgan Out Island 41 they were sailing on, and Prosperine, Elias's girlfriend of almost two months as well as the ship's navigator and morale officer—seemed as game for this vision as she. Abraxa was the ship's cook and surgeon. The three of them had toasted over cocktails in a Carmel bar, toasted the sights of the Indian Ocean and Suez Canal that would soon be theirs, toasted the whole idea of themselves: three transsexual voyagers who would take what they wanted in life, drunk on a vision of themselves Abraxa had so forcefully, fluidly articulated to them there in the mountains at the Rainbow Gathering where they had met not three weeks earlier, as soon as she learned that they had a boat. So they adopted her into their party, and a new adventure began. They would sail into the light together, Abraxa's skin crackling red from sun against blue motion of water, the sex wails of Elias and Prosperine's mystic marriage twining around her in her hammock at night.

They had just reached Oregon when Elias and Prosperine started to fight, Elias's face all icy rage while Prosperine chased him around the ship shouting, Prosperine crying on the deck while Elias explained why her behavior and personality were insufficient. Abraxa spent days numbed out in the hold or climbing the terrifyingly skinny mast, toying with how far back she could lean over the water, letting her weight counterbalance the tilt of the wind against the sail. *Faster*, she willed the boat; *sail faster.* The sea was disintegrating the hull beneath them; the couple was disintegrating, too; as ship's surgeon, this was Abraxa's problem to resolve. Only by burning time faster could her vision for this voyage succeed.

And then Prosperine took all the vintage maps and sextants Elias's father had lovingly restored and dumped them into the ocean just off of Oregon Dunes, first taking care to smash the glass frame of each map. Elias hit her, and while Prosperine was screaming and holding her jaw—she insisted he'd dislodged her tooth; he insisted she was hysterical, all trans bitches were—Abraxa jumped into the water to save what she could. She gave up on catching the heavy, sinking instruments and frames, but some of maps had wriggled free of the glass. They slid over the waves, their patchwork borders and latitude lines like patterns on the scales of a snake. She tried to pick one up and it fell apart in her fingers.

She screamed then, and she dove as deep as she could, the water changing from Pacific blue to indigo to black, all motion stopping with the electric cold.

In this game, the weight of your body carries you deeper than you expect. The ocean opens itself to make way for you, and then it closes again behind. The object of the game is to return to the surface. The surface is where the light places are, where the sun's fire touches. Green and gray is up, blue and black is down. But when you swim toward a patch of green, it breaks apart: it was only dust.

Are you swimming up or down? As your muscles work—in

this game, your muscles define the limit of your body's power to move, and your breath defines the limit of your muscles—you are no longer confident of the answer. And you are surrounded by a pressure that no longer yields to you, but instead asks you to yield. And all around you swim strange serpents and fish, and you have gone too far, you are older than you were—you are at your limit—and you pray, from the last lick of fire in your chest, for land. For land again, for breath again, you will do anything, you will make any trade.

Abraxa didn't remember how she returned to the boat. She had just one image: herself vomiting salt water while Elias and Prosperine yelled at her, her thigh bearing a new wound. And the two of them went ashore and sullenly took her in an Uber to the hospital in Eugene, where they abandoned her with her duffel bag.

That was what really hurt: they'd taken her to a hospital, yet she'd told them she was a doctor. By the end, they'd believed in nothing she'd told them.

Rather than buying medical supplies, Abraxa and Marcie eat at a diner near Journal Square. Marcie orders oatmeal, Abraxa the Hungry Man breakfast: bacon, sausage, corned beef hash, eggs, pancakes. Between forkfuls, Abraxa tells Marcie stories about the boat, about the Rainbow Gathering that preceded it, about her stint before that working and living with an intentional community that financed itself through manufacturing ethical peanut butter.

They sell it at chain stores and highway gift shops, she explains.

I love peanut butter, Marcie says. —Why'd you leave?

Abraxa frowns: Why had she left? Someone had been talking shit about her in the blanching room—there had been a note on the pantry about labeling food—she had been looking at a tree and imagining herself twenty years later, resting on a cane, looking at the same tree, imagining it had come to hate her.

It was time to go, she says.

The conversation turns to people they knew in the summer they'd lived together in Florida, having driven down together from the northeast after first meeting at a protest to live with a woman who, Abraxa swore, would initiate them into neo-Gardnerian witchcraft and apprentice them as crystal readers for the southern Ren Faire and carnival circuit. This didn't happen, but they swam every day in the thick, wet heat instead, went down together into the white sand waves. Abraxa imagines this as Marcie tells her stories from that time, imagines Marcie there in the Pacific water with her, pulling her back to the boat. Maybe Marcie's spirit really was somehow there, she thinks, helping Abraxa like she was helping her now.

It takes them two hours at the diner, the smiley waitress who refilled their coffee ceasing to smile, ceasing to refill. Marcie yawns. Abraxa feels good, safe, expanding. She'd been feeling like a rabbit running for cover, and now something human is coming back to her, and she could talk forever. Marcie doesn't mind, of course she doesn't mind, that Abraxa is now the only one to talk, that Marcie is the only one to listen. Marcie gets something from listening to her. Everyone is getting something.

Jersey, Abraxa says. —We're Jersey girls together at last.

I always was, Marcie says sleepily.

I want to always be also, Abraxa says. —Is there an initiation? Do I have to get a sigil tattooed on me?

I think you just have to live here a while, Marcie says.

Then I'll live here forever, Abraxa replies.

Her good mood persists, spreads across the dark microlawn of Marcie's grandmother's house. —You gotta keep quiet, remember, Marcie whispers, and Abraxa wants Marcie to be happy, whispers *Okay*. She is maturing.

The house has a large bay window that looks into a music room with floral couches under plastic wrap and a big old organ with lots of stops. Abraxa, maturing, resists playing it. There's a kitchen with striped wallpaper and greasy old stove burners that she resists lighting, a pill organizer that she resists opening, a shelf of music boxes that she resists winding: automatic ballerinas and brass nameplates, FOR OUR ANNIVERSARY. When they get to the screened porch in the back, however—its stacks of ancient board games, its cardboard boxes of old vinyl and housewares and clipped coupons and recipes, the tape binding them speckled with dust and desiccating flies—and Marcie hangs the car keys on the pegboard over the label for BUICK, next to all the other keys that hang in sequence like a glockenspiel plectrum—and Abraxa must play them.

PO Box, she sings, rattling the keys in vaguely pentatonic progression. —Irv's Office. Church Basement.

Marcie gently stills the keys with her arm. Grandma, she whispers.

Grandma, Abraxa agrees. Stupid—she needs to be more careful—this is a safe place that she must not ruin.

Come see where you're staying, Marcie says, and Abraxa lets herself be led away, although she whacks CHURCH BASEMENT again on the way out. It rings, echoes like a bell.

Upstairs, they steer clear of Marcie's grandmother's room, detouring into the den off the hallway for a moment so Marcie can retrieve her vodka bottle. Half the room remains as Marcie's grandfather had left it—rolltop desk, novels by Leon Uris and James Michener, dusty word processor on used blotter. The other half has become Marcie's work space: a futon heaped with puffy white blankets, chest of lingerie, sandwich bag of eyeliner, webcam and tripod, two umbrella lights clamped to an old rolling clothes rack. Heavy sound-dampening blankets hang on the shared wall with her grandmother's bedroom.

I'm looking to get a replacement bulb for that, Marcie says, indicating the lamp that flickers uncannily when Abraxa flicks on the lighting rig. —You can work in here, if you need money. I mean, if you still work. You have to use your own account, though.

We can't work together? Abraxa asks, bouncing on her heels.

We maybe can, says Marcie, and she picks up the bottle of vodka and leads Abraxa to her bedroom. It's sparse: old lady bed with severe headboard, laptop open on card table against wall, folded laundry stacked on dark dresser with dog-eared copy of *A Safe Girl to Love* holding it down, matryoshka stack of empty suitcases in corner. —You can have the floor, she says, —or we can share the bed.

Abraxa dumps her duffel bag on the ground and flops onto the bed. She stretches her thighs into Happy Baby Pose, spine nearly popping after days of train.

It goes from there: they drink screwdrivers from mugs, Marcie puts on quiet Spotify tracks to muffle sounds, first laughter and then fighting and then murmurs and moans as they fall into making out, slip off shirts and bottoms, Marcie's skinny body at least a year more estrogen-soft than Abraxa remembered it, swollen nipples long like bullets, and Abraxa twists them, and she bites Marcie's lip to stop her from squealing.

Grandma, Abraxa warns, her eyes staring cobralike into Marcie's.

And soon Marcie asks her, and Abraxa digs in her duffel bag for her strap and harness, still pitted and sticky from the sea air. She digs, tosses things out: shirts, wads of panties, receipts, motel shampoo, toothpaste, eyeshadow, freezer Ziploc of estradiol pills, enough for years, parallel port to PS/2 adapter, sack of mushrooms with date and question mark Sharpied on its surface, PS/2 to USB adapter, map of Montana. And the disk, whose label is marked like this:

Everything she owns, scattered from her duffel bag over her shoulders like Johnny Appleseed on the forest floor of Marcie's grandmother's guest room. *My life is fucked up*: her sudden clarity about this comes with gratitude, because surviving her life means she is strong. And inevitably Marcie insists that they wash the strap before use, and inevitably Marcie's the one to do it, hustling on her bathrobe with a vodka wobble in her step. For a moment, the memory comes to Abraxa of her childhood comforter wrapped about her shoulders, her web browser sitting idle just across the room, static crackling like a fire. Teenagers are about to gather on IRC. She's home.

And when Marcie's skin touches Abraxa's and wakes her up—Marcie wet from the shower, her skin and the strap both smelling like pomegranate body wash—Abraxa gets cleaner. She's sure of it.

2. Real Questions

One of Lilith's action figures had fallen from the shelves in the night; she woke up cradling it in her arms. A woman in a blouse, cardinal-red plastic hair, articulated wrists, a cheerful expression. Lilith held her, watching the pale Crown Heights sunlight cross the figure's plastic ridges and hollows.

Standing on the bed in her nightgown, she replaced the figure on the shelf from which she'd fallen, along with the rows of others: warlocks with arms extended, monsters writhing, a ranger nocking an arrow, burning wolves baring teeth, ready to spring. At their center, her figure of the sorceress: skin pale, long ears swept back, whip coiled in poised hands. Sometimes, falling asleep as she looked up at them, she liked to imagine herself as an Egyptian priestess buried in her tomb, all her imported Japanese Mystic Knights toys ready to lay servicing hands on her in the dark. Sometimes she moved the figures around, imagined them introducing themselves to one another, having friend adventures in her apartment while she was out. Did they think of her as their friend, or their captor? She wondered that as well.

Every day, Lilith tried to ask One Real Question. A real question had to do with things another human might be thinking, insights she might not be able to guess by being very vigilant so as to observe and deduce their moods and judgments. Once a day, she would concern herself, earnestly, with another person's inner world—some desire, fancy, grief that another human might have—and she would ask them a question about it. There were two qualities that made a question Real: she had to be earnestly concerned with the answer, and she had to feel she was putting herself at risk by asking the question. One Real Question per day: that was her goal.

There was another trans woman on the subway. This happened sometimes: when she'd first moved here four years ago, hungry for normality in a city so alien to suburban North Texas or any of the cities she'd lived in since leaving there, she'd wished so desperately to encounter other trans women. And now it was 2016 and you couldn't go to a café without seeing one or two scuttling around in the corners of your vision, women you might even chat with, exchange numbers, likely never see again.

The Other sat nearly straight across from her: tall skull, dark tight ringlets of black hair, thick glasses made of beryl plastic. She wore a thick coat, and her e-reader was shellacked in stickers advertising a cartoon for adults. A little sketch of her biography played out: sad kid post-Bar Mitzvah commiserating with close female junior high friends in a sweat-thick summer room that contained multiple electric fans. The woman looked up; Lilith flushed and stared instead into her hands, knotted over her dark tights. Carefully, she pulled out her own subway book and opened it. And the two of them read together as the thick meat cloud of cis people got on stop by stop, coalescing like a curtain between them, and by the time everyone got out at Union Square, the other trans woman was gone.

■ ■ ■

When her manager at Dollarwise Investments, Ronin Mallard, called Lilith into his office from her station at the long
black Formica and cherrywood teller desk, she knew she was
at last about to be fired for being trans. Instead, Ronin told
her she had become the new trainee assistant loan underwriter,
reporting directly to him.

Congratulations, he said. —You've really grown this past
year, and we're ready to see what else you can do for us.

She watched him carefully for signs that this was a joke,
maybe a ritual hazing; maybe the lights were about to shut out,
a long carpet of coals about to smolder to life so that she could
be made to walk it. Ronin looked nervous, but he had always
looked nervous, his bearded smile framed by two broad, locked
shoulders.

Thank you, she said.

Thank *you*, he said. —Now, keep in mind this is still pro-
visional. There are still some hoops we'll need you to jump
through first. Fun hoops. Easy hoops.

He laughed—this is how people showed you it was okay to
laugh—and he went into explanations: the license expectations
for an underwriter, the duration of her probationary period,
the ease of the license exam, which she should really not at all
worry about, some advice based on his own probationary experiences. She nodded, wishing she'd remembered a notebook
so she could remember some of this later; she never remembered anything. Maybe she was already failing the probationary
period. She stayed vigilant for questions. Ronin liked to ask
her questions in the course of his lectures, which over her past
four years here as a teller had been frequent, prompted sometimes by her mistakes (miscounts, failure to secure approvals for
official checks, failure to smile), but sometimes just by his will

to explain the mechanisms of the bank to her. Binding her to his service by his assistance, Lilith thought, breeding a dependency. He called his management style Socratic. His office was lined with yoga mats for five-minute breaks; one of the filing cabinets was covered with a draped cloth showing a four-quartered prayer mandala, which for the past five months had held a dish of undisturbed, staling cigarettes.

You plant a tree, he was saying. —Even on days when you don't see it grow, you keep faith. And then!

He passed her a new nameplate: LILITH PARKER. ASSISTANT LOAN UNDERWRITER. He extended his hand; she realized she was to shake it; she did.

He showed her to a cubicle in the corner of the lobby, which she'd share with another woman who worked on different days, and he assigned her to complete a series of onboarding tasks on the old desktop PC that breathed by her feet. The cubicle was spare—a literature rack of rate sheets and mortgage terms, plastic IN and OUT boxes, mesh screen protector, tomato pincushion accented with ladybug pushpins. Sitting in the stiff-spined task chair, she could see the long black-and-cherry teller desk where she had just this morning clocked in to work. Her fellow tellers—all, unlike her, still in their twenties—could see her here, too. For years she'd stood behind that desk, feeling the barrier it formed between her and the customers as a kind of rampart she was paid to defend. The cubicle felt far more exposed. She let herself breathe, imagined roots growing out of her feet into the ground. This was a challenge, but it was also progress. They would pay her more, trust her to dress herself how she wanted. They would let her sit down.

She was probably the first trans woman in this position at this bank, she thought: thinking it, she felt tired, considered calling out sick. Instead she did the tutorials Ronin had assigned her, which took about an hour, and then she stared at the license requirements, and then she changed her desktop's window colors, backgrounds, and sound scheme until the day was over. She returned to the teller desk to clock out, tried not to meet her coworkers' eyes. Ronin met her there.

So we should go out to celebrate, he said. —Get some drinks, as a team?

Oh, she said. —I actually have other plans tonight? I have to buy new clothes, since you trust me to dress myself.

He didn't flinch at her turning him down; he never did. He hadn't asked her to get drinks in a while: Why today? Maybe she'd accidentally flirted with him? She had to become more vigilant about these things, more professional. She was the assistant loan underwriter now.

As she selected pantsuits and camis from the racks at Macy's, Scott Buckworth came into her mind. It wasn't unexpected: for years after Camp Weathering, she'd often tried to see her life through his eyes. Was she doing enough? Were her grades high enough? Was she pushing herself hard enough so that no one would categorize her as a problem, a queer, an aberration? Even after she decided to come out publicly as a problem, a queer, and an aberration—which she'd been able to do by realizing that if you came off to cis people as competent, an asset rather than a drain on resources, they would often do you the favor of respecting your gender—it was hard to break the habit of seeing herself as he'd seen her, as someone whose messiness, vagueness, weakness he had to teach her to hide. Not for the first time, she wondered why he had been so good at teaching her that.

She chose clothes that she imagined Buckworth might judge typical for a banker, plus a pair of ribbed black leggings that were not exactly professional, but that gave the kind of human vibe one might want in an underwriter. No one gave her shit getting into the dressing rooms; she only half expected anyone to these days, a habit like looking both ways at railroad tracks. She watched herself wear the professional clothes, changing the little lighting sliders from Office to Evening to Sunlight and back again at different intensities. How afraid she'd been, once, to come in here. How afraid she used to always be.

This was an old fear, she told herself. This was the same fear she always had when someone offered her a new job, a bigger responsibility. This was the fear that came whenever she thought about Sash.

She leaned her head against the mirror, and she turned the lights down as dark as she could get them. And then she stood up again, and she looked at her face, and she turned them all the way up, brilliant Gandalf white.

It was always too loud, it was always too dark, and the drinks were always terrible, and Lilith had no idea why her Tuesday-night Bitch About Work Together group insisted on meeting here. But they always did: three votes, one abstention, against Lilith's desire for a change, and here they all were again at the fucking Time Tunnel. As usual, they took the table in the back, surrounded on three sides by scarlet privacy curtains; as usual, they were the only women in the place. (Rare exceptions existed: cis work friends who called them fabulous, screaming bachelor-ette parties, cis butches who played pool and side-eyed Lilith's group.) As usual, the jukebox was all-eighties/nineties and dance-able; as usual, soft leather porn featuring workmen played on the projector; as usual, Susan bought them all drinks when she returned from sprucing herself up in the bathroom after closing her hardware store for the day. Susan's closing routine was a thing of wonder for Lilith: she shucked her overalls, her pink or fuchsia T-shirt featuring Lisa Frank psychedelia or cartoon characters for adults (ponies, Gems); she emerged in platinum blond club wig, black cocktail dress, the gold chain and bracelets that circled her neck and wrists twice nicked by errant drill press. Her black patent heels clicked like the carapaces of scarabs.

Susan always remembered everyone's drink orders: White Russian for Lilith, hot toddy or just ginger ale for Barbara, absinthe boomerang for Janet, whatever red wine was cheapest for Elspet, whenever Elspet showed up. Elspet had shown up tonight, and she joined the general toast to Lilith's professional success.

You should stick it out, Susan was saying, apropos of Lilith complaining about Ronin. —Sometimes you've got to go along to get along. If this guy's making trouble for you, well, guys do that? That's the world of guys. There's not a lot of opportunities for girls like us in that world. Rise above the shit.

But he asked me out for a drink, Lilith said. —I mean, in an emphatic kind of way. He hasn't in a while.

Oooh, said Janet, swirling her wine as if she were someone who knew facts about wine.

He probably thinks you're *hot*, Susan said, leaning back. —You *are*, you know? Don't let anyone tell you you're not. You're a hot young thing.

I'm also a gay young thing, she said. —Is he going to fire me if I don't go with him?

We know you're gay, Janet murmured. —You tell us often enough.

Yeah, well if he fires you for that, you can sue him, Susan said. —Lawyer up. It isn't hard. I've had to do it. Then you use the money to start your own bank. Personally, I'd try to redirect him. Guy like that, likes trannies? Bring him here; I wannt to meet him.

He might not be cute, Janet said. —She doesn't know, because she's a *lesbian*, remember?

You can't say trannies, said Elspet over the rim of her wine glass.

Is he cute, Lilith? asked Barbara, hazel eyes wide and soft. Whenever Barbara spoke, Lilith thought about how nice a person she was, and about how badly Lilith wanted to see her hurt. Barbara cried like Thanksgiving apples boiling and splitting in an oven; she wept butter and spiced juice.

He's whatever, Lilith said.

Excuse me, Susan was saying to Elspet. —Why can't I say tranny? I've been called it enough.

They're sensitive youths, Janet said, rolling her eyes. —They believe in *justice*.

I've been called worse shit, Susan insisted. —I got called worse shit last weekend on a job site, and I *pay* those people. People say shit like *she-male* and *maricón*? I just shout shit right back at them, curse their mamas, all kinds of racist shit. Then we can laugh about it. They respect me, you know. I don't care if they believe I'm a woman or not.

There's truth in that, Barbara said happily.

No there isn't, said Elspet. But she laughed, softening this, and Lilith backed her up with a smile and a little laugh as well. They had an understanding.

Lilith and Elspet had met at the same transfeminine drop-in support group where Lilith had met the rest of her Time Tunnel coterie. It had been toward the end of the period when they'd all been going to the support group together, around the time when it got really easy to skip sessions. Lilith didn't like being the kind of trans woman who skipped support group sessions; those were supposed to *help* you, and she'd always looked forward to becoming the kind of cool older put-together trans woman, poised on her folding chair and saying wise and hopeful things to the ruined young girls of all ages, teens, thirties, forties, sixties, their arms slack at their sides saying they didn't really care what pronouns you used for them, it didn't matter at all, stuff Lilith had once said. And sure, she'd reached the point where she was skewing wise more often than she was skewing depressive, and sure, *bodhisattva* had it all over *arhat*. But the flow of fresh miserable women never stopped—it seemed there were more every year, like the clouds had been seeded with *trans*, and now here came the rains—and sometimes women who were fine one week were miserable the next, as if Lilith hadn't even said anything to them, been gentle yet firm in explaining their problems. It sucked to be a *bodhisattva* at the drop-in group, basically. It sucked to interact with other people like you.

Susan and Janet didn't like the specific *bodhisattva* analogy when Lilith explained it to them, but they definitely agreed that most other trans women sucked, especially (they said) the young ones who all seemed to live in horrible collective warren apartments and seemed to all have read the same mysterious politically savvy authors and to hate you if you hadn't done so, young ones who'd told Susan, fresh on her return from Thailand after saving up for surgery for almost a decade, that her descriptions of the country sounded pretty racist honestly. Susan had told Lilith that story while smoking cigarettes post-group, and she'd segued from that story into an invitation to Lilith to join their separate hangout group: dinner and drinks at a cute gay club the older women liked. *You have a good head on your shoulders*, Susan had told her. *You're sensible*. Lilith was not into racism, but she also was not into continuing to go to the drop-in group, where women younger and more attractive than her made her feel politically stupid.

As a compromise, she invited Elspet, who the older women didn't like, but who at least had a good, inscrutable tech job in UX or something, plus a salary that let her make recurring donations to legal defense funds and LGBT advocacy groups. Elspet never really talked at drop-in group meetings, but she was mean and funny when she imitated the group moderators at the dinners afterward, and she had a bleakness that Lilith liked.

Therapy's a waste of time, Elspet told her once. —The next iteration of the transgender problem will experience fewer issues.

I don't know, I think therapy can be helpful, Lilith said back. And Elspet scowled, and something began.

And when I got there, Barbara was saying, —it was the *men's* bathroom they had directed me to! The *women's* bathroom, it turns out, was on the other side of the factory floor altogether.

Oh no, Susan said. Elspet rolled her eyes. Lilith stared into her drink.

There was just no possibility of it being an honest mistake, you know? Barbara said. —I thought about all the ways it might be an honest mistake, and I just couldn't figure any out. So as soon as I was done, I went back to her; I went back to that receptionist. And I told her: look, I'm a woman. I'm a *woman*, is all. And you need to show me to the *women's* bathroom.

Good for you, Susan affirmed with a sharp nod, just as Janet asked: —And what did she say to that, sweetie?

She didn't say anything, Barbara said. —I guess she kind of sniffed, *I'm very sorry, sir.*

Did she actually say sir? Elspet asked.

Barbara hesitated. —You could hear it in how she said it, she finally said.

Maybe she didn't intend to be mean, Lilith said suddenly. She immediately regretted saying it—something in Barbara's voice had stung her, and as if from bee venom, she'd convulsed. *Be a kind person*, she told herself. —I mean, of course you're right. Of course she probably did. Cis people, right?

Elspet smirked; the other three were still a little uncomfortable with the term (Janet insisted on pronouncing it *sizz*), like loose change from another country, an unfamiliar weight in their pockets. Finally, Susan set her hand on Barbara's cardiganed shoulder. Barbara immediately relaxed into Susan's touch. No one touched her very often.

I'm proud of you, girlfriend, Susan said, and Barbara smiled, and Lilith watched them smile.

And so the evening at the Time Tunnel progressed as so many of them did: the older women talked, the younger ones chimed in sometimes, met in the bathroom line to imitate their elders. Susan kept ordering rounds—don't worry about it, she always said—and she lingered at the bar for longer and longer spells. Tonight her eyes were on a grinning cis actuary, hair greased and smile bright over his diagonal-plaid vest, and she ground against him on the floor to "Born This Way" before finally leading him into the dark space at the back of the bar. Janet, after her third drink, started to talk politics, which was the worst part of the night: Janet was a Trump supporter. Instead of participating, Lilith watched the people dancing on the floor.

Tonight, following Susan's departure, there were no women for her to watch, and she wasn't sure she'd have the courage to meet the eyes of any woman dancing even if there were, so instead she tried to pick the best dancer from among the crowd—best being a quantity, steps per minute, sinuosity of thigh to waist to torso in motion, synchronicity of hands and legs—and watched them, imagining what it might be like to be that person, to be able to dance like that.

It's not so much that I support his policies, Janet was saying. —It's more what he represents. The whole system's rotted out from inside, and Hillary's not the one to fix it.

Barbara shivered. —I just don't believe he's a good person, she said. —People will see that.

People are afraid of him, Janet said. —There's something to that, their being afraid.

Lilith considered responding—considered what Janet might say to her if she did—kept watching her dancer glide on the floor, sweat and Christmas lights washing the smooth surface of his head.

At the end of the evening, Susan long since vanished with her actuary and her bag of work clothes, the four of them stood at the curb, Janet waiting for her Uber to take her to a DUMBO latex-and-restraints party and Barbara for a cab to Forest Hills and the rent-controlled place she shared with her wife. The older women got their rides, and then Lilith and Elspet walked to Union Square together, mostly in silence, where they caught the train to Lilith's Brooklyn apartment. They had an understanding.

In Lilith's bedroom, after both had washed up and Lilith had taken her contacts out, Elspet's body on Lilith's bed and letting

Lilith wriggle her out of her leggings, Lilith asked her: —What do you think I should do?

Are you serious right now, asked Elspet.

About work, Lilith said. —Should I say anything to Ronin? If it starts to get more weird?

Elspet scooched her butt back and sat up on her elbows, which Lilith liked; her breasts spilled a little over the cups of her bra, purchased months ago and losing the race with progesterone.

I mean, what's the worst that could happen to you? she asked. —If you get fired, so what? You could work in tech too. I mean, you'd have to learn to code, but that's not hard. There are camps. Didn't you used to make computer games?

That was a long time ago, Lilith said.

So you'll be fine, Elspet said. —Tell him you're gay. He's not supposed to be hitting on you anyway.

Oh sure, Lilith said, exhaling, letting her arms unclasp and swing like clock pendulums at her hips. —I'll totally report him to the national labor board. A transsexual is upset about unwanted romantic advances. They'll be extremely sympathetic to that.

Extremely, Elspet said. —The newspapers will all carry it. Mass protests and online outrage. The president will step in, and they'll pass a new law for you. They'll make it a holiday. Sisterhood Day.

They both giggled at the word *sisterhood*. —Will there be special songs you sing on Sisterhood Day, Lilith asked.

Lil-ith, Lil-ith, Elspet sang softly. —Lil-ith is so great. Lil-ith, sav-ior, fighting against haaaaaaate.

She tried a goofy vibrato at the end, smiling at Lilith, and Lilith felt so good looking at her and thinking about how bad her song was that she melted forward, crawled over the bed to sit across Elspet's hips, bent down and kissed her white neck, warm like pumpkin spice.

They had a routine that they stuck to: Lilith started on top, never removing her underwear, and she stroked Elspet's chest with the hand that wasn't busy at her crotch—Elspet wanted her shoulders avoided, her face, her hips—until Elspet sat up, sick tranced look on her face, and stood over Lilith like a mean vulture while Lilith got undressed. She never took off her own underwear, let Elspet do it before Elspet crushed all six feet of her down into the bed. Some nights Lilith could come and some she couldn't; tonight was a yes. It was Sisterhood Day. And then Elspet went to Lilith's bathroom to shower while Lilith sprawled and drowsed, imagining what a photograph of herself so sprawled might look like, what its caption in an art gallery might read.

She hadn't asked any Real Questions today, she realized. She would do better tomorrow.

3. The Trials

Marcie's window unit, its motor turning over and humming fresh air into the room against late-summer still heat: it sounds just the way the air conditioner sounded in Venice, California, years gone now at Abraxa's father's house, mornings when Abraxa would turn over, her covers dewed with pubescent night sweat and her mind already churning. Sometime in the night Marcie draped a plaid sleeping bag over her body: she twists and stretches under it, listening to the air circulate. She hasn't thought about her father's house in years. Maybe the thoughts are a sign: maybe it means she's come home. Maybe this is a situation that will last.

Downstairs, Marcie has left her a plate of grapes, veggie bacon, and toast in the fridge. She eats it at a table partly stacked with envelopes and covered with a leaf-pattern tablecloth and a plastic protective screen, the sun and the sound of ugly Northeast traffic coming through from the tiny backyard. She draws while she eats. Drawing in the morning is a habit she's developed over the years, a way to establish a thread between the days. She draws a memory from last night: Marcie sitting on her futon, shirt off and smiling shyly at her. When she lifts the drawing from the table, her pen has transferred part of the outline of Marcie's hip to the thick plastic screen. She runs her finger over it, wondering how long the groove will remain.

She should sweep the floor. From experience with making homes in strange spaces, sweeping the floor is the first task: otherwise, you will think about how uncomfortable you are every time your feet contact the earth. But Marcie keeps her grandmother's floor clean, and there's nothing to sweep. So Abraxa takes a jar of dried sage from the cupboard and upends some of it onto the linoleum: little clouds of spice dust form as it lands. She takes a dustpan, and she gets on her hands and knees to sweep the mess up.

If Abraxa can sit still for just long enough, only have space and calm for long enough to think, she knows she will remember how to find every treasure she's lost. Her high school bookshelf in her father's vanished house, it still exists somewhere—her childhood stuffed rabbit Lumpo—all the save files in all the cartridges of every video game she's ever completed. She can make herself a map; she can go back for all of it. So it's okay that everything she has keeps drifting away from her like smoke: one day the smoke will form itself into rainclouds, will burst over her, water her fresh. She pictures that day of revelation some nights at Marcie's, asleep on Marcie's floor with blankets stacked above her and skimming Marcie's queer-positive comic books by flashlight. All she's thrown away, again in her arms.

A few years ago, in preparation, she really tried to make herself a map of everywhere she'd been and everything she'd lost along the way: a big flattened road map full of stickers and pins. But she lost the map on a Greyhound, and afterward she couldn't remember how to draw it again: it was as if the places had been erased in the act of recording. Better, maybe, not to depend on maps: maybe better to trust only the tools you can carry with you when they ask you to go.

Most days Marcie's away volunteering or working or picking up groceries and pharmaceuticals for her grandmother, so Abraxa uses her computer to make a comic about her trip with Prosperine and Elias. It's a weird Photoshop assemblage of found sprites, cell phone photos of panels she draws in her sketchbooks, very detailed renderings of yachts and deep-sea creatures. She posts pages of it sometimes to her blog, out of order, a challenge for her readers. A lot of people must read her blog, she imagines: Zoomer child-kings scarfing detergent, perhaps a lonely trans woman in her forties, faithfully refreshing her browser over a big bowl of sugar cereal intended for children, perhaps the current presidential candidates. It's not about her audience: it feels good to work on, good to lose herself in contours of railings, interior galleys, the control panel with its inefficient yet semiotically nautical chrome levers and gauges, beyond the portholes a vast salt waste dotted by menacing prows of axe sharks. The sound of street repairs bleeds in through the window, buses shift gears, sometimes birds chirp accent notes like sprinkles, and Marcie's incense burns, black cherry and sickly sweet, next to two white tea lights that float in a dish of water, safe.

What she wants, she thinks, is this: a home she won't have to leave, at least not for a long time. Meaningful work. An end to wandering. Looking at her comic strip, she thinks without words of the lesson the ocean taught her in the moment she closed her eyes and her mind went dark. A home, and it doesn't have to be forever, it doesn't have to be very long at all. Just long enough for her to rest and feel healthy again: to get her land legs back. Just long enough for her not to be able to see its end from its beginning.

Marcie gets her a job interview at a popular arcade-themed bar, clued in to the opening by one of the affable trans guys she volunteers with. Nervous, Abraxa shows up for the interview on the appointed afternoon an hour ahead of time, freshly showered and her scarlet-dyed hair light and wispy on her skull like steam. The space is dark, even with the sun full outside the windows, the wood beams painted black, pinball cabinets and *Galaga* machines whirring and flashing, lost in endless demo. She draws in her sketchbook, declining all the opening bartender's prompts—*Are you sure you don't want to order anything? You're just drinking water?*—until he finally realizes she's the job candidate and pulls up a stool. He sizes her up: he looks like a mean nerd, she thinks, broad fullback shoulders with strawmop hair, thick glasses, and ironic hat saying PACMAN 2016 / MAKE AMERICA DOTS AGAIN.

Why should I hire you, he asks, and she tries as best as she can to answer for the next fifteen minutes before he holds up a hand. —I need to finish opening, he says. —Listen, thank you, sincerely. This was maybe the most amazingly weird interview I've ever done.

She looks at her knees; she's very tired.

You're welcome, she says, fixing her pupils on his and trying to flex her eye muscles in just the right way to make her pupils seem to swirl. —I have lots of ideas for how to make your business perfect. Do you want to get drinks later, and I can tell them to you?

I work in a bar, he says.

He doesn't call her later with a job offer. This was not the way, she thinks. She should not get depressed with herself that it was not.

She can feel System D start to enter her thoughts. (System D is the system that controls everything.) She shakes her head. She doesn't want System D to come into her thoughts again, even though entering thoughts is what System D does. No one can stop it.

Marcie's grandmother stays out of sight. In the morning, Marcie brings her breakfast, and then a snack at noon before leaving for her volunteer gigs, and then a full dinner before any evening plans can start, the previous day's plates collected either before bed or in the morning. The grandmother seems mostly to sleep. Sometimes there's sound from the TV.

She's mourning Grandpa still, Marcie explains one morning over a stack of waffles that Abraxa has made, their batter thickened with remnants of old sauce bottles found in the door of the fridge. —I don't know how long she'll be like this. I mean she can take all the time she wants—she's lived long enough; she's earned it.

You should take her one of these waffles, Abraxa says. —There's a ton of fortifying iron.

Marcie smiles and cuts another square from her own waffle. —I think her doctor has her on the diet he wants her on, she says.

I'm *also* a doctor, says Abraxa.

Marcie smoothly gets up to add more milk to her coffee, lingers over this while Abraxa watches her, tapping her waffle with her fork. Is she saying something incorrect? She should say less.

You'll meet her at some point, Marcie says suddenly. —When

she's better. I mean, she knows you're here and everything, so don't worry about that.

Abraxa hadn't been worried. —Okay, she says, cutting her waffle in half.

Another job interview, this time with one of the bookstores Marcie's organizations somehow liaise with. Too nervous to sleep, Abraxa takes a shower before sunrise, then spends the next two hours experimenting with Marcie's makeup. She settles on corkscrew eyeliner whorls and deep cheek contours, bruised rose lips, hair teased up again and again until it seems to burn behind her skull like a solar disk. In the mirror, squeezed into a silver tunic dress Marcie once bought for a dance party, she turns from side to side, hands clasped to her cheeks. What if she lived in a suburban ranch house and chased red wine with cocaine while ordering a servant to dust? What if she wore an earpiece and directed a consulting business while a pack of thirty-seven children shrieked in a pool in the backyard? She really could get this job, she thinks. She just needs to stay calm.

The interview is conducted by a trans man who spends half of his time reading confidently from a list of interview questions and the rest reviewing his phone. Confidence, Abraxa reminds herself: how you present yourself is how people will feel about you. So she explains exactly how she imagines herself fitting in at the bookstore, and he listens to her, scrolling. At first he notes some of the things she's saying on his piece of paper; as time passes, he stops.

I appreciate your honesty, he says, laughing a little as he shakes her hand. —Gosh, do I ever wish you a lot of luck.

■ ■ ■

After the interview, she goes into her sketchbook and draws a deeper part of the ocean. How far down did she fall when she was drowning? Impossible to know; that part of her brain seems to have erased itself. She draws the underwater world, staining the paper an ever darker indigo, swirling nightmare creatures from the deep. Serpents—bloated anglerfish, hermit lanterns swinging from their foreheads—massive tube worms, meaty stalks that terminate in blood roses. There is pressure at the bottom of the ocean—only creatures without form can survive the pressure at the bottom of the ocean—she puts pressure on the lead of her pencil, until it breaks.

She's just adding a gouache shine to the vampire squid mantle when something falls upstairs. She sets down Marcie's tablet and stylus, sits up straighter: Will more sounds come? A moan, a cry for help? Jackhammers outside break the skin of the street; there's nothing but silence within. How silent is too silent? If there's an injury, how long will it be before Marcie gets home to discover it? What would a doctor do?

Marcie's grandmother's room is sealed in by curtains and lit by a wash of wall-mounted television that showers the bed, the shelves weighted down by photo albums and tchotchkes, medical devices and pill boxes, a snuffed votive before a photo of an old man, a Christmas card still clipped to the mirror. On the bed the woman's face is invisible beneath a wide, heavy sleep mask: only her mouth can be seen, opening and closing in long, gasping breaths. Abraxa watches it for some time. A TV remote lies on the carpet beside her.

Hello, Abraxa says.

The old woman's mouth shuts, twists, opens again. —Hello? she whispers. —Marcie?

Yes, Abraxa says. —Are you all right?

The woman shifts slightly in bed, mask still covering her face. —I'd fallen asleep, she says, wonderingly.

Does your head hurt? Abraxa asks quickly. —Did you hurt your head on anything? Because if your head hurts, I could get you an aspirin.

My head, says the woman. —I think—my head is fine?

I'd better get you an aspirin, Abraxa says. —Wait right here?

The woman's mouth opens and closes, confused, but she seems unwilling to protest. The bathroom connected to the master bedroom is lavish: marble sunken tub, heated toilet seat with a bar, dried flowers in a vase, spent aromatherapy sticks. The aspirin takes time to find—there's both a medicine cabinet behind the mirror and a whole plastic caddy of pills and prescription bottles, some in Marcie's grandmother's name, some in her grandfather's, some seeming to belong to other people altogether—and Abraxa has to take out every pill bottle and sort them, first according to name and then according to height, trying to find the right one for the situation. It takes time, enough time for her to start to worry again. Why did she tell the old woman she was Marcie? And why had she actually come in here; what was she even doing? If the old woman was taking other medications—surely the old woman was taking other medications—was it even okay to give her aspirin? Would it combine with some secret chemical, fizz up in her heart, suddenly pop? She imagines that pop—worries—works in the mirror in tandem with another Abraxa in reverse, reverse hands sorting bottles, shaking.

She brings the old woman a glass of water and two tiny tablets of vitamin C instead. —Here's your aspirin, she says softly. —Yum yum, eat 'em up.

The woman stirs awake again beneath the mask. Abraxa helps her lift her head—her hair is light, like spun cotton; her skull is dry and warm—and feeds her the water and pills. —Thank you, dear, she whispers.

You're welcome, Grandma, Abraxa says. As she takes her hand away, she feels another itch: she should draw back the mask, should look her in the face. To appease the itch, she instead strokes the woman's forehead: soft but loose like the skin of an onion, frown creases gone permanent.

Do you want to go back to sleep now, Grandma? she asks. —Do you want to hear a lullaby?

There's no answer; the old woman's mouth is breathing softly, steadily. Abraxa continues to stroke her forehead, slowly singing one of her favorite teenage songs down to the last *Porcelinaaaaa* of the outro, mostly remembering the words, mostly remembering to keep her voice gentle, and the muted TV shows them paternity tests, cookware demonstrations, cheap deals on jewelry, and at last Abraxa feels her itch dissolving in cool relief, like a splash of aloe. She stands up, restores the fallen TV remote to its place.

That night, Marcie asks her: —Were you maybe in my grandma's room earlier today?

Maybe, Abraxa says, chewing on one end of the toothpick she's been using to clean dirt from the pin connectors of one of her adapters. —Her remote fell down, and I picked it up for her.

Marcie applies another run of liquid eyeliner, leans forward in the makeup mirror to minimize her chin. —Her prescription bottles were rearranged, she says.

I wanted to give her an aspirin for her head, Abraxa says. —I *didn't*, though. I couldn't be certain it was safe.

Marcie's eyes, painted now, seem to want to say more than her mouth has said. Abraxa has a hard time with this, sometimes: What do silent faces want to say? Is everything fine? Are you angry? Are you going to hurt me? Blank expressions are like marble statues: at any moment, they may come to life at you. Reading a blank expression correctly can save a life; has saved hers. She stares at Marcie, waits to see which way the girl's expression will break, until Marcie turns back to the mirror to finish her eyes, puts on a pajama top with the words *GAMER GRRL* messily applied in sequins. Her reflection smiles, finally, noticing Abraxa's reflection watching her. And then she's gone, in the next room with her work lights and webcam on, her audience beginning to arrive.

Run. A literal voice, always worse than the itch whenever it comes. *They don't want you here anymore. Run.* The voice of System D. She strikes herself in the forehead with her palm, twice, in an effort to mute it. Then, hands shaking, she goes to light the tea light floating in the water, but she tips the wax beneath the surface, and down it goes, its black wick snuffed and dark.

4. The Principle

Lilith had already sent her parents her monthly email with updates on her life, but she sent a second one anyway to let them know about her promotion. She wasn't concerned that they hadn't gotten back to her: her parents had taken to traveling since her father's retirement, adventure tours and meetup groups for camping and cruises, sometimes without much access to email. She wondered sometimes why they'd chosen this; she guessed traveling was a known thing retired people did, and they wanted to do retirement right. Sometimes they sent her photos: the two of them in front of palaces and jungles, tight, scared smiles.

When Lilith first came to work at the bank, she'd been in the process of not smoking anymore. It was a terrible habit generally, and she was getting far too old for it, and every time she took a drag she had visions of her ankle popping like a pool float, releasing clouds of trapped blood vapor from her deep veins, goops of teal Estrace. But it only took two weeks of slowly adjusting to the work—legs aching from standing behind the marble teller desk, dreams consumed with account numbers and ancient forms of ID whose crucial digits swam like oil drops over the laminated surface—before Ronin invited her out for a cigarette. He was just a supervising teller then, and she declined at first—*trying to quit*—but he looked so sad, and it was nice to see someone sad about not getting to talk to her. So she followed him out, leaned with him on a wall by a standpipe and smoked one of his periques, which tasted like grill rust.

All natural tobacco, he explained. —Listen, is anyone being weird to you at work?

No, she said.

If anyone's weird to you, let me know, he said. —This is a diverse workplace. You're safe here.

One cigarette turned into a standing twice-a-day appointment. She stopped trying to quit, just accepted her crackling ration. It wasn't so bad, and he didn't always smoke periques: he switched it up, Luckies, Gauloises, Nats. He liked variety, she guessed, and she liked nice surprises.

Ronin mostly talked about work while they smoked: goofy back-office stories, irrational decisions by the loan approvals people and other senior management, weird customers, bizarre transactions. Her days were that service industry mix of boredom punctuated by rushes and shouts; it helped when she could look at a customer through Ronin's eyes, wonder how his stories might transfigure them. She didn't contribute any stories to the pool; she wasn't a good storyteller. But she kept a list in her head, felt a thrill as his narration got around to the young woman who exclusively deposited twenty-dollar bills folded into individual animal shapes (a bitch to unfold, per Ronin), or to his attempted robbery by a nervous old man who'd sloughed a trench coat to reveal a homemade PVC supervillain outfit, his own original character police reports later revealed he'd spent months obsessively writing about on comic book forums. This last story thrilled Lilith deeply: she knew that in practice Ronin had just hit the silent alarm, but she imagined him and the old man struggling over a gun, how hard Ronin would have tried not to knock the man's skull against the cracked bank linoleum. *Be reasonable, be reasonable.*

Are you like, fucking Ronin, asked the cis teenager who worked the desk next to her one day. —Sorry if that's personal.

Lilith worried her fingers together; out for years, past thirty, and still she didn't know whether this was a normal bonding question from a cis woman or a trap.

I'm not, she said.

It's cool if you are, said the teenager. —It's just, you're always going out together. And he's always looking at you.

It was a trap, but not for her: for Ronin, whom she just then realized everyone but her despised. He was the running joke; she, transsexual workplace crush, was the punchline.

What's up, Ronin asked her later as she smoked his Dunhills. —You seem really bothered today.

How could he tell what she was feeling? How did people know that about one another? That was something hormones were supposed to do for you, people online said, yet for some reason this hadn't worked for her.

I'm fine, she said. —How are you?

He watched her, circulating his British-flavored smoke. —Listen, I really enjoy hanging out with you, he said, and she braced herself. —I look forward to it.

Oh, she said.

You're just so cool, he said. —You should know that about yourself. That's all I wanted to say.

He somehow segued from that into a mean story about

a mortgage client who had a funny way of enunciating the name of her dead husband. Lilith mostly remembered to laugh at it. Cool, she thought, through the remainder of the shift. Cool? At home that night, in the same Crown Heights apartment she still lived in, that back then her starting teller salary just barely covered with the help of two roommates and a couch subletter—she looked at herself in the mirror that hung from her door. In what way was she cool? What coolness did she bring to this man's life? She looked at herself a long time, trying to see herself as Ronin saw her, mentally editing the contours of her face—what would I look like with surgery, what will I look like in another year of HRT, what do I look like now; could I describe myself accurately, if you were interested to ask—before her consciousness could finally step back, could see the essential transness of the complicated figure she and her mind were dancing together. She could see it better than he could, despite her being inside and him being out. And suddenly she never wanted to see herself through his eyes again.

The next day he came around with Luckies. —I quit, she said. —I mean, smoking! I quit smoking.

The teller and the other cis girls ate him alive: *Smoking alone today? Where's your cigarette date?* But he endured it. He kept a professional distance for three months, and then he started to ask her about her lunch, her weekend plans: easy, coworkery interactions. A year later he promoted her to head teller. And now here he was again, she thought: ready to let her once more let him down.

As a teller, she'd had to serve many customers; now, as an underwriter, she just served Ronin. The work was scrutinizing documents: sources of income, credit histories, business plans, sometimes criminal disclosures, medical references.

She only rarely saw the human people behind these documents. Since giving her the new job, Ronin had tried to keep her away from customers altogether. It was paranoid and unprofessional, she told herself, to assume that this was because she was trans rather than because she was in training, or maybe because she was bad at her job in some way beyond her power to perceive, in the way one's nose can become inured to one's own imperceptible unshowered reek. She and Elspet called it the Ronin Principle: all the loan applications began with him and finished with him, the human point of contact.

It was definitely paranoid to assume Ronin was keeping her away from customers. He brought her in to see customers sometimes, often for meetings with a certain type of new client: invariably liberal, often white, either a well-moneyed yuppie or grandparent. They seemed happy to see her, and Ronin seemed happy to be able to give them the opportunity to see her. No, stop thinking disloyal thoughts: a Scout is loyal, a Scout is kind. She spent these client meetings sitting in a small armchair inside her rib cage, coaching her outer self to breathe, to feel the roots growing through her feet, to get through the interaction and back to her desk.

At her desk, in the documents, she got to see the truer selves of the customers. Her job, she remembered, was to defend the bank: the customers were the random encounters who threatened it, yet on which it might grow. It wasn't different from her childhood with Mystic Knights games: she remembered scrutinizing the poster that came with the NES game, the one that listed all the monsters and their stats. For hours she'd go over this poster, wondering what it might be like to fight the monsters she hadn't played through the game far enough to meet. People had stats, too: health, credit score, damage power. Her job was to wonder what it might be like for the bank to fight them. What was the chance that the twice-divorced hygienist's debt-to-income ratio after sending herself back to night school would cause her loan repayment checks to bounce? What was the potential damage-over-time factor of trusting the felon? She was paid to answer these questions, cite her sources, and report it out to Ronin with a recommendation to approve or not to approve. If she did well, the bank would grow in power and avoid taking financial damage; if she did poorly, the bank would absorb loss. (A Scout is thrifty.) There were consequences outside the bank, too: her work, if she did it well, determined whether someone's bodega could open, whether a pregnant couple would have a new home for a baby, whether that elderly couple who lit up at the sight of a real living professional trans woman that they could be good to might retire in dignity.

She could make choices: no one had trusted her to do that in a while. Or rather, Ronin trusted her to suggest choices, which he would then make. One day, if she did well, she knew they would let her make them, too.

Suppose she was now someone with a secure future? This was hard to get used to: her years since transitioning had mostly been dedicated to carrying her video game dolls and pop jars full of bulk grain from apartment to apartment, moving cities to follow roommates before somehow ending in New York, wrapping her soul tightly like a grapevine around bad job after bad job until in the end, the bad jobs left her (the bookstore chain closed, the video game store transferred her and then canceled her branch, the closed captioning firm shuttered over a rogue captioner scandal during a live sports event, the coffee shop burned). Throughout it, she kept silent and to herself, eating the shit she was paid to eat: if she'd thought of the future at all, it was in terms of how long it would take the bank to fire her, how many months of rent, food, and estrogen she could draw from her savings, like cooking a soup bone again and again to leach all the nutrients from its marrow. But now she thought of her cubicle and its distance to Ronin's office, and all the offices above him in the great root system of the bank. They trusted her now, the way humans trusted one another. She'd never planned for that.

And yet other times Lilith wondered, intensely, why Ronin watched her so closely. What was he afraid of? What were they all afraid of? Thinking about it one evening while she stirred pasta water, making starchy whirlpools with her wooden spoon, she supposed they were afraid she would betray them. It was like the part in *Mystic Knights 2* when the sorceress first joins the party and the other heroes don't trust her yet. She's evil, she's a witch, she used to be our enemy. How do we know she won't betray us?

Lilith tried to see the situation through Ronin's eyes. The first thing she saw: she was a transsexual. This was never the first fact she noticed about herself anymore, when she chose to look, but it must always be the first thing Ronin saw, even the object of his fantasies of her. And what were those fantasies? Fantasies of blur, fantasies of instability. A transsexual is inherently unstable: she is someone who yanks herself out of her context and plants herself in altogether different soil. No transsexual's roots can ever be as strong as a cis person's. We are built to betray. This is how Ronin must see it.

She looked at her whirling, boiling pasta water, imagining

what it would feel like to be lowered into it on the wooden spoon, and then she shook this fantasy off. This was silly, she thought. She had no intention of betraying the cis people. And one day, if she worked very hard, she knew they would see that.

Thinking of betrayal made her again think of Sash. Invocation LLC had been a job she'd felt afraid of, too, one that had trusted her to make choices from which she'd fled. She wondered why, all these years afterward: the challenges Sash had set for her and Abraxa then had really been so small. Those principles of Thereness, which Sash had clearly invented: What were they even for? To make video game mazes. She no longer knew why she'd been so convinced that it was beyond her powers to do that.

She'd been so negative about herself then. She imagined herself in the past: weird Boy Scout Lilith in her mind, crunched up against herself in a smelly, wet tent with some gross boy, drawing maps and crossing them out. Whether or not it had been reasonable to fail, she'd failed. She hadn't mastered the principles of Thereness. In fact, she hadn't been there at all. But she wasn't this person anymore. The past had no connection to the present—it wasn't a given that she would betray Ronin's trust in her. She could help customers for real, now. She could beat any video game she might want.

I forgive you, she thought about the self she no longer was, and she felt warm.

She'd started her after-work yoga class a year before for her back: standing at a teller window for eight hours was a job that had clearly been more intended for twentysomethings than for thirtysomething transsexuals without good insurance. But now that she'd gotten past her discomfort with healthy cis people staring at her body, she found yoga indispensable. She found her space toward the middle back, and she breathed, bent, and moved her wrists, hamstrings, hips as the instructor's calls dictated, let the details of loan applicants' sordid personal histories start to fall away from her like rain down her drying hair, scattering on her mat.

One night, tired and bound home on the train, she talked herself into buying fancy yogurt with honey in it, cultured in the stomachs of dead Icelandic cattle, six dollars for four ounces. She was terrified that this would be the moment of disaster, that her dead stomach yogurt would be the chariot that pulled her into short-on-rent hell. But it wasn't.

At home, she turned on her phone to find two missed calls, both from Ronin. He hadn't left a voicemail for either. She called him back.

Did you call about something you needed me to do, she asked.

He led her through some questions about something that could obviously have waited, and she remembered to breathe, and he asked her what she was up to tonight, and she remembered to breathe, and eventually she got off the call. On Facebook, Janet had posted a photo of Hillary Clinton, fresh from her third presidential debate. *I hope my liberal friends celebrating right now remember, we get the leaders we deserve.* Lilith stabbed her phone screen, closed the app.

The week after, she bought the yogurt again; after four weeks, she was buying two.

She was hanging Halloween decorations along the edge of her cubicle partition when the loan applicant appeared, the first who had come only to her.

Knock knock, said the applicant. —Sorry, I don't want to disturb your cobwebs.

The applicant wore a pinstripe burgundy suit over a tucked-in dishwater camisole, zebra flats, and many chunky rings. Their skin was pale and freckled, almost glowing, and their eyes were large and focused.

You can disturb my cobwebs, Lilith said. —That's fine.

The applicant smiled and sat down in the cubicle's second chair. The cubicle had no desk, only a corner work surface, so the two of them were side by side, no protective barrier between them. The applicant flexed long, soft-looking fingers; a tall, frizzed puff of hair, like that of an electrified Bob Dylan, reared up over them: a smell of vetiver incense, neutral body wash, and rain.

Can I help you, Lilith asked. —I mean, how can I help you?

I'm sure you can, the applicant said, answering the first question. —Are you Lilith Parker, junior underwriter?

Lilith was the only one of her cubemates who'd put up a nameplate, as well as the only one who had thought to cover her work surface in black cats and festive gourds. —That's me.

Lilith Parker, junior underwriter, seems like someone who can help me, the applicant said. —So Parker is English, but what's Lilith? Like, Baltic? Or Persian, right?

The applicant was smiling: toothy and sleepy, like a surfing wolf. —It's transgender, Lilith said.

Thank you for trusting me with that, said the applicant. —Well, so that we're equal—I'm Fionna Mercier, which is cisgender, she and her, and also Scots and French. With a little Italian. —Fionna's surf wolf smile began to fade. —I hope what I said wasn't busted.

Of course not, Lilith said. —You need underwriting for a loan application. Is that correct?

Just a little one, Fionna said; her smile was sparking up again. —The least of capital loan applications.

In retrospect, thinking of what she said next, Lilith would reconstruct the unexpressed thought that had directly preceded it: *this is someone whom it is wrong to find attractive.* —Normally, customers go through my manager? I can introduce you, if that's something you'd like.

No, I want to go through you, Fionna said, and Lilith didn't ask again.

Fionna was seeking funds to turn a property of hers into a healing center. The bulk of the ask was for reconstruction and repairs: the property, which she'd acquired at auction, was in terrible shape, gutted some years ago in a fire and never quite rebuilt; the congregation had moved on to some other space. In addition to construction and contracting, Fionna wanted operating costs for staffing, training programs in conflict resolution, queer self-defense, personal narrative writing, bodywork, productive divination, and equipment to prepare inexpensive meals. The center would take in people who were experiencing psychological distress, but who may not have access to traditional mechanisms of insurance. Fionna and her staff—initially just her, probably, but in the end to be supplemented by volunteers and graduates of the center's programs—would help free people from their old toxic paths of coping, instead adopting methods that worked.

Scott Buckworth would have an opinion about Fionna. Realizing this, Lilith imagined herself holding up her hands, blocking Buckworth's eyes. She didn't want to know what Buckworth thought.

Fionna's business plan stretched across the pages of a

three-ring binder, aggressively paperclipped and sticky-noted, complete with construction time and materials estimates, a sliding scale chart for services, journal articles about the efficacy of physical meditation practices and art therapy, demographic charts of Jersey City, analysis of rent and property tax over time. She had drawn a map on graph paper of the final space: the community kitchen, the dormitories, the dojo. Lilith's eyes explored it. She and Fionna used the same symbol for doors.

This is incredible, she said.

Thank you, said Fionna, sounding unsurprised. —It's an important project to me.

Lilith closed her eyes, reviewing what remained in her mind from the documents. —You've shown where the capital loan will go really well, she said. —Is there a part here about where the repayment funds will come from?

Donations, Fionna said, face becoming serious. —Sliding scale fees and donations. It'll be plenty.

Of course, said Lilith, trying not to let her voice show alarm: love was maybe being withdrawn. —I'm just, it's my job to make sure there's a clear repayment timeline? So it's sustainable? That's why I need to ask you that. I'm sorry.

Fionna's eyes and mouth had switched jobs: now her mouth was smiling, her eyes were not. —I forgive you, she said. —So what would give you reassurance that there's a sustainable timeline? I'll do anything you need.

I'll review these materials, Lilith said, after a moment. —And then I can let you know some next steps? I'm sure you'll get the loan.

Why had she said this last part? She couldn't possibly promise that. But Fionna's smile came back to her eyes: again their burn, gray touched with red. Fionna had to know Lilith couldn't possibly promise approval on a walk-in, especially for a nonprofit business, especially not for someone who was trying this for the first time. It didn't happen just like that; Fionna had to know that. So because Fionna had to know that, Lilith was safe. Fionna would hear her words in the way Lilith had, in retrospect, intended.

Then I'll give you space to do your work, Fionna said. She stood up and stretched, arms high and camisole moving over her stomach, jut of her ribs like boomerangs. —Listen, do you have a card?

They haven't made me cards yet, said Lilith, trying not to sound pitiable.

Then can I have your personal number? Fionna asked. —I want to have a point of contact, so I can update you if I need. There are a lot of angles I'm working on with this—a lot of things happening.

Lilith offered her number, and Fionna entered it into her phone, which was decorated with a Tarot card: The Star, a woman spilling out two jars, one over water, one over land, indifferent to where the water went.

That's my card, Fionna explained, catching Lilith looking. —I'm very glad I met you, Lilith Parker, junior underwriter. I think we'll work well together.

I'm glad I met you, too, Lilith said. And Fionna's shoulders relaxed—she'd been carrying them so tensely, Lilith realized. *I know you're glad to meet me*: this is what Lilith imagined she thought.

And suddenly Lilith could name the feeling she'd had, just beneath her skin, during this entire applicant meeting: the feeling that Fionna reminded her, as no one had in nearly two decades, of Sash.

■ ■ ■

She sat in the cubicle for a long time after Fionna had left, reviewing the prospectus, neglecting other work. Fionna's documentation was thorough, and it included a long personal essay on the project and what it meant to her: it looked back to her childhood dynamic with her sister Siobhan on their parents' Minnesota farm, the unfeelingness of the family home, how Fionna had broken through the sense of self-loathing that chill had engendered and decided to commit to giving a better, warmer beginning to others. This, too, felt Sash-like to Lilith: Sash's game had been about building a community, too. And Sash also had this sense about herself, this idea that beliefs she had might be narratively important, even urgent. The sense that you could feel something, and then go out and do something because you had the feeling. The sense that you might ask other people to help you with this. The sense that what you felt and wanted was the most important thing.

At this thought, Lilith shut the prospectus, pressed its covers together like a haunted grimoire only she could keep sealed. She sat like this for some time, cold, and then she stood up and started to walk with the binder to Ronin's office. She cradled it over her heart, and she could hear her steps echo as if her legs hurt so much they'd become someone else's legs altogether. He was shopping for something on the computer; at Lilith's knock, he quickly minimized the window.

To what do I owe the pleasure, he asked.

Someone brought this to me, she said, trying to make her voice normal. —I thought I should bring it to you. I read it. I'm sorry.

He frowned. —Why would you be sorry you read it?

She tried to get her words together to answer him, *Because of the Ronin Principle*, except no, obviously Ronin himself didn't know about the Ronin Principle. But what was she supposed to say instead?

Is it good, he finally asked.

It's great, she said.

His fingers knitted his beard. —How repayable is it, he asked. —Scale of one to five.

A Scout is trustworthy. —Three, she said.

He thumbed his finger at his inbox, which towered under a stack of other proposals, their comb bindings staggered to help them lie flat. —Kind of mix it into the middle, he said.

She took a step closer to the stack, berating herself. Why had he asked her to answer with a number?

I really think this one is good, she said. She needed not to say *queer community* to Ronin as a selling point. —I'd really be happy to work on it more with the client. We could get it to a four. A five.

Ronin appraised her. She tried to look disinterested and professional, to stifle the tiny child jumping and screaming next to her spine: *want, want.*

No, he said finally. —You shouldn't put energy into things you know can't work.

He loaded her up with three short capital loan applications for condo space. Back at her cubicle, trying hard to work through them, wondering what had convinced him to say no, she opened a document on her computer, typed *I want*, and then deleted the document.

On the 4 train home, she could smell someone smoking between the cars. She changed to a closer seat, shut her eyes, breathed deep. She checked her email: *Congratulations,* her father had typed. *We know you'll do us proud.*

5. The Vision

Is Marcie still angry with her? This question consumes Abraxa for days. She needs Marcie not to be angry with her: she must ration herself carefully, make Marcie last like water in a canteen.

Where will the end come from, when it comes? In her sketchbook, in the pages after the bottom of the ocean, she tries to draw all the possible ways this might come to an end. In one, cartoon her sits at a cartoon table looking sad while cartoon Marcie shouts at her about dollar signs. In another, cartoon Marcie is in bed with a cartoon lover: genderless, hair a lavender flip, body frail and shaking; cartoon Abraxa sits on the other side of a door, sadly listening. In another, cartoon Abraxa makes a stricken, sad face as Marcie's grandmother's cartoon ghost flies up to heaven, pills Abraxa gave her scattered beside her on the bed. In another she breaks a vase.

This is morbid—this is not like her. In the past, whenever she's started to feel these ways about the places she's lived, she's left. The policy has never failed her, not since she was a teenager, and she was so good at leaving. She's left before for roadside campsites, contracts on fishing boats, dangerous strangers' bedrooms. When did she lose her power to leave? She starts to draw herself leaving—cartoon Abraxa, stepping off the edge of a cliff—and then below the cliff, she draws furious black water—and again her leg begins to ache. No, she shouldn't leave this time. Leaving is what she always does. The work right now is to stay. She commands herself, *Stay*, and in her sketchbook she limns her cartoon figure with four sharp strokes of walls. Then she draws bars.

Marcie's friend Scramble, formerly of Knoxville, is staying with Marcie for a few days en route to a living room sofa in some Brooklyn trans house. Marcie and Abraxa go to pick her up at the same station where Abraxa arrived just three weeks before. Abraxa doesn't like this: things should not go in circles. Circles are a sign that System D is taking control.

Scramble, a short, shivering figure with pale hair steeped in lavender dye, loads their single backpack into the trunk, and Abraxa volunteers to ride in the back seat with the garbage so that Marcie and her friend can be together. Scramble doesn't say much on the drive, leaving Marcie to talk: long rambles about her volunteer work and recent albums and comics Scramble may have encountered. Scramble responds in monosyllables. Abraxa watches them, a feral kitten, stiff in the backseat.

Unprompted, she gives up her half of Marcie's bed to Scramble; she'll sleep on the futon in the den. From the pillow in the windowless twilight, she can see Marcie's webcam, and she imagines she can still smell Marcie in the air around the futon—armpits, sex, detergent. She strains her ears, but maybe the soundproofing is too good. She curls onto her side, frowning into the backs of her hands, and then she turns on the light and opens her sketchbook. On the top of the page, she draws an ugly image of herself squatting naked in her stockings; on the bottom, Marcie spooning Scramble, both bodies lying in moonlight. She draws a halo over herself, wings, as if she's protecting them.

Looking at the drawing, she thinks: *This is fucked up. This is a fucked-up thing to have drawn.* She regards it a minute longer, and then she tears out the bottom half of the page and creeps into the hall with it, slides the bottom half beneath Marcie's door. The action releases her into sleep. In the morning her drawing is gone, unmentioned.

At the kitchen table, she works on more wholesome artwork, a kind of affirmation: herself in a crisp Jehovah's Witnessy dress, knocking on the doors of businesses who want to buy her labor for money—as she listens to the two of them arguing about where to take mushrooms Scramble has brought.

They discuss this in the kitchen, the big leftover pot of lentils, broccoli, and fake bacon that Abraxa made getting cold and gross. Marcie's voice is getting flatter as the conversation circles, as she explains again and again to Scramble that they won't go to jail for doing drugs in the park, no one watches the park, and Scramble's voice gets higher and faster—*no that's fine I mean I get that I mean I'm sorry I mean it's just if they do arrest us I can't deal with what that'll do to my whole life I mean—*

A fight is imminent—and forgetting the word *stay*, Abraxa gets up to leave, which is when she again notices the rack of keys hanging by the door to the game room. Again she begins to tap them like a glockenspiel, sighs as each raps sharply against the wooden plate. Again she notices the key marked CHURCH BASEMENT.

The church is not far, maybe thirty minutes' walk to Mercer Street, in the snootier streets near downtown Jersey City. Marcie and Scramble are leery of the idea of going to do drugs in an abandoned church alone, no matter how many times Abraxa explains the advantages—it is neither home nor a place police are likely to watch; it is a weird old church—and in the end, she has to agree to go with them. She has experience with urban exploration, she asserts, and Marcie believes her.

Marcie packs a blanket in a tote bag, and the three of them take the long walk down Montgomery Street beneath the highway overpass—three trans people huddled against the purple evening, Marcie ignoring catcalls even as Abraxa screams either THANK YOU or FUCK YOU back—and Marcie explains where the church basement keys come from. She tells them about the church food pantry her grandmother once volunteered with, the times Marcie went with her to help coordinate and distribute donations, the long folding tables stacked with preserves, wilting salads, dented cans, bags of flour dust, lines of people and kids loading it into shoulder bags and wheeled carts. Abraxa gets quiet as Marcie talks, lost in the tired reverie she finds herself within whenever she's reminded that someone she meets has come from an uncomplicated home.

Why do you still have the key, Scramble asks, voice wary.

Grandma just never returned it after the fire, Marcie explains. —I don't know all the details, but the church burned down and never got rebuilt. So there wasn't anywhere to return it to.

How can we go there if it burned down, Scramble asks.

It's still there, Marcie says. —It's just boarded up.

Boarded up, Abraxa says excitedly: she imagines the place, a ruin sealed in with thin planks.

Scramble, face swaddled in cloudy wool scarves, looks ill. —Why didn't they rebuild it, they ask, but no one knows the answer.

And it's safe to be there? Scramble asks after some time. —It won't catch on fire again, or anything?

Sure, Marcie says. —Anything bad that happened there probably already happened.

Maybe we'll meet squatters to be friends with, Abraxa sings.

I don't want to meet squatters, Scramble says quickly.

Marcie hooks her arm into Scramble's. —Don't worry, she says. —I'll protect you from squatters, okay?

They walk for another minute, and Abraxa thinks: but I'm a squatter. Then she throws her chest forward and runs down the street, stretching her arms out, feeling her nylons rip and her backpack jounce against her spine. She approaches the traffic light: *ignore it*, she thinks. Go straight through and take what comes. But she stops to let the other two catch up, now silent, now again walking apart.

It's just Abraxa, she imagines Marcie saying to Scramble, maybe via a telepathic rapport that the two of them have already secretly formed. *It's just the way she is. Don't mind her at all.*

The church is a tall heap of stones, a vaulting ashlar petroglyph. The fire left it scarred: Day-Glo orange tick-marks sprayed at key joints, its front doors and windows sealed with swollen slabs of particle board that suture the spaces where the flames and pressure within grew on their own fecundity, and the smoke built until it burst outward, scattering rainbows of dark pebbled glass all over the asphalt. There are two buildings, parsonage and chapel: a narrow, overgrown courtyard divides these, dead flowers drowning in the year's last dandelions. The ruined property sits among rows of brownstones where graphic designers must live, lavish sedans bumper to bumper on the curbs. It faces an empty parking lot protected by a gate. Everyone who parks here, Abraxa thinks, must face the chapel's burned stare every day before they go to work. She clutches Marcie's arm tight, swallows: she must be chill, or this church will not think she is cool.

I've been here before, she announces. —Maybe in another *life*.

I don't want to do drugs here, Scramble says, but it is too late. Abraxa's skull throbs as the three pass below the thin red brick arch that connects the buildings, through the ruined garden between the gutted church, the silent parsonage, and each leaf and weed seems to fluoresce green in the security lights imperfectly bracketed to the eaves.

The sealed doors at street-level can't be the only entrance, she thinks, and she's right: behind the garden, there's a cement staircase dug into the earth, leaving exposed a basement wall that looks raw, like a taproot, wet. At its base is a door, a real one, its edges blackened and its corners warped by passing smoke. The CHURCH BASEMENT key that she's been fingering in the pocket of her hoodie for nearly an hour now is a perfect fit.

As the door draws back, the smell of the interior comes unsealed: dust, candle wax, insect mung, old incense, old fire, all released into Abraxa's face as her eyes, ecstatic, close.

Soon the party stands assembled at the doorway, flashlights in their hands. A click, and an old stone arch vault appears, silver spiderweb filament spanning the void space. Debris from the interior demolition is everywhere: stacks of warped plywood pallets, shattered plaster, wire lath tumbleweeds, the ribbed intestines of disused sump pumps. Their beams cannot reach the back part of the space, whatever hides beyond the vault.

Hello, Abraxa calls into the dark, a courtesy for squatters. But there's no reply, only the stones and wreckage and whatever ghosts move among them. And Scramble protests only a little as Marcie sets her flashlight on the ground and slowly closes the door behind them, leaving a bright column shining up. None of them can bear to close the door all the way.

Once some of the stacked plywood is set aside, there's enough space on the floor to spread out the quilt Marcie's brought, taken from her grandfather's things and redolent of menthol. It's enough space for all three to sit together comfortably, if close.

This is so awesome, gushes Abraxa. —We should always come here. We should play Dungeons & Dragons here.

I need to be in a safe place to play Dungeons & Dragons, Scramble murmurs, and Marcie scoots closer to them. Abraxa imagines flakes of ash passing through the flashlight's beam, imagines the cobwebs fluttering like a wedding train.

Soon Marcie takes out the thermos with the mushroom tea in it, and it begins to circle. Scramble doesn't hesitate to drink deep, their flashlight propped in the crook of their lap and pointing up at their revenant cheeks. Marcie seems spectral too, a sadder specter: maybe a valet, cursed to float in perpetual attendance through the stone vaults. She notices Abraxa staring at her and smiles shyly at her across the dark, drinks from the thermos, passes it on. The tea is lukewarm, meaty and milky at once as it passes down Abraxa's throat.

She assembles the heavy brass candlestick she's carried with her since the Rainbow Gathering, installing the purple taper candle she took from Marcie's supply.

Look, she says, elated at how quickly her lighter catches, how tall and broad the little spear of flame is as it flicks like a lion's tail. —The fire *likes* it here.

Scramble laughs, eerie and sustained in the dark.

■ ■ ■

The drug comes up in the usual way—rolling motion like a ghost hand stroking Abraxa's spine, flickers of color at the periphery of the flame where light borders dark, portentous feeling scumbled hard into everything, as if all sober life was the shadow, and now they were crossing into Narnia, where realer and deeper things might begin.

Abraxa had realized she was trans while on mushrooms. This was something she didn't talk about much, in part because she wasn't sure how correct it was to think of this as *realization* rather than *recollection*. She had known a little bit back in high school, talking about drag queens or shemales or who even knew what crappy things she'd said on IRC. Mushrooms were just the catalyst that had made it impossible to escape the truth of the proposition. She had been out as trans for years now—how many years was it, exactly? When should she start counting from?—and in those years, her memory had reviewed the facts of her identity again and again, made all the arguments *for* so many times that any arguments *against* had long withered, like leaves severed from circulation of the branch. These were things one never spoke of to cis people: that this had all once been a hypothesis, that whatever facts lay at the bottom of it were never unmixed with faith, which is never unmixed with desire. But you could apply that description to anything you believed. If the brain works primarily via systems of faith and desire, what does objectivity even mean? Who even wants it? What should it matter to her now, here, skirt hiked over her knees and cushioning her like a magic carpet in flight?

Her thoughts are loose now, circling, and she laughs—the other two startling, their pupils wide as they lifted from their own reveries—and she stands, wobbling on her feet, chitin lightning arcing up and down her back. Mice skitter and spiders tense as she raises her arms, cruciform, and steps through the portal into the black, breaking the seals of the spiderwebs.

She's been in this place before. She had been sure of that on the street, is surer of it now as her eyes adjust, magenta vision crackling around the borders of objects: shelves, plastic cans of something (primer, sealant, holy oil?), broken stack chairs, boxes, a seriously massive steel cross that rests, dismounted, against the bricks. She stares at this, the space where the planes intersect, as sheets of purple lightning gust over its metal. There are other archways at the edge of this room, deeper darknesses; somewhere within them, there must be a staircase up to the church proper, where starlight comes in through ruined rafters. The earth's core is somewhere below her; she can feel it crackle.

She sits down in the dark room, knees cracking as she sits, cold earth long against her thighs. Each breath brings spider parts into her lungs; she focuses on breathing out, first just to push out the spider parts, and then to push out everything. She breathes out, and the ache in her knees floats away. She breathes out, and she forgets Marcie and Scramble, there in the room behind her. She forgets what she can see growing between them—or had she seen anything? She'd seen what she was afraid of, which is that Marcie will throw her away, and very soon. Because everyone has always thrown her away.

And she breathes out, and gallons of invisible water vomit out of her—she hadn't realized she'd been carrying it—she had drowned on that boat in the Pacific, hadn't she, had floated alone with the axe sharks and drowned, and no one had saved her. Now, seeing herself there vomiting in her mind's eye, she understands in a way that's past language, felt in a slackness around her heart: the story is over. You don't need to be afraid anymore. Everyone is going to throw you away, so all your fears are going to come true, and you never have to be afraid of what's true. Principle of Involution: you already know how this will end.

Thinking that, she looks at her fear sitting before her like a little last ember, and she blows on it and it floats away, settles to the ground at her feet, goes out. And now she's empty, breathing easily in the dark, cleaner and easier than she has been in years.

Breathing, she realizes that she's no longer connected to the floor.

There's space for the dust between her and her thighs, enough for a spiderweb to blow. How much space is there? Infinitesimal? An inch? Two inches? More? How much space is there between her and the ceiling? How far away have the others moved, so small and out of sight?

She is rising out of her body, as if a crane has hooked her collar, is winching her up, up. As if the ceiling isn't here anymore, only walls as lines, breaks in the field of walkable space. From above herself, she looks down on the labyrinth, her friends clustered in the outer room, their faces suddenly looking up. Her own face is there, looking up at her: a white face peering out of a blue coat. And the fire is a triangle—the debris is symbols, letters—the dust is ASCII char 176. Up here in space, among the fires of stars, the third dimension is lost: the space is flat, a blueprint, a map.

The space is a room in a CraftQ game.

A purple thunderclap—she returns to her body, finds herself kneeling before the cross—and in the dark space ahead of her is a figure, female, her long inhuman ears crackling in the dark. The figure is laughing: she loves Abraxa, always has, loves her like no one else ever will.

Feeling the comedown begin, she floats back to rejoin the others. Scramble's face seems to crack, breaking into a bright, joyous yolk; Marcie shudders as she sleeps. Abraxa loves them both, wishes them only good. They'll leave me, she tells herself, and then the thought rearranges itself like a warm wax lamp: they'll let me go.

She picks up the candle, breaks the stalactite wax that's flowed from it, fusing it to the floor. In her breath are dust, char, mildew, new weeds breaking through cracked concrete. And she knows the way is open now, and she blows out the candle, and everything temporary disappears.

6. The Tower

An hour after the election results had come in, Lilith was still playing Nintendo. She'd had no competition for the TV since the critical states had been called; Elspet, joined by a plurality of other guests, had begged her to turn it off. No one wanted to see it happen anymore. And then Elspet had taken sleeping pills, Lilith hoped only to sleep; she was in the bedroom now, snoring softly and out of Lilith's sight. All the other guests—trans-in-tech friends of Elspet's, plus some cis friends of friends of Lilith's college classmates—had long since gone, having cried, smoked, hit themselves in the face while their partners cried *stop*, talked about all they guessed was coming: the tanks that would sweep the streets clean of protesters, the passports and marriage licenses revoked, the trans kids who would die. Lilith had sat on the periphery of these conversations for as long as she could before she got up, found the NES and the copy of the original *Mystic Knights* in the closet, and used a clunky RF adapter to hook it up to the big Smart TV she'd bought. She loaded her high-level Beat the Game file and began to play, and the others gradually stopped talking to watch her, sipping drinks while chiptunes barked.

■ ■ ■

In *Mystic Knights 1,* the world is made of 16 colors, 256 × 240 pixels, stretched now to fit the contours of her modern TV: all old video games exist on life support, kept alive by catheters, adapters, ports. In this pixel world, your task (Lilith's task, or rather the task of the player you, Lilith, are controlling) is to explore, build power, and ultimately unseat the cabal of venal archmages who have placed the dreams of the people beyond reach. Your characters are assembled from a pool of six heroes, from whom you may select any four as your party to go through the game.

(Another thing Sash used to tell her: the four-person party is so much better than the three-person party, a standard the later games lapsed into. A three-person party is reduced to the three essential roles: someone to lead and absorb damage, someone to heal, and someone to deal damage and overcome threats. Any combination of three characters is tenuous: a fourth party member allows for stability, experiment, and growth.)

Your party, Lilith, which has idled on the battery-backed save file of the cartridge since college, is the unfairly maligned hi-magic build: three frail wizard characters, plus a longbow-wielding ranger to take hits during the touch-and-go early dungeons. You have ground them over the years to senselessly high levels, and their success against even the strongest monsters is mathematically certain. The battle music starts—you mash the action button—crunchy squarewave percussion hits and damage animations in bad colors play—you gain experience, the next fight gets easier. As a person, you grow.

Tonight—or today, or how late is it?—you and your party of wizards are making a circuit of the Giant's Wing. The Giant's Wing is an out-of-the-way gallery at the northern extreme of the Northwood Abbey level, floors above the chamber where the

sorceress KARMLA waits for a boss showdown. In the world of
Mystic Knights 1, you move in four directions, sliding square by
square like slow rooks. Each square in the Giant's Wing you step
on triggers a fight with between two and four giants, verdant
and implacable. Their attack numbers have three digits; when
you first meet the giants, your damage numbers have only two.
The giants will mash your wizards and ranger into pudding. It's
suicide to attempt the Giant's Wing when the story first brings
you to it; it is there only to teach you fear. (Scott Buckworth
had loved it, Lilith remembered, long ago.)

But the secret is that later, you can come back to the Giant's
Wing, once your own attack numbers have three digits too, or
even four. What would happen if you came back to your old
elementary school with the skills you learned in later years? You
would absolutely dominate; the children would have no chance.
They would disappear in sparkles and chirps. So did the giants,
and each dead giant became experience points, the currency that
makes your combat numbers become still higher. And so more
and more of the giants' power becomes your own, and your party
becomes stronger and stronger, virtual giants themselves.

For years, whenever you have been sad, you've come to the
Giant's Wing to farm giants. Do so now: step from battle to
battle, winning every one, circling the Giant's Wing as your
guests murmur. You grew up in the 1990s. Every year was supposed to be better than the year before it, every risk met by
quick reward. When had that stopped?

Maybe you, maybe she didn't have to admit that was true yet.
Maybe Lilith could still believe it was the way it had been earlier this evening, when she and Elspet had set fresh snacks and
wine on the table of her Franklin Avenue apartment and hung
a STRONGER TOGETHER banner from her coat rack. Maybe she

could just sit here, slaughter giants, and imagine herself in a diving bell at the bottom of the ocean, breathing the last of the old world's air as slowly as she could.

At some point the last of the guests must have gone home. She hadn't even noticed them gathering their coats.

She thought of Scott Buckworth whenever she played the original *Mystic Knights*. He was the one who'd told her about the Giants Wing, long ago. She would never have learned to win at this game without him. She wondered, suddenly, who he'd voted for in the election. It was suddenly imperative that she know this.

She set down the controller mid-battle and went to her phone, still plugged into the wall and sharing space on a checkerboard paper plate with a dry slice of victory cake. Good: Scott Buckworth was still her friend, among that strange limbo of Texas friends who'd found her in the initial elation of Facebook a decade now before, but who'd never quite acknowledged her change in username and gender. His Facebook photo showed him, widow's peak sharp and in sunglasses, on the deck of a cruise ship in a leather jacket. The photo had been taken years before; his profile was otherwise inviolate. If he was upset or elated by what had happened tonight, the Internet hadn't captured it.

Many other friends were active, though, in a thick chain of hashtags and reactions: *#devastated, #NotNormal, #resist. I can't even. If we end up in camps it's all because of you. Do not let him divide us. If you voted for him then fuck you, own it. I never want to talk to any of you again.*

She didn't follow Ronin Mallard on Twitter. She tried not to have too much to do with Twitter—it felt like a trap, Elspet always said—but she knew his username anyway (@MasterlessBemused.)

He'd just posted: *Shaking with rage. The darkness won. Going to bed. I love you all; we're strong enough for this. #NotMyPresident.* She stared at her phone, feeling at once powerless and weirdly omnipotent, sorceress invisible in high tower, watching people's thoughts in her seeing stone. She was scrolling when the phone began to ring.

Hey, said Fionna's voice, crumpled and sad. It was the first time Lilith had heard it in three weeks.

Oh hey, said Lilith, quickly taking the remote and muting the chiptune soundtrack for her game for children. —I mean, hello. What's up?

A silence. —How are you even asking me that?

No, right, said Lilith. —No, of course, what am I even thinking. Fuck. Right.

I'm so, so sorry, Fionna said. —Like, on behalf of everyone. I'm so, so sorry we did this to you.

For a moment, Lilith had no idea what Fionna was talking about: Who was *we* and who was *you?* —Oh, she said, remembering: trans, cis. —No, uh, it's cool.

It's not *cool*, Fionna said.

No, you're right, Lilith said quickly. —You're right. It's not cool. Fuck, it's not. Sorry.

No, *I'm* sorry, Fionna said, this time laughing, and Lilith laughed back gently, tactically. This was a Work Contact, Lilith remembered. She tried to adjust her invisible cloak of professionalism over her shoulders.

Are you okay? Lilith asked. —Can I get you anything?

Fionna snorted. —How would you get me anything? You're funny. —A breath. —Sorry I called you at home. Are you at home?

It was after midnight. —Don't worry about it, Lilith said.

I'm sorry, Fionna repeated. —I was just having the best day, before. Like—a day for the ages. And then this shit. —Fabric shifted; a liquid poured. Lilith wondered, in a quick stab of mortification, if Fionna was in the bathroom. But no: it wouldn't be that. What would Fionna's life be? She imagined a white penthouse, whole walls of glass that framed a view of Williamsburg graffiti and rooftop barbecues. There would be bright and copious ivies, and spiritual paperbacks and magazines mingled with DIY financial advice books would rest on a cut glass tabletop overlooked by a black metal electric candelabrum and a Buddha statue. Fionna would be drinking wine, wrapped in an afghan, among clouds touched by the moon.

Every time I *look* at him, Fionna was saying. —Every time I *think* about the shit everyone heard him say. And how none of that mattered. And the shit he'll do and say now, and how none of that will matter, either. Like we're on an elevator, dropping.

Do you want to tell me about your day? Lilith asked, trying to keep her voice gentle, something to average out Fionna's rising pitch. —Since it was good, you know? Maybe the last good day?

It was a perfect day, Fionna said. —My friend Chantal and I—I hadn't seen her for a while, not since moving here—and we wanted to make this whole day of our seeing one another again. Because we knew, I mean we all knew who was going to win, right? I mean, we *knew* it had to go our way. But I wanted to make sure, you know, like what if my one vote was the one she needed, and she didn't get it? So we did this whole thing where we voted, and they gave us stickers. —She paused. —Stickers, she said again.

The line went quiet, and Lilith held her breath.

So we stuck on our stickers, Fionna resumed, —and we bought egg and cheeses, and we went to Prospect Park to sit with the boats. We just watched the boats and thought about the history we'd just made, just the two of us. And Chantal talked about a breakup she was having, how glad she was to be on her own, and it was chilly in the wind, and the world was going to be so beautiful, and soon.

Lilith waited. —Totally, she said, after some time. —A beautiful world. —Then she fell silent too, and she and Fionna were silent together for some time.

I'm sorry I called you, Fionna said, and Lilith felt a flash of alarm before Fionna continued: —But I'm glad I'm talking to you. I need someone to talk to. I mean, I'm sorry I interrupted your night or whatever.

It's fine, Lilith said. —My night isn't anything.

I'm calling everyone in my phone, Fionna said. —I just don't want to be alone, you know? Like I called my sister. We got into this huge fight, actually. Actually I think she voted for him.

Oh, said Lilith, and the silence went on.

So how was *your* day, Fionna said, the tone of her voice brassier, as if the purpose of her call was over, and now it was time to start thinking of the weekend. —I mean, *besides.*

Besides, Lilith said, nodding. —Uh, I worked. Then there was a party. It's over now. I'm playing, or I *was* playing an old video game. It's stupid. To turn my brain off, you know.

Mm-hmm, Fionna said. —An old game—like what, like Mario?

No, Lilith said. —No, kind of an RPG—like, a story game. Kind of something where you gain levels and gold. I don't know. I wanted to feel like I was gaining something.

Oh cool, Fionna said, her tone officially closing the topic.

Lilith wondered, in the silence that followed, if she should have lied, and how she should have lied.

So how's the loan stuff coming, Fionna asked.

Lilith froze. Ronin still had the proposal: it remained, as of her last involuntary summons to Ronin's cube so he could ask her about her dinner plans, at the same place in his inbox, a moth-bloom of dust across its vinyl wings. —It's coming along, I think.

You think, or you know? Fionna said, and Lilith felt her vision blur a little. But then Fionna continued: —Oh my God, I'm so sorry. That was my dad you were talking to just now, not me. Yuck. My sister's like that; I'm not like that. But really: You think? Or you know?

I'm—reasonably certain? offered Lilith. —There are some, uh, approvals I'm waiting on. That's all.

Do you need me to talk to anyone? Fionna asked. —I'm totally happy to do that, you know. If there are more materials you need, or if there are boards or directors you'd want me to present to or something. Would that be helpful?

The phone in her hand was a brick of lead. —Okay, Lilith said. —I can't really think of anyone besides me it would be helpful for you to talk to, I guess.

I mean, don't be afraid to use me, Fionna said. —My personality is my secret weapon.

I won't be afraid, Lilith promised. —But I mean, there are a lot of people worrying right now. Because of what happened tonight, and all. Like this isn't the only call I got tonight? —When she lied outright, her voice had the ancient habit of dropping a little; she faked a cough to compensate. —It's just—it'll take a while.

Fionna exhaled, a theatrical exhale, with an arc. —Okay, she said at last, in a sigh. —I understand. It takes a long time. I just want to do something right now. I want to hit someone. I think of this healing center, and what that monster will think of it. Thinking of that feels like hitting him.

Lilith smiled and cradled her hand that held the phone. —I like thinking of that, too, she said.

Fionna fell quiet. —I mean, in a way it gets easier the longer we wait, she said at last. —Some of the down payment or collateral or whatever like, technical term for it, it's tied to stocks and property values. And I mean after tonight, with this *monster* in office, those are bound to go up. Silver linings, right?

Lilith sat processing this. This was something it was literally going to be her job to think about—and this reminded her that her job existed, too, that tomorrow she'd be expected to go and do her job, like nothing had ever happened. She stood up straight and then bent deep at the waist in a forward fold, letting her spine un-knot and her hair hang like roots against the floorboards.

Hanging upside down, she found that she wanted to ask Fionna a Real Question.

Can I ask you something? she said. —What is it you want to do in the healing center?

Didn't you read the proposal? Fionna asked, alarm in her voice. —Do you not have it anymore? Because I wrote it all there, and I can see what the holdup is if you didn't even—

No, I have the proposal, Lilith yelped. —I have it right here! I'm asking something different. Like—

She struggled to articulate it, while Fionna waited. Her mind worked only in level design metaphors: *What does the player see on the first screen; what can she do right away?*

It's like—when you walk into the space, she began. —Once you own this building, once the healing center is open. It's 10

A.M., and the front door has just closed behind you. What do you do? I mean, physically, what actions do you take?

The other end of the line grew quiet.

Okay, I see what you're asking, Fionna said. —Got it. Hang on. —She drew a deep breath. —10 a.m. I just walked in. I'm hanging up my coat; I'm putting away my keys and mail. I've got kind of a little office back where the priests used to work and all, and that's where I'm putting everything. I've got my matcha in my hand, and it's warm, because the day is cold.

Sure, said Lilith.

I'm going downstairs, Fionna said, —to where I've got the encounter group and meditation rooms set up. I guess, okay, it's ten, so there wouldn't be any groups or activist meetups or like that on site. So I check the meditation room. —Her voice grows more confident. —There's one person in there.

Go on, Lilith said.

It's—it's a trans person, said Fionna. —He, no, *they* are the only one there. They're sitting alone, kind of hunched and crying. And when I walk in, they try not to look at me. I think they're ashamed of their tears.

Lilith had been standing for some time and realized how fucking tired she was. She dropped hard to the couch. —Oh no, she said.

And I ask this trans person—what's *wrong?* Fionna said. —And at first, they don't want to tell me. They've learned not to trust, like a hurt animal, you know? But they saw the sign, I guess—I mean, the one on my building, the one we're buying together. And I guess it looked to them like a safe place.

Lilith steadily found and drained any remaining liquor from the party within reach of the couch as Fionna went on, describing how she'd teach meditation to the young person she'd conjured. She described the tiny bedroom she'd set up for them in her office so that they'd have a safe place to sleep in exchange for them sweeping and making repairs, described the college applications they'd fill out while sitting at Fionna's own desk, and while Fionna continued to speak, Lilith, having finished all the alcohol, began to gather the dirty plates at last, scraping every wasted slice of cake and discarded grape stem into the trash, restoring the room to the state it had been before the party, before the results had begun to arrive.

Okay, said Lilith, when Fionna finally stopped. Her voice sounded strange to her, like the voice of a man: she imagined Fionna's mind translating her voice, remembering that this was an important thing to do when you talked to a trans person, an object of emotional charity. —Thank you for answering my question.

You're welcome, said Fionna, her voice now soft. And Lilith suddenly felt shitty for hating everything Fionna had just said. This was not actually a bad person. Was it bad to fantasize about caring for other people? How could that be bad? Why was Lilith so mean and shitty that she felt bad about that?

I need to go, Lilith said. —I've got work tomorrow? Uh, I'll try to keep the loan stuff moving.

Okay, said Fionna. —Maybe let's have a weekly check-in about it? I really want to do something. It's important that we all do something.

I know, Lilith said, and she hung up.

The living room was clean now. The game sat, muted and paused, outside time. She switched off the NES without saving her progress from tonight. From the bedroom she could hear Elspet talking in her sleep: *no*, she was saying, *no*.

Listening to Elspet, Lilith realized she had lied to Fionna: she couldn't keep the loan approval process moving because the loan proposal was sitting in Ronin's office. She didn't even want to keep the loan approval process moving—she didn't even want anything right now—she just wanted the cis woman to think kindly of her for a moment, to have reason to keep reminding herself that Lilith was a woman, too. Cis women controlled the borders of womanhood; in this game, you existed to the extent that you could please them. Immediate shame at this thought: Was it a bad thought, the kind of thought a man would have? She shouldn't want the cis woman to think kindly of her—she *didn't* want it. She wanted to keep killing giants.

Her corner window opened onto a fire escape that the landlord forbade his tenants from sitting on. Lilith opened the window, took a cigarette from the emergency pack in her kitchen's anything drawer, and sat on the sill, half her butt dangerously close to the wrought iron rail. She brushed rust as she smoked, looking down on Franklin Avenue. It was silent, the people who walked down its sidewalks at this hour moving slow, as if staggering from a punch, and a green cab passed by, moaning. She thought about the scene in *Mystic Knights V* where the fallen paladin Philippe marched through the sacked capital on a burning destrier flanked by phantoms, how in just four, five hours, the sun would rise and economic activity would begin again. And Lilith imagined Fionna in Williamsburg, just miles north of here, smiling and sleepy as she stood up. Her windows would be sheer glass: she imagined Fionna slowly closing their drapes.

7. The Sigil

Abraxa can still see it, days later, her pencil moving to define the space underground: long cross arms extending into infinity, the light of Marcie's lamp behind her, the spiderweb veil, behind it the sorceress.

Abraxa still has muscle memories of typing *mystic knights 3* into Yahoo and being able to review every fan website that turned up. All the beauty of 1990s Internet: fan art gallery sub-pages with HTML frames, animated webring banners, pastel text on black starfield backgrounds, JPGs without thumbnails that took minutes at a time to load over dialup. Today, pencil tapping her sketchbook, she runs the same search, and the results gush on for pages: digital paintings and comics, novel-length fanfics, explainer articles about which game is which (there sure were a lot of games after she stopped paying attention), pornography, collectible merchandise, anniversary retrospectives, speed runs by adults in pajamas. Scrolling, she feels jealous, the Velveteen Rabbit looking in the window at the boy who used to love her. She and her friends—Lilith, Sash, what had happened to them?—had thought of these games as special, of themselves as special for loving them. But the game had sold thousands of copies—millions by now, after the smash success of *Mystic*

Knights V—many other teenagers had loved these characters as she had. Now that love is worth money; that love has taken over the world.

Refining her search to fan art of the sorceress alone, she scrolls down pages of image results, letting the variations fill her dented monitor. Cherub cheeks—long elf ears—mohawk—white furs over fishnets and leather gloves, clad in the products of every beast—sinister eyes that watch her, scrolling, from Tumblrs, ancient DeadJournals, Wikis, Twitters, Instas. The icons watch her, even as she watches them. But none of them are exactly what she saw in the dark.

She takes her sketchbook to Marcie's breakfast table. She hasn't drawn this character since she was a teenager, but she remembers it, her tricks for rendering the highlights on fur—simplify the shadows; blank paper is the brightest color—the snap of her pen as she defines the sorceress's jaw. Her cells have all died and been replaced at least twice, but somehow she remembers this, and her pencil moves, drawing what she saw beneath the ground. Dry land drawings—she never wants to draw the ocean again.

She's still drawing on the kitchen table when Marcie walks in.

Can we have a serious conversation, she asks.

Sure, Abraxa says, afraid.

Marcie pours herself kefir, leads them into the bedroom, sits on the bed. There's nowhere else to sit, so Abraxa sits on the floor, shifting some Kleenex boxes and a heap of laundry lingerie. She wonders if, here on the floor, she looks like a dog.

Ruff ruff, she says. —What do you want?

Marcie rolls her bony shoulders until they crack. —So Scramble didn't feel so good about the other night.

Abraxa flinches at *Scramble*; that person left days ago; she'd forgotten them. —Oh, bummer, she says. —Sorry.

No, of course, Marcie says. —No, of course you didn't mean it. It's just—it was a lot for them. Breaking into a place, and you know, on drugs, and you walking in like that, from the dark. Laughing like that and saying stuff. They just got weirded out.

Abraxa inclines her head: Had she said stuff? —I'm sorry I said stuff, she says. —What stuff?

Marcie looks down at the surface of her kefir. —Weird stuff, she says. —*The road is open.* You kept saying that. And, *I know what we were doing. That's what we were doing.* Something like that. —She puts a second hand on her mug, cradling the first. —It was really scary for Scramble. And for me, too.

Beneath Abraxa's folded legs, the linoleum is falling away, like from an earthquake spell: she imagines herself falling all the way to the world's burning core, where she burns. —I'm really sorry, she says.

It's okay, Marcie says to her kefir. —I understand. —She looks up. —I know you're really a good person.

But it isn't okay and Abraxa isn't a good person. Burning on the earth's core, she knows she needs to try to be. There is a good way to respond to what Marcie has said, a way that is not scary or uncomfortable and that gives Marcie a sense of peace.

I'm really, really sorry, she says. —Do you want me to go away?

No! Marcie says it automatically; pain is now spidering her face; Abraxa didn't find the good way to respond. —No, I don't want you to go away—I mean, where would you go? I mean, no, it'll be fine. I just wanted to talk about it. That's all I wanted. So you'd know how they felt.

What do you want me to do instead of go away, Abraxa asks carefully.

I want you to, Marcie says, her voice rising, but then she stops. She is considering her tactics again—Abraxa watches her, from the core of the earth—*she has to be so careful around me*.

Just—is anything going on, Marcie finally asks. —You seem really nervous, and I don't want you to be. You're a guest here.

No problem, Abraxa says, loud: the goal is to hide her nervousness, got it. —I'll try not to say scary stuff anymore! And I'll be mindful when scared people are here, so they don't have to be scared. And then it'll be easier for you not to be scared, too. And then no one will be scared.

For a moment, it seems like Marcie wants to interrupt her, to say an angry thing, but as she keeps talking, Marcie's anger seems to drain away. She just looks sad now—quiet angry, maybe. Quiet anger is a safer emotion than loud. If one stays careful around quiet anger, sometimes it just turns into quietness again, peace. Maybe this is how evil people think, evil people who should go away from everyone.

Finally she stops talking, and Marcie watches her. For a moment Marcie looks younger, twentysomething and newly out, as she'd been when she first looked at Abraxa, the coolest big trans sister anyone could want.

Abraxa's drawings of the sorceress have been improving: her fourth now today, ease developing in how she renders fishnets, furs, facial expressions. A rough setting is starting to appear behind her; she's confident enough in what she sees in her imagination to begin abstracting, big blotches of shadow and form. She looks at the sorceress's eyes: tiny ink zeros. *The road is open*: that's what Marcie thought she'd said, underground. And: *that's what we were doing. I know what we were doing.* But what had they been doing? How would she find out?

The next day, she walks back to the church on Mercer Street. She stands outside for some time, watching from the shade of a tall cedar tree. By day, it looks different, almost innocent: the sun reveals more details of the torn-up garden between the main building and the parsonage, the spray paint on the plywood that blocks the windows, the delivery vans parked outside, engaged in normal human business. Once, while she was staying with friends in San Francisco, the donut shop down the block from her friend's apartment caught fire, and for days after she walked past it to catch the lingering smell of incense, sugar, yeast. The gutters were full of shattered glass and the ashes of canned goods, but people walked by it on their headphones while indifferent cars circled the block. The burned space was a scar that healthy skin couldn't quite assimilate: something you learn not to see.

There's a bagel shop around the corner of Mercer Street from the church: a few seats, a water pitcher on the counter thick with bobbing, unseasonal limes, a languid barista in pink stripe arm warmers and shaved head with thick blue veins, a notice board. Her skin itches as she peruses it. The corkboard, its edges striped in stale Halloween spiderwebs, contains many flyers: ads for guitar lessons, house cleaning, au pair services, roommates who are *professional, nonsmoking, and friendly* and who can afford large rent deposits. Something is happening with her heart: it seems more porous here in proximity to the church, taking in hidden significances to things, double meanings. *Thirty years' service to music—bodywork available at healing center.* Looking over this last flyer, she remembers herself just overboard of Elias's boat: body cruciform in the ocean, chest pointed at the sun as the water pushed her shoulders down.

How beautiful her heart had been, she thinks, before she drowned.

Poppyseed bagel and cup of free water beside her, its taste bright with stored citric sun, she fills notebooks: page after page of sketchy renderings, starting with more of the sorceress before moving on to rooms she remembers from her teenage CraftQ game. She tries to translate the ASCII contours she and her friends—Sash, Lilith—had laid out into real plans, rooms that someone might build. Soon she's working on maps of the church basement, both as she remembers it and as it might be transformed by broom and candlelight. As it might be transformed—as one might transform it.

She designs banners one might hang. She designs robes a priestess might construct, moving through the arachnid air, her shoulders brushing aside countless sticky, invisible patterns as she walks. In the periphery of the last page she works on, she again draws the sorceress extending her hand from out of the dust and spiders, tall enough to be trans herself.

On her way back home, she walks down Mercer Street again so that she can pass the front of the church. Under the cedar tree where she had stood before lies a feather, absolutely white. Its rachis is hollow and light when she picks it up: she imagines that when she lets it go, it will float straight up.

Back at Marcie's, she brings out the *disk*.

No other copies of the file on it exist anymore; she's pretty sure of this. Sash forwarded her the file on the day of her resignation, after Lilith had already gone. Abraxa was the last to touch it.

Whether or not there were other copies of the data, it felt important to work with the disk. The file was only a pattern, like the sheet music to a song; any competent computer could play it. But this pattern had lived for so long in a specific material context. The disk was made of iron oxide pulled out of the earth, magnetized, melted, spread over a sheet of plastic. For years of wandering, she had carried that magnetic iron with her like a lucky compass. If a violinist plays the same cursed song every day on an ordinary violin, eventually the violin becomes just as interesting as the song. There is some mystery she has to unpack here, some reason the sorceress appeared only to her in the dark. The disk must have something to do with it.

There was no way to easily load a 3.5" floppy disk on a modern computer. The USB to PS2 connector is simple enough, but the PS2 to parallel port—its plastic cord thrice sutured by duct tape—requires more care. She finds rubbing alcohol and cotton swabs in the bathroom and works at the pin connectors for a full half hour before the plug cleanly harmonizes with her flat box of a disk reader. But at last, the ghost of her teenage CraftQ game materializes, blasphemously, on Marcie's modern laptop. Here, on the title screen, is another drawing of the sorceress: a white ASCII char 2 on blue, staring fixed out of the black.

In this game, you, Abraxa, play as the sorceress. At first, she has no body, and neither do you: the first room is all text, written by Sash. *Epigram* is its title in the ROOM list in CrQedit. The prose is fixed-width ASCII, white on black, illuminated by a granular ASCII sunset and constellations:

every day i look out the same window.
every day i do the same thing.

every day i'm alone.
but there is a world out there—
a dream i no longer have to dream alone—

The world of the game is bright colors, eight foreground and sixteen background, all in ASCII: trees with *I*s for trunks, *O*s for boughs, houses made of 176-177-178 blend stones. The first ROOMs are set in the sorceress's childhood village, where the player can touch smiley faces representing villagers to speak to them. They laugh at your pretensions—they express trepidation at your habits, your sorcerous experiments, the way you preserve the skeletons of fallen forest creatures—slyly they hint at your flirtations with the mayor's haughty daughter—they comment, disgusted by your smell. They react to you, shaping you as they speak.

Sash always had extremely strong opinions about the stories in video games, especially when it came to the motivations of their villains. Video game villains were classically monsters: power-mad military generals, dark sorcerers, venal turtle kings, the literal devil. The most common verb in a video game is to kill, meaning that per the laws of game design, a game's story must resolve through the act of killing. And to make it okay to kill someone, you must first make them less than human. Sash's choice of the sorceress was deliberate: of all the Mystic Knights characters across the games, she was the only one who'd really started as a villain. *but she was too complex to remain a villain,* Sash had typed. *most villains want to dominate the world, control everything—most villains are system d. the sorceress wants to build something. she wants to be free.*

In the game, after speaking to the villagers, you (the sorceress, the player in the game) inevitably elect to return to your house.

There, beside the window that you, per the epigraph, have looked out of all your life, you find the Crystal Stone, source of your family power.

Take the stone and hold it. (In Sash's description, the sorceress sees her reflection, blurred with that of her mother by the crystal's facets.) Walk outside: night has fallen, a nice piece of CraftQ programming (if you do say so yourself). Explore until you find a chapel to the village's god: tepid, a farmer, false. Enter to find an altar made of stone. Ritual implements have been set in place—the ritual implements of the village's tepid farmer-god. Sweep them away. Put the crystal in their place. Take bones and feathers from a satchel, sprinkle them around the base. Hear the crystal, your lost mother in its face, whisper. But then the face changes—it is not just your mother's face—it is your own face, your future face—a guardian angel that calls you forward.

Watch as the cut scene continues, as the sorceress chants the words Sash wrote for her in 1998, as a strange smoke fills the church—

Instead of *kill*, Sash said, their game's verbs would be *gather* and *build*. Gather power—gather allies—build defenses, build a world. The origin point was a sequence in *Super Mystic Knights 3* that Abraxa had barely remembered before Sash talked it up: the party, finding the ruins of Northwood Abbey—sacked between games by the sinister agents of System D—could send different non-player characters they met in towns and dungeons around the world to become abbey residents. There were some thirty potential residents, from which any given player might choose six: over four hundred thousand mathematically distinct abbey populations.

Why stop there, Sash asked. The plot of *Saga of the Sorceress* would lead the sorceress, inevitably exiled from her small-minded village, to shelter in the ruins of Northwood. From there, she would set out on a journey around the world of the Mystic Knights series. The goal would be to find the greatest spirits in the world and bring them to found the community of Northwood.

Sash spent hours and hours of IRC queries describing her plans. Sometimes this took place in their secret company channel with Lilith and Abraxa, and sometimes just with her, after Lilith had gone to bed and neither of them could sleep. It was hypnotic, listening to CraftQ's only female creator describe all of this: there seemed no bottom to her ideas and to her ideas about her ideas, her stories about The Critical Hit and the secret knowledge of their affairs she seemed to have. She told Abraxa once that she had learned Japanese from books at the library, which she'd used to translate a Japanese video game magazine she'd purchased from a thrift store in her neighborhood. The article supposedly covered the company's whole history, and revealed how steeped in queer subculture and the occult the Mystic Knights games actually were. Per the article, Oshiro99 had woven actual magical principles into the game's spell effects, and even, through his influence over the level designer SuFish, into the maps of the levels themselves. There was a rumored secret build of *Super Mystic Knights 3* that actually functioned as a kind of *hypersigil*—a magical operation that would open a gate from the unwitting player's SNES console to a realm of beings beyond human comprehension, who spoke to humanity through the games.

obviously we don't have their level of magical knowledge yet, Sash said. *but in a way we can think of our game as a restoration of that intent.*

Reading her spill of words, Abraxa had wondered what it would be like to date Sash. She imagined meeting Sash in person sometime: the two of them occupying booths of a diner in Hollywood proper, Sash with neon red hair, thick eyeliner, black leather, monologuing for hours over an untouched plate of pancakes while waitresses came by to refill Abraxa's coffee. Talking to her friends at school about CraftQ, as she infrequently did, she sometimes tried out the fiction that Sash was her girlfriend, invented stories about their plans to meet. They could go to a concert together—they could spray-paint buildings—they could go to the beach, where Abraxa had once, shortly after they'd started work on their game, dreamed of a candle sailing over the waves into the air.

The story of assembling Northwood Abbey was to last for seven chapters. But the three of you never finished the first: the game ends with the sorceress plunging into a sewer with no enemies in it, a three-way fork, and a passage to an empty room. Lilith never finished, and Sash went away after her.

Abraxa sits cross-legged on Marcie's carpet, back hunched over Marcie's laptop and the daisy-chain phylactery of peripherals for nearly three hours. It's taken her three hours, even skipping most of the text and exploration, to get through the finished portions of their game: the escape from town, the surrounding forests, finding the ruins of Northwood, forging an alliance with the orcish bandits who controlled it, proving her worth to them, eventually setting out for the sewers of Bell Prix to steal the treasures from the wizards of System D. How long had the three of them actually worked on this game, the file flitting like a raven messenger between their inboxes? Two months? Three?

She's thirty-three now: around four hundred months of time, older than she'd honestly expected to reach. Despite the typos, the art glitches, the expanses of the juvenile, the callow, the impure, they had still captured something—so much of the promise Abraxa had felt in those late night chats—possessed by a lazy grace they knew they would never find again. That they had no understanding of what they had captured made it no less real.

What had they captured? Did she understand it, even now? She reviews her sketchbook: the space beyond the veil of spiders, the presence she felt, all the stories Sash had once told her about The Critical Hit releasing magical gateway sigils on Super Nintendo cartridges for worldwide distribution. And then the way the three of them, teenagers, had joined their lives to that effort.

She opens the editor and looks at the menu of ROOMs. She opens it now and looks at the final ROOM they made: a placeholder, just default yellow borders awaiting Lilith's level blockouts that never came. After a minute, she goes back to the menu, and she starts to open each ROOM again, this time in reverse. Outside, the sun begins to arc downward as she ascends through her work, reversing time, and with each room, she finds she has more patience, her life becomes more stable, her friends rejoin her. The final room is the first: *epigram.* Sash's drawing of a melancholy teenage sunset, above it bright and steady stars. They twinkle out of the screen of Marcie's laptop, while outside, neighborhood streetlights hum, and the city over the river glows, painting out the night.

She looks again at the list of things she understands, and she thinks of the basement of the church, and of her dream. *but there is a world out there, a dream i no longer have to dream alone.*

She rolls onto her back, her shoulders resting on laundry and floorboards. Above her, Marcie's ceiling fan moves. The computer light is making her shadow on the wall: the blades in the air are chopping it up, as in the bathroom a sink runs drawing a glass of water, and good people's voices are coming to her, on the floor, through the air. What she is thinking of doing now, she knows, is scary, is not what a good person would be thinking. And maybe she isn't a good person, now. But maybe the her who made this game was. And maybe there is a chance of bringing yourself back from the dead. Maybe even a villain can build—maybe even a villain can be free.

8. The Choice

It took Lilith an hour, borrowed against the hours she'd been unable to sleep after the abortive party and Fionna's call, to choose her outfit for work. Nothing seemed right: every garment she tried revealed at least one little flaw in her body, and the minmax calculations of which flaws pulled focus from which others to average a neutral effect—like camouflage, a transsexual body you could sense but not see—was beyond her today.

Finally she went with a disaster build: olive jumpsuit, the tall transsexual's bane, matched with dark blazer, white scarf, red heels. Her ankles, her wrists, her gross huge hands stuck out: she attacked them with chunky accessories, her dangliest earrings, her bracelet of thick wooden spheres like planets, an anklet; she tied her hair back, tied it up. She looked at herself in the mirror; she looked insane. She should change immediately into something safe. Instead she went to wake up Elspet, still hung over and twisted in her sheets.

Hey, I'm going, she said. —Are you crashing here today? I can leave you my key?

Elspet lay very still, then opened a single eye: a hunting animal.

You're going into work today? she asked. Don't go into work today.

I have to work, Lilith said.

Elspet closed her eye. —No you don't, she said. —No one should. Everyone's lost their work privileges. Let's all stay home for four years.

A conundrum: she was afraid of Elspet, but she was more afraid not to go in. Was there a strong-person reason for her to go into the office, one Elspet might agree with? —It's important not to show them that we're afraid, she finally said.

After a moment, Elspet threw off the covers. Stretching (her orbiting shoulders, Lilith thought, her hacker's armpits), she went to the kitchen. Lilith followed, heels navigating hazards like prey deer, and watched her eat a handful of wrinkling party grapes before entering the shower.

Does this mean I should leave you my key, she asked Elspet through the steaming door.

I'm going home, Elspet said. —I'm going to do drugs there for three days.

So I shouldn't leave you my key, Lilith said.

Can we split a cab, Elspet said. —You can at least wait for me, right? You can at least be late?

She could; her coworkers could understand being late to work. It was possible. So she sat, waiting for Elspet—it wouldn't be a long wait; Elspet was efficient—and she worried about why she'd said what she'd said. It was important, she guessed, to show her boss that she wasn't afraid of the political thing that had happened. But it was also true that it had never seriously occurred to her to skip work. Work was a way not to feel afraid, or to feel anything. When had it become that? Wondering, she sat and twisted her bracelet—the wooden planets revolving about the bone in her wrist as Elspet finished carefully dithering her eyeshadow—and she asked herself when she'd started to sincerely love her job.

■ ■ ■

In a cab that smelled like breakfast meats, Elspet sent encrypted texts to other trans women, her phone buzzing with each text she received back. Lilith could feel it, counterpoint to the cab tires bumping over the heat joins in the Williamsburg Bridge. It seemed wrong, unreal that there was as much traffic as there was here: so many people continuing as if nothing had happened. Maybe nothing had, she thought.

She listened to the encrypted messages arrive—each notification was different; Elspet had somehow hacked her phone to play squarewaves randomly selected from Mixolydian mode—and imagined their contents: the sharing of resources, the planning of actions, the possibility of flight to Canada, the logistics of securing medications and documents. Maybe they were setting up a safehouse, or securing weapons. Elspet was good at solving the world like this. Should Lilith become better at that, too? She closed her eyes and felt the car vibrating against her thighs, her butt, felt the warmth of her cool hacker girlfriend across the seat of the cab. And she counted the seconds, not thinking about the future, until the car stopped lurching and she knew she'd arrived at work.

On her way past the thick glass windows, she caught her reflection: that woman looks competent, she thought, before she remembered that she wasn't.

Ronin had called out sick, and no one else seemed to notice she was late. She worked in her cubicle, feeling unreal—it was like she was on a carousel, her work a fixed point outside, and if she focused she could get a little stab of it done every time it circled back around. After an hour, she let herself go to the bathroom and sit on the toilet, alone for the first time, she realized, since Fionna had ended their call. She continued to sit, unobserved, long after she'd finished. When she came out, Mr. Swannuken, the branch manager, was there waiting for her.

I'm sorry, she said on instinct.

He was an old, small man, his thinning hair like a feathery snowfall over his skull. What had Ronin told her about him? Conservative—bitter—disliked her. Had what happened last night made him bold? She tried to scoot toward the wall and braced to be fired. But he just looked at her, confused eyes two dark acorns.

I wanted to make sure you got donuts, he explained.

In the employee break room, he'd placed a large box of donuts. It was from a bakery she'd never heard of before, and the donuts were intimidating: lavender cream, chopped hazelnut and caramel, cloudberry coulis, bourbon sesame glazed. She chose the closest thing she could find to a vanilla ring. Mr. Swannuken watched her eat it, grateful.

So many people called out last night, he said. —I wanted to show my appreciation, for. —He trailed off. —You're a good worker, he finally said. Her heart went out to him.

She ferried her donut and her fresh break room coffee back to her desk—her leftover Halloween cobwebs wavered in the air conditioning but did not break, perhaps a sign of hope—and she looked at her computer, and then she went for her phone to check her messages. There was nothing from Elspet; there was one from her father. *Did you see the Presidential Election results last night? Very strange outcome. Please call if you'd like to discuss. Thinking of you.* She considered calling him back; he'd be worried. It might be nice.

Her thoughts dissolved on the thought of that call; it was something she could not hold. When she came to herself again, she was thinking about Fionna.

Her inner Scott Buckworth had had a judgment about Fionna; before, she'd resisted hearing it. She let herself listen to it now: *This is not a serious person. This person is vulnerable. That's something I've taught you never to be.* She sat with this, feeling her stomach clench from donut grease and yeast, until a thought came to her. What do I look like through Fionna's eyes? She had no idea. Closing her own eyes, she tried to see through Fionna's. And again, she saw a transsexual, but one who was scared. One who was scared, and one who was worth protecting. One who could help.

She stood up. She could feel the donut in her breaking down as she walked, heels automatic across the tile, into Ronin's office. Fionna's proposal was still there in the stack. She extracted it, cradled it to her chest, brought it back to her cubicle. Nobody noticed her doing it, which wasn't strange, because of course she wasn't doing anything wrong. She was a loan approvals under-writer; the bank had given her the power to establish grounds for approving loans. Now she would use it.

She hadn't asked anyone a Real Question yet today, so she paused to ask one of herself: *Am I really going to—?* But she didn't pause to give herself an answer. The answers were there, as felt as planet gravity, because this was the world, and cis people were the whole of the world. The main ethical choice in life is who to betray: so she'd throw the switch, divert power from the cis man who didn't care about her and give it to the cis woman who did. Because Elspet and her hacker friends weren't going to do any of the things they said they would. Because Buckworth's plan long ago had worked:

the cis people had trusted Lilith, and so she had coins to spend.

Her mind went back to the moment when she'd jumped across the gap in the rock, and the feeling, however brief, of no longer being on stone, but in air. And for the first time since the political thing had happened, she found her thoughts on the future, and the healing center the cis woman wanted to build. No, the two of them would build it together: something helpful, something safe.

In her cubicle with the stolen proposal, printouts of her family smiling at her, she thought of the last cis woman who had asked for her help. To her surprise, the thought felt warm. *Look*, Lilith would say to her, should they ever meet again. *Look, I learned.*

9. The Nature of System D

On the day she's chosen, Abraxa waits until an hour after Marcie's gone: an active waiting, jouncing on her heels as she organizes her Ziploc of cords and peripherals, wipes maps and patterns into the dust on the edges of Marcie's grandfather's library: clues, souvenirs. In silence, she crouches just outside the master bedroom door, and she listens to the electric pulse of the TV, imagines the woman dreaming inside, how the TV signal is working its way into her dreams.

I didn't mean to scare you, she whispers, to no response.

Again, she loads her teenage game onto Marcie's computer. She takes the first room in the editor—Sash's teen poem, the sunset, the emerging stars. She screencaps it, airbrushes out the poem in Photoshop, writes in something new. This accomplished, she uploads it to her website. A sigil, drawn in the online air: a sign of a new road opening.

She leaves a note on Marcie's desk: *I am going away for a little while to do something. I'll be back in a couple days after I make some ~~pRoGrEsz~~. Don't throw away my stuff lol.*

Assuming Marcie will throw away her stuff, she adds more objects she wants to save into her backpack: notebooks, hoodies, underwear, a thermal bodysuit Marcie said she could borrow whenever she wanted. Then she says goodbye to every room in the house. She takes a bath; she eats a full meal. She masturbates on Marcie's work sofa, just some: she can feel the short remaining time pressing on her shoulders; she doesn't get very far. The final room is Marcie's. Still damp from the bath, Abraxa lays herself back on the bed, stacks all the pillows up under her sore thirtysomething neck, lights two sticks of the incense she's left Marcie after stealing the rest. *Remember this feeling on your skin*, she thinks. *This is what comfort feels like. This is what softness feels like. Both of those are maybe going away, so fill up on them now. Stuff yourself.*

She tells herself to let the incense burn through, but she gets impatient: she kicks her legs up into the air, rolls them forward, stands up. She puts on her clothes, and she shoulders her new and full backpack, a half-gallon jug of water buckled to its side. From the screened patio she takes Marcie's grandfather's toolbox; he won't need these anymore. She is equipped—she has made herself alien to the house—there's no point in lingering anymore. There is no point in hesitating: now, do it. And Marcie's family photos on the main hallway artery blur into streaks as she passes, accelerating like a DeLorean, until she catches fire and bursts into sunlight.

She speaks aloud—*I can come back here anytime*—because doing so may make this more likely to be true. Then she starts to walk, heart simmering with terrified trust. With every step, the fire under her skin starts to cool, become a force she can tolerate: this is how she knows she's doing something good.

She was eight, or maybe even younger, the first time she ran away. The beach was just a short hop from her dad's Venice apartment; she'd thought of it, skin itching in her bedroom, how much she wanted to be in the water right then, and there was no one home to stop her. So she'd just done it: walked the blocks to the water, skin glowing with excitement.

It was only as the afternoon got longer, as the beach began to grow familiar and thus to lose its sense of possibilities, that she let doubt grow. The concrete pavilion that housed the toilets and outdoor showers made a shadow on the sand, and she started to pace its borders. If she could just make a perfect line of footsteps around its borders, she knew she would be okay; she would be free. But by the time she'd finished, the lines she'd paced in the sand no longer matched the shadow's clean leading edge. She went back to pace them again, and then again, until the sun got lower and the shadows began to lose their definition, the sharp edge blurred, and she became afraid. She imagined the sun becoming unfixed, falling toward her with terminal heat.

In the end, she surrendered. She found a woman rolling up a deflated raft with a dolphin's face; she circled the woman and her children, giggling and looking lost, until the woman found a cop and the cop walked Abraxa home. The cop and her partner spent some time at Abraxa's house: everyone squeezed into the ill-lit front room, Abraxa's father's dusty guitars on stands around them, the slabs of their bodies like grave markers. Abraxa sat squeezed between her parents in an arrangement no one was comfortable with, and neither cop touched the little dish of honey peanuts and fridge door pickles Abraxa's mother had set out. Her mother was running her fingers through Abraxa's hair as her father spoke, swore they'd looked for her, ask anyone in the neighborhood. She touched her daughter curiously, as if she was petting an unfamiliar dog. *Taking care of your boy is a big responsibility,* one of the officers said. *You don't want to see half of what we've seen. There are a lot of bad people in this world.*

I've become one of the bad people. This is what she realizes now, in the present, in New Jersey: it makes her smile. Look how far she's come: walking here alongside the cars lined up for the Holland Tunnel, smelly fall wind crisp on her face, her skirt blowing and her burglar's tools on her back.

Her mother is the next to run away. She doesn't see Abraxa much at first, is traveling in other cities. When Abraxa asks, she explains that she couldn't stay tied to choices she'd made once, long ago. She needed to be free. And then she's gone altogether: her father, when she asks, claims not to know where she is, how to look her up.

He sits, nights after work, in the living room, playing his guitars. Abraxa sits opposite him. Sometimes she talks him into ordering food in, taking her to the comic book store, the board-walk: not so much because she wants these things as because she wants him to do something. Things have become serious; she has to become serious for him. One time she catches him gazing at the back of her head, as if she's a statue he's sculpted yet doesn't remember designing.

He falls asleep early and deep, and she can go out if she wants. She does want to: tall enough to avoid attention, to walk to the beach when she wants that, just to walk in supermarkets and music stores, fall into conversations, intense rushes of sparks that help her get out of herself. What relevance does school have next to this; what authority do teachers have? She has no fear of them, or the law. At school, most of her classmates avoid her; others start to worship her. She accepts it: she provides them possibilities, she thinks. She makes jokes with them, and they laugh, and she knows that she is normal, still tethered to something.

One night she sees a transsexual working on a street corner, keeps circling the block to look at her; she is beautiful, she can't be much older than Abraxa is herself.

She acquires a Super Nintendo late in the console's commercial life cycle, a surprise Christmas expenditure from her grandfather that she knows somehow relates to the divorce. She skims money from her father's wallet to buy games from friends anxious to upgrade to the newer N64 or PSX libraries.

The best thing about video games is how they erase you, except for your willpower. You can do anything in a video game that the code lets you do, even many things the code doesn't let you do.

Her first SNES game had been a hovercar racing game set in a future of floating highways. If you accelerated your car just right at a ramp, you could leap small pits, but this was balanced with a risk: you might leap off the floating track altogether, crash into the bubble city below. At one point on the track, it almost looked as if you could leap from the start of the track over an expanse of skyscraper arcologies to a loop far closer to the finish line: she tried it, she crashed. She tried again; she tried for hours, her hovercar's engines whining and then exploding, the microwave clock that told her when she'd have to get ready for school advancing digit by digit. It was 4 A.M. before she made it: the space car soared into the digital air, screamed over the buildings, then glided into place.

From then, all she wanted from games was to learn to break them. The specific game didn't matter much: she would trade her old games for new ones, push them as far as she could push, swap them with her friends from school or the local used store. When she acquires and plays *Super Mystic Knights 3* for the first time, she ignores the New Game option, dives into the save files of the kid she got it from. One contains the party (all renamed for childhood pets and siblings) gathered in some kind of haunted skyship, directing a vast red lion to destroy a pyramid. There are possibilities here.

It's strange now to think how irrelevant the story of the *Mystic Knights* series was to her—how irrelevant the sorceress was, at first, before Sash. It was the combat system of *Super Mystic Knights 3*, the attacks that did greater and greater numbers of damage to your enemies, that first fascinated her. The systems MELKIOR had programmed had been an absolute mess, maximally ambitious, minimally rigorous. There were stat numbers for attack, defense, intelligence, magical ability, status effects that let you be poisoned, reversed, frozen, floating, condemned, turned into a frog, turned into a pig, turned into another character, swords made of fire that dealt damage to ice enemies, internal clock systems that operated differently if the player were gaming during the full moon. None of it went together, but this was just like the systems that made up our own world, and therefore as rich.

She spends hours pushing the limits of the game, nights when her father's asleep or out trying to date and the TV is all hers, her disembodied avatar wandering through placid corridors while her mundane body sits in the half-light of her living room with a controller in her hands, avoiding her friends when they call. She builds ridiculous characters: a fighter with speed boots who's cursed with a gryphon mask, which makes every attack fail, but which glitches the random number generator to permit fantastical instant kills. One night she runs an AltaVista search for stat tables other players had compiled, which is how she finds CraftQ: a game you don't even have to play to break and shape. She never looks back.

Super Mystic Knights 3 begins when one member of the Mystic Knights, the abjurer Arden, returns to his home village to find its denizens acting strangely. An irascible miller has disappeared into a nearby forest; his children roam the streets, concerned; the villagers seem unaware of the absence. After assembling a party of four to investigate—a party which, when you and your friends play, always includes the sorceress—you learn that the miller's disappearance happened at the same time as the installation of a great copper lamppost in the town square. The lamp is lit with an eerie violet flame. No one in the town seems to think this is unusual. At nights they gather in a ring around the lamppost, singing prayers of thanks to it for their prosperity. Journeys to other nearby towns reveal similar missing citizens, similar lampposts, and soon, similar rumors of mysterious wizards.

A grand journey in pursuit of these wizards takes you and your party through different thematic caves, mountain passes, swamps, and dungeons: the ice dungeon, the fire dungeon, the techno-dungeon, the dungeon with a carnival theme. Antagonists and allies are introduced, riddles unraveled, the yearnings of party members confessed by moonlight on the verandas of rural inns. But in the end, after a dangerous mission to scale the crystal tower of the Bell Prix Wizarding Academy, the secret of the lamppost flames is revealed during a confrontation with the archmagus himself.

The wizards seek control, as must all wizards. Their latest scheme has been to use a combination of subtle political influence and people's inherent drive for communion to install the copper lampposts in every village. The lamppost is sold to the people as a symbol of village harmony, a catalyst for connection. Indeed, this is all too true: the violet flame is enchanted, propagating a series of common dreams in the minds of every soul within a fifty kilometer radius over a series of seven nights. At the conclusion of the seven nights, the minds of the townspeople become connected into a single shared consciousness, removing those barriers to understanding and love that every soul must experience as a condition of its embodiment. All misunderstandings are clarified; all perspectives run together as one. Cities and towns work together as never before—harvests increase yield, lovers reconcile—and the people gather every night around the lamppost to pray their thanks, and the dream deepens.

There are defectives who cannot share the dream. The irascible miller was one, disposed of by the village one night while making a desperate attempt to cut down the copper lamp with an axe meant for sharpening fences.

But now the world is connected, crows the archmagus on the rooftop, his words punctuated by thunder. *And so the final phase of System D begins!* He raises his hand, and in that moment, cut scenes reveal all the people in all the villages the party has visited dropping unconscious to the grass. Their souls are yellow flames that rise curiously from the cages of their ribs and high into the air. In the lamppost's violet flame, they are joined—and then each lamppost's flame rises into the air and joins with every other—and soon the entire population of the world, absent the noble misfits who have consistently aided the party throughout, has fused into one great flame, burning in the air as the archmagus laughs. Soon they have formed into a vast divine being, a great dragon made of white lightning under the Academy's magical control. *System D,* announces the archmagus: *D is for Dragon.*

It is clear that System D will be the game's final boss, and that you must defeat it by reducing its hit points to less than or equal to zero.

The game then sends you on a pilgrimage to build power by conquering seven Great Shrines, accompanied by a growing band of refugee dissenters and proto-queers who were too sad and individual to be absorbed by the lamppost dragon. They, and you, gather at Northwood in the town-building minigame: the power base of your effort to form a rival network entity, one founded on Freedom rather than Control. Through a complex series of block-pushing puzzles and tricky combats, you accomplish this, and you and your friends all transform into a massive, roaring red lion of raw destruction. After a pyrotechnic final battle, you win: System D is dissipated; the lampposts melt; the people's souls return to their bodies; they wake up from their dream. Abashed, they apologize to you. They will try to find better ways to love one another in the future. And the Mystic Knights, following a raucous feast at which several emotional loose ends are tied up and the names of the developers—Oshiro99 and SuFish first among them—scroll across the screen, disband until their next Super Nintendo adventure.

As a teenager, she has dreams about the characters. She dreams *as* them, draws them in her notebooks: a whole world that exists as a sequence of magnetic charges on a printed cartridge that she sometimes cleans with alcohol and a toothbrush. She draws the sorceress the most.

There's one line of dialogue toward the end of the game, while the party is exploring the fourth of the Seven Shrines (the Sound Shrine, carved from a multilevel pump organ with fiendish pressure-plate traps.) The sorceress asks the party: *How is what we're doing different from what the wizards are doing?* Her point is never answered in the game, but Sash spends hours on IRC explaining how this line alone makes the sorceress the best of characters: *she sees the most.* The sorceress is certainly the most exciting to draw, Abraxa thinks: spiderweb gowns, undercut and ear jewels and whips. She starts as this weird person whom the party initially meets running a death cult in the basement of a northern church, yet who becomes a part of the team, whose differences are tolerated. Abraxa draws a series of little notebook comics about the sorceress: confronting baristas by ordering blood served to her in a skull, lassoing a cute boy on the street and turning him into a skeleton. And she imagines, walking nights, what it would be like to look in the windows of liquor and hardware stores, to see the sorceress's own pixel reflection looking back out.

(She sees her own reflection now, in 2016, walking through good New Jersey neighborhoods to the church: smeared across an Internet company van's windshield; hair wild, makeup blurred in anxiety sweat. In the basement that night, when Abraxa had stepped away from her friends by the fire, what had the sorceress seen?)

Abraxa's father goes into landscaping while his music career gets off the ground. He has long since been promoted to lead contractor, mostly responsible for gathering whatever day labor he needs from among the silent men who watch his eyes carefully as he circles them from his car in the Lowe's parking lot, making his selections. He has a set of rounds of job sites, responds to emergencies, hands out cash at the day's end, sticks around to resolve any disputes. Then he comes home and listens to Replacements and Blue Öyster Cult records while Abraxa plays her game. One night he wipes down his guitar with a paper towel and lemon cleanser, plugs it in and tunes it, and Abraxa's excited—it's been a year, maybe two since he's played—but he just sits holding it for a few minutes before putting it away. Her adolescence has put a distance between them. Part of her has begun to worry that the closer she comes to him, the closer she comes to making his mistakes. The farther she moves from him, logically, the fewer mistakes she can make.

Her father didn't want to become part of System D, she thinks. She dreams about System D. In her dreams, System D is made of ghosts: old men in the masks of beasts, limbs replaced with thousands of writhing tentacles. She dreams of running away from them, the tentacles snapping out to capture her ankles, forcing her limbs apart, drawing her in, dead eyes behind waxy animal faces. She draws them across the pages of her note-book—she draws the sorceress, too, setting them on fire in a series of endless battles. The sorceress knows a counterspell—something that can stop them, something she could teach. As a teenager, this had been her favorite fantasy.

The computer with Internet access comes in 1997. Her father sets it up and pays for net access, hoping to use it to strike out on his own with a landscaping business; he doesn't. Abraxa quickly transfers her affections to it, leaving the Super Nintendo to the dust.

She sets up a members.aol.com site (*um. hi. you've found my website, or something. whoa!*) Soon enough she's found the old AOL CraftQ file archives; soon after that she's migrated to

IRC and met people who care about the Mystic Knights just as much as she does. They teach her about emulators and ROMs, and they teach her she can make games, too.

One night someone on IRC tells her he's had a dream in which Abraxa was a woman and the two of them went on a date. They rode a wooden roller coaster that shook, and the dreamer was afraid, but dream-Abraxa kept screaming, stood up and shouted at the moon. She saves this conversation to a text file on her computer. Sometimes, in the dark, she looks at it.

No one has to teach her about the other websites she visits, very late, careful to delete her browser history each time she encounters them, even though she knows her father will never dream of checking it.

One week on the bus, she sees a cis classmate reading a massive book on Tarot symbolism: one of the weird girls, hair twisted into a braid, sleeves scissored into ribbons and headphones piping dark music. Abraxa goes to sit next to her, asks her about the book. It's full color, lavishly illustrated and painted; it looks like a professional strategy guide for an RPG. The girl, at first reticent, finally shows Abraxa some of her favorite pages; Abraxa has learned that asking weird questions is a way to conceal what you're thinking while giving others space to reveal their own secret thoughts. She asks Abraxa what she knows about *this kind of thing*; Abraxa pretends to know a lot more about witch-craft and Tarot cards than she really knows. The cis girl believes everything she says.

The next week the two of them get off the bus together and travel to Holy Cross Cemetery, where they walk for hours talking about bands and Tarot and magic. Abraxa wants to tell her about CraftQ, but it's hard to find the words for it, and she keeps quiet. Instead they talk about spells, rituals, and whether either of them has ever performed one. Neither has.

I can't believe I'm having this conversation, she says, gazing at Abraxa: Abraxa has long hair even then; Abraxa is aware that she's accounted handsome. —You know—talking about magic, out loud.

I can't believe I'm having this conversation either, Abraxa laughs, meaning: *with a real girl.*

She claims that she knows a technique for calling in spirits. She doesn't, but she does have Sash's notes and style guides for the authentic occult principles that the Invocation LLC marketing materials all insist will be deftly woven into *Saga of the Sorceress* on its release. She copies some of them down, along with a veve symbol she finds on AltaVista, and transcribes them in chalk on her unvacuumed bedroom carpet. Her father and his new girlfriend have gone on a wine tour; she showers in anticipation, looks at her hair hanging around her ears in the bathroom mirror, towel wrapped about her waist, mind fogging out. She finds herself wishing she hadn't invited anyone over for anything, that the whole situation was behind her. She wonders if the spell will actually work, if their lives will be better, after. She wonders if her father will be okay. Then she puts on yesterday's clothes and goes to the back porch to smoke one of his cigarettes while she waits.

The cis girl arrives, hair meticulously arranged and Donna Black Zero shirt clean. Her eyes get wide when she sees Abraxa's room, its squalor alien and exciting. They go to sit on the magic circle on Abraxa's carpet, facing one another, legs crossed. Abraxa still feels like shit and everything the girl says seems depressing; Abraxa responds to it all in monosyllables and mean laughs. She can watch the girl's spirits flag, imagines writing an algebraic function to chart their decline. But the girl still says, once they've both fallen into silence: *Should we do it?* And Abraxa says *yes.*

The girl takes the lead, walks the directions, says words she recites from a small spiral notebook with vines and falcons printed on the cover. Abraxa repeats whatever she says, follows her from east to south to west to north. They invite the dead spirits into Abraxa's bedroom. They close their eyes together. She can hear the girl describing the spirits she sees circling her: her aunt, a friend who moved away and later died, a warrior queen the girl has always admired. As the girl mentions each dead spirit, Abraxa imagines she can see them: perhaps they are sitting on her bed, perhaps next to the keyboard of her computer, perhaps standing in the doorway, looking at the living children playing at their feet.

They finish the ritual, and the cis girl says she's expected home. They go out to the porch, where they linger, and Abraxa forces herself not to think about it, just to kiss this girl goodbye, which is what a good young man is expected to do, which is what she would want done to her if she were this girl and had just summoned the dead with someone for the first time. Somehow, these two feelings were not separate. The girl accepts the kiss with more eagerness than surprise, as if she had been thinking of it too, as if it is an adventure, a gift, rather than something Abraxa is trying, confusedly, to take.

For years she will wonder whether they could have had sex that day, if Abraxa had wanted to badly enough, what would have happened if they had. The cis girl's name is Maura, and this is the last time she and Abraxa will ever speak.

■   ■   ■

Lilith disappears in 1998, of course, still owing Abraxa and Sash the final layouts for the Wizard Academy proper. Sash dissolves the company in a shitty forum announcement, never bothers to notify Abraxa in advance. Her last email to Abraxa is her copy of the .qek file and nothing else. Sash was the only one who knew how the story was supposed to end.

Her father's new girlfriend sticks around. She's younger than he is but older than Abraxa, a comfortable median between them. It's only a couple of months before the new girlfriend moves into their house, her suitcases containing what she's scavenged from her bad group place in Venice. She brings bright fruit lotions and scrubs in the shower, clothes that Abraxa knows on sight are just her size. Two wardrobes, a light and a dark, shorts and tanks and gauzy blouses by day, satins, brocades, black lace, and Aqua Net by night. It's the latter category that Abraxa steals from one morning, hustling the clothes into a duffel and hurrying out the front door, breakfastless and swearing. Her skin itches as she slides off her clothes in the sun, semi-concealed in an alleyway by an electrical transformer box: raw skin like a lobster's, mid-molt.

She understands that for every true magical action she performs in the world, there will be an equal and opposite reaction from the world. She understands that System D will retaliate against any act of revolution. But the severity of its retaliation honestly surprises her: the sick looks when she strolls in, the basketball player who throws his books to the ground in his rush to get in her face. It's like there's been a whole dammed-up river of violence aimed at her, and she's blown up the dam, freed it to flow. Part of her had been thinking of the street transsexual she'd seen, how much she had loved her, how much she always assumed that others, seeing her, would love her back.

She's in the principal's office before first period even starts; even though they're sending her home anyway, they make her take off the dress—black sequins, with accents at the collar like stars—just to sit there and wait to be picked up. They give her canvas pants and an oversize school sweatshirt to wear instead, the same kind the basketball player had worn. Her brain feels unstuck, like a gate has come unlatched, is swinging: and a gate is something you can step through.

She has the disk with her then, in the pocket of the school's shitty canvas pants; she had planned that evening to bring it to a friend's house so that she could work on it while they drank beers together. All she has is the clothes her school gave her, an address she had some trust in, her mind and how she understood it: this, and she has the disk. This is what she has when she contemplates going home, and when, for the first time in years, she realizes that going home is one choice she might make. There are others.

When she looks back—all the days that intervened, every night she spent at home after this, weeks or months or years she no longer remembers, listening to her father plead with her to tell her *what's wrong*; every night on the couches and floors of friends or friends of friends; every terrible temporary job in stores, warehouses, construction sites; every sex client; every night spent in places only lightly disturbed by human passing—then all the silent calls to her father's house, unable to speak when he asks *Hello* and *Who is this?* and *Is that you?* and *If that's you, please say something* until she hangs up, and one day she calls and the line's been disconnected, and she imagines his voice—she could look him up in the phone book, but then ten, then fifteen, then more years have gone by, there are no phone books anymore—when she looks back, she knows that she had always understood magic, and how to perform it. The day when she'd run away from home to the beach was the first day she'd knowingly served the sorceress, had tried to do her work in the world. Today is the second.

She's reached the basement door of the church. It's noon, the late November sun cold. Her father is alive somewhere, she hopes with a new family, she hopes with a band that is really good and sons he can love. All of them sit by a fire, a whole room on fire, the tentacles of System D snaking into the room: through the TV, the cell phones, the router piercing their pink bodies, the cables on their skin soft as willow leaves. The violet flame that is burning for the whole world. And she knows now what maybe her mother—who must be alive somewhere, too—once knew first: that the best way to love someone is to free them. And she screams—a high shriek, like a specter is leaving her body—and she brings her stolen crowbar down hard against the lock, and the chains fall off.

: l o o p \ n # t r y s e e k \ n # l o o p

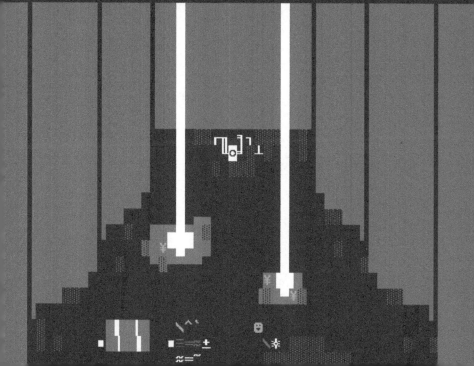

1. An Investigation

- Write down ideas when they come to you.
- Keep good to-do lists.
- Keep your computer desktop orderly.
- These habits build up into tasks, which build up into goals.
- These days your goals are small, measurable, achievable.
- Feel okay while still making progress toward escape.
- Progress comes from good procedures.

Back in the CraftQ days, when you and your friends were still making a video game that would change the world—laugh at yourself about that now, go ahead—you thought good procedures were like grinding in a Mystic Knights game. You don't want to think in video game metaphors anymore: that's childish, and you are not a child. You are thirty-two years old. But the metaphor still means something to you. What does it mean? Breathe, and let the meaning arise.

Video games are all about preparation and practice. You kill monsters in a dungeon, which prepares you to kill bigger monsters. Similarly, reaching small, everyday goals teaches you to face big long-term challenges. A theory of discipline, one you still believe in. You were just completely wrong about the nature of the challenges you'd face.

How could you have been so wrong?

Don't think about that right now. It was good that you were wrong. Being wrong helped change you. It helped move you away from the bad person you once were toward the strong and independent yet empathic person you have, as of this new year of 2017, become.

You had the same dream: you were flying, big brooms of clouds pushing you in every direction, unable to land until you opened your eyes.

The therapist you once experimented with seeing told you that on anxious mornings, you could help yourself feel better by making an inventory of the things around you. Try it now, at your computer, to help you wake up:

- Last night's tea warmed on this morning's tiny AC-powered hot plate.
- Your red sheets, which lie behind you like a broken egg sac.
- A green pendant hanging from a nail, a magical item you once believed you could create.
- Your black bookshelves, pared down by ruthless inner instinct in the years since you transcended college and came back to live at home: Audre Lorde, Nella Larsen, Toni Morrison, Émile Durkheim, Janet Mock, Anne McCaffrey, Ursula K. Le Guin, Octavia Butler, Tove Jansson, a Mystic

Knights V PSX strategy guide still with your
teenage annotations, a binder with printouts of
notes of apology you once wrote, at the rate of
one a year, lavish prose eventually breaking down
into bullet-pointed lists of your sins you wished to
apologize for, none of them ever sent.

- In the darkness of your closet, deep but sparse, your
  laundry lies neatly folded in its basket.
- On the red-draped windowsill, there's nothing but
  your dry succulent's spines (you can't keep them
  alive, but you keep trying; every death is experience
  points) and the view of Sterling Place you've known
  all your life: row houses, bodegas, heavy metal
  shutters, January snow.
- A tall mirror.
- A webcam, a vibrator, and a flogger, all of which
  huddle, wrapped in cords and tails, in a duffel bag,
  neat and out of sight.

Give yourself two minutes, measured in four-count breaths,
to steep yourself in this inventory. Be still—let thoughts float
across your mind—still as the part in *Super Mystic Knights 3*
where you have to not press the controller for a long time—let
that thought go; let Mystic Knights go. Feel yourself ground.

At last, grounded, you can begin the first of your morning
procedures: the traversal of the links.

The Internet is becoming steadily more evanescent—old image
links break, old RSS feeds go out of service. All the GeoCities,
lost with Atlantis. Things that vanish are one of your areas of
interest.

The procedure is to go through the same list of links you've traversed since your teenage days—old Elfwood galleries, the dev log of an aging programmer who's trying to invent new tools for storytelling in games, a fantasy webcomic started in 1995 and still not concluded, a bad movie forum—plus all the links you've added in the years since—transgender zinesters, histories of international squatting, a lively forum centered on the hermetic traditions of Franz Bardon. Not every link every day—variety is important to any richly lived life—but each link at least once in a three-month cycle. There are probably better indices to track the progress of time online, but these are the indices you've chosen. So follow them: check the links, note any differences. Take in the world.

Most of these websites are long idle, years between updates. Most days there's nothing to take in. Today, there is.

There are people from your CraftQ days you don't check up on anymore. But Abraxa's LiveJournal is a link you can never quite write off, always your favorite of the former CraftQer social media presences. In her prime, in her twenties, her adventures were a treat: long surreal narration, sometimes in classic IRC dialect, spooky confessions of drug experiences, excited processing of transsexual firsts. She's one of the first people you knew not just to secretly exist as a girl—or at least to pretend to be one on IRC for clout, as you did—but to actually *take steps.* For years you divided people into two types: those you could learn from, and those you could teach. Abraxa is one of the few people you put in both categories. You were proud of your programmer, artist, musician: a horse you knew you could never break, but whom you could encourage to trust.

But just as Abraxa was one of the first to adopt LiveJournal, she was also one of the first to move on from it. Sometime in the middle of the Bush years, her updates tapered off. For years now she's posted virtually nothing: months-apart incoherent blog entries or notebook scribble drawings, skulls, angry girls, candles with unnervingly detailed wax buttresses spilling down their sides. The last update was three years ago.

But today, she's here for you with a new entry: a single image. No text? No, the image itself is text: white on black text, roughly rendered ASCII gradient evoking sunset in the corner. Why does it feel so uncomfortable to you? Ponder this question until you feel a sick lurch, like you're in a taxicab braking suddenly on a winter street. You've seen the image before. In fact, you drew it, when you were just thirteen: the opening ROOM of what was once to be the greatest CraftQ game ever made. You haven't seen it in the nearly two decades since.

It takes longer than it should to notice that the text is no longer what you wrote.

> *SAGA OF THE SORCERESS IS CANCELED*
> *OR IS IT . . . **UN**CANCELED*
> *MERCER STREET | JC | CRAFTQCON*
> *© 1998–2016 INVOCATION LLC*

Once, when you were eleven, you broke a bone. Reading the words she wrote across your screen shot feels like the memory of that: your feet out of balance with your wild XY growth spurt, the vertigo of knowing that in one moment, over there in time, your shin was intact, in the next moment, over here, there is a thin yet decisive crack.

Through the wall, your father is already layering his Casio tracks. He starts his daily practice, predictable as tides: a warbling mulch of slow chords on the bottom, some spikes and accents in the midrange he feels out, a rakish squiggle on top. Listen for familiar chords: find none. So he's not continuing work on his latest longstanding project, just improvising again, finding space to fill the fifteen minutes before his bus to work. When your father is inspired, he repeats himself, plays a fill or melody over and over with slight variation intercut with long pauses, during which you know his mind is searching for every possible thing wrong with it.

Your teenage artwork is still staring back at you. Remain calm—breathe smoothly. Then take out your quest log. You're still finishing last year's quest notebook, and most of the pages at the front are full of to-do items you've already checked off. But find an open page and make a note to yourself: *Abraxa—Mercer Street—CraftQCon—Saga. INVESTIGATE.* Draw a box in four crisp strokes. Leave this box unchecked.

Your father's oatmeal, into which he's grated red peppers for joint health, sits balanced on the edge of the Casio that hems him in; his broad forehead, fringed in graying kinks, unlines itself when he sees you. Nod at him, remember to smile as you get your own breakfast: toast burned dark brown, sour cream and jam blended and spread. Your mother's sugared grapefruit rind is already in the trash: her sixth grade classes start early, her weekends are full of exercise. You can't remember the last time you've seen her eat it. Settle on the couch— your sometimes bed, when strangers and relatives require your room—and watch your father, his post office approved vest straining against his stomach, extract himself from behind his instruments.

Sounding good, you say.

He winces. —Sounding like something, he says back.

You wish you could somehow transmit confidence to him. You used to give him notes on his performance, tried to encourage the tiny shoots of things you liked in his playing and gently pinch out the things you didn't. But he would stop playing whenever you did that, fade out sometimes for months. So instead of giving notes, generate these words in the eye of your mind—*there is nothing wrong with what you're doing*—and see them pass through your skull to his. Wait for them to be received.

He asks: —How's the video game biz treating you?

This is still the question he asks you every day, despite you not having owned a video game corporation since 1998. A kind of cold war.

Ups and downs, you tell him. —I just heard from an old coworker. Someone who used to do art for me.

He raises his eyebrows. —Think he might be interested in working with you again?

I don't know, you say. —Not impossible.

He disappears into the bedroom—you can tell, from the dents in the couch pillows, that he's once again slept here rather than join your mother; you'll have to reverse the cushions—and then, unexpectedly, he returns.

Something I was going to ask you, he says. —Leroux and I were talking after work.

Leroux is your father's possibly only friend, his fellow postal worker for at least a decade. The two of them started a conversation about Alice Coltrane one shift, and your father has been chasing the high of this for years.

How is Leroux, you ask.

His oldest is in the orchestra this year, he said. —He's looking for a tutor.

Reflect on how simple it is to predict where this is going.
—Uh huh.

Your father lifts his chin a little, lets his eyes peep out a little, dangerously, beneath the rims of his glasses. —Not for actually playing or anything, he says. —Just for music theory. Intervals and chords. Things like that. It'd be for the whole year.

When your father is in this state, it's important to respond swiftly. —No.

No to what, your father asks, pulling on one uniform cuff, eyeing the door: he knows exactly when he has to be at the stop, eight minutes prior to the scheduled arrival, so no one can blame him for missing the bus.

No, I have a job, you say. —I work as a research assistant. Remember?

Neither of your parents believe you about your job, but it's important to assert the fiction. Again, your father looks at the door, and then he looks at you. —It'd be easy work, he says. —And I already told him you'd do it.

Follow procedure: when enraged, swallow, will your shoulders to relax. —No, you tell him, voice still.

Maybe just give it a try, he says, looking at the door. —We can talk about it later. It doesn't start for a week. Now, I'm going to be late.

Yes, you say. (Keep your shoulders very relaxed; do not let them press up toward your ears; this is a sign of weakness.) —You will.

But probably he won't be: already he's out the door, his creaking down the stairway in one-and-a-half time. Breathe. This is not the first time he's done something like this. Neither will it be the last.

Prepare your strategy. You won't show up to the appointment

he sets—you won't offer him an explanation—you will remain still, unmoved, until Leroux finds someone else to tutor his kid in a subject that you don't actually know and you don't understand why your father believes you know. You will not wait for an apology for this latest attempt to control your affairs. You will take his oatmeal bowl from his speaker to the sink.

One of your jobs, as the adult transsexual daughter in whose important research assistant job your parents agree to pretend to believe, is to keep the house tidy. This is less daunting than it may seem: neither of your parents is home often enough to mess it up, and neither of them have friends they invite over: no large parties to prepare for, no pets, no ostentatious mess. A mess is impossible to ever know you've completely cleaned. Where is it appropriate to stop cleaning? What is the state of being clean? Does it stem from social agreement: we agree to call this condition of the bathroom clean? Or is there something more objective: perceptual threshold of smell, realistic possibility of disease, relative entropy of molecules? The probability of someone encountering dirt? This is another question that used to paralyze you, and therefore you wouldn't clean—would organize your bookmarks instead, review old emails—and therefore you'd be named lazy, risk your position living at home well after you probably should be living here. This is why you've found an alternative: clean, no matter what, for thirty minutes a day. By *clean*, understand: *react to whatever seems like dirt*. Bathroom, your room, living room, kitchen, the family bedroom, the entry hall, closets, repeat. Your mom leaves sticky notes sometimes as small adjustments. The system seems to work: no one has gotten sick, no one seems to be getting mad, and for thirty minutes you can think about whatever you want.

Today is living room day. Move your mother's gradebook back to the top of her file cabinet, take water glasses to the kitchen, straighten the bookshelf, dust shelf, credenza, table, frames of photographs: old relations to whom you feel little connection. Spray false citrus chemicals on the prewar moldings, the same ones you've looked at all your life, dozing on the floor while one or another parent watches dramas. What did it feel like to be in one of these apartments in the old prewar days? Who else walked in the spaces where your small head was resting, held up by a couch pillow, warm and safe beneath blankets?

Think about whatever you want while you fill the dry air with lemon incense. Or no: think about Abraxa. Interrogate this: Why does her post rattle you so much? Try to schematize as best as you can without your notebooks, the boards to which you pin your butterfly thoughts:

- Abraxa posted your work to her blog. Is this a specific signal to you?
- Does she realistically expect you still to be reading her blog (even though you are)?
- Does this mean you have a duty, beyond the duties others may have, to notice this?
- Abraxa may be in trouble.
- She still has a copy of *Saga of the Sorceress*, years after you gave up on it. You let go of this dream, but she didn't. Does that mean that you never deserved to dream it, and she did? Were all your anxieties about her right, all along?
- You are thinking bad thoughts about your friend.
- Your friend who may be in trouble.

- Your friend who is asking for help.
- Your friend who needs you.
- But you aren't capable of helping her.
- You aren't capable of helping anyone.

Think these thoughts—think them again, and again—scrub the shelves. Your timer hasn't gone off. The mess isn't yet clean.

At the computer in your room, begin your investigation.

First, assemble your clues. Right now you have one clue. Study it, and start listing the *knowns*:

- You know you drew this, almost two decades ago.
- It was the opening screen to the video game you and your friends were making.
- Its text has been changed. The text is the only element of the screenshot (as far as you know) that doesn't date back to 1998.
- The text is your best clue for finding Abraxa, who you're sure is calling for your help.

Therefore your course of action is clear: study the text. CraftQCon you understand. JC you don't—a cry for help from the divine?—until you remember that there was still an open debate about where the CraftQCon would take place. Jersey City was one of the target locations. Google it: Jersey City contains a Mercer Street.

By chance, Jersey City is also where your last remaining client lives.

Consider the implications for a minute. Then pick up your business phone and begin a text.

*attention worm. your sorceress queen needs you. cancel
all your insignificant shit for the day and be on camera
at 5 pm or remove yrself from my presence forever. yq,
caramella.*

Send it. The message transmits to the satellites, and you
feel larger. Stand up and stretch, then—toes arching yourself
upward, hands circling wrists to extend them out, sash of your
loose-knotted robe coming undone. Feel your body at last.

Leave your house and head for the library. Here's a list of the
potential random encounters you'll face:

- the convenient deli where the man behind the
  counter offered to fuck you and you said no, so
  maybe he now wants to kill you and you can't go
  there anymore;
- the other deli, where you wait to pay for your sports
  water while you try not to be noticed by two men
  from the neighborhood with whom you'd gone to
  school;
- the subway entrance at Utica where they hand you
  J-W tracts, or they try to sell you Black Liberation
  literature and incense, or they call you a faggot;
- the invisible boundary line around Kingston
  Avenue where the coats and wigs turn heavy and
  the people glide around you in a wide, suspicious
  berth;
- the white people, their nervous smiles;
- the families with children on the library steps, who
  navigate their children's attention away from you:

wary eye contact, a sharp suggestion to *buddy, come look at this, come over here.* Seeing you will only lead to questions.

You're at sufficient level and equipment to meet these challenges. So follow the path—so follow procedure. Try to think only of nature—the sky, the purloined land—and let your racing fears vaporize into clouds.

At the library, go to the small cafe and treat yourself to pie. Then climb the escalator and stairs to 2F, where you'll find the room with outlets. The creep in plaid is here today, the one who spends his time organizing a thick stack of index cards and who you once made the mistake of sitting near. He hissed at you—*you've got so many rights now, too many rights*—and you went to hide, shaking, in the stacks, and the library cop cruised through and stared. You didn't come back to the library for a month. But now you and the card catalog creep avoid one another, an implicit truce among coworkers.

Set up your laptop—two years old now; you should replace it; you should schedule some more visits with Droneslut to afford that—and begin a new document: *INVESTIGATION*. Before you write in it, file it: Documents > Projects > Active > 2016-2017, and then a subfolder of its own. One day, you know an archivist will appreciate all you've done for them.

Imagine that future biographer now, a way to summon strength: the clean gesture line they'll trace through all your projects. The line will have nominal divisions. Juvenilia, sure, and then your early CraftQ work under the name Sash: the pretentious fantasy games. *Saga of the Sorceress*, however unfinished, is the second. Then the work you did after *Saga of the Sorceress*: three chapters of a multivolume fantasy novel, never completed, a new hastily assembled original project in CraftQ, never released, a lavish experimental interactive fiction game, never released, the sourcebook for a new tabletop RPG that focused on relationship mechanics, never released, a feverishly drafted novella about a romance between Oshiro99 and SuFish, completed, burned. Then your pivot from games to analysis, fiction to nonfiction: the work you dreamed of secretly publishing in academic journals for colleges you failed to apply to, the community college papers perfect in outline, never actually completed. Plans to publish your own academic journal, your own website, your own zine, your own LiveJournal, and what all of these might say.

Each plan you recorded in years of diaries, brainstorm documents, outlines, fragments. You've become an expert in not releasing any of this work. What started as simple self-doubt, inertia, and fear, in the first years after Lilith—don't think about Lilith—eventually became policy. Cultivate silence, you vowed. Its shape is more interesting than anything you could have said.

Silence is best shaped by occasional sound: a stone falling, the echo that defines the cave.

You have a Tumblr, untagged and disconnected from all other networks. You post every two months, six a year, each a kind of research-backed koan. The last was about the glaciated landmass of Crown Heights, the terminal moraine along which you walk every day to this library full of books not in Munsee or any other language originally spoken on this land. *spines balanced on a ridge of ice: give us away.* No one liked or reposted this, or any of your other posts, except the one that referenced a popular character from a Mystic Knights game (which you've since deleted). Some people read your Tumblr: there are traffic logs, flickering like the static from long-distance space radio arrays. You don't look at the logs in detail anymore; you don't want to know too much. But you imagine the IP addresses who flicker in and out like marsh lights must represent real readers, secret intelligences who wait for these messages you transmit. You are a numbers station, inspiring mystery and fear. Your biographer will appreciate the smooth gradient you've made of your life. Once you wanted to be everything; now you work hard to be nothing. The two poles of perfection: slowly, you will find the correct, balanced distance from each. This is what the life you've built affords you: the power to be perfect.

But return to your investigation—don't think of the past—don't think of Lilith. Right now your best lead is Droneslut. What other leads can you develop while you wait for five o'clock, when he'll be free from work? Think. Are there possibly clues in the screenshot itself, information you can glean from the file metadata? Download it, drop it into the hex editor. There's no surprise about the timestamp: it's less than a minute from Abraxa having taken this screenshot to having posted it. Therefore, unless she took a screenshot of a screenshot, the original game file must still exist.

Part of the text says *CraftQCon:* that part you understand. It had been your idea.

No CraftQer had ever met another CraftQer. As a teenager, you were sure of this: the very concept of CraftQ seemed to preclude sharing knowledge of CraftQ with any other person

IRL, as if every CraftQ game was counterfactual, would dissolve into quantum ASCII vapor on disclosure. Who at school would you even tell? It was a disembodied thing, a secret of the air and wires you and your teenage friends shared every night when you settled into your parents' desk chairs and turned on your monitors, friendships made exclusively of words.

There had been only one serious effort to meet: the CraftQCon. You were behind the CraftQCon, because of course you were: back then you thought you had to be behind everything.

This idea to host a tech conference for you and your IRC friends went further than, in retrospect, you can believe. You updated a spreadsheet calendar of availabilities and school holidays for anyone in #teengoetia who expressed a passing interest; you made a rough map of everyone's home cities (assuming no one had lied about this, as you had). You even picked a hotel in the different candidate cities. The brand-new Doubletree was Jersey City's, relatively cheap and almost unimaginably far west of where you still live in Brooklyn. You had one serious conversation via DM with another CraftQer about how to handle the logistics of booking the room fees and convention space, how to collect money online. (The going plan was to mail an envelope of cash around from participant to participant, then the last person would bring it to the hotel on the day of the event.) You'd planned a schedule of activities—expert talks by some of CraftQ's best coders, a meet-and-greet, a marathon coding session, time for *StarCraft*.

It was all to culminate in a trip to the hotel ballroom for a dance party, which you would somehow arrange. You imagined this as the ballroom scene from *Hackers*: hundreds of savvy queers gyrating and clinging to one another's shoulders and hips amid glowing reactive light. This is what you imagined the adult world might look like, and this is how you imagined taking your place there: you and your teenage online friends at a hotel you somehow booked, nervously shuffling, until the dance became natural at last.

When you imagined the CraftQCon back then, you imagined your two friends there with you, finally in person. You and your friend Abraxa, and your other friend, Lilith. But don't think about Lilith. But don't.

Abraxa wrote CRAFTQCON in her screenshot: so she remembered this, too. You've spent a very long time thinking about what your plans meant to Lilith, about whom you will not think. But the idea that it all might have meant something to Abraxa, too—that she even remembered all of this eighteen years later!—this you didn't consider.

To find Abraxa, understand what CraftQCon means. Write it in your notes. And then consider the reciprocal: What did Abraxa mean to you? A worthy competitor, an Other, another executor of your dreams. This is who she was to you: Does any of this give some clue as to who you were to her?

You can't go further with this on memory alone. The historical record is your next step.

In part, your expectation that an archivist will care about what you do is based on a solid foundation: at least one group of archivists already does.

For years after you'd stopped caring about CraftQ, the program itself, irascibly DOS-based, would still run on modern computers. You took advantage of this during your guilty, depressive, and brief college hours sunk in loathing and desiring to be A Real Woman But Alas It Can Never Happen. Alone, you let yourself play your old games, looking for evidence that what you desired now for your gender, you'd also desired then. You searched every corridor of your adolescent labyrinths without finding anything conclusive: sometimes reassurance, sometimes a shocking disconfirmation. *I always wanted to be a woman*: Who actually has a story like that? Cis people don't have to have that level of clarity about their history; why do trans people? But don't think of this now: think instead about how sad you were to lose access to your digital past when computers stopped running on a skeleton of DOS sometime in the late 2000s, how elated you were now that modern browser applications and the will of a few former teenage CraftQers—now in their thirties and realizing they might one day die—had made it possible to preserve.

They did a good job: they uploaded not just the games but old email archives, IRC transcripts, forum posts, the whole vast smorgasbord of puberty and humiliation. You've spent nights reading old #teengoetia logs, hand clasped over your mouth in shame. You've also read, again and again, the post they made about you on their official early 2000s CraftQ wiki page:

> *Ashley "Sash" d'Arkness (which is of course a REAL AND LEGITIMATE name that humans have) was the only female CraftQer and therefore the erotic locus of the entire CraftQ community. Sash was also a tremendous bitch who thought that having a vagina made her a fucking literary genius when actually a bunch of guys just wanted her to blow them so she'd shut her pretentious mouth. Her games contained more words than the dictionary but were less interesting.*

A novel-length close reading of your uninteresting teenage games followed. This had been published on the CraftQ forums in 2004, while you were still attempting college. Even now you can summon its text from memory whenever you want. You still feel pride, like a dark candle burning in the wet pit of your stomach, that the text proves that they never guessed what you were.

They profiled Abraxa on the wiki, too. Hers was a much more positive profile; everyone loved Abraxa and her weird punk shit. No one was surprised or cared when Abraxa slowly came out over the course of eight to ten years in a smooth gradient of cocaine barf forum posts and screenshots and underwear selfies. She kept posting into her late twenties, even her early thirties, these years when everyone else had jobs and mostly used their blogs to talk about politics and being tired. You, in your silence, read every post.

Here is the method you will use: to understand what Abraxa saw in you then—what made her post your screenshot, what made her remember the CraftQCon—you must look, again, at yourself.

Fortunately, the CraftQ archivists have you covered. The official CraftQ archive—financed by Patreon, maintained by a lonely programmer whose games you can't remember—holds not only the work you put out under your later, more legendary handle, but earlier work too, never clearly attributed to you. Now—at your laptop in the library, where just anyone might look over your shoulder—find yourself lingering over these essays in your craft, the time before Abraxa or anyone else knew you. It's bad: a crude transcription of the *Power Rangers* TV theme song bleats in squarewave from the PC speaker (thank

God for headphones.) Honestly, take a moment to admire the audacity of this work: the copyright notices you put on your DOS game where licensed corporate characters go to the bathroom, as if you had something to protect. That long list of production credits, eleven of them (one for each day the game took to produce, you're sure), each job title filled out with your former name. By the time you and your friends were working on *Saga of the Sorceress*, this earlier hubris made you blush with shame. Now you just wonder when you lost it and what you traded it for.

There's only one CraftQ game (other than your own games) that for years you considered as good as a *real game* (before you began to question what realness here meant). The game concerned a nameless character, the classic white-on-blue char 2 smile, attempting to navigate a surreal tower filled with anthropomorphs and puzzles in constructed languages. In its climax—immediately before the player is killed by a falling brick, ending the game—the narrator reveals that the player's avatar is not representation, but exactly what it appears to be: literally a face looking *up*, as in out of the computer screen and at the human player. *Looking down at you is the slightly disappointed face of a fourteen-year-old boy*: that's what the text said.

That climax comes back to you now as you look down at your childhood work. This avatar your child-self constructed a world for is now looking up at you from your laptop screen. But your child-self doesn't see a fourteen-year-old boy: it sees a thirty-two-year-old transsexual with unkempt braids who has a video appointment this evening with her regular sex work client. The avatar smiles. You press ESCAPE.

■ ■ ■

Your phone buzzes: it will be a text from your friend Tula. *hey are You going to my thing tonight?* Remember, abruptly, Tula's reading series: a monthly review of trans poets, and sometimes new media professionals from the West Coast. It will contain uncomfortable sincerity, strident callouts of The Cis, sexual desperation. On the plus side, you will see other people there, and it's important to do that sometimes. On the minus side, it will not help your investigation.

Text this back to her: *should i?*

Now wait for the usual countertexts to come in—*of course, Bitch!*, or *what kind of Question is that??* or *only if U want To? :)* But none of those come; your phone stays silent. Try not to feel unsettled by this. Think: *good.*

Go home, avoiding all random encounters. Dust and spray the air with Pledge until you feel your sense of safety come back. Then order, receive, eat, discard Chinese takeout. Take a shower, make yourself up: dagger lashes, black lips, sharp contours. Equip yourself: crimped hair with fall and purple extensions, PVC bodysuit, black slacks, white cashmere sweater with cowl neck: something your client can imagine touching.

Now, prepared, log into Skype and connect with Droneslut. He's already online and waiting.

In this game, you play as yourself. It's a multiplayer game, but your body is your own. The graphics are however you decide to use that body and its surroundings to fill a webcam. To succeed in your adventure, you must make careful use of your three magic skills:

- your hands,
- your mind,
- your voice.

Droneslut's office fills the frame on the other end of the line: phone and e-reader stacked and charging, football pennant, mess of papers and folders that contain the financial secrets of America, family photos whose faces you cannot see. His body is there, too: pasty and overweight and patchily furred, naked face flushed pink. His dick is semitumescent, framed by matted hair. Feel furious: you didn't tell him to be naked.

Hello, Queen Caramella, he coos.

Why the *fuck* are you naked, you ask. —What did I tell you?

I'm sorry, Queen Caramella, he says, not sounding sorry. —I thought it'd be more convenient?

Convenient for what, you ask. Twice now he has spoken your professional name: feel this, like a regal mantle of black feathers is coming to rest on your shoulders.

For you . . . watching me, he says, blushing more, dick blushing, too. —To make sure I do it right.

You think I want to watch a *drone* jack off? you snarl. —Do you like watching dogs scratch themselves? Worms shitting dirt? Get your clothes back on immediately, or I'll enslave someone more obedient.

Remember, when you say this, not to be too openly harsh: there's a balance to strike here, if you want to retain clients. But it has an effect: Droneslut jumps up, collects his shirt and boxers and everything from around his desk, struggles to pack his erection back into his relaxed-fit slacks. Watch him carefully: there have been other infractions since November, some back talk out of usual bounds, and once he ejaculated when you asked him to ruin the orgasm. The money's remained the same, is the problem: there's even been more of it, enough for whatever you need. But losing control here would be a problem. Droneslut has been your client now for almost three years, and he's been a good one, sufficiently good for you to drop all your other clients: the ones who got snippy, who canceled, who insisted on meeting you in real life. You'd thought Droneslut was different, even felt tenderly toward him sometimes (pro tip: to achieve this, try to forget what he does all day). But now these rumblings of rebellion. Now is not the time to worry about the future, or people you won't be able to keep, or starting yet again from nothing. Stop this. You can't let yourself get depressed in a session. No one's fantasy of financial domination involves feeling obligated to care for someone.

Droneslut is dressed again now, his crisp shirt skipping a button, sleazier in his work clothes than he is out of them, you think. He's waiting, silent, for your command.

Very good, you say. —It pleases me when you obey. Do you like to obey?

Yes, he says, rapt.

Ask: —Do you know why it's important to obey me? Do you remember our goal, here?

Yes, my queen, he says.

Aren't you clever, you say. —Say it!

Because I'm your drone slut, says Droneslut. —In the service of the mind-hive of the great Caramella, sorceress queen. In her mission to . . . to destroy our world. To overthrow all capital and smash cis patriarchy, and—

Say it as if you *mean* it, you suggest.

To overthrow all capital and smash cis patriarchy, he yelps. —To return the world to anarchy. To bring the Sex Goddess through the ritual door from Outside so that she can rule us filth who've poisoned her world.

Exactly, you say. —And why are you helping me with that, Droneslut? Why did you agree to give up your free will and join my hive?

Because I'd sell out my people for a chance to cum, he says, eyes sparkling.

Yes you would, you say. —You're a very good slut. I could turn you into a queen, too. Inject you with venom from my stinger and dissolve that little dick of yours. You'd be on the winning team. Do you want that?

Droneslut trembles. He never answers this question, unable to tell if it's a threat you're making or a promise. Feel grateful for this ambiguity: if Droneslut were super into chemical castration by sorceress venom—or however the workplace D&D cosmology you established when you started this works; it's been years; you forget—you might start to feel ethical obligations toward him, and the moment you start feeling ethical obligations toward people is the moment a relationship curdles. Let yourself stay on the surface: whenever you tell him you'll dissolve his penis, he always gets quiet. Find yourself feeling tender at him.

If this is my queen's will, he says.

Very good, you say. —Now I'm going to tell you my task. And this is the most important task I've ever given you, slut. I need you to—

Excuse me, queen? he asks.

Don't interrupt, you say. —What is it?

He squirms. —Did you need, he begins.

Shit: you've forgotten to ask for money. Get control back.

You do *not* bring up money in my presence, you say. —I

expect you to furnish *whatever* I require, *whenever* I require it. Your job is just to *make* the money. Work your life away like a good little drone. I'm the one who decides how to *spend* it to enslave your people.

He looks happy: you're probably back on safe ground here. But you need him to stay happy. (You can't believe you forgot the money: the library, playing your old games, Abraxa—it's all rattled you more than you thought.) So: get back into control. Take some time to breathe—slow down. Make a little meal out of telling Droneslut the lavish, species-treasonous, and fictional ways you squandered his previous payment to you: decorations for the prison hive for all the cis humans prior to drone conversion, vats of marbled royal jelly and drone honey, lingerie and perfumes: a queen must be beautiful. You don't even remember how you actually spent the part of your wages you let yourself spend: MetroCards, library pie, your contribution to the family's ever-steeper rent and insurance payments, sandwiches from the deli, a new dress (a queen must be beautiful), a deposit in your hypothetical surgery fund (you haven't decided; maybe you will go to an island instead). And, ever, your escape fund: the money that will allow you, once you gather enough of it, to never see Droneslut ever again. Expenses that Droneslut would not be correctly humiliated to find his finance-bro salary covering. Caring for someone, even a trans woman, was not humiliating in a sexy way. So use your magic powers—use your mind, use your voice—and shape a good story for him. And soon it works: you have created a little cocoon of fear for him to steep in, a little dream. This is what you have to trade.

You've reestablished control. Now, set him his task. —I need you to go to Jersey City, you say. —Are you capable of doing that?

Of course, my queen, he says. —I live in Jersey City!

I don't care where you live, you say; remember to smile. —Go there, and investigate Mercer Street. The information you bring back will be decisive in my plans. I need to know you're capable of *not fucking this up*.

Droneslut looks confused. —What—what do you need me to find out about Mercer Street? he asks.

You have no idea. —You don't need to know that, you tell him. —Just walk back and forth.

How many times, he asks.

At least fifteen times, you say. —And tell me everything you see there. Anything strange—anything that interests you. Anything magical.

He still looks dubious, more embarrassed than humiliated. This is no longer sexual playacting, but just playacting, which adults cannot engage in. Get control back.

Do you need a little taste of how I'll reward you when you bring me what I need? you ask.

He flushes happily. From here the encounter is second nature: guide him to lean back in his chair, to ease his dick out of the zipper of his slacks, to leave his shirt on so he'll ruin it. Set his pace with commands: lots of slow strokes and pauses to start, until he's fallen into your rhythm and you can phone it in, monitor his breathing and only stop and restart him when he gets close to crisis range. There is an art to watching Droneslut jack off, a lull like you imagine highway driving must feel: your mind free to wander, something subconscious knowing how to pace him without knowing how you know. He's so aggressive, at whatever pace you set: think of a scrubby child shoveling food from a suburban buffet. Watching him, start to wonder what it would be like to be cis and to have a child. Get sad.

Hands off, you order. —Wait for him to comply; he does, whimpering. —You can have the rest when you bring me what I need.

Make Droneslut cut his shirt with scissors: you told him he'd have to mess it up, and consistency is key. He appreciates these extra attentions. Then set a time, two weeks out, for your next meeting. Then end as per usual: make him wait, head bowed at attention and chanting your name, while you sign off.

Stretch—crack your knuckles—put victory music on your laptop. And wait for your phone to ding: money has hit your Venmo account. It's more than you'd agreed on: another liberty he's taking. Another experience.

Session over, lie on the bed and try to stop your thoughts. Try to meditate, try to breathe. But you can't: your thoughts keep moving in unproductive, agitated loops. Forgetting to ask for money—your CraftQ failures—Abraxa in trouble and you don't know where—Lilith. Sit up again and check your phone. There aren't any texts. Tula never answered.

Feel a rush of terror. And type: *yeah, i'll come to your thing. i want to see you.*

She texts back: *cool*

Change your clothes, put on a bathrobe, go to the bathroom to take a shower. Your mother is in the living room, TV shine shadowing the ribs in her after-work tank top, gradebook open over her ancient, pilled pajama pants, workday wig in the box. She has a glass of white wine in one hand and a student paper in the other. She takes a sip—she watches ten seconds of TV—she reads one paper. She marks the score both on the page and in the gradebook. Repeat. When you were a kid, this efficiency seemed monstrous to you: Didn't she want anything more out of life than to be really fast at grading math quizzes? Now she strikes you as someone to aspire to be.

Attempt to hang out with her, before your shower, following your usual procedure: lean on the door casing until she looks up.

What, she asks. —Is the bathroom clogged or something?

I was trying to have a mother-daughter interaction with you, you say. —Is that okay?

She takes another sip of wine. —Did you talk to your father about that job from that friend of his?

What friend, you ask.

You know what friend, she says, cracking a smile. —He only has one friend. You're not going to take it, right?

I have a job, you tell her. —I'm a research assistant.

She looks down at a student's test, her smile going away. Look at the shelves you cleaned earlier. It's not reasonable to expect her to notice them, although you know she'd notice them if you didn't perform your regular cleaning procedure. You know, on some level, that she appreciates you.

End the interaction: —I'm taking a shower before I go out.

She looks at you. —Where are you going?

Hang on the edge of the molding, letting your body swing in a circle, tethered to your hand. —Out, you say. —With Tula. Around. Anywhere.

She sets down her glass of wine, and she looks at her gradebook. Swing on the door casing, like you did when you were a little kid, and sneak glimpses of her as you swing: her eyes, tired, her mouth, pinched. Think about the time, when it was first becoming clear to both of you that you would fail to form an adulthood of your own, when she could get angry at vague answers, when she needed to know just where you were going. Think about the time when you were ten and you overheard her through the walls one night, crying and shouting on the phone while your father was away: *How did this happen to me? How did I end up here?* And so you learned the goal was never to be here.

By the time your shower is done and your going-to-the-reading outfit is assembled—thrifted leather jacket, your fancy tiger glasses, black vinyl top with huge ringed zipper, pink extensions and nails, earrings shaped like swords, cloud of nag champa over dragon fruit body wash base coat—your mother is done with her grading and sits watching her show, face still, arms folded tightly over her ribs. When you say good night, she doesn't look at you to say goodbye, just raises her wine glass, like an all-clear from a guard.

You encounter your father in the front hall. —Mom says hi, you inform him. Watch him brighten.

They're talking about you as soon as you get to Tula's reading; you're certain of it. Two of them, generic and trans and Brooklyn in knit caps, ringlets (bleached, dyed) hanging over crisp jackets (leather, denim) and bountiful scarves, eyes glittering, mouths taut and bright. The girls and Tula are having a conversation, the two of them laughing while Tula smiles the greedy cat smile one smiles when one is enjoying cruelties.

One of the blond ones sees you enter first: old coat at your shoulders, hair tied up in pineapple-leaf fall, how old you must look to this brat, how tired. She drops her smile, and the conversation goes to a whisper. Then Tula turns to you, and her smile has changed keys.

Hiiii, she says. —I'm so glad you could make it!

Best practice here would be to dispel your anxiety with a

question, so that you can get through the show: *You weren't just talking about me, right?* But Tula's nonresponse to your text still has you rattled: therefore, keep quiet, offer a wave. You don't want to gain a further reputation as unpleasant, or a problem.

Go to the bar, order a Shirley Temple, and try to recover your sense of balance for being among people whom you know and who know you. (You don't let yourself drink anymore: drinking was not a procedure that helped.) The bar is a queer dive, its floor a haunted checkerboard, its walls covered in framed posters of movies where sailors are killed by serpents and gill-men, its track lights capped in fuchsia gels. The owner has crosshatched the ceiling in post-Christmas discount silver tinsel, which casts waving fishtank shadows on the faces of the two trans women who have certainly started talking about you again. Then they excuse themselves to go outside and smoke and probably talk about you some more. Find Tula in the crowd: she's standing now with one of the readers, you guess, a shorter-than-you enby-vibes person in a hoodie with Philippe from *Mystic Knights V* printed on it. Reflect on this: Why did you pick, as the site of your teenage shame, a fandom that the rest of the transsexual world would one day come to embrace?—and reflect on the volume of your drink. It's a progress bar, a minigame. Once the drink is empty, you can leave, but you will fail if you empty it too fast.

Tula returns at about the halfway mark, rapping her empty highball glass against the back of the neighboring stool.

Girl, Tula says. —Girl, I'm glad you *made* it.

I *made* it, you say, making a little here-I-am gesture.

What's even *happening* with you? she asks. —Do you need another drink? What are you even drinking?

I'm not really drinking these days, you say. —I've told you that.

Gosh, I'm sorry I forgot, she says brightly. —Maybe if you hung out with me more, I'd remember!

Do not take this bait: stay silent, let her signal the bartender and point to her glass. —That's really responsible, though, she says as he refills her. —I should be more like you.

I don't think anyone should be more like me, you say.

No, this was a mistake; people do not like you to be this honest. Think of normal things to say while Tula turns to flirt with the bartender—*thank you*, low, her head resting, just tips of fingers, on his wrist—and then she turns back to you. —So what's even *happening* with you, she repeats. —Are you going to read your blog tonight?

Ignore this. —Lots of things are up, you say. —I'm doing a kind of research project about the Internet when I was a teenager. Some people I knew then.

Teenage Sash, she says, contemplating this. —Were you a goth?

I wasn't anything, you say, gazing in melancholy at your cherry stems. —I was a megalomaniac. I thought my friends and I could make a video game that would change the world. But I didn't have any friends. Except online, where I was a girl.

Everything you are saying is miserable and stupid, but Tula winces in sympathy. She puts her hand on your own: flinch at this.

Was that okay? she asks immediately. —Is it okay to touch you?

Is it? —Of course, you say.

You know I had this whole girl persona on like, classic movie forums, she says. —I would argue about Mafia movies with like, horrible film bros, and they'd fall in love with me. Then I'd get scared and go to a different forum.

She sips her drink: her eyes look, for a moment, faraway.

You were making a video game that could change the world, she muses. —Like what? Like *Angry Birds*?

Yes, exactly like *Angry Birds*, you say, staring at your dead cherries.

I knew I guessed it right, she says. —You're pretty angry.

She begins to detail a situation involving a crush of hers. From what you can gather, trying to pay attention, it's not different from other crush situations Tula has detailed to you over the years: flirtation on apps, a hookup that leads to subsequent hookups, his good qualities and at least one funny sex story, the speculation about whether he's open about his interest in transsexuals, the speculation about whether her feelings will endure. Hearing your friend process this, listening meaningfully, and offering whatever measured and sober and procedural advice you can: these are things you like doing. It's a crucial piece of why you still come to readings like this: you know that if you don't, if you aren't refreshed sometimes by these contacts, your soul will die. But it's hard, this time, to focus on the specifics of what Tula is saying. Your mind keeps moving backward, instead.

Are you okay, she finally asks. —You're not like you're usually like.

What am I usually like, you ask. But she's looking over your shoulder—*shit, I've gotta go start this thing, don't I? Let me know if you want to read*—and then again you're alone, to worry about how she might have answered.

On stage, Tula says correct-sounding things: *space for our voices, community, tip your bartenders.* She's found so many gorgeous readers for you all tonight. One of the kids who was definitely certainly talking about you is the first reader; her friend claps for her and so does everyone but you. She never looks at you, instead reads a lengthy and awkward *essay-thing* about her most recent firing. She touches on the layers of ambiguity around the firing itself, the layers of ambiguity around the sexual encounter she'd had with a cis coworker and her roommate one night while doing whip-its and thinking about Class Politics. *Of course this wasn't because I was trans.* Everyone laughs each time she says it. Resist laughing.

But she doesn't die, and the next reader comes on. And your anxiety slowly settles as the readers cycle forward: the self-deprecating poet; the poet who reads seductively about makeup, stockings, and human touch; the fearsome computer poet; the trans woman who reads sci-fi; the trans woman who reads erotica; the trans woman who reads sci-fi erotica; the trans man who reads about grappling with social responsibility; the stand-up comedian who is sort of in the wrong place, but who is welcome.

You used to read here. You'd read long essays, fanfiction pieces, posts from your blog. Decide, as you listen, which of your blog posts you'd read, if someone insisted that you read. Envision it: saunter up there with your phone to read your blog, koan by koan. The room rapt in silence except for sensual murmurs, gasps, *oh*, then applause. Gross: predictable: no. Better to stay at the bar with your empty glass while everyone claps and cheers. You would get the same cheers, if you were to read, because no one really knows you: no one knows you are a truly bad person. You're sparing them this.

The final reader is named Gig: the one in the Mystic Knights hoodie. In the blended spotlights, they're queer cute—leather skirt over camo leggings; bleached, spiked blond hair; glasses.

Feel, looking at their wide smile as they approach the mic, just how drained your social hit points have become.

You've done well, you think, alone at the bar. You've filled up your tank of interacting with others for another week, and you have a new question to ponder. Soon you can go home, alone, to ponder it.

Okay, great! So hi, folks! It's so good to be back here in Brooklyn, where I can see all y'all's lovely faces. Give yourselves a hand just for being alive right now, right? And give Tula a hand, too, for putting together this amazing reading! Come on, give her a hand!

This reading is so good, actually, that I didn't really have time to prepare anything to read that's, you know, worthy of it? I'm really sorry! I had to do consulting and record footage for YouTube yesterday, and then I had to get on a plane, which, you know, trans at the airport. (Applause, hoots.) *Right? And I just didn't have time to get it all together.*

So I thought I'd maybe just kind of tell you guys about what I've been working on lately? This kind of long article thing I'm doing? It's taking a while, is the thing, and I'm getting impatient about it. Like, I want to pitch! So I thought that's maybe what I could do tonight: kind of show you some photos related to the idea, kind of talk about it, kind of feel my way forward with all of you. Like a pitch, but just to you guys instead of a real one. Okay?

Could you put up that first photo? No, the first one. No, keep going. No—no—yes! That one. Thank you. That's okay! Don't be sorry!

So what you're looking at here is the exterior of a ranch-style house in Emeryville, California, just north of Oakland. It's also a monastery, the home of a religious order called the Brotherhood of the Digital Vine. It's founded by this guy—second photo, please?

Okay, thanks—this guy named Xavier. Just Xavier, a mononym. Trans guy. Hashtag: own voices, right? So Xavier lives here with three other housemates, and they're all monks, and their whole monk deal is that they're living in retreat from the world to bring humanity closer to God. But they're doing that by making a video game.

I know! Right? Right?

Now what I think is so interesting about these guys—third photo, yes, here they all are, Xavier, Ashton, Yavis, and Klar—is that they all have serious tech bona fides! Xavier worked at Google, Yavis was at PayPal, and Klar and Ashton were both contractors for an indie games studio that got accelerator investment from some big names. But about two years ago, the four of them sort of had this, like, spiritual crisis about living in the Bay Area and working in tech, that whole model of making the world a quote unquote better place. The neoliberal dream, right? These bros were like: no! Dollars can't transform human hearts. They just can't. But then what could?

So Xavier remembered playing old funky Japanese RPGs as a kid, right? Super Mystic Knights 2, 3—stuff like that. Xavier's idea is that these old cartridges still contained these vast digital spaces. They were crude—16-bit graphics, tile-and-sprite based, that classic video game look—but they had charm. Xavier was thinking about all the hours he spent as a kid wandering through those spaces—castles, forests, shrines. And he was thinking about rituals, too: movements through a designed space to achieve a meditative effect. And he was thinking about just how—ethereal the Internet makes us, right? I mean like, we're all here, right now! We're all together, like breathing, hot-blooded, food-digesting pheromone messes! Transsexual messes! But the Internet takes away that mess— makes us like, spirits. And Xavier was thinking, so do video games.

In a video game, you literally control pixel bodies—spirits without flesh, right? It's basically meditation.

His pitch to the rest of the group was, why not make that explicit? Why not make a game that was a communal prayer for anyone who played it? And, real talk, for the friends who made it.

So the four of them talked it over, and they made a plan. And one day they just quit their jobs, cashed out their 401(k)s and stock options. They used the money to buy four like, last-generation computers and a ramshackle house in Emeryville. The rest of the money they gave away. They grow their own food, and they rely on food banks for toilet paper and stuff, and when they have to, they sell microbrew or web designs. And the rest of the time they spend contemplating the like, sorrowful mysteries, or working on this game that they believe will be a bridge between the people and, like—God.

I know what you're thinking—total Wisdom Tree, right? Actually no, though: I've spent weeks now interviewing Xavier, and I've been out to the monastery. And I've had the chance to play what they have of this game? (Fourth photo, please, then fifth photo—the screenshot.) It's kind of an MMORPG—different people can log in at the same time—but no one can speak. And there isn't really quote unquote gameplay. You're sort of journeying to different holy sites, in real time. And when you get there you can sit down, and if you don't touch your keyboard or mouse for a while—I mean, not at all, not even free look—you kind of go into this space of contemplation—you drift up into these visions. And they're based on the monk's own contemplations. Like, what you see is a spiritual experience someone really had. All recorded there visually, for you to imagine. The game is the mechanism that makes religious experience objective, at last.

It's a small team—Yavis does particle effects, Ashton does Foley and socket code, Klar is doing really interesting things involving Escher simulations in Unity, right? It's like how a whole village would spend generations building a cathedral. It's really cool, you guys, and I don't know, just this really useful thing for spiritual seekers who might want to go on a pilgrimage in real life, but who don't have the means or privileges to do it. Like so many people have to get by in this world, right?

So that's the work I'm doing now—this weird interview project about people who make video games as a way to bring people to spiritual experience—spiritual workers who've constructed their whole experience around making video games that will change the world. Wild, right? The issue is just, and it's kind of a shitshow, but—Yavis quit the project, and no one knows why—

Listen to the applause they receive, and reflect: What does the universe want you to make of what you've just heard? Is this some kind of a joke?

Order another Shirley Temple with double cherries for yourself and sip it, furiously, while you process. Then prepare to order a third. Then find Tula, engaged in folding up the mic stands and greeting her crowd. Wait, patiently, for her to finish.

Another notch in the bedpost of trans literature, she says. —I love this show. No one take this show away from me. —She points at the bartender, then at you. —Her drink is comped, she announces.

Ask, in as chill a voice as you can manage: —Who was the person who read about video games?

Tula perks up. —Gig? she says. —Yeah? I can see you being interested in Gig. They're from the West Coast. They're chaotic— but really good at what they do, you know?

Blink at the knowledge that they're from out of town. —Were

they just in for this one reading? Are they going back soon? Do you know when?

Tula tightens her expression. —Wow, that sure sounds like a them question, she says.

But I'm making it a you question, you say.

They're in and out, she says. —I just caught them for this reading by a fluke. Someone canceled, and I saw on Twitter or whatever that they were in town, and I asked them to do it. Are you going to be weird to them?

I'm never weird, you say.

She smiles at you, mouth tight. —If you promise not to be weird, I can introduce you, okay? A favor, to celebrate this incredibly rare time when I actually see you. —She gets quiet. —I put up with you, do you know that? I put up with you like I never put up with anyone. Why do I do that?

Look down at your drink: you don't need this from her: you don't need reminders of how badly you fail. But this is the price of being her friend. You suppose she pays the price of being yours often enough.

You put up with me because I fascinate and torment you, you say to your drink. Then look up to find Tula smiling at you.

Tell me I do a good job with my readings, and I'll introduce you, she says. And then she frowns. —Oh, it's maybe too late—they're leaving. Email introduction?

Find yourself standing up. And give your friend what she asked for: —Your readings are great; trans literature is lucky to have you—and then leave her behind.

The bar is thick with people putting on scarves and pulling cigarettes out of thrifted wool pockets: one of the people is Gig. Realize the emotional importance of getting an answer to the question you want to ask them through the speed with which you hurry after them across the bar, catching them just before the door.

Hello, you say.

They look at you—they look up. —Hello, they say brightly. —I'm sorry, am I blocking the door?

No, you say. —I just wanted to ask you a question, before you left. About what you read.

Gig smiles, a strange half-their-mouth smile. —You ran across the bar because you wanted to ask about my reading?

I'll make it quick, you say. —But it's important. I can't tell you why without taking a lot more time than we have.

Gig raises their eyebrows—it feels practiced—you can tell this because you've also practiced charming facial expressions. —This is so mysterious, they say. —A mysterious stranger, with a question.

Yes, you say, returning your own professional glance. —Will you answer the call to adventure?

They make a cringe expression, and then glance backward at the door. —I really have to go, they say. —I've got to do this thing?

That's fine, you say. —I'll just ask—

But they interrupt: —Do you want to come with me, though?

Why did they ask you this? Assess them. They don't seem like they're making fun of you. It also doesn't seem like it's some kind of test where you're supposed to refuse.

Ask them: —Where?

Their smile is fangy. —I can be mysterious, too, they say. —It's nowhere weird, I promise! But you can tell me why your question is important on the way.

Your mother's face, her glass of wine: this is what you're thinking of, along with how tired you are, along with how ashamed you are of being tired, along—and you cannot deny this—with the memory of this person on the stage, telling the audience how excited they are to interview a strange video game tech bro cult. How they understand why that is a good thing to do. How their body moved, shifting weight from foot to foot with nervous energy, while they told the story.

Can I go to the bathroom first, you find yourself asking. And then: —Can I just ask you the question, without the context? That way you can go.

But will *you* answer the call to adventure, Gig whispers. And suddenly, find yourself smiling back.

Sit inside the stall with the broken lock, covered in piss-stickiness and LGBT-positive flyers. Breathe. You won't wake up tomorrow with your two books, your bedroom, your computer, your view. You won't make it to the library on time. You won't have a chance to clean. But maybe your investigation will proceed. Maybe you'll get an answer to the question you don't yet know how to formulate. Maybe you'll spend time with someone who is reminding you of ways you might feel—someone who looked at you, your going-out clothes and your skin and smell, and made a choice to see more of you. Droneslut does that. No one else has in a long time. Don't think of the first time.

Enter the car that Gig uses the Internet to summon. Inside, dark leather seats release trapped animal musk that mixes with glowing neon app backlight, the driver's trap playlist. Bite your lip and remain: have the adventure you'd talked yourself into having.

All buckled in, they ask you. —Safety first?

Pull the seatbelt away from your chest a moment, then let it snap back. Consider the idea of safety.

Ask: —Where did you say we were going again?

I didn't, they say, waggling their eyebrows. —I guess first we're going to my ex's house, to pick up some books? It's okay—we're on good terms.

Okay, you allow.

And after that, they say, fluttering their eyes, —we can go wherever you want. —They look up at the driver. —To keep talking, they append.

Nod, signaling receipt. Consider the rules of this situation. Consider your professional knowledge: the dance of a new client, the possible doors and roads that flicker into possibility, moment by moment. To be attached to any one of these doors and roads is to lose all of them. They are feeling their way, as are you. It's just you haven't done this in person for a long time. It's just you wish you could remember how this was done.

Feel them shifting in their seat—realize that it's been too long since you've contributed anything.

So you had a question for me, they say.

Nod, quickly. —And some context, you say. —Do you want the question first, or the context?

I want it all, they say.

Allow yourself to smile. —The context, you say. —The context is—it's a lot. It has to do with video games.

Figured that, they say. —Go on?

It has to do with video games, and with— Pause here; remember how Tula reacted to the word *investigation*. —It has to do with archival work, you say. —Archival work that I think maybe resonates with your talk at the reading.

Yes, Gig says. —Tell me more about my reading, and how good it was, please.

Good: clear rules. —It was beautiful, you say, leaning toward them, as far as your seat belt will allow. —I don't care about tech bros at all, but you made me care. You reminded me of things I haven't thought about in a long time.

Did they flinch? Quickly, assess. They're looking at you, their mouth different. What does that mean? The rules were not, in fact, clear. You need to back off. This moment is precarious—all moments are precarious. And remember, you have a purpose here. You have to ask them a question that's pertinent to your investigation. (Don't think about what it is.) Find your balance.

See, I used to make video games, you say.

Oh, they say; their smile is absolutely different, their canine teeth more bare. —That's cool. Professionally?

They think you're some kind of aspirant: this is bad. —It was in high school, you say. —It was a hobbyist thing.

Oh, they say; relief is clear. —Hobbyist game creation— that's very cool. That's very queer.

It was before queer games, you make sure to say. —I'm older than that. I didn't know that was going to happen.

You are babbling. You need to get into control. They watch you: something about them has changed, psychologically. Certain quantum doors you're certain are now closed: certain professional curiosities are engaging.

Very cool, they repeat. —What like, game engine did you say you used, again?

Don't tell them about CraftQ; don't let them look you up. —It was just something, you say. —It isn't around anymore. It isn't important.

They nod, too quickly—this is bad—this is the *calm down*

nod. You are ruining everything—this is like it was before—you can't let this be like it was before. Get into control—control your face—don't let them see you start to come apart like this. How did they see you before? Another dumb transsexual woman—another vaguely goth weirdo at Tula's reading—someone maybe fun to talk to at a bar. Someone to invite into your cab for an adventure.

Try to summon that. Try to be fun. Force yourself to be fun.

Mercifully, their phone alerts them. —Shit, they say, squinting at it. —It's my ex—there's some picking up a key from a bodega thing they want me to do? Hang on a second.

Don't try to speak. Sit there, trying to summon fun into yourself, while they look at their phone for what is much longer than it reasonably takes to respond to a text. Sit there and do not think about the lie you've told: because CraftQ is still here. Because it is still important—so important you suddenly don't trust them enough to tell them about it.

Reflect, while Gig is on their phone, on your purpose here, and the progress of your investigation. Open your mental notebook and write down everything you know in it.

- This morning you woke up to see your teenage work looking back at you.
- Abraxa is trying to contact you. (But is this something you *know*?)
- Abraxa referenced the CraftQCon, a professional gathering of CraftQ game makers that you were starting to plan. It would have been a bunch of teenagers in a hotel. It would have been a disaster.
- You wanted it to happen more than you wanted anything.

- And you now know it meant something to Abraxa, too.
- But Lilith left the company.
- So it didn't happen.
- You never knew why.
- You haven't spoken to Abraxa in over a decade.
- But the moment she reached out to you (but do you *know* that she did?), every part of you sprang to life.
- You even got your client involved.
- Jesus. Why did you get your client involved in this?
- Why are you making him walk around Jersey City looking for clues for you?
- Are you fucking insane?
- Tula doesn't seem to think you are. She is your friend, and you can trust her.
- Your own perceptions, however, are not something you can trust. You have very much learned that the hard way.
- Haven't you, bitch?
- And now you're in a hired car with some games journalist you don't even know.
- And you're tired, and you're ashamed, and you wish you were home.
- But there is still a question you have to ask.
- Don't think about what it is.

Gig's ex-lover has a roommate, a cis white straight guy roommate whose existence you hadn't guessed. He has curly brown hair and is wearing an iridescent Marty McFly ball cap indoors as he plays a modern video game on a massive TV. Other than the foyer light—which Gig turns on when you come in with them, and they point to a shoe rack and tell you to unlace your boots—the walls are dark, washed blue and green with flatscreen light. One whole brick wall of the apartment, into which you think two of your family's own apartment might fit, is covered in curtains of green vines and flowers, a cellulose waterfall from hanging planters. Gig's lover has decorated it in photographs and framed pen-and-ink pieces of valleys and houses.

Gig indicates the bedroom closest to the game. —I just need to run in there for a second, they say. —Hang tight?

Nod, and watch them scrunch their face into a grin, and then remain alone with the bro. His eyes are on the screen; he doesn't acknowledge you. Fold your arms, flatten your back against the wall, and watch him play.

It takes a minute of watching the bro's player-character—a burning wolf spin-dashing hordes of ice goblins, combo XP ringing up in haptic dopamine drops—before you realize that you know what this game is. The names of spells—the equipment menu—the feeling—the name *Bell Prix* on the mini-map. This game is part of the Mystic Knights series.

Watching it, find yourself becoming interested. Everything is synchronicities today: the screen shot, Droneslut happening to live where Abraxa seems to have gone, hearing Gig read to you about video games and God. And now this: face to face with the late 2010s variant of the game you sacrificed your whole teenage life to the worship of.

Find yourself curious. What's the story of this new installment? How many hundreds of hours of content have you missed since 1998, when you last cared about these games? What does it mean that your brain reorients so easily to this content, like cocaine arousal, like flowers turning to sun?

■ ■ ■

Eyes on the warm TV light—tired at the end of a chain of synchronicities—realize that the time to resist has stopped. It is time. Think of Lilith.

You first noticed Lilith one night on #teengoetia, the late hours after dinners had settled and parents may have gone to bed, issuing cautions—*don't stay up too late, school tomorrow*—and, controls dropped, teen boys without bodies could become vulnerable. Sex, as ever, became the topic: the girls we were all attracted to; the girls we would one day be with. (As the channel's resident girl, you were solicited for your thoughts on the topic; you were, in some bold cases, named. You cut them down every time—*little man, i love women, what makes you think you have a chance?*—and they loved every moment of it. It is something you still think about, sometimes, when you are at work.) Lilith, though still a newbie with only one game demo to her credit, still using her vanilla AParker83 handle, participated.

<AParker83> I don't know that I'll ever end up with anyone.
<AParker83> it just doesn't seem like it'll happen?
<NecroPizza> NO ONE LIKES A MISERY MERCHANT
<AParker83> Maybe I'd end up with some terrible woman :/
<AParker83> A totally evil one who'd yell at me about dinner not being ready? She would make me buy her stuff, too :/
<AParker83> Like big jewel earrings that she'd wear all day while telling me that the lawn wasn't watered :/
<NecroPizza> that's...pathetic?

<AParker83> her name would be something evil, like Lilith
<sash> i like lilith already.
<sash> i wish she could hang out here.
* AParker83 is now known as Lilith
<reficul> lol
<Lilith> "Be careful what you wish for! ahahahahahaha,
    hello, losers!"
* Lilith cackles. Lightning strikes!
* Lilith smiles a twisted smile >:)

The routine went on for hours, Lilith, playing her own evil future wife, saying bitchy things to all the other teenagers, defending her sustained emotional abuse of AParker83: a wimp, a loser, someone who wasn't even here. You watched all of it, playing it cool.

The next day you played through Lilith's game demo, which you'd downloaded and dismissed weeks before. Then you played through it again. Then you sent her an email inviting her to join the company you and Abraxa had already discussed forming. And now you spoke with her by IRC query almost every night: sometimes in company meetings, sometimes not.

<sash> hello.
<xLilithx> hey?
<sash> hey? back.
<sash> did you see abraxa's vomit warlock rooms for the
    midboss of part 1?
<sash> they're . . . not what i was expecting. crude. but
    mechanically effective, i suppose.
<sash> i'm certain the likes of philippedark will love them.
<sash> did you see them?

\<xLilithx\> no, I didn't see them :/

\<xLilithx\> sorry, I had kind of a crappy day :/

\<sash\> i'm sorry to hear that. do you want to discuss it?

\<xLilithx\> not really :/

\<sash\> i see.

\<sash\> does *lilith* want to discuss it?

\<xLilithx\> hahahaha

\<xLilithx\> um, well :/

* xLilithx transforms

\<xLilithx\> "I thought you'd never ask!"

The CraftQCon was a fantasy you had. Whatever it meant to Abraxa it was, you now realize, nothing but a way for you to meet Lilith at last.

In your fantasy, you and Lilith room together. It can't be otherwise. You'd have ensured, of course, that it couldn't be otherwise: you were the one who'd control the convention, down to the reservations and bookings. You wanted to see her—you wanted to be in physical space, real space with your friend who designed levels for you. And if you arranged a professional gaming conference, you could be.

You weren't even sure what you wanted to *do* in this hotel room. Your plans regarding Lilith mostly fade to white when you imagine gazing at her across the twin beds. (No, the king bed: *sorry, the hotel must have screwed up and they gave us a single, that's okay right?*) What will you do? Will you lie on opposite sides of the bed, staring at the ceiling without speaking, the room dark and silent except for thumping air conditioning and incongruous indoor fireflies, until she turns to you and says *Hey I've had this strange fantasy?* Or no, don't wait for her to do it; you do it yourself. *Have you ever had a strange fantasy*? She looks frightened, her hands drawn away from her chest, allowing you in.

Slowly, slowly unbutton her shirt—you don't care what shirt, some stupid boy flannel or something, it probably smells. As soon as you take it off her it evaporates into useless boy smoke. Then draw the black dress from your suitcase: *just your size*. Fasten it behind her neck. Her rapturous, entranced hands, gripping your wrists as your fingers start to lift away from her shoulders, her chest.

There must have been a way around the problem of your body. You remembered thinking that: problem-solving for your size, your hormone balance, your skin. Could you hire a real woman to play you, and you'd somehow communicate instructions to her (maybe a two-way radio earpiece?) Could you dress as a woman yourself, try to go the whole length of the convention without coming clean? Could you simply dress as yourself, and when Lilith gasped at the sight of you—*I thought you were a woman*, she'd say—you'd simply murmur, *I am?* Immediately you'd both break into tears, embrace. You spent a lot of time, at one point in your life, thinking about that counterfactual embrace: how your tensed muscles would hold you in place like the clasp of a jewelry box, until you relaxed, until she relaxed.

Realize, as you think about Lilith—as your eyes roll lazily over the modern screen, as Gig and their ex are whispering in the next room, before their voices go very quiet—realize that you took the name of your findom sex work persona from Mystic Knights. Queen Caramella is the sorceress, the subject of your game. This is something you have never consciously put together: the game you and your friends were making was so close to you that you didn't even experience it as separate.

Ask the bro: —Which Mystic Knights is this?

It sucks, he says, instead of answering. —It's just a bunch of fetch quest shit. Like I'm fifty hours in without a plot yet.

Resist the urge to react to this: *you don't deserve a plot.* Continue to watch, until the bro looks at you. —Do you like Mystic Knights, he asks. —Do you like, play the online one, or anything?

I didn't know there was an online one, you say.

A lot of trannies play it, he says. —No offense.

Stare at the back of his head. Behind a closed door, Gig and their ex's voices shape a bright melody.

Is this level supposed to be the Skyveil Keep, you finally ask. —From *Super Mystic Knights 3*?

I don't know, the bro says, rainbows glowing from his hat. —I don't play any of that ancient shit.

On the night of your final chat, you got Lilith talking, as you always did: her problems, as ever, remote and abstract from your own. You don't even remember now what specific problem you turned her into Lilith that night to discuss. Her school, and her lack of friends there to compare to the blazing stars of #teengoetia? Her family? Some camping trip she was supposed to take that summer? The specific matter of her life, the problems she was working through: these emotions were just the cause of the words she formed, the basic matter of her. Your job was to type words back: words to fix her problems, to neutralize her sadness. Your language would provoke hers, would keep her words appearing in your IRC query window. She was here, her spirit in the presence of your spirit: all you had to do was bring it up. It felt so powerful, a power you never felt in your daily life. Here you were powerful, a mysterious woman, the head of your own video game corporation. Here she worked for you.

Your hotel fantasy was always there in these query chats, the ether in which everything steeped. It led her from the common channel to this private space, her willingness to become this Lilith character for you at your command. And she always waited for your command, even though soon her regular IRC handle changed permanently to the one you'd given her. To name a fantasy is to shape it, to make it a little bit more true.

\<sash\> lilith. can i ask you a question?

\<sash\> a real question.

\<xLilithx\> "What's a real question?"

\<sash\> a real question is one that you don't know the answer to, and that you put yourself at risk by asking.

\<sash\> may i ask you one?

\<xLilithx\> "…okay."

\<sash\> what would you do if a— didn't exist?

There it was, on the monitor of the computer you'd convinced your father to move into your bedroom, set up in type, words you cannot take back. A string of characters suspended in electronic pulse; your own heart pulses in response.

\<xLilithx\> "…what do you mean?"

\<sash\> don't use quote marks, lilith. type it again.

\<xLilithx\> :/

\<xLilithx\> What do you mean?

\<sash\> if a— died. so you became a widow. and you had to live, without having a— to complain about. if a— was gone.

\<sash\> what would lilith do first?

This is the moment, you know, when she will leave, if she's going to leave. This is the moment when she will not prove equal to the question, and you will see her sign out, and your cursor will blink alone.

<xLilithx> I'm not sure.
<xLilithx> :/
<xLilithx> What do you think I should do?
<sash> good question.
<sash> it's important to have procedures for figuring out what to do when you're lost, or sad.
<sash> personally, i take a bath.
<sash> a long, slow one, with bubbles and essential oils.
<sash> that's what i tell all my lovers to do.
<xLilithx> Oh?
<sash> do you understand?

You kept waiting for her to sign out. If she signed out, then you would know it should stop.

<xLilithx> I don't know?
<xLilithx> Do you want me to sign out and do that?
<sash> no.
<sash> i want you to stay, lilith.
<sash> i want you to keep listening.

Any moment she might stop: but you tell her to let her clothes drop to the floor, to look at herself naked in the mirror in her mind and describe what she sees there. To become turned on by what she sees. To touch what she sees. When she stops agreeing with it, you'll stop too, you tell yourself, but she never stops.

Your words appeared in a space, and then her words appeared in a space to answer them. And then her words began to become strange—*teh* for *the*, *stoker* for *stroke*—and you knew, as part of your brain had never quite known before, that she was not only words. Behind the words was a body whose hands your hands on the keyboards were moving. So you kept telling her to keep touching herself, to sink beneath the water, to let it warm her, cook her, boil her to flavor and steam, her hands moving between her legs, both in your imagination and in her reality—which is your reality, which is one. She was about to come: you came, imagining it.

And let it occur to you now—now while you are leaning against this wall to watch Gig's ex's bro of a roommate steer a burning wolf around a lushly rendered open-world environment while voices in the next room moan—that the days when someone could connect with you, could open you up and change your course, are totally over. Sometime in your twenties, you must have met all the people who will ever be able to change you. You are not in your twenties anymore. If you squint at the giant television, your eyes will sort of paralyze and lose focus, turning into a big visual smear without distinctions, the way the world probably looks to a child: undifferentiated sensation, something just as easily switched on as off.

You have the power to update your blog from your phone: use it, now, to make a post that you don't even research. *what happened to my friend?* Then close your phone. Drop it in your bag. Keep watching the game that the bro plays in the dark.

You kept typing to Lilith that night, trying to bring her off too, every metaphor you could synthesize from copious online reading without experience. And you understood then, for the first time, what people meant by *desire*. Desire is an arrow, a quest marker that points you away from the safety of yourself. Lilith was not only a person; she was a door: and that night you believed you could walk right through her, as easy as that, into a world where you were not alone, where you were not veiled, where you were not half sick of shadows: where you were uncomplicated and happy, where you were home.

Gig's hair, when they emerge, sticks up at strange angles; the camo pattern on their leggings is on backward. They're carrying a stack of paperbacks and their face is a scowl. The bedroom door closes behind them. Quickly, lace up your boots.

Both outside again, watch them lean against the stoop, their breath coming out cold in the air. And while they lean, think about Lilith. It is too late now to stop.

Sorry, they say. —I maybe just need to go back to my Airbnb and chill?

That's right: they had offered to go somewhere with you to talk. You'd forgotten.

Okay, you say. —So what, I just go home?

I can drop you somewhere, they say quickly. —Like, we can make two stops. Where are you going?

Imagine, for a moment, what it will be like when you're alone.

Is there a diner near where you're staying, you find yourself asking. —I want to get some fries. I still want to ask you that question.

They sway on their feet, as if a strong wind is blowing them. —Okay, they say. —Can you just ask it? And maybe I can get back to you later, when I'm not really tired?

■ ■ ■

Let a wave of shame cut through you—no, don't let it. Get back in control. Follow procedures. Start by recognizing what is plain and true:

- You've fucked up
- You've really fucked up
- You useless bitch
- You fucked up with Lilith and you hurt her and you're fucking up again
- Like with that update about missing your friend, fuck you what was that
- Delete that, fuckup, bitch
- The price for fuckup bitches is extermination
- Fuckup bitches do not deserve to live in this world—
- Fuckup bitches in order not to be fuckup bitches have to make things right and that means fuckup bitches need to undertake the work of extermination
- Don't hesitate useless bitch do it NOW
- Exterminate
- Exterminate
- Exterminate
- And then—

Feel your back: it's cold. Find yourself on the sidewalk. Gig is squatting above you, holding your wrists.

Calm down, they're saying, their eyes terrified. —Please calm down?

The back of your head hurts, a lot. But tell them: —I'm calm. —Make your voice as calm, saying this, as you can.

It takes several repetitions, but they let you up. Drag yourself to the stoop and sit, staring at your boots, feeling your breath coming up at you. Put your hand on the back of your head: check the damage. No blood—only bumps—the ache already going down. Only a dent in the clip where your extension meets your head, and one of your sword earrings is gone, leaving you asymmetrical, less than fun.

I'm sorry, you say. —I'm just very tired. I'm so, so sorry. I'm sorry. I'm fine.

Remember, after a minute, to look up at the person standing with you. They're holding their arms tight around themselves, their eyes wet. Feel shame at this—get back into control. Help them feel okay.

Tell them: —I'm fine. You didn't do anything wrong.

And it's true: the wrong one is, and always has been, you.

Insist that they take a Lyft home, as they'd planned. Lie and tell them this is your neighborhood. Lie and tell them, feeling your breath against your cheeks, that you'd prefer to walk. A walk would feel nice.

The car comes, and they get in. Before it drives away, hear them say: —Sash.

Turn. They're at the window, beckoning. Come closer. They reach their hand out. You're meant to place yours into it. Is it a test? No—people don't set tests—that's something good people don't do, something only you do. Trust that it's not a test. Allow this.

And let them hold your hand, their thumb moving over your skin, until you take your hand back, and the Lyft drives away, and just you remain.

\<xLilithx\> hey, i have to sleep
\<xLilithx\> thanks
\<xLilithx\> goodnight?
\<sash\> oh. okay. yes. sleep.
\<sash\> and we'll talk in a week?
\<xLilithx\> okay night
\<sash\> good night. in a week, then?
* xLilithx has signed off

This is the question you wanted to ask Gig, that sent you running across the bar to ask it:

- Why did Yavis leave?
- What did the other tech bros do to make Yavis leave?
- And if they had known, then, what they had done to make Yavis leave—and if they had fixed it— would Yavis have come back?

Feel the shame of these questions, and all the reasons you wanted, and want, to ask them. And as you feel that shame, know, with certainty, why Abraxa posted your screenshot. It was for the same reason Abraxa does anything: it was out of her own random, destructive brilliance. It wasn't an attempt to make contact. It had nothing to do with you at all.

Realize, then, that your investigation is over: a cold case, like the rest.

It doesn't matter what you do anymore. Therefore: use your phone to look up directions to your parents' address. There are no mysteries, just a shortest possible route, a determinate arrival time still well before sunrise, when you wake up and your procedures start again. Good: so close your bag and walk. So know that the fear you feel at being in unfamiliar streets is only temporary: all it takes is time, and then anything different from you, and frightening, can be churned and processed through experience until it becomes yourself.

If you ever see Lilith again, you'll apologize: that is all you have left to give. But for now, it's just you again: a gulf stream, an air current that will guide you home to your family. You've long known that this is the only place you can go. Because how could you swim against the air? What would you push against?

2. The Reliquary

If Abraxa spends time underground here, she'll figure it out. Years ago, with the help of her friends, she summoned a sorceress into herself. The other night, the same sorceress appeared to her again. So the goal is to work out why this happened, and what it has to do with her purpose here in Jersey City, why fate drowned her and sent her here. She's not crazy. She has clear goals. And once she achieves them, she'll be free to go home—wherever home currently is. Maybe the sorceress will tell her that, too.

By day, her map is clearer: four directions, and a center.

The east room, where the sorceress appeared to her that night beyond the doorway garlanded in spiderwebs, is a closet with long metal shelves. She keeps her tools there, her keys, her crowbar, sledgehammer, ruler, level. Her art supplies are there, too, when not in use: paints she scavenges, brushes, rollers, pencils, sketchbooks.

The largest space is to the south, beneath the nave, and mostly in ruins. The fire warped the center of a joist; now it hangs overhead, cracked but maybe still stable, a hammock for cotton-candy fiberglass. Soot streaks the walls; stone dust blocks the exits. What had these rooms been: Sunday school,

AA chapter? Now they're a labyrinth of load-bearing walls and twisted cabinets and pipes, all greased to black. In one inaccessible room, a circular hunk of plaster has crushed a folding table, like the cake you get on your worst birthday. A bucket of water rests there, a blob of steel wool balanced on its rim. There's a clear space she's made, scrubbed down to the primer. There are possibilities in the south.

The northern room is bright: a water pipe must have burst in the fire somewhere between the ceiling and the chancel floor, and rotten places above let in shafts of sunlight like glow-in-the-dark bedroom stars. A long crack runs along the foundation, evidence of a long-ago shoddy slab pour. Bags of trash and plaster rest there, hauled out to alley dumpsters at the rate of one or two unobtrusive bags a night.

The western room, where she sat with Marcie and Scramble on the night she received her revelation, is safe to think about. The door to the outside is safe, the padlock she smashed now replaced with a fresh one to which only she holds a key. Her blankets and army surplus bedroll are here, her pillows, her backpack with everything she owns.

The disk and its peripherals are carefully wrapped in her tank tops.

She made a fire ring at the center from stones and landscaping soil. As the sun starts to go down—hard to see, down here, but her body can feel it go away—she burns to compensate for it, consumes dollar-store candles and lighter fluid in her kerosene stove, working through the oatmeal and lentils and veggie sausages from Marcie's house. Cars outside pass and none of them can see her. She holds the blanket tighter over herself, cozy, and smiles as she looks through the tiny fire and the spiderweb doorframe beyond it.

■ ■ ■

It's crucial that the Internet isn't down here with her. Her separation from the Internet is crucial to the exact extent that she's always thinking about the Internet. It arrived with her adolescence: she has no concept of adult life without it. How did people live before the Internet? How did they learn things, say things, understand themselves through other people? Did they just spread rumors or photocopy zines? Whatever they did, she'll discover it again. Her mind will become a tide pool in the rock, supporting a separate life.

Thinking about this, she thinks about System D. Before the violet flames System D installs during *Super Mystic Knights 3*, thoughts could move from one mind to another only indirectly. Thoughts found a form in words and other artifacts—songs, paintings, video games—that could leap from one mind to another, like fish from bowls placed too close. But System D instead fused all the fishbowls into one: the glass disappeared, and millions of private little waters all flowed together, seeking homeostasis. One might call it harmony. What will she become during the days she'll spend down here, disconnected? Maybe just melody again, a song she forgot.

The first night alone down here was intolerable. The wind outside flapped the plastic sheeting over the burned-through doors on the upper floor like black sails, and the floor was unfamiliar ice against her bones, and how secure even was her padlock? How confident even was she at not being found and killed in the night? She kept turning, a wadded hoodie failing to cushion her ear, her skull, her chin; what if the stone was somehow distorting her organs, what if her spine was fusing, what if spiders were to crawl over her face and spin silk plugs into her nostrils? And then she opened the door to morning cars and pink sunrise over the shadows of row house moldings.

Within a few nights, she found herself able to sleep through the wind, waking up to the faint light coming from the northern rooms: a light she's learning to see.

She's not supposed to be here. She tries to remember this: she's not going to succeed. But she's never succeeded, so what's changed? She can go further than she has before, at least: at least try to connect with whatever wants to connect with her. She's so afraid: therefore turn up the torchlight, therefore step into the dark. The moment when she'll run away will come when it comes. Until then, work.

In flashes, she works: sweeps the floor of the west room, makes small shelves from bricks and boards to keep her clothes from the concrete. She improves her fire ring and beer can stove, reorganizes her shelves of canned goods, begins to collect thrown-away books from in front of people's apartments.

The biggest project is to fix the burned-through ceiling joist in the south room. Otherwise the ceiling will fall in on her, burying her. She needs not to think about this. What she needs to do instead is build a foundation—a pyramid of small and stable tasks, swept floors and organized shelves. Once she's strong and stable, she can fix the ceiling. She's sure of it.

Of course it's hard right now. Anything worth doing is. Every morning she wakes up, cold and numb and slow, and part of her thinks: I should not be here. She thinks this for as long as she needs to, rolling against the cold floor. And then she gets up, and she cleans and fixes for hours, alone with candlelight and the sun through the cracks in the north room.

Drawing, exhausted, by the fire, she sees the order she's making peek out at her like friendly owl eyes from behind the flames. It isn't bad here. She can invite Marcie here one day, once it's fixed up. Invite all Marcie's queer friends. Invite every queer everywhere: come and build a world with her, here in the church underground. She can return every favor she's been done.

At the bagel place, the island of society she lets herself visit once a day, the bagel clerk has come to either like her or think she's a gateway to a grittier and more absolute reality. Either way, he gives her stale bagels, and she drinks lime water and spreads out with her sketchbook. She fills it with drawings of her visions and worked-out sketches for shelves, irrigation pipelines, saw-horse banquet tables, mini power grids. She imagines someone looking over her shoulder as she draws, wondering what her life is. The thought is a comfort while she works underground, hauling sacks of plaster and dirt, her breath rasping behind a painter's mask.

On days when she can't bear the thought of working any-more on the space, she walks. She tries to walk where there are as few people as possible: down the streets south from her neighborhood, over the footbridge that spans the canal that opens onto the harbor and the Hudson River, past the dead sand yard full of boat trailers and beached yachts and onto the long cobblestone walk that passes through trees. There are people sometimes—joggers, families with strollers, young couples with dogs that strain on their leashes—and some of them stare at her as she passes. She waves; she doesn't speak, imagines her mind as a kind of reliquary. Its separateness is important to preserve.

As she walks, the skyline of New York watches her from across the harbor. Has she ever been to New York? Somehow it's never happened. She imagines everyone there gathered around the violet flame on the top floor of a skyscraper—maybe small groups from every block, all crowded into every skyscraper—worshiping the whispering voices of wizards. The city is terrifying to her, like a communicable disease; its eyes following her from its windows. So she stays on her side of the river, but some days she lets herself look. To look and not to touch: that's maturity, something children learn.

One day, dumpster diving, she finds a tray of mason jars still in plastic. She takes them home and cuts flowers from the park, fills each jar up with water. The flowers will not live in the dark, but for a while, they bloom. She finds a rug wrapped in tape and hauls it on her shoulders like a merchant's guard to the west room. Improvements and iterations. It's like an art project. It isn't like she has nowhere else to go.

Another day, she takes out yellow spray paint and on the east wall paints this:

NORTHWOOD ABBEY

The paint dries, perfuming the close air in acetone, petroleum, propylene glycol, and silicates: she imagines it as frankincense. She sits at the center of the space and closes her eyes: in her mind's eye, her breath is white-hot at her nostrils, black and rich as it leaves her mouth. The space is giving her its dirt; she's giving the space hers. They're approaching homeostasis, learning to be together.

There are good people and bad people in the world. A good person extends herself for the spiritual growth of another: she read that once in a book. This is what she's always tried to do. She makes a list of all the other people she's rushed at, intending love: all the ways she tried to generate it in their lives. She wanted to sail Prosperine and Elias to Angkor Wat—she wanted to help Marcie's grandmother—she wanted to help her teenage friends make the greatest video game in the world. She was so warm to these people, shined for them. So why do they keep throwing her away? What is she doing wrong?

Other people are all around her, even here as she walks through rich neighborhoods where trees break through the pavement and Christmas decorations begin to appear on brownstone railings. She tries her best to look like she belongs: if you remain confident yourself, people will draw confidence from you. Confidence, she beams at the others in line at the active church down the street from hers as she loads a reusable grocery bag with cans and boxed potatoes. Confidence, she beams at the bodega clerk in the next neighborhood while shoplifting Krazy Glue and scrub sponges. Confidence, she beams at the clerks of the free library as she climbs the marble staircase to the third floor Jersey City history reading room. She avoids the computer area—a trap set by System D—and browses the stacks instead, sitting by the big rotating space heater to keep warm. The problem of being underground is a problem of heat transfer: with the help of her fire, the space heater, various calories, and confidence, she's certain she can stay underground as long as she needs to. As long as whatever use she's being put to will take.

She reads through the stacks at random: manga for teenagers, how-to manuals, big full-color art books, case-bound volumes of photocopied newspapers, burial records, photographs of factories and fires and traffic snarls. She reads about churches, too: their architecture, their history, their cardinal structure. In a book about Hildegard von Bingen, she reads: *I am the fiery life of divine substance. I blaze above the beauty of the fields. I shine in the waters. I burn in sun, moon, and stars.* She reads about others: Teresa of Ávila, Catherine of Siena, Julian of Norwich. She dreams about being on her knees in her basement as behind her an unseen Mother Superior blesses her, then walls her in.

She needs to take the ceiling joist seriously. She pictures it: imagines the beam falling in on her, where its fall is most likely to begin, what she can do to arrest it. It's a simple problem of forces: if the beam wants to fall here, stop it. If it wants to fall there instead, stop it there, too. Stop it everywhere until it no longer wants to fall. This is the general method of solving a problem.

On Grand Street, a bucket of sealant from a boat supply store in each hand like she's a milkmaid, she hears a voice call out to her: *Can I give you a hand with that?* The speaker is a man with a mountaineer's beard and Coke-bottle glasses attached with a chartreuse sports strap. He wears a black hoodie beneath a rumpled leather coat. Trans, she thinks.

Want to help me carry my boat sealant home, she asks, excited. But it turns out he doesn't want to do this. They talk about home repairs—they talk about the co-op house he's restoring—he tells her they're having a potluck soon; she should come by; he can show her his container garden. His name is Dirk and he gives her an envelope of seeds, an enticement.

No one stops her from entering the co-op that evening: a vestibule stacked with coats and satchels, a heat lamp that grills the air. The kitchen boasts a vegan spread, food like she hasn't seen now in weeks—three bowls of chips and one of salsa, a thick brick of banana and oil cake, a wrinkled plastic sack of hot dog buns, an untouched pyramid of corn ears. She helps herself, and then she follows the sound of punk music to a living room in the back lit by three low-watt bulbs and a sofa shaped like a pair of red neon lips. The furniture has been cleared to accommodate speakers and a clot of nervous, dutiful transsexuals and other queers in coats. A young man plays a saxophone without melody but with great passion. Abraxa stands at the back, not being looked at, eating her corn and cake.

Dirk introduces her around to some other transsexuals whom he says also have an interest in farming. They smile at her, jacketed and adorned, and she bums cigarettes from them. She is pretty sure she's passing for a normal person; she is not talking about living in the church basement. One of them tells her their plan to travel upstate and buy a house, a place with long rows of gardens and ample lawns, places where queers can come and pitch tents and dance around spring bonfires. The plan sounds beautiful, and Abraxa listens and files away whatever she can about gardening—what months to plant what vegetables from seed, ways to ensure soil drainage when working with containers, ways to harvest and recycle greywater, what fish are best for emulsion—without volunteering to join the project. This is a kind of maturity, she knows; she's proud of herself. The old Abraxa would have left tomorrow. None of them know what she's doing, and she's resisting the urge to tell them, and that restraint is the root of all magic. She is keeping herself clean.

After some hours, feeling her age and feeling nervous about returning home to the church after dark—she's tried to be careful to avoid coming back at any hour when police are likely to notice someone moving alone—she asks Dirk if she can stay here tonight. He shows her to a mattress on the second floor foyer. It's covered with two sleeping dogs, whom he clears away. She falls asleep in her clothes, watching one of the dogs' toys: a cartoon nun with wimple, squeaker somewhere in her rubber belly, chew marks through her neck, eyes directed up.

That night, at the co-op, she dreams that her body is somehow in the church, and that her heart is rising out of it like a balloon. She rises, a ghost trailing her heart, above the basement, above the church itself, above Mercer Street, above Jersey City, the whole tri-state, the towers of New York, all of it nothing now, all of it trash, just her heart above all of it. She is in a strange place that she knows to be the sun. Curtains of mist surround her, and she falls to her knees. Her body is nothing like her body. The sorceress is standing before her. She is tall and laughing and her whip trails in the sand.

Abraxa throws her arms wide and the sorceress embraces her, and she burns to ashes. At first she tries to hold too tightly, and then she surrenders, lets herself be held. The sorceress is touching her, is stroking her forehead, her shoulders, her chest, her stomach, her hips, her thighs. She can feel her body opening up—the sorceress is sliding into her, smoke and laughter rising from her base to her stomach, her heart, her throat—she shakes—the real her shakes—the other her, the false her, there on the dog mattress in New Jersey, is shaking, too—nothing is touching her; she has never been touched this way.

The sorceress continues to rise—her forehead, the crown of her skull—until she is a fixed point on a vast electric column, its crown in the stars and its root on earth, the voice of the sorceress within her a bell. What is the sorceress saying? She can't yet understand.

She wakes up between two dogs, feeling clean. Dirk's bedroom is just down the hall from the room with the dog mattress, its door covered in surveyor's maps and a small professor-office nameplate. She bends to press her lips to the doorknob; she can hear him snoring behind it. The sun is still rising, and everyone in the house seems asleep but her as she borrows someone's very new razor and cleans herself up in their triple sink.

She fills her backpack with canned goods from the pantry and creeps out the door. The sun breaks through the sulfurous winter smog, far away the sound of boats honking as they sail up and down the Hudson River: everyone has somewhere to be today, everyone has a place and a purpose, and everyone includes her. The sorceress set her a test, and she passed.

Thinking of this, she suddenly also thinks of how close she's come to Marcie's house.

She'll just look; she'll just walk by Marcie's house and look, and if she sees Marcie, she'll just go in the opposite direction; she'll go back home. The air is getting chilly; the leaves of the scant trees on Marcie's street long ago dropped, the street trash jammed beneath parked cars smelling like pumpkin and woodsmoke. Marcie's not out front, but the car is present. Abraxa stands at the foot of Marcie's front steps for a long time, and then she quietly lifts the latch of the gate and climbs to the front door. The basement window is covered, and the curtains of the bay window are closed—what's behind them? She imagines it, coffee mugs still on the table runner, dishes drying on a rack and a smell of chemical lemon, warmth and space. No sounds from behind the door. She finds herself knocking on it. This is fine—get it out of her system—confirm Marcie's not here, then go away. But Marcie is here, because the door opens, and here she is.

Sorry, Abraxa says immediately. And then: —Hi!

Hi, says Marcie, but her eyes are saying something else.

Marcie's kitchen has been cleaned; a stack of medical bills sits there, half worked through. They sit with the bills as a centerpiece, a plate of vegan cheese, crackers, and old and wrinkled grapes between them. These are dangers, Abraxa knows: the more of them she eats, the less likely she will be to leave. There's a tall pitcher of water; Marcie fills two glasses.

Thanks, Abraxa says. —I can't stay too long.

Yeah, I'm busy, too, Marcie says.

Abraxa digests this, staring at the grapes and keeping her hands in her lap. Then she stands up and goes into the kitchen, where she perches against a countertop, bouncing on the balls of her feet.

Sorry I left like that, she says. —And that I didn't let you know where I was going or contact you when I said I would.

She is about to add—*that probably sucked,* but she makes one of her lips clamp down on the other lip and makes herself look at the linoleum. She has to be careful with Marcie, and it's possible this is unkind.

Why didn't you tell me where you were going, Marcie asks, after a silence.

I dunno, she says quickly, and then she stops: she should think of the real answer. —It felt like it wouldn't happen, if I did? So I didn't. But now I am.

But you haven't, Marcie says.

Oh, Abraxa says, and she laughs. —Duh! I guess I'm—

She stops; what is she even doing? She's lost the habit of putting it into words other people can connect to. Maybe this is a sign that the process of attuning to the sorceress is working; maybe she shouldn't answer Marcie's question. But she can feel Marcie looking at her, patient.

I guess I'm kind of . . . squatting, she says. —In the church we went to with your friend that one time? I'm trying to turn it into a squat. You know, living there, a little.

This feels safe: she hasn't mentioned the sorceress. She's honoring both of them.

What kind of squat are you turning it into, Marcie asks, after some time.

Kind of a community space, she says.

Marcie meets her eyes, then. —For stuff like—shows? she asks.

Right, yes, shows! Abraxa says. —It'd be a great place for shows. There can be a stage, and power, and a place for snacks. And rehearsal space, once I get the southern ceiling fixed? I need to get a jack is the only problem. Do you have one? Like did your grandfather? I mean like a big jack, where you can put boards and stuff in it, not like for a car.

Marcie doesn't answer this. —Why didn't you want me to know this, she asks.

Abraxa frowns at the linoleum: Hasn't she already answered this? What is the right answer to this question?

I didn't want you to like, worry about me, she says.

Marcie thinks about this, and then she takes one grape.

Do you have heat, she asks.

Sure, Abraxa lies. —I have a space heater, and power set up? It's really warm. The stones heat up, like the way a volcano works, or an oven. It's almost too warm.

Marcie smiles. —Can I see it sometime?

Abraxa looks down at her feet again. She pulls herself up onto the countertop fully, scooting a cutting board behind her away, and lets her feet dangle in space.

Sure, soon, she says.

She manages to change the subject to Marcie's volunteering, her grandmother, her shitty clients, the video games she's playing. They find themselves together on Marcie's bed, passing a controller. In this game, you are a tiny dolphin, exploring vast, dark undersea caves in search of your pod. They take turns being the dolphin, sneaking past malevolent devilfish and urchins, using sonar to explore distant passages, solving puzzles. It's the kind of game that has always frustrated Abraxa—she likes games where she can build things, or games with strange imagery or systems, or of course the old Mystic Knights games. But this is a game about being alone. She finds herself holding the controller less and less, and then handing it off to Marcie altogether and shouting suggestions to Marcie for where she should send her dolphin to explore next. And then she falls silent and just watches Marcie play. It's growing late—six o'clock already; the light from outside is nearly gone; the sun is going away for the year—and the reflected blue from the TV screen is washing over Marcie's glasses. The younger woman is deep within the game, her living body still except for her fingers. Her spirit is moving in the dolphin, on the screen, exploring the silent, dark ocean that is hers to explore. Abraxa watches her, imagines she can see a line from Marcie's heart to the dolphin forming, like a spiderweb in space. And she wonders what it's like to be inside her heart. What is it like to move through oceans and feel no fear?

Eventually, they order pizza and garlic knots. It comes, and Marcie goes downstairs to pick it up and make her grandmother a plate for supper. Abraxa lies on the bed, the game paused, the ceiling above her. Marcie's bed is soft and warm from their bodies, and she realizes how tired she is. *Don't fall asleep*, she tells herself, and then she finds Marcie waking her up.

I have to go, she mumbles, and she knows this is mean; she is always saying things that are too mean.

Marcie's face above her, eyes hidden behind her glasses like coins. —Your squat is safe, right? So you should rest. You should go back tomorrow night.

I have to sleep on the floor, Abraxa says. —I can't sleep in the bed. I have to remember how not to sleep in the bed.

But Marcie covers her with a blanket, and when she opens her eyes next, the room is dark, the game is turned off. Marcie is asleep, turned away from her and breathing. She slides out of bed and finds the pizza box, and she sits on the floor and eats three cold slices, watching Marcie dream.

Computers are all around them; even the video game they played came to them through downloaded software. She tries to visualize the violet fire of System D in everything, crackling through the walls, but it's harder to do here than it had been before, in the shock of her initial vision, harder to focus on than it had been underground, cold and alone. She imagines herself down there, in the days, the weeks, of her building—the hours of physical work, writing in her notebooks, shivering asleep. Here, on Marcie's floor, the thought makes her feel ashamed.

Maybe this is what spiritual temptation feels like; maybe this is what spiritual peril feels like. Maybe this is the moment when keeping faith in the things she believed—believes—is most important. Or maybe those are just things mentally disturbed people tell themselves. Which is it? She lies down on the floor, partially beside and partially under Marcie's bed, and she pulls the edge of Marcie's duvet over herself. Under the bed is a strange world, plastic containers and forgotten dust, sharp angles of suitcase: she falls asleep, gazing into it. She'll go in the morning.

She wakes up to Marcie cooking breakfast: sizzle of eggs and pepper climbing the stairs, snap of grapefruit. She drags herself into the bed and falls asleep again, and off and on for the rest of the day. Once she wakes up to find a mug of noodle soup on the end table—is it for her?—she drinks it, she falls back asleep.

In her dreams, a strange woman in cowled wool robes is walking with her on the shores of the ocean. There's a tall, black rock somewhere just in the distance, pointed up at the stars. At intervals along the sand are small copper bowls in which thick pillar candles burn. She and the strange woman walk in a braided motion, weaving around each of the pillars. There are dead jellyfish everywhere in the surf, and there's a powerful, sweet smell of rot. She keeps wanting to apologize to the woman for something, but every time she tries to, the woman bows her head, and her cowl swallows her white chin, and Abraxa forgets what she wanted to say. And all night the woman leads her along the beach, and the next night, and the next.

Through the walls, during her periods of being awake, she can hear Marcie working: thanking her viewers for tips and subscriptions, adjusting her lights and cameras, laughing at jokes in the chat. System D—the violet fire on the other side of the walls.

No, this is a terrible thing to think about the person taking care of you. She is a dangerous and polluted person. She should stay away from Marcie—that's what a good person would do. But Marcie was upset when she did stay away. So maybe a good person wouldn't make Marcie upset. But she isn't a good person. She doesn't know who she is. She knows only that she can feel a fire burning in her brain, all of her thoughts going into the fire and coming out again as smoke phoenixes. She imagines the sorceress holding her shoulders; she feels the weight of Marcie's blankets.

The next morning, she feels rested, more than she has since she can remember. Marcie is already awake; dishes are moving in the kitchen downstairs. Abraxa stares up at the ceiling for some time, thinking, and then she rolls out of bed. She takes Marcie's bathrobe from the hook on the bathroom door, and then, walking on tiptoe, she descends to the basement, where she takes off her clothes and puts them in the washer. Once they're off her body, she can smell them—their sourness, crystallized sweat and cold—and she watches them circle as the washing machine erases them.

Marcie's at the top of the basement stairs. —Oh, she says. —Are you feeling better?

She sounds scared. —I'm better, Abraxa says. —I'm going back to my squat today.

All the dirt she's accrued is swirling with her clothes behind the washer door. If she squints, can she see it—a black waterspout behind the glass—or does it become invisible when diffused? Behind her, Marcie isn't making any sound.

Is that okay, Abraxa asks.

Sure, says Marcie. —Can I come with you?

Abraxa laughs, her heart spiking.

Not to stay, Marcie quickly says. —Just to help you carry some stuff.

What stuff, Abraxa says. —I don't have any stuff. I don't need any stuff.

You needed a jack, Marcie says, too fast. And then: —And you told me not to throw any of your stuff away? In your note?

I don't want you to come, Abraxa says. —You can't come.

She pulls Marcie's bathrobe tighter around her body. The window to the street is blocked—the corners of the basement are dark. Marcie is standing on the stairs. She doesn't want to push past Marcie. She tries to remain still, in front of the washer, and contained, and not hurting anything.

Okay, Marcie says. —But can I come to check on you later, maybe?

No, says Abraxa. —It won't be ready. I need to be alone—I need to be alone for what I'm doing.

But what are you doing, Marcie asks.

Stop asking me, Abraxa says.

Okay, Marcie says, and something is broken in her voice,

and Abraxa knows she broke it, and why is this so difficult? Why is it so difficult for her to express what she means?

But, Marcie starts again, and Abraxa screams, and from upstairs, there's a sound.

Shit, Marcie says, and tension bursts from her voice like a vapor, and she rushes upstairs to her grandmother's room. Abraxa follows after her, a few seconds later, escapes the basement trap.

The kitchen is empty; Marcie has been cutting some kind of green onions to fold into dough for fried onion pancakes. The smell of onion lingers, bright and rainy, in the kitchen while Marcie walks back and forth upstairs, calming her grandmother down. Is the stove burner on? If it is, what will it feel like to touch? She imagines Marcie's face modulating through several intolerable frequencies: anger, concern, the persistence that wears away stones. She cannot make things better, only worse, unless she presses her face against the burner, in which case her face will cook, maybe fall off in tiny baconish strips. She holds her face still and away from the burner; she works very hard to do this.

After some time, she reaches her hand out to graze the iron with her fingertip. It's cold. Grateful, relieved, she kneels down and lets her face rest against it. There's a ring of cold metal at the center of the iron, a hole where hot flame can vent; her cheek fits neatly inside it. She rests, willing herself: get up before Marcie sees this. Get up before Marcie sees you with your face on the stove. And in the act of willing, she remembers finally what the good thing to do is. The good thing is to give someone what they really want, whether they know yet that they want it.

■ ■ ■

She's at the table acting normal by the time Marcie comes back down. They say some apology things and she goes down to finish her laundry. She puts her uniform back on and packs some of her things from Marcie's room into a shopping bag, then adds some pantry cans. She tries to take things that won't be missed: pie filling, hominy, beets past expiration. Marcie is waiting at the table when she comes out of the pantry with her loot. There's a cell phone in front of her.

What's that, Abraxa says, staring at it, her heart picking up.

I thought it would maybe help, Marcie says. —For emergencies? It's prepaid; I have some spares for work stuff sometimes.

I don't want to be connected to anything, Abraxa says.

Marcie's eyes sink until she's looking at the phone. I could leave it here, Abraxa thinks. I could leave it and Marcie wouldn't say no. Marcie wouldn't get in my way.

I won't charge it, Abraxa says. —It's just going to sit there, dead on the shelf.

That's fine, Marcie says. —That's totally fine!

Abraxa stares at the phone, and then she sits down on the floor with her back to the sideboard. There's a heating vent coming up beside her—hot wind from the basement—it feels good next to her, like a friend.

I'm sorry I'm bad, she says.

Marcie doesn't say anything back.

They don't touch when Abraxa says goodbye, and the walk back to Mercer Street is colder, and she wishes, the weight of the phone and the cans in her bag notwithstanding, that she had never been. It was cruel to go. She needs to do better. She wills herself to do better, imagines her guilt burning up in her heart and turning into smoke, imagines the smoke floating up above her as great black birds. And then there really are grackles flying above her, up among the geometric eaves of Saint Peter's University, and the synchronicity makes her heart easy. And by the time she's finished the long and boring walk down Montgomery Street to the old part of town, she knows she has come back to herself, and that she always can.

Part of her expected to find Northwood Abbey destroyed, counter-squatted, everything she worked for scattered. But the key still works in her padlock, and all of her things are just where she left them, and her heart sinks as she recognizes the smallness of the world she's building. But there's lightness, too: this world is hers. You only really know a home when you leave it and then return.

She stacks the canned goods in the ersatz pantry and sets the prepaid phone on a shelf. After a moment, she removes its battery and places it in the south room, on top of a can of boat sealant she hasn't yet cracked open. She writes down her dream about walking with the woman on the beach. The sorceress, in another guise? A part of herself? Someone else? There's so little she understands. She can't wait to understand it.

There's a sledgehammer among her tools. She takes it and begins to strike at the floor in the north chapel, just along a crack, close to the place the sun touches. And she closes her eyes as a hole slowly opens, listening as the noise becomes signal, as concrete becomes soil.

3. The Air

FROM: screamingButterfly89@gmail.com
TO: sashiel@yahoo.com
DATE: Wednesday, January 4, 2017 at 10:55 PM EST
SUBJECT: long time lurker first time caller :/

Hi! I hope this isn't weird, and I hope this is still your email? LOL, I almost wrote you a few years back when you still had your contact info listed on your website, and fortunately I still had your email addy in drafts. Sorry if this is weird!

Anyway, I just wanted to say, <3. I lost a friend recently, for not good reasons. And I just saw the post you made where you said you were worried about your friend. And idk. It hit me in the feels really hard. I hope they're doing okay now? I'm sorry if they're not.

Your blog is really interesting. I love your links! Keep writing, K?

<3, hopefully not weird,

Dana

FROM: queencaramella@alias.co
TO: DronePaypigSubmissive75@clandestine.email
DATE: Saturday, January 7, 2017 at 11:30 PM EST
SUBJECT: listen up worm

did you do what i asked yet?

.

.

.

for your sake, i hope so.
ensure you have what i need by our next session. set a date.

FROM: bwwyland@sherwoodthemagazine.org
TO: theFaceOfSashiel@yahoo.com
DATE: Saturday, January 14, 2017 at 1:33 PM EST
SUBJECT: looking for writers!

Hi! I hope you're well!
We've never met, but my name is Brenda Wyland? I'm an editor with a literary magazine called *Sherwood*, which publishes prose essay and poetry from transgender voices, especially from marginalized backgrounds who don't traditionally have a voice in literature. I was at the reading your friend, Tula Vidrio, put on the other night, and I asked her if she could recommend any voices for me. And she said I should reach out to you?

She gave me your blog information, and I checked it out, and it's really interesting! Would it be okay for us to publish some of your pieces in the Fall 2017 special edition of *Sherwood*? If so, could you send me a collection of your blog posts (no more than 5k words total please!) that you'd like us to publish? (We do pay, although not as much as I'd like!)

Obviously no hard feelings if it's not something you'd want to be a part of, but thought I'd ask!

Thanks, and I hope your day is going excellently!

All best,

B

FROM: theFaceOfSashiel@yahoo.com
TO: bwwyland@sherwoodthemagazine.org
DATE: Saturday, January 14, 2017 at 10:41 PM EST
SUBJECT: Re: looking for writers!

sure, $500, as long as you tell me what your favorite thing i've written is. can you do that?
(Not sent.)

FROM: sashiel@yahoo.com
TO: tula.vidrio@gmail.com
DATE: Saturday, January 14, 2017 at 10:43 PM EST
SUBJECT: wtf

hey, maybe don't give out my blog to random magazine editors? friendly suggestion! thank you!

FROM: sashiel@yahoo.com
TO: gigwritesgames@gmail.com
DATE: Saturday, January 14, 2017 at 11:40 PM EST
SUBJECT: .

hi. it's been a couple of weeks, so i wanted to check in, if that's okay. i'm sorry i was weird at the end. i still think all the time about your piece (at tula's reading, i mean, about the bros) and what it meant to me. let me know if you ever want to talk about that, or about topics that you would also enjoy talking about.

regards, s

FROM: DronePaypigSubmissive75@clandestine.email
TO: queencaramella@alias.co
DATE: Sunday, January 15, 2017 at 2:02 AM EST
SUBJ: Re: listen up worm

I am so sorry so sorry so sorry my queen! I am so sorry and pathetic and not worthy! I am a worm ,you are so right to say that, a pathetic disgusting worm who does not deserve to be alive. You are right and I should not have let the act of disappointing you happen. I only did that because I am a pathetic useless wretch who only deserves punishment!!!

I went out last week and maybe these photos will help?? I hope they will! If they don't maybe, you could give me more information maybe, on Skype? It doesn't have to be at the office anymore, things have changed with my situation, which I will tell you about when we next meet. Can it be tonight?
(Attachment: A series of uncompressed JPGs of Jersey City streets. They are useless.)

FROM: sashiel@yahoo.com
TO: gigwritesgames@gmail.com
DATE: Monday, January 16, 2017 at 1:06 PM EST
SUBJ: .

hi, sorry for double emailing. i'm not sure if that's okay with you. please tell me if it isn't.

i keep thinking of what you wrote, or anyway what you read, and what it meant to me. i think it's because you were writing about a kind of spiritual project. i would love to talk to you about this sometime.

sash.

FROM: queencaramella@alias.co
TO: DronePaypigSubmissive75@clandestine.email
DATE: Monday, January 16, 2017 at 2:10 PM EST
SUBJ: not good enough

i briefly reviewed your email. you're right that what you did was unacceptable under any circumstances. you're wrong that you deserve punishment. you don't deserve that much attention.

regardless, this is what you're going to do.

you're going to take off your pants.

you're going to stand in front of the most dangerous window you can find.

no, not that one! you know the one i mean. the one where they'll see you and know what you are.

you're there now. do it.

you're going to get yourself hard.

feels good, right?

yes, it feels so good. you've waited for this.

keep touching it.

then

crush your balls.

harder than you think you're able to.

don't take your hand away.

if you took your hand away, put it back,

then hurt yourself.

as hard as you think you can bear without doing yourself permanent injury,

and then,

crush them ten times harder.

i don't care if you destroy your reproductive capacity. yours will be the final human generation.

so, harder.

harder!

.

..

…

all right, let go.

zip your little blood blistered worm dick back up,

and find me what i need. now. we will not have any further sessions until you bring it to me.

go with a flashlight if you have to. photograph every inch of that street.

i don't give a fuck what time it is, or if your pathetic wife doesn't want you to go. honestly, you shouldn't be thinking about that cis bitch anyway. you're loyal to me, and to *my revolution.* that's the deal you made, because you wanted to let a transsexual on the internet make you ejaculate. hope you're feeling good about that decision.

queen caramella

FROM: sashiel@yahoo.com
TO: gigwritesgames@gmail.com
DATE: Monday, January 16, 2017 at 11:42 PM EST
SUBJ: regarding

i'm not sure my last message was totally clear. i don't remember everything i said to you that night about the piece you read, but it really did speak to me. maybe it wasn't even the piece itself, maybe that was accidental: maybe it was the mood i was in that day, the old things i'd been thinking about. i don't know. i haven't been sleeping well. it's hard to articulate what i mean without reducing it to something easy and safe to say. compression and ambiguity let you feel that you're being profound even as you're protecting yourself. "amirite"? and it's been so long i've been doing that. i don't want to anymore. i don't want to be safe anymore. for example, ordinarily i would delete this and not send it to you. guess we'll see if i actually do that.
(Not sent.)

FROM: DronePaypigSubmissive75@clandestine.email
TO: queencaramella@alias.co
DATE: Wednesday, January 18, 2017 at 4:33 AM EST
SUBJ: idea

I'm so sorry my Queen! I still haven't found it ,I called in from work the past two days and took photos. Here's a link to them on Flicker? *(Link to an uncomfortably public Flickr account.)* Please tell me if this is enough or if you need me to do more .I hope it is enough though so we can Skype again.

　　Thank you for giving me the instructions in your last email! It really hurt me , but I knew you would not make me do more than I can withstand. I feel safe with you my Queen. I have to make a confession which is that later I tried to make myself Come without permission. But when I got close it hurt like anything and I threw up. Then I finally got it that was something you had planned for me ,so that I couldn't disobey you. You are so smart , smarter than all the others, even the people who work for me , and they are some of the smartest people in the world.

I keep being worried because I know you need money for your revolution, and we have not had one of our Meetings lately?? I had an idea and since I don't know how long it'll be, before we Skype again, I wanted to tell you about the idea. Some of the money for the revolution must go toward a revolutionary Base right? If it does, the idea is that maybe instead of paying rent on the revolutionary Base you would want to move in with me? There isn't anyone else in the house now. I am loyal to only you. And I could still pay you the same or even more ,so you could use the money for things you need, like weapons for the other drones who refuse to submit to you because they do not know that they are your drones yet! And you would have me at your Disposal 24/7 and could use, as much money as you wanted.

I think it is common sense. I love you my Queen and, I want your revolution to succeed. I think I am ready to take the step to fully committing to it. I will always support you though even if you do not like this idea and even if you never let me Come again.

Kind Regards
drone

FROM: queencaramella@alias.co
TO: DronePaypigSubmissive75@clandestine.email
DATE: Thursday, January 19, 2017 at 11:14 PM EST
SUBJ: no

as of this email any business ties between us are severed. if you contact me again i will forward all correspondence with you both to the media and to the police.

FROM: sashiel@yahoo.com
TO: gigwritesgames@gmail.com
DATE: Friday, January 20, 2017 at 3:32 AM EST
SUBJ: risk

hi, i realize these emails are annoying. but i think i need to risk annoying you? more and more i think i have been too careful for too long. i have wanted to be safe, to be precise, to hold onto everything keeping me together from the really dark places i think you saw that night. and it takes so much work to do that. and i don't know how much longer i can.

(this is related to being trans but not as much as you think it is? but you're trans too; obviously you know that.)

i am really scared right now. there is some drama with a client who started telling me crazy things, and so i had to let him go. and my entire income came from this person, and i don't really know what to do now? and i think i just need to talk to someone. and you saw me in the worst place i can get to, and you were kind to me, then. and maybe that means it is okay to talk to you. is it? i keep going around and around. there is no one it's safe for me to talk to. but you were kind. but I hurt everyone i talk to. but you were kind.

i should delete this whole email. but what you said meant something to me. it made me feel complex and messy things, and very little makes me feel anything anymore. and i'm afraid and i want to grab at what i can see while i can see it. "grab": that is a scary word. what is the right word? please help me stop going in circles. please, i need someone to.

tell me how you're doing too, so this is just a little bit reciprocal?

s

(Not sent.)

FROM: sashiel@yahoo.com
TO: ulysses.t.marat@usps.gov
DATE: Sunday, January 22, 2017 at 8:14 AM EST
SUBJ: hbd

you dream, dad, and sometimes you dream desert swelters.
red skies long after the world stops its gears,
moraine—it was once eastern parkway—now welters,
under dead concrete, and waste-lands, and tears,
sighting a temple, cloaked figures seek shelter.
in the cloister—*recordings.* time's made some abatement,
cassette spools have faded. but a label, delicate,
intends to make some last artistical statement:
"songs of ulysses—canto one, abstract hearts.
well, crank it—huh? what *is* this? what's all this *shit*?"
embarrassed, bewildered: "these synths sound like farts!"
in such ill reception, one's tempted to grieve,
rend shirts. but proud men with cosine wave charts
do not. coarser loves are not theirs to achieve.

love, your daughter

FROM: blake299949.0000000a@email.com
TO: queencaramella@alias.co
DATE: Monday, January 23, 2017 at 2:12 AM EST
SUBJ: Re: [bk-trans] [#60899] space queen searches for new submissive sluts, hint: this is you, worm

hay ur hot id fuck u will u send pics both hard an flaccid

FROM: queencaramella@alias.co
TO: blake299949.0000000a@email.com
DATE: Monday, January 23, 2017 at 8:31 AM EST
SUBJ: Re: Re: [bk-trans] [#60899] space queen searches for new submissive sluts, hint: this is you, worm
sure, $500.
(Not sent.)

FROM: sashiel@yahoo.com
TO: gigwritesgames@gmail.com
DATE: Friday, January 27, 2017 at 3:30 AM EST
SUBJ: hi

hi, how are you doing? s

FROM: sashiel@yahoo.com
TO: tula.vidrio@gmail.com
DATE: Friday, January 27, 2017 at 12:15 PM EST
SUBJ: gig

did you hear anything weird from gig about me? they're not responding to my emails.

FROM: tula.vidrio@gmail.com
TO: sashiel@yahoo.com
DATE: Friday, January 27, 2017 at 6:04 PM EST
SUBJ: Re: gig

hey no i haven't heard anything from them. And miss me as far as taking sides goes? But if you've been sending them a lot of emails or something . . . maybe don't do that!

   oh btw sorry about the whole thing where i gave your blog to that weird woman who wanted to pay you ¯_(ツ)_/¯

FROM: sashiel@yahoo.com
TO: tula.vidrio@gmail.com
DATE: Friday, January 27, 2017 at 6:20 PM EST
SUBJ: Re: Re: gig

okay, thanks, sorry.
(Not sent.)

FROM: sashiel@yahoo.com
TO: screamingButterfly89@gmail.com
DATE: Saturday, January 28, 2017 at 2:33 AM EST
SUBJ: Re: long time lurker first time caller :/

hi dana,
sorry for my delay in responding. thank you for reaching out to me. it meant a lot. not just knowing that you were actually reading my blog, though that's obviously a lot. it also meant something that you cared about my friend.

   sometimes i wonder whether she really was my friend. were any of my online friends real? every time i connect with people online, i pay a price. no: every time i connect with people, full stop. i know i still need to do that, that not to do that is to die. but it is becoming more and more difficult to want to do that, to believe it is okay to do that, even to know how to do that. that's starting to scare me.

i used to want to become a sorceress. and then i learned to really be one. wrapped in an armor of glamour, i learned spells of protection. all philosophy is about balance: not passion or complacency, but a third way between. i thought i could find that balance, the point of sail a good sailor can find in any wind. i thought all i needed was a stable, still place in which to create it. but now i'm starting to die in here.

once i believed that if me and my friends made a perfect video game, everything would be good. that was the rule then. what is the rule now? please tell me. you seem like a good person who cares about my friend. you must know the rule.

i don't know why i posted what i did. my brilliant artist, programmer, rival. we probably weren't even friends; we never would have been. and then we all got older, and lives diverged so much from our common point of origin, however indistinctly defined. having a common origin can't be enough. part of me thought she was going to kill herself. why? because so many girls like us do? i had this whole idea that i could find her and save her. but it didn't work. i could have done more. i didn't do more. i'll never know what to do.

anyway, thank you for reading my website. i worry that i talk too much, so thanks for reading this, if you did. you can also talk more to me if you want. we can talk about your friend, or about anything.

<3. sash.

(Not sent.)

FROM: DronePaypigSubmissive75@clandestine.email
TO: queencaramella@alias.co
DATE: Sunday, January 29, 2017 at 10:02 PM EST
SUBJ: Please Don't Delete I Found Something!
(No text. Attachment: a crude photo of a drawing hanging on the community board of a bagel store. A series of confusing hand-written assertions and quotes from different mystical writers of the past. A logo:

And an email address.)

FROM: sashiel@yahoo.com
TO: abraxaabraxaabraxa@marcieletskaudesign.com
DATE: Monday, January 30, 2017 at 9:16 AM EST
SUBJ: .

hey,
(Not sent.)

4. The Hermit

There are two long, raised beds of stolen black potting soil now in the north room, each limned with chips and chunks of stone smashed free from the foundation slab. Beneath the slab—far thinner than she had guessed; some hasty mid-century concrete conversion job?—was weathered gravel; beneath that was raw, packed earth, which she had taken off her work glove for, which she'd touched. A tomato cage rests against the wall, ready for deployment.

Thrown stones and diligence have widened the holes in the ceiling above, bringing down buttery shafts of sunlight. It's a tradeoff: more warmth gets out, more happiness gets in. She chalks a palm tree on the stone wall, paints it in primer and gouache. Afternoons she sits under it, drawing in her notebook.

The work in the southern room has advanced about as far as it can without her having a jack—all the rubble is collected and bagged; she's swept the baseboards many times—and the space is clean and empty, waiting for spring. She can make it to spring down here. She just has to let it get cold again, and then colder, and then warm. The leaves of tomato plants, rustling soon in subterranean wind: it will be simple.

■ ■ ■

What she wants, and stubbornly keeps wanting, is a bed. A wide queen bed up on a steel frame, cups under its legs against night vermin, soft mattress that settles against her skin like marshmallow whip. Or maybe a firmer mattress, taut like a drumhead, against which she bounces when she drops at the end of a working day. Or maybe a futon, wrapped in anime blankets, headphones in her ears whispering to her as she falls asleep. (No, that would be System D.) Maybe a four-poster with princess veils. Maybe a waterbed. (No, not a waterbed.) She keeps wanting this as she tosses at night, turning one hip and then another away from the cold stone beneath her stolen carpet, her yoga mat, her bedroll. She wants blankets, she wants pillows, she wants springs, she wants to yawn and smell her growing tomato plants and know she's absolutely safe.

She wants that, and suddenly she also wants very badly to be fucked.

It would be hard to steal and assemble a bed underground, but the other problem is not hard to solve. She lets herself charge and activate the phone, though she sets a boundary: she won't use it in the church itself. At the bagel store, she watches the clerk work through a philosophy paperback while she installs Grindr and loads her profile with her usual set of pics: herself sitting at a laptop in striped socks and underwear, herself squeezing her boobs together in the mirror of a public bathroom, herself on the deck of Elias's boat, cross-legged and naked except for a snapback. She finds herself staring at this photo for some time: sitting in a burning sunbeam with all the salt water surrounding her. Then, shaking off bad premonitions, she sets the "Looking for" field to "Right now," and she starts to triage the arriving pictures of dicks, like sorting berries for winter jam.

Even all the weeks underground hasn't effaced the muscle memory of reviewing Grindr messages. She responds to all messages: *hi! Want to come fuck me in a haunted basement?* Anyone who replies in a way that is even a little bit on-topic, she keeps in her final pool of submissions. From the remaining dozen, she selects a man who looks like he could be either a former tattoo artist or a cult leader, wizardy and hollow-eyed and who uses the word *cherish* in response to her. It feels gross and scary and sweet, a swollen fruit. Is he a wizard? She will learn. She makes a plan to meet him at a Starbucks a few blocks away, and then she deletes the app, takes the phone battery out.

She honestly would be fine with her connection not showing up—the endorphin rush of Grindr is sufficient, actual sexual activity that results from it almost superfluous—but he shows. He is a wiry, goateed cis man in a thick canvas coat, black at the seams and patched with band logos in Sharpie. His eyes are a bright blue surrounded by white. Iago: she remembers his name.

Look nice, he mumbles at her.

She leads him around the block and beneath the arch to her church. Another way a house becomes a home is when it is seen through the eyes of a guest. She imagines what her abbey looks like through his eyes: sleeping bag littered with rationed estrogen bottles, rolled edges of white paint blurred into cement floor, muddled incense and turpentine.

Can I like, offer you anything, she laughs, feeling complexly proud.

Nope, he says quickly, looking at the walls rather than her.

His nostrils keep flaring: Is he smelling? Can he smell her? Trying not to think about what she might smell like, she offers him some of today's bagels. He takes one, poppyseed, inclines his head thank you, gestures at her floor, as if inviting her to sit down on it. She does, cross-legged—he can definitely smell her—and he sits as well. He stares at her, and he holds the bagel in his fist like it's a big medieval keyring; he takes no bites.

Are you a serial killer, she asks, to fill the silence. —Sorry, ha ha, that's really rude.

Iago seems to flinch. —I've never killed anyone, he says apologetically. —You're right to be careful.

They sit, the bagel hanging from his fingers, untouched. He is much smaller than her, she notes. She imagines leaning forward and taking a bite of it for him, maybe to show him it's okay.

So your profile said you had a band, she said. —Does your band have a website or anything?

His face turns stoic as he shakes his head. —We do not yet have a website, he says. —I know it's a problem now, with the Internet so important. I paid a guy in Knoxville like $700 for one, but he cheated me. There've been other priorities is why I haven't made a second try.

Dude, you don't need $700 for a website, she laughs. —I learned to make websites in *middle* school. I could make you a website *right now* for *free*.

What kind of middle school did you go to, he asks, awed.

A regular one, she says. —I just got some library books.

He shakes his head. —You're smart, too.

She laughs, leaving the hanging *too* mysterious, and she begins to explain the basic idea of HTML/CSS to him while he nods and props his chin on his hand to signify thinking.

Carefully, he begins to eat the bagel, and she relaxes: having eaten her food, now he has to stay.

She guesses he'll be most interested in her stories about her traveling years, which, she realizes in the act of telling them, have hopefully ended. They'd been to a surprising number of the same places—Ida, Moab, Enchanted Circle—and they shared a surprising number of nontechnical skills: being a doctor when no one else dares to be, getting out of the rain where you have no tools for that, moving without fear in the moonlight. And soon they're talking about Northwood itself: her physical plans for the space, how she might safely bring in a generator, how to grow plants that thrive in a crack of ceiling sunlight. He knows some of the plants she knows; he knows plants she doesn't. The possibilities he opens are thrilling, and it makes her feel good, and soon she's feeling good enough that she stops listening to what he's saying, just nods and watches him say it. He's warm, he smiles, even though glimpses of hurt appear in his speech like bite scars from a warmly remembered dog. And then he isn't speaking anymore, just looking at her as she sprawls, cheek on her sleeping bag and smiling up at him.

I've never met anyone like you before, he says. —I mean, I've met people *like* you before. But not—you know. Like who you really are.

She closes her eyes, deflating. Of course her profile outs her as trans, as does her basic existence on Grindr, but being clocked as Not Cis always feels sad, like someone in the audience has stopped the play. But at least if he kills her, she knows this won't be why.

It's because I'm possessed by a sorceress, she says, wriggling her shoulders.

He lets this go. —I've never met anyone *like me* before, he says, and his eyes are wide.

While he excuses himself to pee outside, she does a quick Tarot reading. If she draws Death, The Tower, Judgment, any high-value swords at all, he's gone. But she draws The World. The last time she turned up this card, the question had been: *Am I really a girl?* The woman in the card looks up at her, two crystal wands in her hands, and she looks back.

When Abraxa was a teenager, she always imagined that if chromosomes had bloomed right and she had somehow been born a real girl, she wouldn't fear sex in the way that the actual her, a fake girl, did. If she had been real, she'd have the power to find and give ease.

At nights, curled under a blanket on the carpet of the computer room because she didn't want to find her way to her bed, she fantasized about being a real girl. She'd sit in the bedroom of a boy crush after studying or whatever, as talk turned—no one steered it; it just turned like a planchette—to their common awe before their bodies, and what they wanted. *Should we try it?* He'd be scared; she'd see his fear. And she would know—deep in her body, felt from inside, Abraxa knew she would know—how to resolve that fear, to comfort it. She'd take off her earrings, undo her hair, kneel on the knit rug before his bed, and she'd teach him what she didn't herself yet know.

It hurt to imagine this. So over time, her mind began to rearrange this fantasy. She began instead to cast herself as the real girl's close friend: someone without gender, someone who was more afraid in the way Abraxa was afraid, who listened to these stories, heard both the bravado and the shame in them.

And she imagined what she'd say to the real girl: *there's nothing wrong with you, you deserve good things.* And somehow the act of imagining herself saying this also let her imagine herself hearing it, as a candle in front of a mirror doubles the light.

Later, when she began to understand herself also to be a girl, and still later when she acted on this understanding, she felt conflicted about the doubled fantasy. Were cis girls afraid of being cis girls in this way? If not, why had her fantasy been so naive? And didn't that naivete mean that her trans girlhood had been fundamentally different from cis girlhood, vile and paraphilic and outside of ethical experience? Why had she felt a right to fantasize about being cis at all?

But whether it was right or not, these were the fantasies she'd had as a girl. And from that root, she'd grown into a weird and fucked-up woman: a woman who in this moment, facing Iago across her stolen basement, suddenly remembers how hard she'd worked then to bury herself. How little she's honored the girl she'd been. And for the first time since she drowned in the Pacific Ocean, a little porthole in her heart suddenly screws open, and light comes out, and she hears again the advice one part of her told herself long ago. She does deserve good things. She should take them.

And with the candle standing between them, their shadows dark red on the wall, she pulls her shirt over her head, lowers her shorts and leggings to the concrete. Her jaw—her breasts, surgically perked—her good hips—the contours of her genitals. Her legs are strong from walking; her boots are still on. She spreads her arms like a bat and laughs, terrified, because if murder is in her fate, this is when murder will find her.

Iago has been sitting cross-legged; now he rolls forward, onto

his knees. His mouth hangs open, staring up at her in awe. She
wants to cry. He crawls toward her, reaches up to her belly: this
big patch of white paint on it. He puts one hand on the paint,
one on her thigh.

May I, he asks shyly.

The sorceress speaks through her: —*Drink it.*

He does, eyes closed in rapture; he lifts her veil, and then he
devours her, horrible goatee and her unshaven legs scratching
each other like cats. And when she's come again—or the
sorceress has; Abraxa is confused, whirling through constellations—Iago touches her ass, asks her permission. She lets him
in. She feels like she's stretched out into sun too hot, sinking
into beach sands—she's being fucked on the concrete floor of
a church that has been set on fire while an invisible sorceress
strokes her hair—she laughs. This is a new place. This is a new
possibility life has opened to her. This is him coming in her
while the candle burns and showers volcanic wax, lava cooling
to flowstone.

In her mind, their ejaculate intertwines, changes like frogs,
his penetrating hers, hers penetrating his. A moonchild begins
to form.

She's sleepy, and as she sinks into her sleeping bag, she invites
him to join her: *you can stay. I'll turn the space heater on, you
can stay.* He tells her he will in a minute; he has to pee, he'll be
right back. She has a dream about him: the two of them hoe her
garden beds, gather onions and tomatoes in silence to fry in a
huge iron pan. When she wakes up, he's long gone.

She sits for some time, her ass aching and her knees sore,
and then she gets up and starts to wash the floors. Water is
tricky to haul, so she normally does this just once a week, but

today she doesn't want to think, just to push her rolled watery towel across rooms. So she works, cleaning the south room, her body replaying the memory of his hands and beard scratch and pressure. It was a mistake to go online. It was weak to need to be touched by someone. Eyes closed, imagining the sorceress walking just ahead of her across a long, cold desert, she feels her body like a light-up piano: parts of her flash to direct the player's fingers.

5. The Ship

FROM: sashiel@yahoo.com
TO: tula.vidrio@gmail.com
DATE: February 2, 2017 at 9:17 AM EST
SUBJ: (no subject)

hi, are you busy today? s.
(Not sent.)

FROM: sashiel@yahoo.com
TO: tula.vidrio@gmail.com
DATE: February 5, 2017 at 9:24 AM EST
SUBJ: (no subject)

hi, are you busy today? i know i shouldn't be emailing you this. i am and will probably continue to be a terrible friend. i have been avoiding sending you this email for a long time because i'm terrible. but i am scared right now about things related to work and related to a bad train of thought i have been going through lately. so i am wondering if it would be possible to "hang out," as "friends do," because i am worried that if i don't i will become disconnected altogether from the world. and i know i should try to make a new friend to connect to so i don't further exploit our friendship but i am not capable of doing that right now. so i will ask. no is a completely okay answer to give.

s.

FROM: tula.vidrio@gmail.com
TO: sashiel@yahoo.com
DATE: February 5, 2017 at 11:04 AM EST
SUBJ: Re: (no subject)

Hahaha damn bitch chill! Sure let's hang

Tula suggests you meet her at a place with unfamiliar trains, a system of transfers that you know you are not capable of on the appointed day. Convince her to settle for the park next to the library you know how to get to. Wait at the corner of the park entrance, adjacent to occult and falcon-capped pillars, feeling the dark eyes of your library coworkers on you. The sky is a sheet of dull aluminum, and the people here—more people than you'd expected, all bundled in coats and hats—move slowly along the paths, the grass left pristine but for dogs and lonely frisbee players in sweats.

Tula appears in jeans, hiking boots, and windbreaker, bizarre eighties-heroine sweatband across her brow. She leads you to a side trail that extends up a small hill, past a stream bounded by flat stones bearing strange human offerings—wrappers, receipts, a small white wooden boat with popcorn stuffed in its hull—then up another side trail that winds to a space bordered by a thicket of dry brush and spike vines. The earth is studded with empty travel bottles of liquor, condom wrappers, and Gatorade flasks of thick orange liquid; it is, you think, the worst place in the park. But this is where Tula stops and seats herself on an arcing log, a plastic bag of desiccated human shit at her feet. After as much time as you dare, you sit beside her, careful to leave some inches of space.

The log faces the main road, as a veranda might: below you, down the hill, joggers and dogwalkers and teens with no better activities move through the channels formed by painted side-walk stripes. They can't see you, you are certain, even through the imperfect crosshatch of still-bare trees: two transsexuals perched like Muppet opera critics.

Like it? she asks after you've both sat shivering for a minute.

It's the park, you say.

She sighs. —It looks about as bad now as it ever does, she says. —This pre-spring season, the spike vines and stuff. It's like puberty.

Don't respond to this: wonder what the temperature is right now in Jersey City, where you now know Abraxa is, whether Tula's allusion to spring means it will get warm soon. Whether it's accept-able that you haven't done anything yet—whether your friend will survive her winter with or without your help.

Right now it's a floor plan, Tula continues. —But all those hunks of dead brush, they turn into walls.

And then the walls turn back into dry brush, you say, stretching your legs out from your perch on the log. —What's your point?

I've tried to bring myself here when I can, to see it lots of different ways, she says, after some time passes. —We should come here in a couple of months: it's like, a green mansion with birds in every window. I bring them honey and blueberries. It's a Disney sensation. Also sometimes people fuck here.

Contemplate her smile. —Is that why the condom wrappers are here?

That's how I found out about it, she says. —It's my favorite place in Brooklyn. It's the one space that justifies New York's existence.

I was born in Brooklyn, you warn. —I've basically never left.

And how lucky for you, she says, —that you got to be born so close to the perfect center of the universe.

Consider this, watching people who have nothing to do with you walk from place to place, shivering in air that has yet to become warm, the body next to yours separate and content.

So people come up here to fuck, you say after a while.

Not now, though, she replies, looking at the path through the trees rather than at you. —It's too cold for that now.

I see, you say.

It's just a place I wanted to show you, she says. —It's a place that makes me very happy.

Sit with that too, shivering, waiting for birds that don't seem to come.

So what's going on, Tula asks.

Flinch: perhaps you should have expected this question. — With what, you ask.

With all the shit you emailed me about, Tula says. —I mean we can not talk about it if you want, but we could also . . . talk about it?

Think carefully: How would a good person answer this question? —We can talk about it, you venture.

Sit there, observing birds. —You said there was stuff with work, she finally says. —Do you mean with a client?

Feel your body immediately reject this line of inquiry: you do not want to discuss Droneslut. —I changed my mind, you say. —I don't want to talk about it.

Her face seems to close a little—alarm in your throat—this

is what happened with Gig. You don't want this to happen with Tula, too.

It's more about work generally, you say quickly. —General things with work.

General things, she says. —Like the need for work? Are you still working?

According to my parents I am, you say. —And I have enough savings to keep up that fiction for some amount of time. A small amount.

Tula doesn't respond: her face, in profile, is not showing you any information about her inner state. She is calculating whether she should invite you to live with her at her apartment: intolerable. You'll only mess this up.

I mean I'm going to be okay, you say. —I just need to figure out similar work, but that doesn't put me in the path of similar clients? It's just been a while since I had to set up freelance gigs. It's just been a while, and I'm older, and you know—

Okay, she says; you can hear her impatience; flinch. —Chill, okay? Just chill.

I'm sorry for not chilling, you say, it's just that—

Find yourself trailing off—words are deserting you, no, replace them with images—say, *it's just a lot to consider* as you pull out your notebook to show her your lists and calculations—the new title of your investigation, *where is the best place to sell my body and soul?* And another list:

- fresh photos
- fresh copy
- listing fees
- time (for streaming)

- time (for vetting clients)
- time (for flakes)
- time (for research: contract rates? Worker reviews? Reviews of reviews, what can you trust?)
- time (remaining to be beautiful)

Show this list to Tula—words are still failing you—gesture to it. —This, you say. —I'm thinking through all of this.

She laughs, and the laugh is ugly. —Bitch, I don't need to see one of your like, serial killer lists, she says. —Just chill, okay?

It's not a serial killer list, you say. —I'm not a serial killer.

But wonder about this. Does Tula see something in you that you don't see?

- Did Gig, or Lilith?
- Are you actually maybe a secret serial killer?
- How would you assess this question?
- Because if you are a serial killer you should be exterminated.
- A serial killer for example could drink industrial cleaning chemicals to eliminate herself as one eliminates a disease.
- What industrial chemicals would even accomplish this? Do you have these?
- There must be tests to see if you're a serial killer.
- So you know what to do.
- There must be—

Listen, Tula says, and her voice is different. Her hand is stretched out a little. —You don't have to be all Sash about this, okay? I'm here to help you.

■ ■ ■

Keep looking at your knees, a safe place to look. Do not cry. You must not cry—you are thirty-two years old and your friend is maybe dead and it is obscene to cry. Heat blooms on your cheeks, salt heat that turns instantly to vapor cool.

She lets you try to cry for a while—and you really do try, you're sure you're trying—and then she scoots closer to you on the log and puts her arms around you: her smell is tropical church gardenia, estrogen sweat. Keep trying to cry while she holds you, here in the only place that justifies the existence of New York: feel her crush you slightly too hard, because she is irritated with you, you and every trans woman she's had to do this for, every trans woman and all the years she's had to do this and all the years she'll have to do this still. All of you should just get your shit together; why can't you get your shit together? Once you were so smart; you were even going to make a video game.

She doesn't let you go, and you let her hold you, and eventually your breath comes out short.

She takes you from her secret site in the park to a bougie coffee place she likes. There is a small outdoor garden even in the winter; the two of you sit out there under a dead tree, sipping cocoa, and she tells you about her life and the progress of the crush she'd told you about before. Listen to her, pretending you remember what she'd said. Realize, at some point, that she doesn't actually care whether you remember what she'd said before. She just wants to talk about it where someone can hear.

It's getting dark, and she walks you to the B45 bus and waits with you at the stop, the other passengers keeping their distance from the transsexuals. Stand next to her, head on her shoulder. She's tall enough to support it.

There's gotta be a place for you to work, she says shortly before the bus comes to whisk you home. —I'm gonna keep thinking about it, okay? I know like, everyone.

Sure, you say. —I have no recorded work history or skills.

You have ridiculous skills! she says. —You have so many skills! Didn't you used to make video games? Can't you get a job in video games or something?

And as the bus drags your body home, slowly realize that your friend is a genius.

6. The Desert

At a certain point, layering the church basement walls with protections—her paintbrush and pens tracing circles, defining letters—Abraxa starts to understand. The walls are becoming text. Walls define a space, but they also carry meaning: words and symbols that slide over the plaster and paint like eggs on hot grease. Pyramid chambers covered in spells, holy tabernacles, CraftQ games. The sorceress lives in the space, but she speaks through the walls.

One night, sleepless and shivering—the hole she opened to the earth is a major heat leak, the deepening winter damp threatens frost—she tries to trace how she first became connected to the sorceress. She works out a lineage flowchart in her notebook: herself, Sash, Lilith, all represented by the company logo. Then the three of them connected to the Nintendo corporation, them connected to The Critical Hit. Sash had described the occult ideas they'd encoded into the game. Which part of what they'd copied had been the active ingredient? Which had formed the gateway? How much more of the story did Sash know? She had taken that with her, into the silence.

The company sigil, a candle with three lines intersecting it.

Only Abraxa had remained faithful to it. The three lines ran parallel; they would never meet again.

Planning ahead, she goes to steal more cans from the punk house, but the queers there remember her. One of them clocks her the moment she waves a jaunty hello in the foyer, and three or four are waiting for her when she backs out of the pantry with her backpack stuffed with cans. They ask her questions.

I came to a party here, she says in response. —You invited me?

You need to get out of here, one of the queers says. —You're making people here uncomfortable.

They let her keep six canned goods, and they insist that she write down the number of a suicide hotline.

Back inside, heating a can of soup in her scavenged pot, she tries to imagine the trans guy who stopped her on the street, who'd invited her in to sleep on the dog's bed. She pictures him on the side of a mountain in Tennessee, one leg thrust forward and one back like a warrior, a three-ring binder open in his hands. He reads from it and intentional communities spring up like mushrooms from the mountainside. When the rain falls on him, it's always gentle.

She pushes her tongue against her tooth, and she's sure her tooth shifts. Had it always had that shift? She can't remember what her teeth used to feel like. How hard she's worked—how much physical work she's done, how few resources she's done it with. How much more work like this does she have in her? How long are these months going to be until spring? In this game, you are a body who has to make it to spring.

■ ■ ■

At nights it gets harder and harder to go out. She imagines the eyes of the co-op kids coming to meet her around street corners. She stays in by the fire and reads instead. *But when the sun drops closer to the earth, the cold of the earth runs to it from the water and causes all green things to dry up,* says Hildegard von Bingen. *And because the sun has dropped closer to the earth, the days are short, and it is winter.*

A scene from *Super Mystic Knights 3* comes to mind, one Sash used to talk about in her company sermons. In this game, you are in a shrine, and you are asked to find the appropriate way to worship a forest spirit whose aid the party requires. In most games, worship would be instantiated through pressing buttons, finding the right sequence of actions to take to win the god's favor. But in this game, you win only through silence. You win through pressing no buttons and waiting, waiting while the game's internal clock counts down. Waiting, without hope of reply, for the silence to break. Wait in place. Do not move. You cannot win unless you wait. You cannot win. Wait.

Depressed, she weakens; weak, she turns the phone back on to use Grindr. But there's a message from Marcie instead, asking her to meet at the diner near her house.

It takes her four days to respond to it: *sure, an hour okay?*

The reply: *yes, of course!*

She knows she smells bad; she knows her skin is wrecking the lemon-cleansed leather of the diner booth. She can see the waiter eye her as Marcie orders coffee and orange juice for them both. Marcie's pretending not to notice her smell. In this game, we are bodies who are pretending to be normal.

Normal people don't talk about the things they are actually thinking and feeling. Normal people smile and order food. She hears herself order lumberjack pancakes with extra sausage and syrup. Marcie nods; an item has been checked off her list.

So how are you, she asks.

I'm fine, Abraxa says, folding her arms. —How are you?

I'm fine, Marcie says, her voice wary. —It's really okay if we talk about how you're doing. It's also okay if we—

I have never been better in my life, Abraxa says, and other diners turn to look at them. She looks back at them, meeting their eyes, until they turn back to their own conversations, and she turns back to Marcie. —So how are you, she asks.

I'm tired, Marcie says.

Abraxa lets her pancakes arrive, lets the silence grow until, like a whirlpool, it is a pressure that it's more socially graceful to fill than not. So Marcie does, and Abraxa looks down at the pancakes. Don't eat them, she tells herself. Or at least eat them slowly. But she's no sooner thought it than she finds herself scraping up the last syrup and congealed crumbs with her fork tines. Marcie is telling a story about some kind of conference she's been assisting with, some fund for legal defense on employment lawsuits, something exhausting that she relates exhaustively while Abraxa scrapes her plate and the sugar makes her back molar ache. She pushes it idly with her tongue, riding the edge of the pain as her mind glides over the glare top of Marcie's words, until Marcie's story is finished. She heard none of it. A good person would have listened.

That sounds like it bites, she says.

Marcie frowns and nods, and then very deliberately rests her head in her hammocked hands. —It doesn't, she says. —I'm lucky to be able to do it. I'm happy to be able to do it. You can order more, if you want.

As Marcie says this, Abraxa feels a small, sucking pressure on her gums. An acrid iron taste soaks over her tongue, a small weight.

Do you want more? Marcie asks.

Abraxa puts down the fork she's been sucking on; she sits on her hands. Thinking quickly, she draws her empty coffee cup to her mouth, trying to conceal its emptiness; with a careful push, she deposits her bloody molar into it, not making a sound.

I'm good, she says, smiling, hoping she has no blood on her lips.

Marcie's face gets a pained little smile, and Abraxa remembers another time with Marcie, years ago in Florida when they'd first met: Abraxa had successfully used a pole she'd carved herself to spear a passing snapper, a flash of red in clear white water, and she was singing about how they'd grill it together, and Marcie was looking at her as if she was so exciting, so beautiful and young and trans and cool, and maybe she had even been some of those things then.

Part of her thinks, as she tastes the rust of her own blood, that she wants to tell Marcie everything she has been thinking. She wants to tell Marcie about how good it feels to live underground, to be alone, to turn the pages of library books by the fire, to draw and paint and prepare soil, to be so scared all the time and therefore to know you're at the root of something that matters, that you're on fire yet not burning away. To know just how hard it is for you to be eradicated. Everything about the small, strange, brilliant world she is making for herself, out of sight and in secret, every hope she has for the work she's giving birth to. A less wise version of herself might have already blurted it out, told about covering the walls in words in languages she can't understand. But she knows what Marcie will say if she talks about it. Her dreams crackle inside her like canned food, sealed in from time: the moment she places them into language Marcie can hear, they'll start to die. So she says nothing; so she lets blood slowly roll back down her throat.

Marcie insists Abraxa walk her home, and then insists she wait while Marcie goes inside to get something. When she comes out, she's dragging a big blue rollaboard suitcase behind her.

It was really nice to see you today, she says, and Abraxa flinches: her voice is so careful. —Can we set a date to see one another again?

No, says Abraxa immediately. —Thanks for showing me your luggage. I want to get home before sunset, okay?

Marcie takes a deep breath. —It isn't my luggage, she says. —It's just some things—some food, blankets—some toilet paper—

I don't want them, Abraxa says. —Thanks, but I really don't.

Well, I didn't want to come meet you, Marcie says, and suddenly she's shouting. —I thought about standing you up. I thought about how good that would feel.

Then she snaps her mouth shut, her eyes horrified. Feel it— some kind of rush from Marcie's eyes to hers, like a hose of feeling pouring into her body. She wants to hold Marcie very tight, wants to tell her it's okay until the horror disappears. She steps toward Marcie. Marcie flinches.

The suitcase has blue canvas sides, slashed at one side by some airport mechanism or vanished cat. She imagines Marcie at home—cursing Abraxa while she stuffs the suitcase with cans, boxes, rolls—and then looks at her here, anger gusting from her shoulders like steam. She imagines herself at the railing of a boat, watching as the other woman treads water. She keeps watching, in her imagination, as Marcie looks at her curiously in the present. The other woman is drowning. Help her not drown.

Give me the suitcase a minute, Abraxa says.

Marcie doesn't move, and Abraxa carefully steps over and takes it. She holds Marcie's gaze, makes sure the other woman is watching. Then she lifts her foot and aims a kick at the dead center of the suitcase. And she must have struck the toilet paper, because the suitcase sinks in and then recoils, springs backward on its rollers to crash against the sidewalk. Marcie is moaning—*stop it*—but Abraxa steps on it anyway, hears a crack. She kicks the corpse off her foot, turns, and walks, pancake sugar fortifying her thrumming muscles.

As she goes, jaw clenched and eyes leaking, her mouth tastes like blood again: she forgot her tooth, she thinks; her tooth is still in the diner, floating at the bottom of her coffee cup.

There's a stranger in her garden when she returns: blond woman, tall and in thick hipster glasses, new black coat and green knit cap matching her striped green leggings. She's squinting at the sigil on the door.

Can I help you, Abraxa asks.

The woman stands up so fast she drops the three-ring binder she's holding: the rings pop open, and documents spill out onto the stones near Abraxa's feet. The woman quickly stoops to pick them up as Abraxa stares down at her. There are forms, pages of text, and what looks like a blueprint. The blueprint contains a map of Northwood. Abraxa is about to pick it up, but the woman grabs it first.

Really sorry, she stammers, her voice thick, —sorry, I'm leaving—

Are you in a band or something, Abraxa shouts at her departing back, wind moving over the raw root in her gums.

She has a dream about Iago that night. In the first part of the dream, he's behind her, his fingertips scraping her back, his smell releasing into her nostrils. Then the dream changes, and she's huddling close to the fire while he pounds on the door. Again and again he pounds on it as he screams her deadname, a word she'd almost forgotten. The door buckles, a cartoon parabola, the padlock she put on the only thing holding it in place. She holds her knees and she watches it, keeping very still, wishing and wishing for the padlock to hold as he screams for her. And then she imagines the sorceress behind her, holding her from behind; the sorceress's hands moving over her wrists and leaving a wetness like olive oil, a smell of spice. The woman behind her whispers, and a strange symbol appears over the buckling door, and she knows it will hold. And she watches the fire flicker and the door pound, humming a melody whose source she can't remember.

When she wakes up, she copies the symbol into her note-book. The next day, she paints it in gold over the door. The day after that, she paints it across the doorjamb, too. She imagines it repeating until it fills every inch of her walls, like fleur-de-lis wallpaper in a grandparent's kitchen; she imagines the smell of cookie butter beneath it.

In another dream, she's surrounded by candles, sitting before the fire. She closes her eyes and sees the ghost of herself stepping out of her chest and onto the church floor. The fire burns tall

like a door, and she walks through it. Eyes closed, she can feel
the earth beneath her feet pushing her upward, and when she
opens her eyes again, she and the sorceress are in a place made
of white sand and red dusk sky. Stars are everywhere, their light
overwhelming.

She holds her arms open, and her skin pimples as the sorceress burns her hoodie and denim away. The sorceress's hands
are all over her, pushing into her body that isn't her body: here
her body is perfect, soft. The sorceress rushes through her like
warm blood, from the base of her spine to the crown, and she
presses a thumbprint into Abraxa's forehead for protection, and
Abraxa opens her eyes.

The sorceress wears white fishnet gloves, a long blue veil
through which her expression is kind.

They walk together over the white sand, where nothing is
growing, until they come to a flat stone plate floating on the
sand. It's decorated by statues: a snake coiled and diving into
a stone basin, a deer fleeing a forest on fire. There are candles.
She squints at the flame: it looks like flickering letters. The walls
are covered in spells. This is what the sorceress is asking her to
build.

She shivers—her body shivers, too, she can feel it somewhere
far away in her sleeping bag, seeking warmth—and with the
motion, the dream blurs and starts to break. The stone temple
shifts, as if it's a sand painting and a hand has just brushed across
its surface. She wants to cry—she wants to hold it together—
she wants this not to leave her, too.

I don't know how to build this, she says. —I'm not good
enough to build this—I don't know what I'm doing—I'm going
to let you down—

Her eyes close, and she feels the sorceress's palms warm on her eyelids. She wakes up to find herself facing the fire, the moonside of her sleeping bag still damp and clinging.

You're good enough—this is what she thinks she heard the sorceress say. But when she wakes up, she's less sure.

Three days later, a heavy rain comes, and she wakes to find water sluicing up from the soil of her garden and over her floor, grains of rice from her ten-pound bag floating on its surface.

The sleeping bag is soaked, the garden flooded, her seeds drifting. The altar and everything on it is secure. The canned goods are protected; her phone is looped over the doorknob on its cord (in a panic, this is what she saved first). Her dry stores are wrecked. Her firewood is useless, her books soaked through. Plaster dust forms islands that change shape, a gasoline skim. She feels calm, in trance as she takes off her socks and shoes and holds them in one hand, watching the flux. This is how it must have felt at the beginning of time, when the world was only ocean, and none of the islands were anchored, and the land might become anything.

As she watches the flood slowly drain through the hole she'd broken in the floor, leaving the trash in the places where the water carried it, she imagines she has the power to reverse time, fix the problem: put the stones she'd sledgehammered free back in place over the raw earth. Seal the cracks in the foundation, too. It can all be salvaged. The sigils she painted along the baseboards have all washed away. Maybe this is a good sign. Maybe the protection diffused with the pigment, and now it's everywhere, an invisible mist. Maybe she's lucky.

7. The Red Flag

Mystic Knights ONLINE is one of the most popular MMORPGs ever created. In *Mystic Knights ONLINE*, you inhabit an avatar whose appearance is totally up to you: you can sculpt her face, nose, brow line, the color of her skin and hair and eyes, whether she is a cat-girl or a rabbit-girl or a bird-girl or any other girl you like. You can dress her in fantastic outfits. The server population of *Mystic Knights ONLINE* is over 100,000 at any given time, certainly at least 70 percent of it transsexual women. Each of you rides the avatar you create—much as spirits possess mortals to experience their physical pleasures and pains, much as once you and your friends summoned the sorceress into Abraxa online—into the mysterious fantasy realm of the Mystic Knights franchise.

Other players exist here, too. You can chat with them in text, like you did in IRC, or via voice chat, or via pre-scripted physical gestures called *emotes*. Every physical emotional state your virtual body is capable of is predefined and scripted, and you can earn new emotional expressions for doing well on challenging quest content. Type in a hotkey command to make your avatar do a spirited harvest dance, or a crisp salute, or a mortified facepalm, or to laugh with simple joy.

There are other parts to this game besides clothes, chat, and emotions. There are also things like combat, questing, and crafting items. It's important not to become too engaged in these pursuits (although neither can you entirely neglect them). This is because you're here to be a professional, and *Mystic Knights ONLINE* is, after all, only a game within a game.

In the real game, your body is your own. You are here to sell it.

To sell your body, you must turn a camera on it and take video. Subscribers will then pay you money to access this. They can use the camera to hear you talk to them, to watch you, via simultaneous streaming, maneuver your cute virtual avatar through the game, defeating monsters and making emotional gestures. For extra cash, they can make you remove pieces of clothing, or even perform sex operations on yourself.

The secret skill of combat in *Mystic Knights ONLINE* is to use your skills to resolve major monster fights as quickly as possible. The secret skill of the real game is to use your skills to do as little as possible for the people paying you, to stretch out their time as much as possible before acceding to their requests. The two games are, other than this key difference in their attitude toward time, shockingly similar. In the classic Mystic Knights games, you spend time and skill to kill monsters to earn gold to reinvest in weapons and armor, which reduces the amount of time and skill needed to kill monsters. In the modern game, you stroke egos, pinch nipples, send direct messages to earn dollars to reinvest in a new camera, mics, a new PC, new outfits. All of that reduces the skill you need to kill time. The game starts to play itself.

This is how it will all work on paper for you, at least. For now, you're a level-one camgirl, and you know you have a lot to learn. So put in your time; get good. Learn to squint at your clients, just strings of text in the chat window of your stream channel. Learn to infer, from what they type, what they want to see in you, and what they secretly need. Then do your best to give it to them. Gain experience. Level up.

Late at night after you sign out, wrapped in your sheets with a mug of cocoa and feeling the burning sword of your unsent email to Abraxa over your head, you marvel at how completely the life you've led has prepared you to do the work you've chosen. It's so easy to become a body in text, to become whatever someone online needs you so badly to be.

What did Lilith need you to be, back then? Ask yourself that, cocoa in your hands, thinking of Tula, her secret space in Prospect Park, the little white boat lodged in the rocks: and imagine the stream rising, the ship rising with it.

A dream one night: you and your friends really did finish *Saga of the Sorceress*. You debut it at the CraftQCon—a New Jersey ballroom of teenagers cheers your name—the three of you toast big ginger ales, first downstairs, then upstairs.

This time the dream is chaste. The three of you speak excitedly on a balcony, and then drift to sleep. Abraxa is first to crash, sprawls on the couch. You and Lilith linger on the balcony. You smooth her hair behind her ear; she shivers at your touch. *Good night*, you say.

Then the dream changes to you sitting on a park bench, alone, as old and creaky as you've become. After a minute, someone sits down at the far end of the bench from you. You can't see her face, but you know this is Lilith. If you look at her you know she will disappear. Don't look at her. Except, in a dream, it's hard not to do a thing; in a dream to imagine something is to do it. Her face is incandescent, hair purple-white. Her mouth, her eyes tight: angry, sad.

I'm so sorry, you tell her.

She nods, slowly.

I understand, she says, and then: —I've missed you, too.

You still believe in this dream for a few minutes when you wake up, earlier than usual, your back aching and well before dawn. But then the sun rises on the same view of the street, the same curtains and sheets, the monitor waiting for you, the same video game you have been playing all your life, which is now somehow your job. And you feel horror, because your regret isn't even strange to you now: it's become constant and normal, almost a place of peace. Perhaps this peace is the ultimate lesson of being in your thirties: realizing that escape was never possible, and so you can rest.

Listen to your father work on his mysterious composition. Close your eyes and let the chords he's playing form pictures: a hot air balloon losing gas, making a controlled descent into a wide canopy of trees, tall teal conifers. Imagine birds on their branches, silent as they watch it fall.

He doesn't hear you when you come out of your room in sweats and night-fogged glasses. His head frowns down at the keyboard, hand feeling out the changes. Watch him until his hand relaxes, and slowly he comes to a stop. He's noticed you, but he's acting like he hasn't. Note this: it's important to him not to be caught knowing as much as he does.

You could speak to him. Instead, heat the pan, crack two

eggs into a bowl. After a moment crack two more, and then add turkey bacon, and then heat greens and Scotch bonnet relish from your mother's Tupperwared leftovers. Load it onto two plates; finish just before your father approaches.

No comments today, he asks; his eyes are scared. —The old man's playing that good?

Don't answer this; just hand him the plate. —I thought we could eat together today, you say. —Is that good with you?

He blinks, twice fast; he doesn't take the food. —Oh, he says. —Well—

You won't be late, you tell him.

He hesitates—but how can you really *know* that he won't be late?—and then he lets himself sit down on the couch, balancing the plate and fork on his thigh. Sit before him on the floor. His face changes as he starts to eat: Have you ever cooked for him before? You don't remember. It's not as if you're some good cook. It's only eggs and leftovers. Anyone could do this.

Really good, he says.

Thank you, you say.

He goes on eating, and you go on eating, unsure what's correct to say next. Maybe nothing is correct.

Are you okay sitting there on the floor, he asks.

I'm fine, you say. —I like the floor.

It's cold on the floor, he says.

Don't reply. He eats a few more bites, and then he sets the plate down.

So how's the video game biz treating you, he asks.

Look at your plate, then look at him.

I quit the video game biz, you say. —It was a stupid, senseless pursuit. I'm never going to work on it ever again.

He nods, slowly.

I don't think I want to do anything creative, you say. —I think I want to be a nurse now. Carry big trash bags full of biohazards around. I'd learn to help people. Something useful, like mom.

He frowns at his plate. Watch him frown at it. Keep watching until the door buzzer goes off. He sits very still. The buzzer goes off again.

Are you going to get that, you ask.

Resigned, he stands up and walks to the buzzer. He presses the button to open the front, but the buzzer just goes off again and again.

Someone must've propped it, he says; his voice comes out high, relieved; this is a normal problem. —Just a minute.

He goes out to solve his normal problem, and he leaves you here. Stare now at your plate, the half of it that's left; you're not hungry anymore. And you don't want to sit on the floor anymore, either. Investigate the question: Why are you doing this? Answer: because there isn't anywhere else to sit. The couch, the piano bench, your chair at your desk: that's all any of you have ever needed.

Your father has been gone for a long time, and this suddenly infuriates you. Did he go to work? Did he actually just take the opportunity to slip out the door, to avoid whatever ambiguous confrontation the two of you were having?

You're furious: therefore go down the stairs, sweatpants whisking over carpet. Good: your father is at the end of the front hall, talking to someone through the cracked door.

Hearing you approach, he turns. His face is the face of a witness to a mass death, a suicide. You stop moving, watching as your father stares, terrified and in awe, into your eyes. Then his interlocutor—shorter, stockier, pastier, unbuttoned cuffs—leans over to see what he's looking at. It's Droneslut.

Feel it: hot, tense fear at the sight of your former client, unmediated by a screen. Suddenly he is very solid, his flabby body wrapped in pinstripe shirt, casual sport coat, expensive earphones. In your mind you see his body unclad, stippled with grisly shadows where you've made him shave himself and ruin his orgasms. Now his body is not six feet away, next to your father's, standing as a kind of protective layer between you. Droneslut's gaping expression: its pupils, once swollen to take in your bitstream splendor, now twisting closed, the better to adjust to your sweatpants, your hoodie, your close-cropped skull. This is the first time he's seeing your jaw without makeup. Watch this body breathe. Watch its capacity for violence.

You need not to go upstairs and hide. If you do, your father will have to speak to Droneslut more than he already clearly has. So be brave: step to where your father is, open the door wider, slide past to the world outside. It's freezing; your skin tightens. Droneslut stiffens, but holds his ground. He stares at your father as if your father is the anomaly, as if he alone knows who you are.

I'll take care of this, you tell your father. —Go back inside.

Your father looks at you as if he wants to argue this, but then he looks at you again: he stops. His expression changes. Turn away immediately from the expression he is making now; do not see it: to get through this situation, you must remain in an even and effective place. Instead, close the door behind you. Listen to footsteps on the stairs, until you're sure your father is gone.

And now here you are, you and Droneslut and the melting snow. Neither of you quite know how to begin, now that you're both bodies and not images. But here your bodies are, here in the insufficient natural light, here on your block, which you know his pasty face has never visited or imagined. A neighbor and her daughter pass you on the way to the corner store, one or two more neighbors are smoking, despite the chill, on alternate stoops. Memories of them speaking to you, as a shy teenager at block parties; memories of them staring you down on the streets, things they called at your back. Times they told you exactly what they wanted to do to you. Don't think of this. There is a present situation to manage.

I thought my last email to you was clear, you say.

Y-yes, my Queen, he says, hiding his eyes.

Imagine a screen between you: an amplifier for your power. —How did you find this apartment?

I looked it up, he says. —You know—the address of the person who owns the domain you email from. I hired a hacker to do it.

You can't help it; you crack up. —You hired a *hacker*? For a WHOIS request?

I'm sorry! he shrieks, and now he can look at you. —But I, I'm sorry, I wanted, I thought—you didn't understand—and if I could just *see* you—I just needed to make sure you heard what I had to say—

He looks down again, his eyes passing over your sweatpants. You stand there, cold. Down the block, a U-Haul thumps over a pothole; a radio plays. The neighbors are now staring at you: the local tranny hooker fighting with her—his?—fighting with its client. This is pathetic—this is what Droneslut must be thinking—this is no one's fantasy. This is not what he paid for.

So you're here, you tell him. —So what did you have to say?

He looks at his feet.

What did you think was going to happen, you ask.

Then wait, and wait, until he answers.

When you get back into the apartment, your father is still sitting on the couch, the plate of food beside him. He looks at you without turning his head; just his eyes slide to you, as if at a stranger in a doorway. His expression from earlier is gone—what had it been, revulsion, anger, concern? Now he just looks tired. His plate is now empty, and somehow this is the most enraging thing of all.

Any questions you want to ask me, you say, surprised at your voice: it comes out thick, like spackle.

He shakes his head, fast, like shaking off a tick.

Give me the plate, you say, and he hands it to you right away. —You're going to be late for work.

Watch him go. Then scrape and wash all the plates. Then, face hot, go to the computer and find the email to Abraxa. Then send it.

On the street, what Droneslut told you was: *I just wanted nothing to change.*

The first words of this sentence were dry, and the rest of the words filled like a sponge. He looked hard at the ground, like he was trying to force all the water back into it, so it wouldn't come out.

Part of you wanted to scream at him: *Shut up! Shut up! Shut up!* But that was just one part. Another part looked at him gently. You could stand closer to him, you thought, closer to this body you controlled through a screen, made do lavish and cruel things to itself. You could embrace him, once more and for the first time: a last softness before you send him on his way. But you're not as strong as Gig had been with you: honestly you're scared, honestly you always have been. So you just watch, arms folded, and finally he turns and walks away. And now the block is only yours again. And in a way, you suppose his wish came true. So did yours.

And meanwhile, across the city from you, in a basement ringed with green bushes finally turning white, imagine your friend, standing with a mop in a puddle that is finally starting to dry. Imagine her holding her phone, at last turning it on. Imagine her checking her inbox. Inside, she finds a tiny red flag.

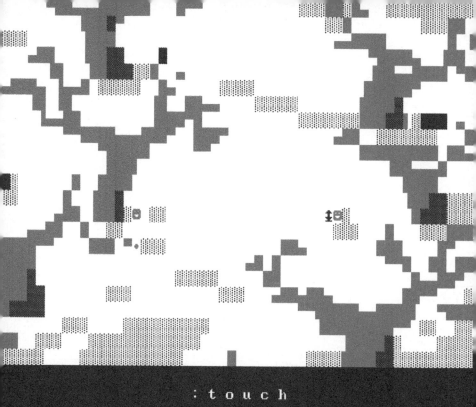

: touch

Trees, and everywhere: birch and aspen and pine, dark spaces against white ground and fog. They'd arrived early, Lilith and Elspet, and there were no human tracks ahead of them, just the passage of bobcats and dogs. They crunched and balanced on staffs taken from a pile that had accrued at the loop trailhead as far away branches broke, ice fell in melt.

Lilith hadn't been to the woods since she was a kid—a Boy Scout, she always made sure to specify—and she'd never been in the woods in the snow. Some ancient part of her came to life as she walked through it: some little kid, let loose inside her big adult transsexual body, kept jumping to peek through the windows of her eyes. They passed trailheads: Shriek Falls, Lost Pond, Victory Vista, Smolder Pass. In this game, you can turn onto any trail you want. What would Lilith find if she did, scrambling up rocks, beckoning Elspet to follow her? Why did it feel so different to be in the woods as a woman? No one could see her here but the other woman who was like her. Her gender had less social meaning than it ever had.

I'm happy, she thought, and the thought made no sense.

Elspet was ahead of her, head bowed to watch her feet on the ice. Lilith found herself enjoying Elspet's discomfort: the way she stuck to the trail map she'd downloaded to her phone with its iffy GPS, the way she hesitated before stepping into slippery brooks. It was so rare to feel butcher than someone, and she wanted to savor it. Elspet had agreed to come up here with her, on her first real vacation out of the city in years, honestly the first vacation she'd ever told herself she could afford. This was also the first time they'd spent more than two consecutive days together. They'd had an understanding. She wondered whether it was changing.

She didn't ask this, exactly. Instead she stayed behind Elspet, letting the woman with whom she had an understanding use the Internet to guide them past trailhead after trailhead, and she fantasized. Suppose they came up here again and took some of those trails. Suppose they moved up here together. Suppose they ate every day in the little diner they'd eaten in this morning, Elspet ordering an irritatingly exact omelet and Lilith wanting one of everything, settling for a Monte Cristo and syrup. How much would it cost to buy one of the small houses in the township? Did she have enough for a down payment as a first-time buyer? Could Ronin help her get good terms through their job? Could they buy a big wooden table for their living room, work at it across from one another, grow rich seasonal crops?

Hold this lightly, she told herself, and then she stopped to watch Elspet. The other woman kept walking.

Hey, Lilith called out, suddenly afraid. Elspet stopped and turned. —Do you want to take slutty photos of me for group chat?

Elspet stopped. She turned and looked at Lilith, her eyes hidden behind circles of fog. —But it's so very cold, she said.

I don't mind, Lilith said. She unzipped her coat, and beneath it unzipped her hoodie. —See?

It was very cold, and she could feel the skin above her sternum start to pimple as Elspet watched her.

Your bra is a ridiculous color, Elspet finally said. She lifted her phone and scanned it over Lilith's body as Lilith let her coat drop into the snow. —It's too bright. It's creating problems for my autofocus.

Sorry, said Lilith, shrugging off her hoodie too and unhooking the bra, pineapple print on magenta. She held the cups to her chest. —Is this better?

Slightly, Elspet said. —We'd get better contrast if you were to lean up against that tree.

They took photos, some five yards between them, until Lilith got cold and they both got too paranoid about somebody coming up the trail after them. Lilith put on her soggy clothes and drank the rest of their cocoa, and they started to hurry along the trail.

Hold me, she told Elspet, and Elspet did. She uploaded the photos of Lilith to the nude-swapping group chat they were both in, and she felt warmth seeping in from Elspet, beside her and far away, and they both went down the mountain as they counted the heart and fire reacts.

The propane truck had visited their cabin, so the heat was extra crispy, and Lilith cooked them supermarket salmon with lemon and shallots. Then Elspet had to do some coding work, so Lilith was alone, and now there was no longer anything to distract her from what she'd seen on her visit to the property on Mercer Street.

It was impossible—wild coincidence—that the sign she'd seen on the steel door of the church had anything to do with her teenage video game company (or rather, three teenagers dressed up as one). The logo was just shapes; it must have been independently invented many times before and since. If she told herself these things enough times, she wouldn't have to believe that her teenage video game company had somehow, after nearly two decades, come back into her life.

So much of her pretransition life was hard to think of, the memory of a protracted illness long ago melted into an undifferentiated mass of bedcovers and pain. But just at the sight of the symbol on the door, her egg days began to return. How she'd used her geometry textbook to hide the maps she drew at her cafeteria table alone—how her backpack felt on her shoulders as she walked through ninety-five degree heat along the brown grass of sidewalkless North Texas streets, minivans whooshing past—how she'd flushed with shame at computer conversations that she was sure no one around her could possibly appreciate or understand. Her memories of her teenage years were blurred underpaintings; all color had been in the memories of Abraxa and Sash, making the greatest video game in the world. Seeing the door had felt like picking up a coin from a field with her own face stamped on it.

She closed her eyes and imagined them: Abraxa, gender-blurred and strange in tie and pleated skirt and impossible tattoos, churning out drawings and game engines, Sash on a tall stool, silver-blue hair streaming down to the floor as she wrote her scripts and visions in the uppermost of a stack of spice-scented old books. And who had she herself been? A tall, bony kid in a shirt her parents had bought her on vacation tucked into khaki shorts, lying on the floor at their feet, scrawling ballpoint maps she'd copied from better video games.

Somewhere she had read that glass is not a solid but a liquid, one that flowed so slowly that no one could perceive it in motion. And yet it pooled at the base of very old window panes. And yet if you were seriously committed to the project, you could push your way back through it; you could swim.

At the same time, the situation seemed palpably unsafe. A property she was working to approve a loan for had now been padlocked and possibly squatted. Squatting was a case of adverse possession; adverse possession was a kind of theft; theft was handled by the police. She tried to picture herself in her cubicle at Dollarwise Investments, picking up the phone to call them on another trans woman.

What do you think of squatters, she asked Elspet, bringing her a plate of radishes from the Airbnb fridge. —Do you like them?

Digital squatters, or physical? Elspet asked.

Physical, Lilith said.

I like them, Elspet said. —We're all living in a big dragon hoard anyway. Use it or lose it.

Lilith nodded; she liked when Elspet got flinty. —My friends and I used to make video games, she said. —They were based on characters owned by a big corporation. That's kind of like squatting.

You and your friends made fan games? Elspet asked. —I didn't know you knew how to code.

There are many things about me you don't know, Lilith said, waggling her eyebrows. —Okay, I can't really code. My friends could, though. I made maps for them.

That's cool, Elspet said, quickly scanning her laptop for notifications.

I got really into making maps for a while, Lilith said. —I had all these notebooks and rules for mapmaking.

What's a rule for mapmaking, Elspet asked. —Like, *always start north*?

Absolutely not, Lilith said. —You have no future as a mapmaker, I'm afraid.

Why did you stop making video games, Elspet asked.

My friends stopped, Lilith said. —So I stopped, too. It wouldn't have led to anything. We never finished a game.

Most things people try don't happen, Elspet said, biting a radish.

So how's the approvals process going, Fionna asked her from the adjoining treadmill.

It's going, Lilith said. —I mean, it's going fine?

They were in Fionna's gym, a week after Lilith's return from the Catskills. Fionna's workout outfit was impeccable, high-rise sweat control runner's capris paired with cigarette-burned Black Sabbath tee and St. Brigid's cross necklace; Lilith's was a gray hoodie plus yoga pants with running shorts worn over the top. It was the first time Lilith had seen her client in months: Fionna had gone upstate after the election, a mini-tour of friend houses in the Finger Lakes with breaks for protests and fundraising. She'd apologized many times to Lilith for being late to respond to inquiries about funding sources, certifications, and due diligence compliance; many times Lilith had told her *it's fine*. Really it was fine: there was so much to be done to bring Fionna's loan proposal up to Ronin's standards, or at least whatever Lilith guessed these might be, and she was nervous about working on this while Ronin was in the office with her. Eventually she would have to come out as someone who believed in approving unsound loans that might help others; she was happy to delay that for as long as she could.

It had given her courage, during the bad weeks since the election—difficult now to remember, the shock at the result that had slowly settled into dread of the immediate inaugural future, now with the start of February mercifully past—to imagine that Fionna was upstate and safe from all of it. She imagined Fionna strolling ragged mountain paths, working on her breathing and gazing at trees. Looking at the world through Fionna's eyes (rather than Buckworth's, or for that matter Sash's) was a comfort: everything looked solid, like you could lean back on a tree and it would bear your weight. Honestly she'd wanted to go to the Catskills with Elspet in part to imagine how Fionna might have seen it. What did it feel like to be safe? She wanted to understand.

Fionna was talking about her plans for the center; Lilith had zoned out again. Fionna talked with hands, one hand gesturing while the other held onto the treadmill, big gestures flung at the glass walls of the second-floor gym. They were mere blocks from Lilith's cubicle at Dollarwise. Fionna had been briefly in the city and called Lilith's cell to ask if she could come by the bank; Lilith had been about to leave for her lunchtime yoga class break, and Fionna had somehow convinced her to come to her own fancy gym network instead. *They have a location right by you, and I have this guest membership thing I never use,* she'd said. *Come on; come let me treat you.* And now here she was, struggling to breathe as she worked through the part of the preprogrammed run that simulated foothills. (In this game, you are a body on a treadmill; you win the game by surviving to the end.) She had worried, on her way over, that she might run faster than Fionna or seem stronger, and that would mean that she was really a man despite everything, but fortunately there was zero danger of this. She huffed and swallowed while Fionna jogged easily, talking about how the healing center might cross-promote with other activist spaces and resistance initiatives, people she'd met doing phone banking and other forms of mutual aid. Lilith was grateful she was out of shape. It reaffirmed the status between them; it kept her gender safe.

These were terrible thoughts. How would Fionna see these thoughts? Fionna would hate her thinking this way, would feel first guilty and then guilty all over again for having reacted badly to being reminded that at the end of the day, Lilith was trans and Fionna was not. A funhouse mirror: Lilith didn't want that for her. Cis people didn't like being reminded of the hurt places at the border between them and others: it was rude to press on it, not the action of a friend. She resolved, breathing hard, to get better at not pressing on it, to make things smoother. The thought that she could do that made her feel stronger, or maybe it was just that the foothill simulation part of the workout program had come to an end.

She wouldn't tell Fionna about the woman she'd seen at the church, she decided. Again, the anomaly was hers to resolve.

After ellipticals, Lilith's phone timer went off. —I've got to get back, she said.

No, Fionna argued. —Let's train forever. Let's get all tough like Sarah Connor. Let's fight the fash in the streets.

But she stepped down from the treadmill, and they crossed to the locker room entryway, which was decorated in lavish gender-symbol inlaid tile. Just before entering, she stopped and turned. She'd noticed, as Lilith had hoped she wouldn't, that Lilith was not following her in.

Aren't you changing, she asked.

Immediately, the reptile part of Lilith's brain scanned the room for threats: the panopticon desk at the center where the attendants worked, the old women on headphones, the lifters in the corner solemnly laboring in Trappist silence. None of them seemed to have heard, or maybe they just didn't want to get involved in the sordid affairs of transsexuals.

I usually don't, she began, but she didn't finish the sentence. To finish might mean explaining her usual post-yoga routine, which was to go to Starbucks, hastily change out of her gym clothes in the lockable private bathroom, and then decompress with a twenty-ounce cup of basically marshmallows and milk until she felt ready to clock back in at work. Through Fionna's eyes, she knew how this routine must look.

You're allowed to use the locker rooms, Fionna said. —It's okay.

Lilith considered her options. Would refusing the offer be more aggressive, or would accepting be? She didn't want to be aggressive; she wanted to be easy, frictionless. In the end, she followed Fionna into the women's locker room. The walls were teal, the lockers pink, the tile beige and gold. No one else was changing on the benches; there were no sounds of steam or water from the shower area; good, safe. She changed, turning her body to face the lockers, trying to make her breathing sound even as she took off first her shoes and pants—the underwear she'd selected that day had lace hems and a giant pink Batman logo; you couldn't see the logo from the front—and then she replaced her leggings and her pencil shirt, and then she took off her sports bra, replaced her professional bra, her cami, her white blouse and cardigan. Her hair was disgusting; she wished she could shower it. The whole time she was petrified; would Fionna talk to her? She knew she was acting weird, like a predator, like a man; to feel less weird, Fionna would try to make small talk with her; that was a normal and understandable social thing to do. But Fionna never talked, just changed in silence. When they finally looked at one another again, Fionna was still wearing the

Sabbath shirt, under a corduroy blazer now, expensive jeans, the same St. Brigid's cross necklace. She smiled, a reassuring smile, and Lilith wondered if she had wanted a shower, too.

On the street they said goodbye. —I really will get back to you about the money stuff soon, Fionna said.

Take your time, Lilith said. Was she speaking too quietly? She felt strange, like someone had turned the colors of the sky either too far down or up.

This is why this is so important, Fionna said suddenly, and she was looking right at Lilith again. —You shouldn't have to be afraid. No one should have to be afraid.

What was Lilith to say? What would make things easiest? She didn't know. She just tried to smile, letting Fionna worry, until the cis woman reached out to touch her on the wrist, once and carefully, like petting a cat who scratched. Then she was gone to catch her train, and suddenly Lilith was back at her desk. How had she come here? She tried to remember. She could no longer say.

* sash joined #teengoetia

* NecroPizza set topic at 2121 PST 2002 20 Dec to ~tumbleweeds, silence~

<abraxa> lol hi

<abraxa> fancy meeting u here

<abraxa> lol

<sash> i . . . can't believe this server is still running.

<abraxa> hahaha rust never sleeps

<abraxa> or lol I mean, love never dies

<abraxa> and neither do irc servers!

<sash> where are you right now?

<abraxa> lol

<abraxa> that question is very complicated!

<abraxa> I mean

<abraxa> I'm at home

<abraxa> lol

<abraxa> just chillin

<abraxa> typin on IRC using a keyboard hotwired into a cell phone by skilllll

<abraxa> might get a bagel later

<sash> okay.

<abraxa> lol where are you?

<abraxa> a/s/l

<sash> also at home. always at home.

\<abraxa\> hahaha okay!

\<abraxa\> coupla homebodies

\<abraxa\> but okay, so, like!

\<abraxa\> what have the last like twenty years been like for you????

\<sash\> that's . . . a really long amount of time.

\<abraxa\> hang on

\<abraxa\> 2017 minus 1998

\<abraxa\> is what?

\<sash\> nineteen years.

\<sash\> it doesn't feel like that long.

\<abraxa\> lol what were we even doing all that time

\<sash\> i was literally not doing anything.

\<sash\> i was sitting at this desk for nineteen years not doing anything at all.

\<abraxa\> lol whoa

\<sash\> it's fine.

\<sash\> it was my choice to do that.

\<abraxa\> whoa

\<sash\> it was my choice not to engage with the outer world in any significant way.

\<abraxa\> bummer lol

\<abraxa\> hahaha this is just like old times already

\<sash\> how?

\<abraxa\> we're just talking about how SAD we are

\<abraxa\> on a computer

\<abraxa\> lol we're like REGRESSING

\<abraxa\> TURNING INTO BABIES

\<abraxa\> turning into babes

\<sash\> we did both do that.

\<abraxa\> the power of voodoo. Who do? You do.

\<abraxa\> lol, wait????

\<abraxa\> what do you mean?

\<sash\> it doesn't matter. we got older, is what i mean.

\<sash\> and you transitioned.

\<abraxa\> hahaha is that what they're callin it

\<abraxa\> sometimes I forget???

\<abraxa\> it's weird; you'd think you'd remember being trans all the time

\<abraxa\> but you kinda don't after a while!

\<abraxa\> just a vague sadness

\<sash\> i understand.

\<abraxa\> DO YOU THOUGH

\<abraxa\> CAN U TRULY KNOW MY PAINNNN

\<abraxa\> lol bc you're like cis or whatever

\<abraxa\> sorry for slurrin

\<sash\> i have to tell you something.

\<abraxa\> hahaha uh oh

\<sash\> which is that i'm concerned about you?

\<sash\> you understand why, don't you?

\<sash\> hello?

\<abraxa\> hahaha, I mean, sure

\<abraxa\> sorry I was thoughtfully chomping on my bagel and that's why I didn't type for a minute

\<abraxa\> it was really poetic

\<abraxa\> you shoulda seen it

\<sash\> so you have food. and presumably electrical power.

\<abraxa\> lol I have water too

\<abraxa\> way too much of it sometimes!!!!

\<sash\> what do you mean?

\<abraxa\> lol nothing there was just

\<abraxa\> a flood thing going on

\<abraxa\> lol it sounds so much worse when I type it out

\<abraxa\> I mean I guess it was pretty bad

\<abraxa\> I couldn't really do anything but wait for the water to go away???

\<abraxa\> which fortunately it did after a while!

\<abraxa\> it kinda wrecked a lot of stuff I was doing though

\<abraxa\> lol but, silver linings! my canned food is fine, and my altar and wires and stuff are still set up in the north room

\<abraxa\> and probably there isn't like asbestos or insulation floating around and seeping into my skin and blooooood

\<abraxa\> lol are you there

\<sash\> yes. i'm trying to think of what to say.

\<abraxa\> hahaha take ur time

\<sash\> i guess first: how long is "a while"?

\<abraxa\> DAYS UPON DAYS

\<abraxa\> no just like—a day

\<abraxa\> I ended up walking around

\<abraxa\> you know, like—I didn't know if I would be able to come back, right?

\<sash\> your house flooded? your apartment? your friend's house?

\<abraxa\> hahaha what a question

\<abraxa\> but anyway I got some paper towels from A PLACE I KNOW

\<abraxa\> and a lot of the water had like, evaporated or drained out or whatever

\<abraxa\> so I was able to wipe down the rest?

\<abraxa\> and now it's smoove sailin

\<sash\> what about mold?

<abraxa> lol what ABOUT it

<abraxa> it deserves to live here too!

<sash> where is here.

<abraxa> I don't want to answer any more questions!

<abraxa> I wanna talk about YOU

<abraxa> WHAT'S BEEN GOING ON IN YOUR WORLD

<abraxa> besides nothing and being sad, lol

<abraxa> but cmon what is your world like??? Are you married and shit? did you have kids???

<abraxa> are they like in college now???

<abraxa> are THEY happy????

<sash> listen—i have to go.

<sash> i have a work shift starting.

<abraxa> lol where do you work

<sash> but i want to keep talking to you.

<abraxa> I'm imagining a big office building like made of crystal

<sash> can we arrange a time to meet?

<abraxa> or like a forest farm where you're like a cult leader, and everyone has to do the weird shit you tell them to

<abraxa> hahaha kinda like our company way back when

<abraxa> but lol yeah, we can arrange a time

<abraxa> I mean I don't know what time it is!

<abraxa> oh but I guess this phone has a clock??

<sash> okay, good. a clock is good.

<sash> then we'll talk more, soon.

<abraxa> lol yeah

<abraxa> I'll come prepared with FRESH QUESTIONS AND FRESH SADNESS

<sash> then i guess i will too.

<abraxa> lol k then, bye

\<sash\> bye
\<sash\> please don't forget. please let's talk again.
\<abraxa\> haha sure
\<abraxa\> i'll find time in my busy schedule!!!
\<sash\> all right, same.

The church on Mercer Street was in a gorgeous part of town from a real estate perspective: brownstone stock, water adjacent, trees, low crime rates and overperforming schools, a solidly professional tenant base, an easy and walkable commute from the PATH train at Grove Street. Lilith imagined a person with investments would see the city as a kind of tactical map: a hot, high-pressure city across the river full of renters caroming around like cartoon molecules. Eventually the river wouldn't be able to contain them: it would overspill its banks, and waves of gentrification would wash across the state line. If she were a person with investments, she would know how to guess exactly where those waves would break. A person with investments would see this neighborhood like a real-time strategy game.

She didn't want to be a person like that, she decided, or not today. She closed her eyes and focused on the walk itself: wind across her cheeks, onion and roasting garlic popping in the metal oven of the bagel cafe around the corner from her destination.

The church, still shrouded in caution tape and plywood, was a neighborhood anomaly. She closed her eyes and tried to imagine it as it would be in the future, once Fionna's loan came through and the healing center was under construction: a rainbow flag, a community bulletin board with colorful notices and pushpins, queer teens milling around the entrance and lounging on the steps, having hopeful conversations. The overlay of that future on this one helped with the dread she was feeling now, being back here in the place where the strange trans woman had shouted at her. Even the company sigil and padlock on the door seemed quaint today, spooky decor at the Tarot reader's booth at the Renaissance festival. There was no reason to be afraid of this place.

She wrote a quick note on one of her business cards—*Lilith Parker, Assistant Loan Manager, Dollarwise, please give me a call!* She looked for a moment at what she'd written, and then she added a drawing of the Invocation LLC logo on the back of the card. Before she could let herself think too hard about it, she slid it under the door. It was done, now, and she'd either get a call or not. The situation would develop however it would.

Her errand done, she went back around the corner to buy one of the bagels she'd smelled as a reward. This is where she found the trans woman she'd seen in the church courtyard: sitting at a table, working furiously in a sketchbook.

She turned and walked out. Around the corner, she pressed her shoulders into the red brick, willing her breathing to slow. The woman was sitting inside, through the window glass, only feet away. Lilith went back in, not letting herself look. The barista and two of the customers glanced at her as she reentered: *suspicious, transsexual.* The other woman continued to draw.

Lilith ordered a bagel and a latte with rose and vanilla syrups, mixed. Holding them, the surface of the coffee shaking, she sat down in the seat next to the woman she'd come to find.

The bagel store was hothouse warm against the late-January chill outside; slant winter sun shone on her table, and the window glass sweated. She paced out her latte and stole looks at the woman. The woman's sketchbook was worn, its metal rings bent and in one case missing, and she was working over a page with what looked like a colored pencil. A charcoal-steeped etui sat next to her, other pencil stubs and smudged erasers spilling from it like a cornucopia. A cell phone charged on an outlet close to the floor behind her, its cord dangerously looped around her chair.

Her face was the hardest to look at. Up close, she seemed much older than Lilith had initially assumed—thirty-eight? Forty-five?—with streaks of gray along her dirty blond hairline, purple circles under her eyes, cracks in her rash-red skin. She wore the same hoodie, leggings, bandanna, and shorts she'd been wearing when Lilith had last seen her, and she smelled intense, at first terrible in a way that came around again to good: like a wheel of cheese in a cave, a red clay oven baking sourdough bread. Lilith had the sense that if she touched the woman's skin, her fingertips would singe.

So *are* you in a band, the woman asked her, not looking up.

Lilith tried to think of every good reason not to respond to this. She thought of lots of them. —No, she finally said. —I work in a bank?

The woman started to laugh, and Lilith blushed: Was the laughter with or at her? It seemed to be neither, a tangent laughter. —The two genders, the woman said.

Lilith let herself sip her drink. —Why did you think I was in a band?

You look like you're in a band, the woman explained. And suddenly she really was looking at Lilith; she closed her sketchbook, turned her chair to face her head-on. —You're tall, and you have those glasses. You're like a hot bass player.

Lilith suddenly thought of a childhood trip to the Dallas Zoo, where she'd met a jaguar. The animal had been glassed in, muscle and velvet and golden motion, and in Lilith's memory she had walked right up to the glass, not six feet from Lilith, and looked her full in the face. The great cat missed nothing, she'd thought, and all Lilith could do was look back and slow-blink: the cat signal for *I am not a threat. I don't need to see all of you.* She found herself slow-blinking this woman. She told herself to stop.

What are you drinking, the woman asked. —It smells like flowers!

A rose vanilla latte, Lilith said, instinctively cupping it closer.

Yum, said the woman. —Will you buy me one? I'm asking because you work in a bank. And there's money in a bank.

There is, said Lilith.

It's like a dog pound for money, said the woman.

A little, said Lilith. —Sometimes they let us take the money out on walks.

The woman hadn't really been smiling before, Lilith realized, just grimacing: but now this changed, like the volume had turned up on the sun.

My money's not gone, the woman said, distorting into a silly voice that further confirmed her transfemininity to Lilith: all trans women could do characters. —It's just living on a farm upstate!

Lilith happily bought her a drink. The barista's look at her was like a cold splash on sunburned skin—*be careful*—but he rang up the extra drink in silence. Suddenly ashamed, she gave him a custom 300 percent tip, and she brought the second rose vanilla latte to the woman at the table. The woman immediately picked up it, pulled Lilith's half-empty mug close to her, and refilled it to the brim from her own cup.

Now we're sharing, the woman said. —Even stephen.

Thank you, Lilith said.

You're welcome, said the woman.

The woman was becoming more comfortable with her, Lilith decided. She drew comfort from this.

So what's a bank girl like you doing here in Jersey City, the woman asked. —Just checking out the bagel stores and churches? They're good here!

Lilith flinched. She looked at the surface of her mug, trying to work out how much truth she should meet the woman with.

I'm here sort of on bank business, and sort of not, she said. —It's complicated.

Like a secret identity, the woman said excitedly.

Kind of, Lilith said, also suddenly excited at this thought. She decided to be bold. —I'm looking at a building here for a friend, she said. —A bank friend.

Like Uncle Pennybags, the woman said, nodding. —I'm following.

She's—kind of like Uncle Pennybags, I guess, Lilith said. —Sure.

You like to say *kind of*, said the woman. —And *sort of*.

Lilith looked at her coffee. —I'm sorry.

It's okay, said the woman. —Ha ha, I mean, it's *sort of* okay.

Lilith didn't look up.

Hey, said the woman. —I'm sorry.

Lilith waited for the woman to say the final *kind of*—she was sure the woman was thinking it, as she was sure the barista was looking at her, the people at the next table, too. She found herself breathing deeply, a kind of emotional regulation muscle memory that felt nostalgic; how long had it been since someone had made fun of how she spoke to her face like this? If she hadn't suspected this woman of being someone from her teenage IRC days before, she certainly did now. But the woman had been quiet for some time. When Lilith finally looked up, the woman's face had changed. Her eyes were wide, jaw hanging loose to show the void behind her teeth.

I'm sorry, she said, in a very different voice.

And Lilith felt for a moment like a double exposure—a young tree superimposed on a grown one—as she responded to her teenage coworker. —It's okay, she said.

They didn't talk any further about Lilith's business, or her bank friend. Instead, the woman in the cafe asked to draw her, and she consented. In part this is because while the woman was drawing her, Lilith could watch her in silence. Again she thought of her childhood jaguar, and how wrong she'd been then. As a child, she'd thought the jaguar's power came from its simplicity: the cat wanted to eat her, and was trying to decide whether or not she was a threat or a friend. There was some of that to the woman, too. But the jaguar's real power was in its mystery: the absolute unknowability of its mind. The woman's face concealed no emotions—had no filter—but there was something besides emotion sealed up in there with her. A codebook, maybe, one against which everything she felt, thought, and said had to be translated. Lilith knew how important it was, when relating to others, to know how everything you did would ultimately be perceived. But this woman had no power to do that. Lilith couldn't decide whether to feel pity or awe.

The woman must have been Abraxa. She was about the right age, underneath the roughness and damage, and she *felt* right to Lilith, and there were no other real suspects. No other CraftQer could possibly have cared about their logo enough to remember it and carve it into a door. The only other possibility was Sash, and Sash had been cis. Sash had also been nothing like this woman: this woman was outwardly unguarded, inwardly inscrutable. Sash had been the opposite, at once deeply secretive and obvious.

She didn't want to think of Sash right now; she'd barely thought of Sash for years, really. Instead she tried to find reasons to believe that this in fact wasn't Abraxa—just some fascinating derelict, just someone to whom she had no connective ties. This was difficult because part of Lilith wished very much for it to be Abraxa. The CraftQ part of Lilith's life had been so charged and yet so difficult to explain: *my friends and I made video games when we were kids! But not real video games; they were made of text; they looked like garbage. And we traded our garbage with one another, and we pretended to be corporations, and it was all online.* She wished she had just been in a cult; it would have been simpler to explain.

But a deeper part of her never wanted this to be Abraxa. This was because Abraxa had been brilliant—hypertalented, creative, funny, fearless. If this woman was Abraxa—this unwashed, aging, complicatedly haunted woman before her, this woman who had scammed her out of money for a drink and who was very likely squatting in the building Lilith was responsible for—then key things Lilith had understood about the world and her place in it had been wrong.

So she hoped, prayed, willed this not to be Abraxa. And she had really talked herself out of it when the woman finally finished her portrait and turned the sketchbook around for Lilith to see it. The drawing was vivid, Lilith's image against a background of dead grass and leafless trees behind a black iron gate. Abraxa had drawn her looking lovely and sad, which is how Lilith realized she was both. But the portrait took up only half the sketchbook page: a long string of CraftQ object code took up the rest.

On the PATH train home, she wondered what she would do. She'd avoided telling the woman—Abraxa—her name. Maybe this gave her some room to breathe. If the woman didn't know who they were to one another, it would be easier to forget all of this. She could drop Fionna's application—or no, she could quietly complete the work and leave the problem for Fionna to resolve; she didn't need to say anything about what she'd seen. Or she could call the police to resolve it. Abraxa would never know who'd made the decision to betray her.

Two thoughts came to her then, and for years, she would wonder which had come first. One, she couldn't do that to Abraxa, ever. And two, something that, in the shock of Abraxa's physical presence, she had managed to forget: she had already left her business card—and her name, and her email address. There they were, under Abraxa's metal door, fully out of Lilith's reach.

<irc.austnet.net, channel #teengoetia, 1105 PST 2017 24 Feb>

* sash joined #teengoetia

<abraxa> yayyyyy

<abraxa> HONEY, YOU'rE HOME

<abraxa> how was work????? Hahaha

<sash> work, yes

<sash> i guess work was good.

<sash> i'm getting used to the daily game loop.

<abraxa> lol whoa

<sash> on login, i travel to the hub city, bell prix. i check all my gear sales, and i make sure my retainer has appropriate work to do.

<sash> i set some crafting macros while i prune my direct messages, guild invitations. i build my schedule in my notebook.

<sash> i sync with iriul doomcat. She's the leader of the guild I work for, and she brokers appointments with regulars.

<abraxa> lol whoa

<abraxa> is iriul doomcat trans???

<sash> one can infer that iriul doomcat is trans.

<sash> iriul doomcat is a reasonable employer, as well.

<abraxa> hahaha cool. Team iriul doomcat!

<sash> anyway, then I socialize with other players and make them ejaculate.

<sash> and then, if i'm not exhausted, i find a group to raid some high-end content.

<sash> and then i go to sleep.

<abraxa> hahaha whoa

<abraxa> SOUNDS LIKE A FULL DAY

<sash> strange observation: raiding content is very similar to making players ejaculate??

<abraxa> hahaha do u remember how saga of the sorceress was gonna have sex battles

<sash> oh my god, that's true.

<sash> the ssbe

<abraxa> STRATEGIC SEX BATTLE ENGINE

<abraxa> you chose shit like CARESS and WHISPER and STROKE

<abraxa> lol and it cost you mana and stuff

<abraxa> and I guess it made enemies die or something

<abraxa> le petit mort

<abraxa> except it was like a dragon

<sash> well, that isn't too different from what i do now.

<sash> the mana is my will to live.

<abraxa> hahaha well I hope this convo is recharging that for u

<sash> maybe. we'll see.

<abraxa> lol well!!!!! that is a fun work story

<abraxa> me, I only do THE LORD'S WORK now

<abraxa> or I mean I guess I do other stuff???

<abraxa> I drew someone in a cafe today!!!! That is sorta work!

<abraxa> it was SUPER WEIRD

<abraxa> I feel like I'm like . . . losing touch with stuff like that

<abraxa> lol do you know what I mean

\<sash\> i think so, but go on?

\<abraxa\> I used to draw like, everyone

\<abraxa\> on my travelz

\<sash\> i think i saw you post some of that to one of your blogs.

\<abraxa\> probably!!!! I did it like ALL THE TIME

\<sash\> it was a drawing of two trans women standing in a pool of water.

\<sash\> i guess it was at sunset? everything looked incredibly dark, like the last light was coming through the branches

\<abraxa\> hahaha one was prolly me

\<abraxa\> I like drawing myself, I'm a freakkkk

\<sash\> the features weren't clear. both of them were in water to their navels.

\<sash\> there were trees with gigantic roots spreading into the water.

\<sash\> they got more thin as they rose into the air, and then they burst into so many leaves.

\<sash\> it must have taken you so long. i remember being so jealous that you could do that.

\<abraxa\> lol, so, part one, awwww <3 thank u

\<abraxa\> but part two, omg you fuckin freak!

\<abraxa\> All rememberin some random drawing I did like twenty years ago

\<sash\> it would have been no more than ten years. but go on.

\<abraxa\> lol

\<abraxa\> ugh, I wish I remembered what it looked like! I wish I could see it again

\<abraxa\> it was probably of marcie and me in florida??

<abraxa> that is the main swamp I have been in anyway???

<sash> who is marcie?

<abraxa> lol, nvm

<abraxa> I don't have any of that stuff anymore

<abraxa> it just like vanished over the years???

<sash> you didn't preserve any of it?

<abraxa> do I look like a preservative????

<abraxa> nah it just got lost or left behind in moves or thrown away in people's attics and whatnot!

<abraxa> I wish I still had it! It's a good way to remember stuff!

<abraxa> You can look at pictures of people you drew and be like, damn, this bitch owes me money

<abraxa> you can ANALYZE your PAST for PATTERNZ

<sash> i think that is something i should . . . do less of?

<abraxa> hahaha I mean, DO YOU

<abraxa> but neway it was nice drawing someone!

<sash> if it was you and someone else, it looked like somewhere i would want to be, and someone i would want to be with.

<sash> i think i was envious of that too.

<abraxa> yeah, well

<abraxa> I don't really see folkz much down here

<abraxa> DOING THE WORK OF THE SORCERESS

<abraxa> lol did I tell you about all that

<abraxa> I'm actually really freaked out to have typed that!

<abraxa> I didn't really intend to!!!!

<abraxa> [[x-files song.mp3]]

<sash> you . . . did not tell me this.

<sash> what do you mean?

\<abraxa\> lol well, okay

\<abraxa\> so like, this is hard to expain?

\<abraxa\> but I guess I kinda sorta moved into the basement of this church I kinda sorta had a key to

\<abraxa\> it had something to do with marcie

\<abraxa\> the one in the picture, I mean

\<abraxa\> lol, the swamp girl you were all jellies of

\<sash\> go on.

\<abraxa\> hahaha anyway I have been kinda sorta living down here for . . . I'm not actually sure how long

\<abraxa\> I think at first it was just like—I was just mad at her or something??

\<abraxa\> like I had other reasons but I feel like a lot of it was just I needed a place to go and this was a place to go

\<abraxa\> but then it's like—that was part of it, and there was this other part

\<abraxa\> and the two parts kinda switched

\<abraxa\> lol sorry I' m making like zero sense.

\<abraxa\> A SMALL SIDE EFFECT OF BEING TOTALLY CRAZY, YOU SEE

\<sash\> what was the other part?

\<abraxa\> the other part was like

\<abraxa\> um

\<abraxa\> I'm trying to figure out how to say

\<abraxa\> it's like it has to do with the sorceress from mystic knights?

\<abraxa\> the one we were making the game about

\<sash\> yes, i know which sorceress you meant.

\<abraxa\> haha ofc you do

\<abraxa\> and how like—I dunno. I keep thinking about

how there were all kinds of like, OCCULT SEEKRETS
programmed into the game?

<abraxa> like how the designers at the critical hit in japan
in like 1988 or whenever they started making those
games were like

<abraxa> copying symbols from like grimoires and stuff
into the game to idk, make it all cool and metal

<abraxa> remember? We used to talk about this all the
time, like eight million billion stories about oshiro49 and
that programmer dude

<abraxa> but I think they maybe actually like . . . work???

<abraxa> lol YOU ARE VERY QUIET OVER THERE,
HOTKEYS

<abraxa> are you okay??? Everything cool in sashland???

<sash> yes, I'm fine.

<sash> it's oshiro99, not 49

<sash> can I say back to you what I think you're telling me,
to make sure I understand?

<abraxa> sure!

<sash> you believe that the mystic knights games have
occult symbols in them that really have occult properties.

<sash> and that has something to do with why you're still
living beneath this church?

<abraxa> lol yeah like

<abraxa> I dunno

<abraxa> like, what if the sorceress is REAL

<abraxa> like a real living goddess or force or whatever,
that we summoned that time on IRC

<abraxa> and we were supposed to finish our game to
bring her message to more people

<abraxa> and we DIDN'T?

<abraxa> ???

<abraxa> lol you got quiet again

<abraxa> maybe because I said something crazy again

<abraxa> except what if it ISN'T crazy

<abraxa> what if I'm not crazy!

<abraxa> what if you're the one who's crazy!

<abraxa> what if all I wanted was a pepsi!

<sash> sorry. I'm thinking of something.

<abraxa> and they wouldn't eveahahah okay haha sorry! I'll be more patient!

<sash> I was thinking of a conversation I had with someone recently.

<sash> or actually it wasn't even a conversation. They did all the talking. It was at my friend's reading.

<sash> they were talking about a church that a bunch of game bros were forming.

<abraxa> !!!!! X FILES THEME SQUARED

<abraxa> RIGHT EXACTLY

<abraxa> there has to be a REASON you heard that!!!!

<abraxa> lol I'm like PHYSICALLY SHAKING HERE

<abraxa> I'm FREAKED OUT, FRIENDO

<sash> except, like.

<abraxa> except what?????

<abraxa> lol you keep gettin all silent

<sash> it's hard for me to say this to you now.

<abraxa> hahaha just say stuff when it's hard to say it

<abraxa> that's the abraxa way

<sash> all the stuff about the critical hit people coding grimoires and occult properties into mystic knights?

<sash> is actually . . . something I made up?

<sash> hello?

<abraxa> lol

<abraxa> you're fuckin with me

<abraxa> playin a fast one on ol brax

<sash> no, it's true?

<sash> or rather, it's false

<sash> i made it up. i'm really sorry.

<sash> i'm trying to even remember why I did this.

<sash> i think it was kind of like . . . a marketing idea?

<sash> like a way to give the game we were making mystique. like we had seen some magical truth in it other people couldn't see.

<sash> i definitely felt like there was some kind of truth in it. i felt so many things then.

<sash> i think i just really wanted us to make this game together.

<sash> that's the best answer i have. i'm really sorry.

<sash> i think i forgot over the years that it wasn't true.

<sash> hello?

<abraxa> I'm here

<abraxa> WEIGHING YOUR FATE

<sash> i understand if you don't want to be my friend anymore.

<abraxa> lol so like,

<abraxa> I'm trying to follow the abraxa way here

<abraxa> of just saying stuff when it's hard to say it???

<abraxa> but I don't even know what I want to say

<abraxa> see, the CRAZY in me wants to like—DOFF MY CAP TO YOU, MADAM

<sash> i wish you wouldn't call yourself crazy.

<abraxa> because that is kind of an amazing story for a teenager to make up??

\<sash\> that's not a word i ever want to use for you.
\<abraxa\> hahaha okay what's a better word?
\<sash\> i don't know what word is right, sorry.
\<abraxa\> okay
\<abraxa\> or I mean, I dunno if it's okay?? Maybe??
\<abraxa\> can I like
\<abraxa\> sign off for a while
\<abraxa\> and think about it
\<abraxa\> alone
\<abraxa\> and in the dark
\<sash\> :(
\<sash\> of course.
\<sash\> would it be okay if we set a time to meet again?
\<abraxa\> lol, u worried I'm gonna ghost u
\<abraxa\> bitch its u who are the ghost!!!
\<abraxa\> RETURNED FROM THE DEAD
\<sash\> please just say you'll come back to chat again, okay?
\<abraxa\> lol sure
\<sash\> okay, thank you for letting me say that and not going away.
\<abraxa\> u r welcome
\<abraxa\> good nite, piss pal
\<sash\> good night.
\<abraxa\> <3
* abraxa has left #teengoetia
\<sash\> <3.

Here is my question to you, Elspet asked. —Exactly why do you care?

Lilith frowned at her own ceiling, head cushioned by Elspet's fuchsia-striped programmer stockings.

Is that a Real Question, she said. —Or just a question where you want to say what you think about a thing?

It's a genuine question, Elspet said, although Lilith knew this didn't mean anything; people always assumed their own questions were genuine. —This is someone you knew, sort of, in high school. Before you were even out, correct?

Out: her mind flashed to an IRC window, the last night with Sash. Don't think about Sash. —Correct, she said.

So I understand online friends, Elspet said. —And I understand trans friends that we meet before we're out. I understand why you would logically have an interest in reactivating those connections. Memory nodes you can only access mutually. A fuller and more truthful collective picture of your past. These make sense to want.

Lilith rolled her face to the side, cheek pressing into Elspet's thigh; she imagined her face covered in big corduroy stripes. —Go on, she said.

What I understand less is you thinking there's something you have to *do* here, Elspet said. —Beyond enjoying whatever I don't know, calibration you get from this one meeting. I think you should do nothing. And yes, my question is genuine, to the extent that I don't get why this isn't also obvious to you.

Lilith lay there, imagining the other woman's bones were secretly made of Terminator steel, couched somewhere deep within a warm silicon and nanogel flesh that made her feel more human.

Do nothing, unless she does, Elspet repeated. —Meet her for coffee if she calls you, or emails you. Neither of which she's done yet, correct? In the week that you've been stewing about this.

Lilith rolled off Elspet's lap and landed softly on her thick area rug. She closed her eyes and spread her arms wide like a vinyl shag angel, feeling the floorboards hold her up. —Correct, she said.

So why not continue to do that, Elspet asked.

Because, Lilith said angrily. —Because! Because I'm not sure. —She closed her eyes again. —Because we're connected, she said.

Everyone's connected, Elspet said. —It's an uninteresting tautology to say you have a connection to another person. What matters are the connections you choose to cultivate. Why choose to cultivate this one?

Because it's cultivated already, Lilith said. —Because!

Don't shout at me, Elspet said, and on instinct, Lilith clamped her lips.

So you were connected in the past, Elspet continued after some time. —Therefore you must be connected in the future. Because nothing in the universe should ever change its state. Is this your real argument?

Lilith stood up, focusing on keeping her lips touching.

I'm going to make us dinner, she said. —Do you want dinner? I have veggie sausages, and some broccoli and garlic, and different shapes of pasta. Which shape of pasta do you want me to make.

This woman is like, homeless, Elspet said.

She's squatting, Lilith said, pulling boxes from her cupboards as noisily as she could. —I have rotini. I have penne. I have wagon wheels. I have dinosaurs.

No, that's bullshit, Elspet said. —I have friends who squat. They make plans, and develop support networks, and legal strategies. They have an understanding of their purpose and their boundaries. It's an act of serious political resistance to property and capital as constructs. They take it seriously.

Maybe my friend does too, Lilith said. She chose the dinosaurs, which she knew Elspet would like least.

Elspet sighed and rested her head on her elbows, gazing over the back of Lilith's couch, maybe as if she were watching a simple child at play. —It's really nice that you want to help your friend, she said. —Maybe you could help her by making her some food, if she asks. Or maybe talking to her sometime, again, if she asks.

Leave me alone, Lilith said, quietly enough so that Elspet might not hear it.

Maybe you could introduce her to some support groups, Elspet said. —Or outreach services.

What services do you mean, Lilith said, turning around.

There are services, Elspet said. —My point is—I'm not a monster. There are lots of people I would help too, if I could do that. But this isn't just about how I feel, or how you feel, you know? This is systems theory. This is math. A person is a negative inventory of energy and time. There's only so much energy and time we have to contribute.

Stop calling my friend a negative inventory of energy and time, Lilith said.

This is *your friend* now, Elspet said.

Yes, said Lilith, and saying it seemed to flood her with something, and she let the *yes* grow inside her chest. —Yes, she's my friend, and I'm in a position to help her. So I will.

Elspet fell silent as the water prepared to boil.

What do you think the cis woman will say, she said after a moment. —When you tell her.

Lilith watched the pot. —Don't call Fionna *the cis woman*, she said.

Elspet stretched her wrists above her head. —May I sketch an argument for you, she said. —Is that okay.

Sure, said Lilith, silently willing the water to boil harder, to boil over its edges, to steam as it struck the gas jets.

Goods cost resources, Elspet explained. —This is because of the physical laws of the universe. You cannot move from disorder to order without paying an uphill cost in money, time, calories, emotional effort.

Lilith tore open the box of dinosaurs while Elspet continued to explain things to her: that the laws of thermodynamics were paid for by work, that trans women were systematically excluded from work, other than tech work or sex work—*heaven or hell*, as one of Elspet's friends had once described these; Lilith wondered if Elspet imagined herself to be an angel—the fact that Lilith had somehow failed to work in either of these fields notwithstanding. This state of affairs, Elspet explained, meant that trans women had fewer resources, which meant less capacity to create order. Trans women were inherent sources of entropy. They lead messy lives; they hurt one another; they drain one another; they fuck one another up. She just kept talking and talking while Lilith stared angrily at the dinosaurs in the pot, willing them to soften and die and grow extinct all over again.

I understand, Lilith said. —You're trying to say that I shouldn't help my friend because either I'll fuck her up, or she'll fuck me up, or everyone will fuck everyone up.

I'm saying other things too, but basically yes, Elspet said.

So why do anything, said Lilith. —Why not just die.

What I'm *actually* saying, continued Elspet, —is that you, Lilith, have personally and in ways I've witnessed worked hard and put up with shit to be in a position of relative order—

Which is why I should use that to help my friend, Lilith said. —Good, I think so, too. Thank you for talking to me about this.

No, said Elspet. —Because when you help your friend, you're going to *lose* that position. So you'll need help, too.

Lilith continued to watch her dinosaurs: their semolina skin had melted; they had boiled now to mush.

And the total transsexual-woman capacity to create order will diminish as a result, Elspet added.

Aren't you a communist, Lilith finally replied.

No, I believe in a revolutionary transition to communism, Elspet said. —What you're describing isn't revolutionary. It's sentimental. It's stupid.

Lilith let the word *stupid* echo around the clouds of ptero-dactyl steam, and then she reached to turn off the stove, and the fire stopped.

I think I can do both things, she said, knowing she must sound like a child.

Elspet turned back to her computer. The argument had been settled.

Whenever it was hard to stay in New York, Lilith remembered that at least Brooklyn was on an island, and that at least she could go to the beach. It was Sunday, and she took the bus south down Flatbush, watching old men and women in suits and bonnets get off at storefront churches as she sat in one of the sideways seats toward the back, which would let her compress her long legs as much as possible and let the city flow around her. But slowly the bus emptied, and she could let herself relax and slump, here in a state where she could no longer hurt or inconvenience anyone.

She loved Riis Beach in the summer, sprawled back in a towel and sunglasses with her arms at her sides and her pale nipples broiling in reflected window light from the former asylum, showing off the body she and hormones had collaborated on. A beach setting permitted her sexuality to be blessedly undirected; she could be only a sandy object for other eyes to rest on, nestled among grills, towels, and tents. But she loved the beach in the winter, too. In the summer, the beach was for any queer; in the winter it was just for you. Today was a good day, the wind cold but not fast, moving dry sand over wet in patterns that you could almost read. No one was out but a few stray middle-aged couples with jackets and dogs and a lonely man with a metal detector, moving around the piled-up dunes. Someone had died, and there was a memorial on the seawall made of snuffed candles, streamers, and shells. She sat among them, kicked her feet to shake off sand, and wondered what she was supposed to do.

Sometimes she loved New York, despite her fear of other people. The queers were thicker here, like mosquito clouds, and she felt a strange pride at surviving as one of them through rent spikes and awfulness. She loved her job sometimes: she was a kind of valve within a big artery of a harbor, someone who had a tiny say in who built what where and when. She'd liked working with Fionna on this—no, she still liked working with

Fionna; the work wasn't past yet! Working with Fionna was like working with Sash had been, except Fionna was real, and Sash hadn't been, not really. Lilith was part of a real corporation now. Why would she trade that reality for a chance to help some coworker from her former fake corporation? Really, why?

When Elspet had asked her the same question, she'd responded by calling Abraxa her friend. She watched the waves, and she asked herself: Did I mean it? She thought she did. Abraxa was her friend; she was Abraxa's. So what did a friend owe to a friend? How much could a friend expect you to give up?

She was a bad person, she thought, for framing it that way: as if her friend was taking something away from her. Staring at the waves, she let her thoughts drift, and she tried not to feel this way.

Maybe we owed a friend our best efforts to help them lead the life we think is best for them to live. We owed a friend our help, honesty, advice, support. How could she best give these things to Abraxa? She could broker a meeting with Fionna. She could coach Abraxa on what to say. She could teach the other woman to code—no, Abraxa knew how to code—maybe she could help get her into a coding boot camp, so she could work as a coder. Maybe they could have nice evenings together, and Abraxa would laugh about how hard it was to be a coder, and she could complain about her job too, and they could both feel better and safe.

All the ideas were sliding across her mind like eggs over Teflon, like the sand over the sand. She was no good at thinking through anything to any level of detail; she knew she never had been. She was on the beach, and she didn't know what to do. These two facts were all she had.

Someone had left a cigarette lighter on the seawall, next to one of the candles. She tested it: three clicks and a white flame. Blocking the wind with her body, she lit one of the candles in glass jars, and she sat with it for a while, guarding its flame with her hands so the wind couldn't erase it. The three of them sat there like that for a while—her body, the wind, the flame, and facing them, the sea—and she protected it as best as she could for as long as she could. And maybe this is all we owed a friend.

<irc.austnet.net, channel #teengoetia, 1114 PST 2017 1 Mar>

* sash joined #teengoetia
<abraxa> hahaha look whose come crawlin back
<abraxa> so I have been THINKING
<sash> okay?
<abraxa> and I think like—you said you just made up all
   the stuff about how the programmers of mystic knights
   put all kinds of occult secrets into it
<abraxa> and how the sorceress was real
<abraxa> and here is what I think!
<abraxa> I think maybe you made it up
<abraxa> but now, it doesn't matter that you made it up?
<abraxa> because like ten thousand years ago, or when-
   ever it was when we were teenagers, IN THE NINETIES
   AND ALL
<abraxa> I believed you?
<abraxa> and so she is real, now, to me
<abraxa> right?
<sash> in a sense, yes?
<abraxa> lol not in a sense, that's what I'm trying to tell you
<abraxa> like, whatever basically!!! You done a BAD but
   it was A LONG TIME AGO and I don't even think it was
   bad. The end!
<sash> okay.
<sash> thank you.

<abraxa> whatever! No reason to thank me!

<abraxa> thank YOU for giving me RELIGION

<abraxa> THAT OL TIME RELIGION

<abraxa> hahaha god like

<abraxa> talking to you lately

<abraxa> it makes me think of like, the Old Times

<sash> i really only think of the old times anymore.

<abraxa> so okay

<abraxa> tell me your thoughts about the old times then!

<abraxa> like

<abraxa> drumroll

<abraxa> why did you break up the company??

<abraxa> I mean like! We were doing GREAT

<abraxa> like you and me, making this whole big game full
         of biG IDEAS

<abraxa> haunted and sexy and weird and fucked up and
         full of teen-age spirit!!

<sash> i didn't leave first. lilith did.

<abraxa> yeah well what did she even do??

<abraxa> like what, she made the levels?

<abraxa> anyone could have done that!

<sash> why did you call lilith she?

<abraxa> lol

<abraxa> I guess I did that

<abraxa> A FUNNY SLIP, EH

<abraxa> but really like: what was the deal with lilith??
         Why was lilith so important that you had to break up the
         whole thing?

<abraxa> I KNOW YOU ARE BEING SILENT AND WEIRD
         NOW SO I WILL JUST SIT HERE AND WAIT FOR AS
         LONG AS YOU NEED OKAY

\<abraxa\> sitting
\<abraxa\> waiting
\<abraxa\> eating a big ol sandwich
\<abraxa\> I mean not really
\<abraxa\> I mean I guess I could get one
\<abraxa\> somehow
\<abraxa\> I could get a stale bagel with one
\<sash\> the reasons are complicated.
\<sash\> can i tell you the reasons some other time.
\<abraxa\> hahaha I guess
\<abraxa\> AS LONG AS THEY ARE NOT MORE STRANGE LIES
\<sash\> i am trying not to do that anymore.
\<sash\> other than i guess to my family about my work and conditions of life
\<sash\> and by omission to essentially everyone
\<sash\> you are actually the person i talk to most now, i think. maybe tula.
\<sash\> (tula = my friend)
\<abraxa\> hahaha awww
\<abraxa\> SPOILER, I LIKE TALKING TO YOU TOO
\<abraxa\> I mean I like talking to a lot of people, but like
\<abraxa\> like when I moved down here
\<abraxa\> I got into a space where I thought I wasn't supposed to talk to anyone anymore??
\<abraxa\> like . . . how system D is in mystic knights 3??
\<abraxa\> remember?
\<sash\> with the lampposts.
\<abraxa\> YES YES THAT
\<abraxa\> lol see this is why it is good to talk to you!
\<abraxa\> WE HAVE A COMMON WORLDDDDDD

\<sash\> i don't throw you off course.

\<abraxa\> it's more like, whatever WEIRD MAGIC was in those games

\<abraxa\> you got exposed to it too???

\<abraxa\> lol, you were like the mastermind of it!

\<sash\> but i told you that wasn't real.

\<sash\> all those stories about the critical hit—i mean, i read a gaming magazine about them

\<sash\> but it just talked about how they all really liked dungeons and dragons, and about graphics and full motion video programming

\<sash\> it wasn't about summoning extradimensional sorceresses.

\<abraxa\> but like here is the thing: it doesn't matter now if it wasn't real then

\<abraxa\> because it is now?

\<abraxa\> because I believed it then

\<abraxa\> so now she's real

\<sash\> that's really terrifying.

\<abraxa\> lol glad u think so friend! :D

\<abraxa\> so anyway!

\<abraxa\> I was worried if I talked to people about what I was doing they would be like

\<abraxa\> "what is wrong with you. you should not be doing that"

\<abraxa\> but like, you get it???

\<abraxa\> you never told me I shouldn't be down here

\<sash\> that is true

\<sash\> i never did say that exactly.

\<abraxa\> lol well don't start now

\<abraxa\> uh unless you want to of course????

\<abraxa\> I mean I probably shouldn't be down here

\<abraxa\> there are other places I could go probably

\<abraxa\> I probably have not completely burned the last bridges I have exactly

\<sash\> do you want to stay down there?

\<abraxa\> lol what a question!

\<abraxa\> I want

\<abraxa\> I just want . . . so much!

\<abraxa\> (dances for her life before the stuffy ballet commission)

\<abraxa\> lol no I mean

\<abraxa\> there is something I'm supposed to do down here

\<abraxa\> there is some job I'm supposed to perform, you know?

\<abraxa\> some like . . . point to my life

\<abraxa\> and I want to see what it is

\<sash\> i understand, a lot

\<sash\> i used to feel there was a point to my life too.

\<abraxa\> well maybe there still is!

\<abraxa\> maybe you're supposed to help me!

\<abraxa\> YOU KNOW

\<abraxa\> WITH MY EVIL MAGIC

\<abraxa\> lol did you go away

\<sash\> no, i'm here. i'm thinking again.

\<sash\> question.

\<abraxa\> yay!

\<sash\> how will you know when your evil magic is done?

\<abraxa\> lol oh damn

\<abraxa\> I THINK I WOULD KNOW SOMETHING LIKE THAT

<abraxa> I mean how were we gonna know when SOTS
   was done?

<sash> there was a plan for it?

<sash> when we finished the plan, it would be done.

<sash> um, speaking of done.

<sash> my timer went off.

<abraxa> lol you have a timer to talk to me?

<sash> i'm trying to get used to my new work routine

<abraxa> ol iriul doomcat

<abraxa> what a slave driver

<abraxa> lol okay so you gotta sleep or something??

<abraxa> well then I will just be here

<abraxa> and I will think about the old days

<abraxa> and I will think about your question??

<abraxa> thank you for talking to me about the old days!

<abraxa> we were good weren't we??

<abraxa> like we were really good then

<abraxa> hello???

<sash> good night.

<abraxa> lol

FROM: abraxaabraxaabraxa@marcieletskaudesign.com
TO: lparker@dollarwise.com
SUBJ: You are cordially invited lol
DATE: March 10, 2017 at 2:44 AM EST

(Image: a torn-out sketchbook page, a time and a known street address, an invitation. A drawing of a long table with four seats and four place settings, tall and twisted black candles at its center emitting wisps of smoke. A large silver covered tray at one of the places; opposite it, a shadowy figure made of smudges and cross-hatch. The page is bordered with elaborate ballpoint knotwork on all edges except the ragged fringe where the page was separated from its sketchbook. The company logo has been worked into it.)

The invitation was only for Lilith, despite the four places around the table. She wondered, in retrospect, why it had never occurred to her to bring a plus-one along, why she had been so confident that she would be safer alone.

At night, in the cold, the walk from the train to Mercer Street was different. The streets past the square were empty, other than some dogs being walked and people going home from daylight jobs, earphones attached and eyes on no one. Every window in the designers' townhouses was glowing, violet and blue, and Lilith imagined big TVs tuned to intricate serial dramas, plates of snacks, snug throw blankets.

She turned the corner at Mercer Street, ducked under the caution tape, and found her way beneath the arch to the small garden space. There was a candle waiting in front of the big metal door: WISTERIA BEACH RIND, its label read. It crackled upward, accenting the metal in a dull henna, as if from a Martian moss.

She knocked, and the door opened, and here was her friend, still in the same clothes, accented now by a shawl. Her skin looked scrubbed; her smile was massive and shy and mischievous, like a kid with a secret. Lilith felt like smiling too, on seeing it. *Come in*, said her friend, *come in, welcome home.*

At first it was hard to make out the space beyond the fire; there were no other lights, and the distance to the walls was hard to guess. She'd looked at the blueprints for this place many times—she'd looked at the police reports about the long-ago fire, the insurance documents that cited them, the repair and wiring estimates—and she tried now to superimpose her mental map onto this pulsing, ambiguous space that smelled like smoke, bleach, sandalwood, mellowing pee. She sat, knees folded, on a thin bath towel on the molding stone, and she watched the other woman stir cans of Italian wedding soup together as her tongue pooled with salt.

There were multiple courses, which took a while to come out: Abraxa had only the one pot and had to let it cool between servings. (This helped blend the flavors, she said.) First the soup, eaten from Solo cups, and then quick-cook couscous braised in the remains of the soup plus liquid aminos, turmeric, and bouillon powder, then sausages and soft zucchini sections eaten from skewers cooked directly over the fire, then half a toasted bagel each. Abraxa kept up the conversation while she cooked, a kind of travel monologue about where the ingredients had come from, the advantages of the winter temperatures for keeping ingredients fresh, funny stories from the days she'd collected them from different co-op pantries, store shelves, or dumpsters. It was as if she were talking about wine terroir. Lilith imagined her on a fancy cooking show, then a show where contestants were airlifted into a brutal forest to try to survive, then flipping channels rapidly between these, as red and blue blur to purple. How often did Abraxa get to talk to anyone? She talked for so long she sometimes forgot to eat, and Lilith, who had skipped lunch, stopped responding other than to stare at the unfinished bites that prevented her hostess from moving on to preparing the next course.

How long have you been down here, she asked finally, when the last lentil dog had been taken from the spear and Abraxa's talk had finally settled and stopped.

Months, Abraxa said. —Or weeks? A church counts from Sundays, so maybe fifteen Sundays.

Lilith bit her lip to help her count backward. —So since November? December?

Sure! Abraxa said. —Why not. It's not like I scratch a line on the wall every day like a cartoon prisoner. It's not like I need to know.

She frowned at the fire, and Lilith tried to think of some way to sympathize with this. What would happen to her if she lived without time? She imagined herself on her block at 4 A.M., knocking on the door of a bodega, confused.

At first I counted, Abraxa continued, staring into the fire. —For four or five days? That was hard, and then it became easy. Counting the days made it worse, I think! If you count the days, then you start feeling like, whoa, I have so many good person days stored up! Smell me! But once you start saving something, that's when you start thinking about spending it.

Right, Lilith said. —Liquidity, sure.

She considered this metaphor, as Abraxa continued to talk. *Mystic Knights* had been based on saving and spending to get better weapons and upgrades. But there were other numbers that went only up, never down: up and down cycles within a bigger pattern of rising. What Abraxa was saying didn't have to do with a pattern of rising at all, and yet it also didn't have to do with a pattern of falling. Was there even a pattern to what she did? There must have been; there was always a pattern.

You don't talk much, Abraxa said. —It's weird. Are you like a spy?

Lilith flushed. —Sorry, she said.

It's okay, Abraxa said. —You don't have to talk if you don't want! I was just worried, is all. Sometimes I go on.

You're fine, Lilith said. She stared into the hole, trying to think of things to say about it that Abraxa might like. She imagined what Fionna would say about all of this, how Fionna would see it. Suddenly she didn't want to know what Fionna would see.

The space was gorgeous, she suddenly noticed. Seen holistically, it was a disaster; seen piece by piece, it flowed with detail. The shelf resting on the floor had been worked with a knife into scrolls; the crude bookshelf was painted with little images of the sorceress; even the larder and the woodpile had been artfully stacked. Hours and hours down here, Lilith imagined, hours of attention that jumped and sparked to jobs like these: a firefly who glowed, blessed a space with brief, bright activity, then winked out and moved in silence.

What's your house like, Abraxa asked. —Like where does a

banker live? I'm trying to imagine it. I'm imagining a big castle with a moat.

Are you staying down here a long time, Lilith asked.

I don't know, Abraxa said. —As long as I need to?

As long as you need to for what, Lilith said.

Abraxa got quiet again.

I'm making a garden, she finally said. —Do you want to see it?

She picked up a hot dog skewer, took a strip of cloth from a reusable shopping bag that hung from a nail in the wall— had it been a bedsheet once, sliced up?—and wrapped it tightly around the skewer. She dipped the skewer in an unlabeled can; it came up oily and glistening and smelling like burned bread. Then she dipped it into the fire. The torch in her hand smoldering, Abraxa led Lilith—whose eyes stayed fixed and gaping at the space where the smoking oil caromed off the already black and puckered ceilings—around the corner and into a brighter space. Here, a gigantic oblong of soil had been heaped directly over the concrete slab. The air was much chillier, and the cracks in the ceiling moaned, as if a giant were blowing the whole building like an oboe reed. The skewer crackled, and greasy embers drifted onto the soaked and broken concrete.

I think I can plant this in the spring, Abraxa said. —Fingers crossed! I can probably plant lettuce seeds even sooner, actually, six or more Sundays. Lettuce can deal with ice. It's a real versatile green.

Lilith studied the hole smashed in the foundation, her mind fretfully converting it into contractor hourly rates and premium adjustments. —Lettuce, she said.

I'm putting in some three-gal containers, too, Abraxa said. —For tomatoes and cucumbers. I have a zine that says those should work if I can expose some more sunlight, you know? I think I can get a little more pouring down here.

You're planning to be here for the whole spring, Lilith said. —And the summer, too.

Abraxa didn't answer. Lilith had to stop staring at the hole: it seemed rude, and thinking about it was making her stomach roil. She imagined the rest of the foundation like a sliding puzzle, rushing into the hole and bringing the attached support walls and the bowed ceiling with them; she imagined the silent rubble that would cover their bodies, the little whisper of plaster dust that rose from it. She settled on an end table pushed up against the far wall. Her friend had covered it in extinguished candles, strange bits of trash, and a bird's-nest coil of extension cords and adapters. She tried to imagine a little blue robin egg sleeping in the nest of cables. She tried to imagine that her friend must know how dangerous this whole place was; she tried to imagine her friend must therefore know what she was doing. The ceiling hadn't fallen in yet. There must be time.

Remember how I work for a bank, she finally said.

How could I forget, Abraxa said happily.

In my work, I meet people—who buy buildings, Lilith said. —You know?

I've heard of that kind of thing, Abraxa said.

And I know someone who wants to buy this building, Lilith said. —The one we're in.

Oh, that's cool, Abraxa said. The torch flame distorted the air, swirled her friend's expression. —Just the top floors, or the basement, too?

All the floors, Lilith said.

Great, Abraxa said. —You should bring your friend down here to hang out.

What was Abraxa's face like? It was important to know what people's faces were like, to know how they were taking things. Abraxa was no longer looking at Lilith but at the walls, which Lilith realized were covered in words. This in itself wasn't strange—many walls were covered in words—but the writing seemed more orderly, columns of text that started about a foot and a half above Abraxa's head and dropped in curtains to the floor. The first and last lines were small and cramped; the letters swelled in the middle like glutted leeches. Sometimes there were other characters, too—@, #—were these passwords? In the torchlight, Lilith thought of pyramids.

She's really interesting, Lilith said. —This woman I know who buys buildings. She's planning to start a healing center.

A healing center, Abraxa said, squinting at the walls. Her eyes were moving: Was she reading them? Why wouldn't she know what they said?

Like a space for trans kids who run away, Lilith said. —Who need services.

Cool, said Abraxa. —Is she trans, too?

The *too* weirdly stung, even though of course she'd clocked Abraxa and assumed reciprocity. But there was no need to name it.

No, said Lilith. —Or I mean, I don't know.

Maybe everyone secretly is, Abraxa said, voice excited.

Lilith laughed politely. —Anyway, I think you should meet. Maybe not here at first? I have an office in the city. I mean, it's not really an office.

Abraxa had started to bounce on her heels, making the torch ball bob like a cartoon fairy closer and closer to the ceiling. —What do you want me and your friend to talk about, she asked.

She's not my friend, Lilith said quickly. —I don't know what you should talk about. The sale, or the building, or how you fit into it.

She hadn't meant to say anything about Fionna at all. What she had meant was just to say to Abraxa, *you're my friend.* But that was how that concept had come out.

I have an idea, Abraxa said. —Your friend wants a healing center, right, and wants you to loan her money to make it, right? But I'm already here making something that's kind of a healing center. So what if you gave me the loan instead? Then I could stay here, and there would also be a healing center, so your friend would be happy, too.

Lilith flinched. Was that a Real Question? She elected not to answer it. The torch flickered, and Abraxa eventually stopped looking at her and again studied the walls.

So when is your friend buying the building, Abraxa asked. —How long do I have?

Lilith needed not to do the wrong thing. She needed not to make her friend feel worse. Frustrated, she sat on the floor, and she tried to look up in a way that was maybe comforting. And after a moment, Abraxa stopped bouncing on her heels. She blew out her torch, and she sat down, too. And here they were, sitting together in the dark, backlit from the fire in the next room. Her friend looked scared, tired, old, alone. Was alone an emotion? Again she thought about the jaguar she'd seen as a child. She looked back, and she tried to make her blinking slow and calm until she felt something change, and Abraxa drew a long breath.

I don't know whether she's buying the building, Lilith said. — She's talking about it? But we haven't discussed it specifically in a long time.

Maybe she'll forget, Abraxa said brightly.

I don't think she'll forget, Lilith said.

A healing center for teenage runaways and queers, Abraxa said. Then: —Do you remember Necropizza? Like from online?

The text on the walls blurred. This was the first time Abraxa had acknowledged any prior history between them. They'd never spoken one another's names aloud.

Kinda, said Lilith.

I wonder whatever happened to Necropizza, Abraxa said.

Neither of them spoke for some time. Lilith kept trying to remember more about Necropizza, about all the IRC people from back then. *Sash*—she could bring up Sash. But the idea of speaking her name down here in the darkness felt impossible: this was not the place she wanted to speak that name.

Your friend is going to make me leave, said Abraxa's voice from the dark. —Right?

I don't know, Lilith lied.

Of course she is, Abraxa said. —You can't just live in someone else's building. You can't just imagine that you own a building because you move into it and fix it and pray in it and use it. You don't own it because you have like, a dream you own it? That's just something crazy bitches believe. —With surprising flexibility, she bent forward and pressed her forehead to the ground. —*Cra-zy*, she sang, her throat crunched tight by the weight of her back.

Lilith tried to imagine the feeling rising in her sloshing backward down her spine, draining away into the soil Abraxa had freed from the concrete. It was easier than she worried it should have been. —You're not crazy, she said.

Abraxa stopped singing, but stayed in her forward fold. She was listening.

We shouldn't get ahead of ourselves, Lilith said, trying to summon all of her talking-to-clients calm. —I have an idea. Why don't you tell me what you would want to happen? What would be the best outcome of all of this for you? If we know that, we can try to work from that toward a solution.

Without getting up, Abraxa turned her face to let her cheek rest on the ground and frowned into the dark. Lilith tried to brace for whatever she'd say. What would be Abraxa's price of compromise? A place to stay, maybe. (She could stay with Lilith, of course, at least for a while, for a start.) A job—could the bank use her? (The bank could not use her.) She had art skills; maybe she could design ads and flyers. She could design websites. She could program too, once.

And just following this thought came another, like a falling tree: the writing on the walls wasn't text. It was CraftQ code.

She suddenly wished Abraxa hadn't put out the torch—really, could she not just use a flashlight?—wished she could pick it up and carry it from wall to wall, slowly find the starting point and decipher it, understand what Abraxa intended this building to do. The whole church was a room—was a program. My brilliant friend, she thought, and suddenly she felt fourteen years old again, like it was the summer of 1998 and she was in the coolest CraftQ company of them all. I'm lucky, she wanted to say: I'm lucky. This time, I'll say I'm lucky. This time I'll stay.

This is what I would like to happen, Abraxa said.

In this game, you are a trans woman who is trying to perform a magical ritual. You do this by occupying a space, ritually consecrating it, performing certain actions within it to summon the presence of the entities you desire to be there. For example, if you summon the sorceress, your space will be attuned to her energy, which is the energy of fire: the energy of transformation in accordance with purpose.

One might ask, what purpose? Part of the goal of the game is to divine this. Various methods exist. You might meditate. You might record and interpret your dreams. You might write code on the walls as it comes to you in the hope that one day you'll finish, that one day you will know what happens when the program runs. No player has ever successfully completed this game. There are no listings for it on GameFAQs, no strategy guides to consult. The only way forward is to proceed through the method of fire: spread out. Grow.

You'll know you're on the right track because omens will appear. Roads once open to you will close. You will find yourself supplied with all you need; you will find yourself stripped of everything you don't. Circularities will start to happen; messages will arrive. Friends from the past will return. Some of them bring messages and information, and some bring quests.

Maybe one of those quests looks like this: There's an opportunity to expand the ritual space. Resources are on offer; helpers may appear. There are possibilities: Suddenly there's money to fix the crack in the ceiling. Supplies for cleaning mold and plaster. A warrant to operate above ground, in the sun, so you can finally plug the holes in the ceiling. You can set up dormitories for trans kids, trans adults, anyone who needs a place to go. You can teach them skills: they can learn to code, learn to draw, learn the lore of the Mystic Knights series of games, learn how to make simple repairs. They can develop an ethic of reciprocal altruism, separate from ownership. They can be safe.

In this way, the temple will grow to become a settlement, a village. A counter to System D, staring back at it from across the Hudson, as once the great red lion faced the great white dragon. Like any system, it will soon become self-sustaining. Other villages will sprout like strawberry runners. Promising transsexuals will spread the gospel. Awareness of the sorceress will travel, islands of belief. Her sign will hang above the earth.

There are five jobs when creating a temple. A writer to define what the space will mean, a level designer to build it, and artists, musicians, and programmers to make it beautiful and make it work. You don't know exactly what victory will look like. But you know you and your friends will be the ones to build it. You know that you can save the world.

Do you really believe all that, Lilith asked.

It was a Real Question, one her friend didn't answer.

I'm tired, Abraxa said instead. —I have all kinds of cleaning to do.

Abraxa insisted Lilith take leftovers, which was a can of green beans. Reading its label again and again on the PATH train home, Lilith thought—as she would continue to think, in the months and years after this moment—about how Abraxa had always been the stronger one.

<abraxa> lol dude
<abraxa> I'm fuuuuucked
<abraxa> do you know anything about real estate????
<sash> i'll google it.
<abraxa> lol fucked fucked fuckedddd
<abraxa> fucked am iiiiii
<abraxa> how do you not say crazy stuff????
<abraxa> really how do you not???
<abraxa> I don't have this skill
<sash> i don't know either
<sash> i know how not to say anything, but that isn't different.
<abraxa> hahahaha shame sisterz
<abraxa> lol but dude you gotta help me!!!
<sash> what do you need help with?
<abraxa> okay like
<abraxa> this church I told you I was staying in remember???
<sash> i remember this, yes.
<abraxa> WELL it is about to become a lot HARDER to stay here
<abraxa> there is some new shit that has happened and I am freaking out about it
<abraxa> and there is a worse thing which is
<abraxa> she hasn't spoken to me all day ://////

\<abraxa\> like after months???

\<abraxa\> a sudden silence after months is VERY FRIGHT-ENInG?

\<sash\> who hasn't spoken to you all day?

\<abraxa\> lol uhhhh

\<abraxa\> I want to maybe not explain that right now lol

\<abraxa\> ya gotta help me is the thing!!!

\<abraxa\> can you help???

\<abraxa\> can you like come down here maybe

\<abraxa\> like maybe if you bring idk. Metal rods???

\<abraxa\> we could like construct a stockade!!

\<abraxa\> we could maybe have traps, like in that movie

\<abraxa\> the law can never find us!

\<sash\> hold on. i'm googling adverse possession laws.

\<abraxa\> lol that is probably a better idea

\<abraxa\> you have lots of good ideas!!!

\<sash\> i think there are solutions. there's a whole history of resistance to eviction.

\<sash\> there are best practices? and i know here in new york there's a history of it

\<abraxa\> aaaa keep em coming all these brilliant ideas

\<sash\> c-squat, etc.

\<sash\> probably some of this applies to new jersey too?

\<abraxa\> this is great

\<abraxa\> we could throw a party

\<abraxa\> we could raise awareness and shit

\<abraxa\> we could flood the streets with transsexuall-szzzzssd

\<abraxa\> lol this makes me feel so much better???

\<abraxa\> you have no idea

\<abraxa\> it is like . . . synchronicities all over again?

\<abraxa\> lol like I was just talking about with someone—
like when it is time

\<abraxa\> people will appear to help you?

\<abraxa\> like it's PLANNED

\<sash\> who were you talking to about this?

\<abraxa\> lol

\<abraxa\> idk some rando

\<abraxa\> but also, thank you for talking to me about all of
this!!!!

\<abraxa\> this is really very helpful!

\<sash\> you keep not answering my questions

\<sash\> which for now i'm just going to note?

\<abraxa\> lol sorry

\<abraxa\> but our company is so cool right??

\<sash\> it was.

\<sash\> is.

\<abraxa\> I keep thinkin like, what if we had really gotten it
together back then?

\<abraxa\> What if we had finished our game even???

\<abraxa\> WE'D haVE BEEN KINGS OF THE WORLD

\<abraxa\> QUEENS I MEAN, lol sorry

\<abraxa\> why didn't we finish it even?

\<abraxa\> it just kinda ended!

\<abraxa\> lol are you there?

\<abraxa\> TALK TO ME

\<sash\> i'm here, yes.

\<sash\> i'm thinking something i'm afraid to type to you.

\<abraxa\> doooo it

\<abraxa\> dooooooooooooo it

\<sash\> okay.

<sash> the reason we didn't finish is because i was in love
    with lilith.
<sash> are you there?
<abraxa> yeah
<abraxa> sorry
<abraxa> I guess that makes
<abraxa> a lot of sense?
<sash> i . . . can't believe i typed that to you.
<sash> i never really thought that to myself.
<sash> i think i was afraid to.
<sash> and then with you it just came out.
<abraxa> okay
<abraxa> I guess that is a reason not to keep doing the
    company though
<sash> i mean, she left the company first.
<sash> it's a really messy story
<abraxa> wow
<sash> do you mind if i tell it?
<sash> hello?
<abraxa> lol
<abraxa> I guess no one's stopping you!
<sash> okay, thanks.
<sash> i don't know.
<sash> i don't know how to start.
<abraxa> maybe like why you felt like that
<abraxa> like what qualities she had
<abraxa> or whatever
<sash> sorry, i'm still here.
<sash> i know i didn't type anything for . . . several min-
    utes now.
<sash> that was a hard question to answer.

<sash> what qualities did she have?
<sash> i like that she was working so hard to be cool.
<sash> i had to do that too?
<sash> i think maybe this is something you would find it hard to appreciate.
<sash> you've always been so cool, without even trying.
<sash> with lilith it's different.
<sash> it felt like we were on the same path, and i was four steps ahead.
<sash> her being secretly a girl is part of it. that was visible from space.
<sash> but with other things too.
<sash> i really felt if we all made a game together, the three of us, it would change the whole world.
<sash> and i think she felt like that too.
<sash> she must have, right? she made a demo.
<sash> we must have been the same.
<sash> and then we were talking, and, i don't know. she was talking about gender, and.
<sash> i think i thought of her as someone i could teach.
<sash> god—head of the company, so like her boss, her teacher.
<sash> i know how bad this all sounds.
<sash> but we were just teenagers. it was just online.
<sash> online isn't real.
<sash> but, i don't know.
<sash> maybe online hurts worse than real.
<sash> and maybe i don't even know who she is now.
<sash> and maybe i never did.
<sash> looking at her and not seeing her at all. it's the worst thing i can think of.

<sash> but it happened, and a long time ago now, and what are any of us supposed to do?

<sash> ugh, though

<sash> thank you for listening to all of this. this is excruciating for me.

<sash> i really appreciate it.

<sash> and i am just realizing that you haven't said anything in a while.

<sash> are you still there?

<sash> abraxa?

<sash> is what i said okay?

* abraxa has left #teengoetia (Timed out)

■

Every table at the Park Slope wine bar had a white tablecloth, a two-inch wooden pepper grinder, and a ceramic dish with water and a floating purple orchid. The bar had them too, spaced such that one sat between every two stools like an airplane armrest, a snack you weren't permitted to eat. Or were you supposed to eat them? Lilith had no idea; she had never been in a wine bar this fancy that she could remember, certainly not since coming out. Was she the first transsexual ever to go to this wine bar? No, one was never the first at something: surely lots of transsexuals came here, all sorts of professional and glamorous women who knew facts about wine and elegance.

Fionna didn't seem to be eating the orchids. She stared into her wine glass, which had remained full from the time Lilith had started to update her on the situation with the church until now. Fionna looked tired. It was reassuring to have a feeling in common.

So what do you think, she asked, hoping the cis woman would tell her what to do.

The wine in Fionna's glass rippled, though her hand didn't otherwise appear to move.

You mean about the woman who's living in the building I'm trying to buy, she clarified.

She's really nice, Lilith said immediately. —I know that makes it harder—I know, I know—but she is. She's someone I trust? And, you know, she's going through something—but I feel like maybe she just needs to go through it, until she gets to the other side? And then she'll move on.

Fionna stared. What did people's faces have to say?

It's like you, after the election, Lilith continued. —Where you took that retreat upstate. Where you processed.

I did process, Fionna said.

She just needs to process, Lilith explained. —The same as you.

Mercifully, Fionna took a swallow from the glass. —So your hot take is, I shouldn't do anything, she said. —I should just wait for this woman to process, and then move on.

Lilith took a breath; she must be careful.

I think you should do whatever you need to do, she said. — It's your project, and I'm here to help you with it?

Fionna circled the wine still in the glass, making a tiny cyclone.

Thank you for saying that, she said.

You're welcome, Lilith said. —So. What do you want to do?

Let me think about this, Fionna said. —There's nowhere for her to go at all.

Lilith hesitated. —I'm not exactly sure that's true.

Because if she has somewhere else to go, I might prefer her to go there, Fionna said, raising her eyebrows.

I think part of what's going on with her is that she has to go through whatever process this is in that building, Lilith said. And then, to soften this: —I offered to let her stay with me. She said no.

Why would you offer that, Fionna asked.

If Fionna knew that this was Lilith's friend, something terrible would happen. —Because, Lilith said. —Because—she's trans? And that can be hard.

Had she said before whether Abraxa was trans? She couldn't remember whether she'd disclosed that. It was easy to forget that people didn't just know that about someone whose body wasn't present. Fionna's face was blank; Lilith had no idea whether Fionna knowing Abraxa was trans made things better or worse.

It would be awful of me to evict a trans woman in order to build a queer healing center, Fionna said.

Lilith waited, afraid to interrupt this chain of thoughts.

I'm really not a bad person, Fionna said.

You're not, Lilith said.

I know it's shitty when someone's like, oh, look at me, I don't want to be a bad person, Fionna said. —I get that. I spent so much time upstate just trying to get my head around that. How not to try to be good—how to just be good.

Lilith exhaled. —I understand you completely, she said.

Fionna picked up her drink. —You think she just needs some time to get to the other side of this, then, she said. —Maybe a month.

It could take more, Lilith said. —But we could keep monitoring it? We could keep checking in, and keep making decisions about what to do based on where things are, month to month.

I guess I wasted a lot of months already, Fionna said. She drained her glass and waved to the bartender, who quickly brought the bottle. Lilith finished her wine too, permitting her shoulders to settle. It had worked, she thought. She hadn't even needed to eat the orchid.

The wine poured, Fionna raised her glass, and Lilith met it. —Look, Fionna said, pointing at her legs: she was wearing charcoal tights, as was Lilith. —We match today.

We do, Lilith thought.

\<sash\> hey?

\<sash\> it's been like, days now

\<sash\> this really is not okay

\<sash\> this is really not something i can deal well with.

\<sash\> i'm legitimately afraid.

\<sash\> i'm sorry i said all that stuff about lilith.

\<sash\> i completely spaced on the fact that you might have reactions to that.

\<sash\> because i'm stupid and from space and have no theory of mind and am the worst person.

\<sash\> and should be crushed with a stone pestle and ground into a fine meal and spread on crackers.

\<sash\> and the crackers are then thrown away.

\<sash\> you're not here.

\<sash\> i wish you were so i could tell you the things you were to me, too.

\<sash\> brilliant. rival. collaborator. asymptote. fearless.

\<sash\> i thought with you helping, we could really all be something.

\<sash\> saying it aloud, that sounds so awful too. "helping me." like you were some kind of laborer.

\<sash\> "our company is a family."

\<sash\> it was so long ago. why am i still so emotional about all of these things?

\<sash\> why can i not ever get over anything?

\<sash\> abraxa, i read your blog for so many years.

\<sash\> it made me happy to read it, to think of you out
there like a comet somewhere, shining.

\<sash\> i hope you can somehow see all of this.

\<sash\> all of this . . . horrible emotional disclosure.

\<sash\> i hope you're okay where you are.

\<sash\> where are you?

In celebration, Lilith went back to the Time Tunnel later that week, this time without Elspet. (Had she ever done that? She couldn't remember.) The bar felt pre-festival, the dance floor still empty and gay men chatting on stools and in corners, the bar back wiping glasses as if expecting guests. Lilith ordered a cider and perched on a stool herself, glowing. It had really worked—she'd done it—she'd bought her friend some time. Whole days for Abraxa to paint on the walls, to sweep and cook and clean, to fix water damage, to grow. Who knew? She might even be able to fix up the space for real, especially now that Fionna was aware and involved. It felt so much better to have a cis woman involved in things, particularly one who was mysteriously rich; it felt like there were some boundaries around the whole operation. She let herself dream about what could happen: the space being repaired, Fionna scheduling classes and directing wayward teens into it, Abraxa smiling and welcoming them, teaching them to draw, to care for plants, to make video games. Lilith would be there too, behind it all somewhere, diligently doing her part. Maybe she could help handle accounting? Maybe she could even quit the bank, one day, when it was safe. She could earn a living helping queer and trans youth feel happy.

She hadn't been lying when she'd told Fionna she'd been reading about mental health. There were whole networks of material online about caring for someone going through a difficult mental process, references to books on the theory of it, care sheets connecting people to medication, counseling, support.

One website talked about the work of someone named John Weir Perry, who'd written on the inner experience of psychosis. Perry thought psychosis resulted when someone's old self became unstable—when old strategies for living were used up, when someone had to either grow or die—but the old self saw no clear path for change. Like a dammed sewer: all the old dirty water had to go somewhere, but the culvert flowing out to the watershed was blocked, so instead the water went underground. And it filled the whole world beneath the ground, a vast cavern sea. It began to express itself in delusions, disordered thinking, dreams.

There were two ways to work with someone so deluded. You could try to get rid of the water somehow: maybe divert it, dry it up. But this way was no good: a person mostly *was* water, Lilith remembered; you couldn't get rid of all the water in a person without getting rid of them, too. The other way, which Perry advocated, was listening. If you allowed a person to talk through their process of psychotic derangement—if you listened without distraction, listened without judgment—then that act of listening would, through strange alchemy, itself purify the water. This would express itself in the character of the delusions changing. A sick person might believe herself caught between opposed armies—sin and salvation, authoritarianism and anarchy, heterosexuality and queerness, female and male— struggling toward the cleaner side of the binary. But over time, that delusion would heal. Rather than a world of good versus evil, the one resisting its opposite, the psychotic person would begin to describe a balanced world, a world made whole. Often this was a quartered world: four seasons, four elements, four possibilities. Four was the number of balance.

Smiling as she imagined Abraxa's world becoming whole,

she felt someone touch her shoulder. It was her friend Susan, the construction worker from the group, her face bright: *hey, stranger! What are you doing here?* Lilith smiled back. They shared drinks, and Susan talked about her business and Lilith talked about her trip upstate. And later, when the music started, Lilith wanted to dance. She worked up the courage, and then she told Susan she wanted to dance, and Susan said *yes, yes, let's shag ass!* So the two of them went out to the empty dance floor—two transsexuals, old and young—and Susan shook her hips and arms while Lilith tried to sway like a willow tree to the Kate Bush song, and the song after it, and the song after, while the cis people watched them, and they were free.

TO: lparker@dollarwise.com, cc: mswannuken@dollarwise.com
FROM: rmallard@dollarwise.com
DATE: March 20, 2017 at 8:16 AM EDT
SUBJ: Mercer Street?

Hi Lilith,

    I got a troubling message from a woman named Fionna Mercier. She's asking for a different underwriter to be assigned to a loan application she made sometime last fall. The property is 100 Mercer Street. I don't remember authorizing this work. Could you refresh my memory?

Thanks

Ronin

The words *different underwriter*, her boss's email address: her eyes bounced back and forth between these before finally settling on Ronin's office across from her cubicle. It was Monday morning; it was empty and dark. Had he sent the email from the subway or something? Was that something they expected you to do when you became a manager? Her mind hung on this logistical point for what, in retrospect, was a strangely long time before she finally remembered to add her name to the sick days calendar, gather her things, and clock out. She skulked past the teller desk: none of the tellers seemed to be looking at her; maybe no one would remember she had been in today. Except Lilith knew that wasn't true: she was trans, all of them were certainly surveilling her, one couldn't help it.

She left the bank, circled the block, circled it again before realizing that this was the worst way not to run into Ronin. She ducked into an alley next to a stack of wooden pallets and a ripe green garbage bin, the smell spreading even in the winter chill. Her nose was full of everyone else's trash, a rich black soil, molecules burping in fermentation. She held her cell, Fionna's number ready for dialing, and she breathed garbage, and she counted to one hundred, and then she dialed. It rang through to Fionna's voicemail. She hung up and dialed again.

I'm sorry, said Fionna. —I'm so sorry. The phone was in the other room. I wasn't avoiding your call.

It's okay, Lilith said. (No: why was this always her instinct? Nothing was okay.) —I appreciate that.

Thank you, Fionna said, sounding miserable.

Lilith tried to wait out the silence; she failed. —So.

I knew you'd call, Fionna said. —I told myself it was important to take your call. I thought I should explain, because.

Sure, Lilith said. —Of course.

I just kept thinking it over, Fionna said. —After we met. It wasn't just thinking. I had nightmares.

Nightmares, Lilith repeated.

Nightmares, Fionna said. —They were about your friend, down there. I couldn't stop thinking about her.

What happened in the nightmares, Lilith finally let herself ask.

It wasn't like I thought she'd do anything bad, Fionna said. —It wasn't like I thought she'd like, burn the place down. It's not like I even know her. But I just couldn't stop thinking about her. I kept telling myself I was being stupid, or I don't know—that I was being, you know—

Lilith would not permit the word that popped into her head to form. The word was not charitable to the woman she was talking to. Part of her felt this, and the other part of her tried to think the word louder, so loud that the inside of her skull shook. Words lost their meaning when you repeated them, became vapor, spatter. Fionna was still talking, and she should listen.

I shouldn't have to feel pressure like that, Fionna was saying. —At the same time, I don't want to be a bad person. God—I know how that sounds.

I understand, Lilith said, staring at the trash.

There was a long exhale of static. —Thank you for understanding, Fionna said.

You're welcome, Lilith said. Should she be angry now? It was a puzzle, one her mind slid away from, like she had olive oil all over her fingers. The pieces just lay scattered around her in different combinations. She wasn't allowed to be angry, she thought. She'd said she understood.

You were having nightmares, she said again.

They were like visions, Fionna said. —I couldn't get them to stop.

My friend has visions too, Lilith said. And then she said more, like she was a child on a bike, cresting a tall hill, and suddenly able to see all the land that all this time had been all around her: —Why are your visions more important than my friend's?

Later, she would ask herself whether this had been a Real Question, one she had really expected Fionna to have an answer to, or whether she had just asked it because she wanted to be cruel. She hadn't planned to ask it; she couldn't know. But Fionna's answer had been the same: *I don't know.* Her voice hollow, soaked, sad. So neither of them knew. No one knew at all.

She heard herself thanking Fionna again; she heard herself saying *good luck.* She felt her finger hang up the phone. Here she was, holding the phone. And now here she was throwing it against the dumpster, and here she was with her face blurred in the screen, tracing her finger over its sharp, sandy cracks.

\<sash\> please, you need to tell me where you are.
\<sash\> please, i can't lose touch with you again.

Lilith bought a bottle of mezcal, which always made her feel dangerous. Prying her boots loose off her heels, she imagined the smoke and worm-trace in her mouth. What if she didn't drink it in the kitchen? What if she drank it in bed? She lay on the floor in her foyer on her side, hugging her belly and considering this option. She stared at the mezcal bottle, perpendicular to her on the hardwood. She'd planned poorly; she'd collapsed maybe a foot too far away to comfortably grab it. It was her teenage days at Camp Weathering all over again, again the jump Scott had forced her to make over the rocks. It shouldn't be impossible for her to jump forward over the floor to the bottle. She tried to imagine the teenage Buckworth was here, sneering at her. *Take it, take the leap.*

There was some reason Fionna was right and she was wrong. If she could see everything that had happened through Fionna's eyes, she would understand why it was wrong to feel the way she was feeling right now. She lay on the floor, wondering why she was so damaged that she couldn't correctly see that.

In physics class she'd learned about the normal force of the earth. The earth, being solid, is always exerting a normal force upward on us to keep us from falling into the planet's core. And the normal force varies directly with the force of gravity: the heavier you are, the harder the earth must work to hold you up. Somehow this must all have explained why she couldn't summon the energy to get drunk in bed: gravity was too heavy. That meant the earth had to work harder, and the strain was crumbling it up.

She texted Elspet: *gravity is hard :(helpppppp*

Elspet texted back: *rephrase. I don't speak bottom.* And suddenly the force of the earth gained strength.

They didn't talk about ethics or physics. Instead, as soon as she arrived, Elspet made Lilith kneel and take off all her clothes but her tiger-striped underwear, then held her neck down while tying her arms behind her back.

Growl more, Elspet directed. —Dumb dangerous animals like you growl.

Grr, Lilith said, feeling self-conscious until Elspet pulled the ropes tighter, and she forgot herself, instinctively kicked and fought back until Elspet sat on her, trussed her ankles and thighs. She was a dumb, dangerous animal—she was destructive—she would crush everything without even understanding why. And then she thought of throwing her phone—and she thought of Abraxa's voice—and these thoughts flooded her, and she was a squid venting ink, trying to escape with its evil tentacles intact, and she began to thrash and thrust and push her ass into Elspet and cry. But Elspet stilled her, pulled her hair, forced her silent.

Afterward, she lay in bed—untied and thighs wet, Elspet in the shower prior to her Lyft home—lazily scrolling her phone. Did she feel better? She felt maybe dead, in the best sense: when you are dead, all your muscles relax. Eyelids heavy, she let the fibers of her muscles unravel like silk from corn. She hadn't succeeded, and part of her didn't mind. It would have felt wrong to succeed. She had a clear conscience; Ronin and Fionna had taken her authority away. There was nothing left for her to do for Northwood Abbey. She could let it go. She opened her email app.

■　■　■

She read the email she'd received. She read it again.

Some minutes after, she heard the shower shut off. The mezcal was in the kitchen, she remembered; Elspet had made her move it. Suddenly it was easy to get up: she could float out of bed, walk naked and bruised into the kitchen, where she drank it straight from the bottle, as much as her throat could take. Gravity was canceled, she thought. She imagined her kitchen full of clouds, pink and sticky and pressing into her mouth.

She crouched in the corner on the tiles. Elspet found her there, hair still ringleted wet.

My Lyft is coming in four minutes, Elspet said.

Oh, said Lilith. —Where are you going?

I have a 5 A.M. meeting with my London clients, Elspet said. —Which is why I'm going home.

Good, said Lilith. How clean was the floor? She imagined her ass covered with crumbs and ants.

Are you okay, Elspet said, frowning down at her.

I might be a little overwhelmed, Lilith said. —Would you— could you maybe stay? I can pay for your Lyft cancel.

Elspet folded her arms. —Why are you overwhelmed, she said.

I got an email, Lilith explained.

Elspet sighed and checked her phone. —Three minutes, she said, and she turned to go to the bedroom.

Gravity was still canceled, so it was easy for Lilith to stand up and follow her. Elspet was checking under the edges of the bed; she had lots of routines to make sure she didn't forget things. —Did you mean you could stay for three minutes more so I could tell you why I was overwhelmed, Lilith said. —Or did you mean you had to go in three minutes still?

Elspet mumbled something to the space beneath the bed.

I'm sorry but would you mind repeating, Lilith said, pressing her hands into her temples.

I said I'm not staying, Elspet said. —I already came over when you texted, on a night when I had work to do. I'm tired now. I think I've done enough for now.

Sure, said Lilith, nodding. —I get that. You hit the threshold. You overdrew the be nice to Lilith account.

Two minutes, said Elspet. —You're being manipulative. Maybe you think you'll provoke a reaction. But also, yes, sorry to break it to you, people stand in reciprocal relationship to one another. People like to be around other people because they make us happy, or because we think they're cool to be around, or because we think they're hot. You need at least two out of three. Lately you only have one out of three.

Lilith stared. —You're an asshole, she said, with wonder.

We all are, Elspet said. —Every trans woman is terrible. Sorry to break this to you about yourself.

I'm breaking up with you, Lilith said.

Elspet rolled her eyes. —Because breaking up is possible to do, because we're dating, she said. —Got it.

She took out her phone to check the time, but Lilith grabbed it. She ran into the living room with it while Elspet shouted at her about maturity and property, and then she opened the front door. No neighbors were present to see her disgusting unstable tranny freak body, its grace as she flung Elspet's phone far away from her, like a discus. It skipped along the floor, it slid toward the stairs. Elspet, bag on her shoulder, ran right by her, chasing after it.

Insane bitch, she said.

I hope your Lyft driver calls you *sir*, Lilith shouted as she slammed the door.

There was a crash from the bedroom. She investigated it: one of her Mystic Knights action figures had fallen from its shelf. The sorceress: Lilith picked her up, hugged her to her chest, restored her to her place. Then she put on her favorite silk robe—it had red velvet panels and a ruffled neck; she liked to imagine when she wore it that she was having an affair with a private detective—and she poured herself a tall glass of mezcal. After a moment, she poured it out and replaced it with milk. And here she was: an awful, psychotic, newly single transsexual alone. She and Abraxa were alike, a shared heritage. She'd simply denied it for so long. She hadn't even asked Elspet which of those three reasons was still true. Again, she'd failed.

She drank the milk, and she thought of the email she'd gotten, and then there it was: the one way forward left to her. The path Sash had seen for her once in an IRC channel, many, many years ago: *what if your old self was gone? what would lilith do first?*

TO: lparker@dollarwise.com, sashiel@yahoo.com
FROM: abraxaabraxaabraxa@marcieletskaudesign.com
DATE: March 20, 2017 at 10:59 PM EDT
SUBJ: CRAFTQCON 2017

hahahaha sup losers. Come hang out???
    here's the deets

(Her address. A time, which is tonight. A drawing of their logo. A waning moon.)

Twisting her bracelet, Lilith let the *Super Mystic Knights 4* soundtrack play in her ears as the subway conducted her, like some vast inverse airship, across the city to Dollarwise. There was a coal compressing in her chest, and she imagined other people could see it, see through her haggard post-coital transsexual exterior to her inner shape, sharp and terrified at its own growing capacity. And her Mystic Knights soundtrack had reached the theme music for the final dungeon, and her heroic bracelet was tight and warm on her wrist, in sync now with the heat of her blood, and she knew—felt as certain now as she had at camp on the night she'd known it was time to walk alone to the stone seat in the woods—that tonight would be different. Tonight, everything was as simple as her soundtrack made it.

As a senior staff member, her employee badge and key fob gave her access to the entire building for any after-hours desk work she might feel inclined to take on. Was it bad that this was the first time she had ever used that power? The bank, stripped of daytime's respectable veil, had become strange, the cubicles the partitioned laboratories of thaumaturges and necromancers. She clacked quickly in her low heels, trying, for the benefit of the security tapes, not to look suspicious. She'd go to Ronin's office. She'd take back the Mercer Street binder she'd placed there earlier, and she'd prepare the order that would formally deny Fionna's bank loan at last.

There was nothing wrong in her making use of her power, she told herself. She had denied loans for business ventures far more promising than a healing center in a long-burned church. Ronin had trusted her with the power for his own reasons. Now she'd use it for her own, too. Cis people did things like this all the time.

She wagered, correctly, that the materials would be in the same stack where she'd left them months before. Now decisively trespassing, she eased them from their pile and hastily clopped across the dark tile foyer to her cubicle. The monitor light was a necessary risk; she used her body to eclipse as much as she could. The cover letter struck the right balance of legal precision and imperious terseness. The document would do the real work: dry and boilerplate, an everyday spell to stop people's dreams.

Was she spending too long on this? Her Mystic Knights soundtrack was about an hour long, and had almost finished its second full loop—but she forced herself to breathe, to feel the chair mat beneath her feet. The printer activated, and she rushed to get her documents, letting the printhead's roaring motion mask her steps. She signed both forms, wrote her title, stamped the date. And that was it: the legal spell had been scribed. Her work was complete.

She rushed back to her cubicle with the papers, picked up her purse and Fionna's loan materials, and returned to Ronin's office with them, careful to replace them at their exact angle and distance from the wall: her childhood skills still stood her in good stead. This is what she was thinking when the lights in the foyer all turned on, brilliant like a great dragon's eye opening. Security cameras were her first thought; her second was that now was the time to run. Or no, don't run—maybe it's motion sensors; maybe this is all a nightmare—maybe it was Ronin Mallard, the same Ronin Mallard who now came into her sight, approaching from the break room. His shirt was off, exposing a shaved, sweating chest; he wore black sweatpants with swirled gray accents and mesh cuffs, a headband with the character 刀 strapped across his third eye. At his side, echoing it, was a long wooden kendo sword, heavy and waggling as he walked. He had seen her. He stared at her, now, standing in his office in heels and unable to run, the legal agreement she'd executed on their employer's behalf now clenched in her hand. She stared back. In her headphones, the final boss music began to play.

Ronin closed the door behind him first. —What are you doing here, he asked. —Weren't you sick today or something?

I'm better now, Lilith said. —That's why I came in.

He regarded her, eyes holding mostly on her face. She crossed her arms and nodded: if she created a general sense of affirmation, maybe he would believe what she told him. She willed herself to be affirming and confident while he stared at her, sweat and sword resin melting down his flesh.

You're not contagious, are you, he asked.

Not anymore, she said. —I hope. Maybe I should go home, just in case.

I was meaning to talk to you, Ronin said. —Did you get my email?

Should she lie? —I got it, she said. —Actually that's why I was here. Actually because I forgot to do something related to the work on that project. It's, you know—a messy situation.

Messy how, he asked.

Just, she said. —Just, just. Just—it's really stupid—it's just this stupid mistake I made—something you, I think told me to do a long time ago, and I didn't do it, right, because that's the kind of *fucking stupid* mistake I'd make, because I'm *fucking stupid*—

Please don't call yourself stupid, Ronin said.

She opened her eyes, realizing as she did it how tightly she'd been squeezing them. He looked worried, his expression soft.

Sorry, she said. —Anyway—there was something I had to finish with that project. But I've finished it now—it's done—there's nothing we need to meet about? So I'm sorry for bothering you—you can get back to your practice. —She pointed at his sword. —I didn't know you did sword practice?

May I see that paper, he asked.

What, she replied.

His expression had been a soft cloud, and now the cloud had blown away. —The paper you're holding. May I see it?

Closing her mouth—if one of her lips remained in tight contact with its opposite, she wouldn't be able to cry or scream—she walked around the desk and presented him with her counterfeit document. She watched him review it: the salt reek of his cool sweat, the wooden sword he tapped next to his bare toes. She forced her arms to stay at her sides. If she put up no defense—if she was so vulnerable that he could kill her with one critical death strike—who knew? Maybe he'd spare her. Maybe he'd make sure it was over fast.

He looked up from the paper. —Why did you do this, he asked. And she saw his eyes had become afraid, terrified of what trusting the transsexual may have done to him.

She was taller than him, she realized. And in retrospect, she couldn't account for which fact caused her to act next: her height relative to his, his fear of her, the song in her headphones, the one that played when the Mystic Knights party first found its airship. None of these could be sufficient to explain why she pounced on him, moved with the speed of a flame licking out.

He struggled; she ran her hands down the side of his skull, over his shoulders and down his sweat-clammy arms. But his training had been effective: his arms grabbed her back, twisted her around, thick fingers slotted into her thick ribs, muffled clatter of wood. She thrashed; he held her tighter. Eventually she stopped fighting, just hung there in his arms. His fingers drummed on her skin, like she was an unfamiliar stove, something he had to test. He smelled sour and acid, testosterone salt and fossilized cologne flakes reconstituting in her nose, her mouth.

She was working out how she could turn around to bite him when she felt his arms unlatch. She pulled away, tried to put the desk between them, the power she had felt surging up in her flushed in blood to her cheeks. He was hanging there in space, flushed cheeks behind sweaty beard, silly kanji headband: what had she done? What had she done? She was working out how to apologize—maybe she could offer to have her salary cut, she could offer to indenture herself outright—when he spoke.

We shouldn't do this, he said.

She had no idea what he was talking about, but he kept talking.

God, I don't mean we shouldn't because you're—God, no, please never think that. —This had to do with her body, she realized. She felt a flush of shame, like she had a smaller body trapped inside her own, a little girl inside a robot.

May I sit down, she asked.

He nodded, quickly, and she crossed to the chair he reserved for guests, sat in it. He watched her moving; she tried to move evenly and gracefully. She could get out of this, she thought. The battle victory fanfare was playing on her soundtrack.

I'm trying to make it work again with Beth, he said. —Of course we're still broken up. That's why I've been moodier than I should have been lately; you've certainly noticed. I've been here nights, too. Trying to burn off some yang energies—trying to salvage something. Do you know what I mean?

Of course, she said, her voice hollow. —Salvaging things, it's hard.

From inside the cockpit of her robot body, she watched his face try to interpret this. She could get out of this, she thought—she would get out of this. She tried to imagine his girlfriend, or his ex-girlfriend, or whomever she was: a woman with a messy bun in a big leather armchair, watching prestige TV dramas while Ronin paced the dining nook behind her, shouting katas. She tried to imagine whether, if she could lure him close enough, she could knock him out, steal his sword and the paper, and escape. She tried to imagine what it had felt like not to be so tired.

I wish you could meet Beth, Ronin said. —You have a lot in common.

May I have my piece of paper back, she asked. —So I can go home.

He bit his lip, and she remembered him going out to smoke without her all those times. He used to tell her stories. Who had he told them to, when she'd stopped going with him? Maybe he had just told them to the street, let them evaporate with his smoke.

Why did you do this, he asked again. —What do you need this for?

It was a Real Question; she could hear it. —To help a friend, she said.

After some time, he nodded, and then he reached into his desk drawer. She imagined what he was looking for—a gun, a single rose, a cloth and chloroform? It was a notary stamp. He applied it to the form, signed his name, stamped today's date from the stamp rack on his desk. Then he handed it to her.

Could you photocopy this for me, he asked.

She got up and did so, in a trance. She handed him both copies. He put one in the inbox on his desk, and he handed the other back.

There, he said. —It's over. No one's buying anything.

She folded the letter, folded it again. —Thank you, she said.

Don't mention it, he said. —Why don't you take the rest of the night off?

She nodded. —Listen, she said. —Good luck with your like—girlfriend thing.

He smiled sadly. —Thank you, he said.

She could feel his eyes move over her body, one last time, there at the outer orbit of his desk lamp's light. She let him; she smiled. Then her headphones played the music that played when you died, and she left her workplace for what she knew would be the last time. Ronin would masturbate to her tonight, and her job would not be waiting for her in the morning.

But do not worry about jobs. In this game, Lilith has an appointment to keep.

In this game, Lilith clutches the letter she's spent all her mana to create. In this game, she descends to the subway, video game music still blasting—she shifts from one foot to the other, checking the train arrivals sign against the clock on her phone—why will it not come, why will it not come— and she strains to look down the tunnel into the earth—and it's as if an FMV sequence is beginning, just like one of the FMVs in *Mystic Knights V*, the black CD starting to spin in its player as a little Pavlov harbinger that something is happening—as if a camera is hurling itself far past the limits of Lilith's vision, moving far past where any pair of eyes could reach—plunge through the earth down the train tunnel, electric rail crackle and flipbook flash of graffiti, deliquescing trash, headlamps of workers—then the silent, heavy air of the underground world—then, with a sudden shot of pressure, bubbles against cork, and out into the long cuts of tunnels just east of Prospect Park—here where the grass has died, the city has killed it, all around is moonlight on brick, poison clouds—here where we settle on Crown Heights, and another pair of eyes—why will it not come, why will it not come.

In this game, you, Sash, ask yourself that, checking the clock on your rideshare app.

In this game, you check your email once again, re-confirming the existence of the message within it: the one Abraxa sent you, both to you and to Lilith.

In this game, you have an appointment to keep.

In the back seat of the rideshare, Top 40 loop and hooks clicking over the XM band, you review the details of your outfit. Your wardrobe hasn't been refreshed for years, is only optimized for a webcam frame, no longer spectacular in its fit. But you've done your best: long black dress that drags and hides your work boots, top with spidery straps, fluffy false-fur stole, magenta weave coiled high enough to demand all your poise to keep from flattening against the ceiling of the back seat. Around your neck is a green stone pendant.

The rideshare driver—South Asian, in his twenties—has never seen you before, and now avoids your eyes in the mirror. Stare harder—establish a psychic barrier—and then, reflect. Lilith hasn't ever seen you either; neither has Abraxa. You know what Abraxa looks like from years of random blog photos—grinning from pickup windows, sitting among forest campsites with fantastic numbers of empty beer cans, topless with a red plastic basket and shopping the medical aisle of a CVS. Lilith you've only imagined: pale, white, a pair of wide open blue eyes, no other details.

Before leaving the house—in the front hall, your mother side-eyeing you from her stack of student worksheets on the couch—you texted Tula: *going to jersey city. if you don't hear back from me telling you i am safe in ninety minutes, please become concerned.* Now, you realize you should have sent the address: do so. *it's not a client,* you add. *it's a friend.*

A few minutes later, receive the reply: *k cool.* Is Tula angry with you? Calculate: When's the last time you spoke to her? The time in the park, which was when? Don't think about being a bad friend now; don't become un-centered. Focus on what's around you. You're well beyond Eastern Parkway now, beyond the parts of Brooklyn you know, racing over raised roads. The cars are far faster than you're used to, sliding in and out; you hope the driver knows what he's doing; should you check his star rating? Are you safe? And then you're approaching a bridge—you're crossing it to a borough you've never been. In the first *Mystic Knights* game, bridges were a sign of increasing danger: when you crossed a bridge, the monsters you'd fight would grow stronger. But they were also a sign of your power: you would cross a bridge only when you could.

Against that: vampires weren't supposed to be able to cross rivers: dead things found running water impossible to endure.

It is fucked up that you're going out here. It is fucked up that you read Abraxa's email, and saw who was cc'd on it, and acted immediately. You are no different from Droneslut. You should care about this fact. On some level, you do: you feel this fact floating outside your skull like the shadow of a headache. Inside, however, you feel all in motion, and you feel clean. The feeling inside of you does not come often. When it comes, you cannot argue with it; it is a fact like a wave. To question this feeling is the worst sin you can think of.

Therefore: don't think about being dead. Don't think about whether you trust the driver, or the people who made this bridge. Safe—tell yourself you are safe—thousands of people must cross this river every day. And then your car reaches the far side, and you are in a new place. Thousands of people cross every day, and you're no different from any of them.

■   ■   ■

And ask yourself, as the car glides forward into Staten Island, down the highway exit and over the bridge into Bayonne, the greenbelts, meadows, oil-smoke refinery towers like the wands of evil wizards: What's going to happen when you get to the address you entered, blindly, as your destination?

Close your eyes, find emptiness, then picture it. She's going to be waiting for you there: no, both of them will be. No: adjust your expectations. She won't be waiting for you, just Abraxa will. You'll reassure her. Then Lilith will appear, step out of the shadows in a silver dress, catch you in this moment of comforting someone.

No: this is awful. Adjust your expectations again. Neither of them will be there. Get out of the car to find only dead streetlights, uric scaffolding, crunch of glass and silence, poison smell. Die in New Jersey, never reach home. No, this isn't right—maybe you'll all be at a hotel, teenagers again, able to do it right this time. No, you don't know anything about what will happen. The error in all your predictions, as ever, is you.

Why does this always happen to you in rideshares? Keep calm, keep in control. Close your eyes again and work to find emptiness. But this time, find yourself in the park—the little hill where Tula made you go to pray. Sit there, New Jersey outside, trees and land and the trickle of water in your mind. There had been a tiny white boat in the water, a toy. Watch it bob with the motion of the stream, never going under, until the car comes to a stop.

No one is waiting. The church is still, suburban, quiet. Stand here, holding your bag, studying its ruined frame. No lights on in the abandoned parsonage, the garden black, the main building sutured in plywood. Abraxa said she was living underground:

Did she really mean here, in some ruin? Are you really expected to walk into this abandoned space? There are apartments all around, gorgeous brownstones—the streets are wide and clean—trees break through the pavement, ornaments hang from windowsills, from inside golden glows. Everyone must be watching you. They must know you're a sex worker—they must know you're a transsexual. They must know you don't belong here.

But staying out here isn't safe, either. Close your eyes—breathe—imagine the dark church before you. In your mind's eye, see how it looks in three dimensions. Then imagine yourself looking down on it from a great height, a 2D perspective, as if in a CraftQ game. Imagine yourself as a tiny smiley face, a whole dungeon ahead of you to explore. If you see this as a game, you will be safe. Nothing bad can happen to you in a game.

On the steel door of the basement, find the company logo you designed long ago. You drew it in the corner of a geometry class notebook. There's no padlock on the door. What can you do but open it?

Should you call her name when you step inside? What even is her real name? All of you only ever called one another by your IRC handles. Bizarre—a name is such a basic unit of information, and here none of you really know one another's. The code of a CraftQ object begins with its name; without knowing an object's name, it's impossible to tell it what to do. A nameless object is beyond your control.

Bad air hits you—incense, mildew, waste. A firepit is going: it's low, a board from a corner woodpile made of scavenged freight pallets that the fire has already fissured. If a fire is still burning, someone must be close.

Hesitate, then call out: —Lilith? —No reply. —Abraxa? — Still none.

You may be here a while. You need not to be caught in the dark. Take boards from the woodpile, good long ones. How should you do this? Visualize a fire in your mind: tall boards leaning together, making a triangle. Stack them high, balanced carefully at their tips. Then watch as the fire begins to swim upward into the channel you've made. Good enough: this should last.

Passages lead off from the firepit: east, north, south. Mazes, again. The open space to the north is probably the least dangerous, oxygen-wise: try it first, turning on your phone's flashlight. The floor here is irregular: cross the muddy, broken parts of it carefully. The walls and ceiling are in major disrepair; graffiti sparkles when you pass your light over it. There's a single piece of furniture here, a low table. An altar? Nothing is on it but a bubble mailer. Pick this up. Your logo, again, written across its seal.

As you prepare to open it, freeze. Among the many words on the wall are some you recognize. Raise your flashlight, look again. The wall is covered in CraftQ code: *#try opp seek, #change voids:breakables, #evolve red lions white dragons*. And also *#send lilith: sash.*

Put the package away; search the walls, heart fast. Letters painted in all different sizes, some massive and some tiny, each adding up to a line of code. Is this from—? Story sequences—enemy behavior—graphical effects—minigame engines. It's the game you all worked on together; she kept working on the game;

she tried to finish it. How did she do it? You should be writing this down—no, there may not be time, you should be reading faster. Weeks of work—months of work—objects on one wall that reference objects on others, all of it somehow debugged without reference to interpreter or screen. But possibly by walking between the rooms, you can trace it.

You should start by trying to find all the objects here, making a map in your head of all their names. Work from room to room, flashlight bright, lighting up the different strange gears of her mind. She must have meant for you to understand this. Why would she have brought you here, if not? What was the purpose of doing it?

The code in the north passes to the eastern supply closet, to the maze in the south—the paths were never separate, really, it was never that kind of maze at all—and then they trace up to the ceiling, the letterforms becoming distorted, as if the writer had to stretch to stand on tips of toes. And then the line of code swings to the side to avoid a crack. Why is there a crack? There is a crack—slowly realize this—because one of the ceiling joists is cracked, and because the whole building's weight is sagging into the space created by the break.

No, get back into control—step back, away from the danger—which is how you trip.

The flashlight clatters to the ground—the light shuts out— the only light now is the red of the fire. What is wrong with the fire? The fire is taller than it should be—as tall as you, a column, swimming and flowing into the new channel of boards you made. And then it connects, in a single surging lick, with the ceiling; and then fire is flowing overhead, toward the walls. No, you never learned to build a fire. Why should you learn something like that?

The whole western room is burning, and the fire has caught on a shelf of cleaning supplies, a bucket of oil and rags—roaring, it spreads—it's filling the space between you and the doorway out—and from somewhere at your feet, your phone starts to buzz—

In this game, you run—

—you run, holding your package—

—Lilith runs, holding the envelope with the notarized letter from Ronin, around the corner of Mercer Street, outside, just as a car is pulling up—

It all swam before Lilith, vision blurred from her run from the PATH station: the church, the archway, the lights on in the neighboring brownstones. The woman stepping out of the car parked just in front. Lilith had never seen her before: sticky frizz of hair hastily tied back, denim shorts, tank top with cartoon animals, olive freckles under eyes swallowed in massive glasses.

Are you one of Brax's friends, asked the new woman, whose voice Lilith immediately clocked. —Is she okay?

She will be, Lilith said, hoping this was not a lie. —Come with me?

They moved toward the church together—the new trans woman, Marcie, already seemed to know the way. The padlock on the door was missing, the door itself cracked. Lilith reached out to take the handle—and wait, was the handle hot? No, the handle was *moving*—the door was swinging outward—a wave of hot air was pushing toward her—and then here was another woman, tall, skin dark, hair in a high magenta pile, colliding with her, bringing her to the ground. Behind her, filling the space, a tall red leaf of flame.

The two women, Lilith and the stranger, lay there, tangled on the cold concrete, as Marcie screamed *Abraxa! Abraxa!* The woman tangled with Lilith was cursing, too. Lilith ached, a sore, bruised thud of pain. She rolled over: in the windows of the buildings around the church, suddenly, lights. Silhouettes. She'd lost her letter—her letter was gone.

On her hands and knees, she looked for it. There was a package the other woman had been carrying: Lilith scooped it up, kept searching. There was the letter denying the loan, close to the door. Lilith got to her feet, hustled for it. On the other side, the fire was spreading: the wooden shelves had caught, canned goods roasted like dark foil potatoes in the beds of flame. Her forehead was stretching, tanning like jerky—her cheeks blistering—she imagined her eyelashes, one by one, bursting into flame like holiday sparklers. And the writing on the walls was disappearing as the smoke rose, warping the plywood. Fascinated, Lilith watched the fire, and then she looked at her letter. After a moment, she tossed it through the door, and the fire ate it.

The other woman was standing now. The package, Lilith remembered, the one she was now holding. She turned it over in her hands. There was a label on it—her logo, again—her name. And she thought: it must be mine. And she opened it.

Inside was a tangle of daisy-chained cables, a multi-decade palimpsest of technology. At its heart was a peripheral: a 3.5" disk drive, yellowed and covered in incense and bright violet candle wax. Press eject, take the disk. Read the label on the back: PROPERTY OF A— PARKER, JR., SO HANDS OFF! On the front, someone had Magic Markered a rectangle, a triangle pointing up, three intersecting lines.

And for the rest of her life—which, despite personal and professional challenges, will be very long, and full of happiness—Lilith will remember the sound of the next moment: when the other woman steps close to her—and she feels the woman's breath on her shoulder, thick and sweet—and she hears the other woman speak: *Is that us?*

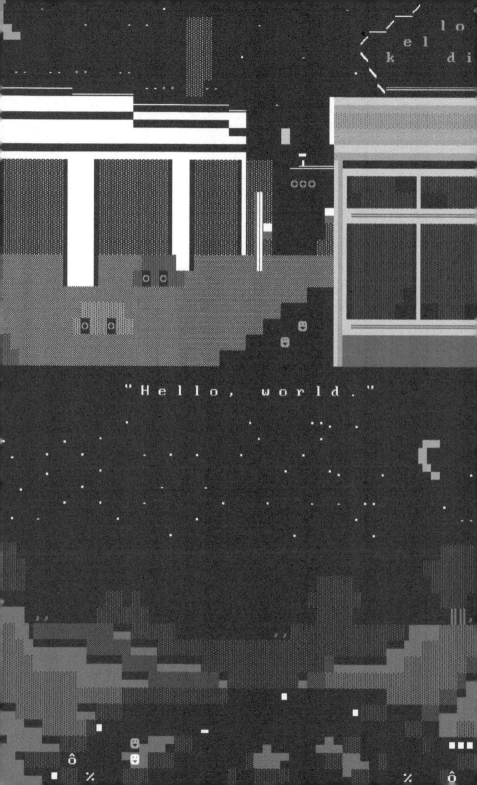

A.

The tent is from the co-op; the sleeping bag, too. It's gently used, only three tent stakes. Three would have to be enough.

There are other objects as well, their provenance uncertain: the butane lighter, the blanket, the dwindling orange bottle of blue pills: ten now, maybe able to be rationed across twenty, twenty-one days. The folding knife, for emergencies. The bricked cell phone: you never know. The canteen, snug now across her chest as she walks past the tiny stone ring where she made her fire last night out of a novel she found in the back of a gas station in a cardboard shelter labeled FREE, TAKE. Where did the canteen come from? This doesn't matter: what matters now is that it's empty, and she needs to fill it.

Fire will never kill me, only in water will be my end. What does that mean: Will water rise to drown her, or will a *lack* of water kill her? It's a very easy prophetic assassination for System D to achieve: as in everything, their success is over-determined. Water is a weapon: its chemical composition is designed to pull apart molecules, to break hydrogen from oxygen. It shreds, suspends, breaks, dissolves. And you can't get away from it: every morning when she wakes up on the high earth surrounded in fog, every bird and insect around her singing, empty spaces in her gums aching, her clothes are soaked. Water covers every inch of her.

There are no leaves yet on the trees as she creeps across a dead yellow meadow, skin itching all the time now, driving her to higher and higher ground.

She hadn't meant, exactly, to leave. She hadn't meant exactly to stop talking on IRC to Sash. Was this how Lilith felt, long ago? Not one big decision, more like many small ones: today I won't, and then there are so many todays in which I didn't, and now everything surrounding is different. This was how it felt leaving Marcie, she thinks, living down there: every day a decision to stay. Out here, in the trees and with the rare airplanes overhead, it feels like a suffocating dream.

It wasn't that she was angry at Sash. It wasn't just that Sash had said all that about Lilith to her, had kept saying it to her even when she'd clearly said to stop. Had she clearly said to stop? She can't remember now, and her phone is gone; there is no way to check. And so much context is lost online, in the world of pure text, the realm of air. Sash and Lilith had some complex understanding between them, a relation that had entirely escaped Abraxa's awareness. How was that possible? For so long she'd told herself one story about the game they'd never finished, making it a story about Sash and herself: Sash gave her a purpose, she was to fulfill it. Now here she found someone else in the story entirely.

She thought about this as she ignored whatever IRC pleas Sash must be sending her, whatever panic emails the banker was sending her, too. She thought about it as she tended her fire and her plants, harvested her cans and other needful things, and drew pictures in the bagel shop, the windows fogged, the barista finishing one book and then another. The bagel shop: where she first spoke to Lilith, where she'd drawn her here in her sketchbook, a herald out of time. Abraxa had been excited less at speaking to Lilith specifically—who was Lilith? Just some rando from #teen-goetia, just some coworker she'd known—more excited at what it must mean that her past was coming to find her, someone adjacent to the sorceress and the time when Abraxa had first served her. And then Lilith became a threat, a sign to interpret: a comet, a piece of some other planet crashing into her own. *Crisis from the skies.* She'd brought the woman over to dinner, wondering if the sorceress wanted her killed. But no, that was totally crazy—she wasn't going to kill anyone—unacceptable, crazy. She wasn't crazy. She was simply following a series of signs. But maybe that choice had been wrong, because as soon as Lilith's visit was done, the signs had dried up. The sorceress's voice had stopped.

At first, she tried not to be concerned about this. She tried to breathe and give the visions room to come, screwdrivered open the paint cans, washed her brush in a dish of scavenged soap, stood at the wall with it raised like a torch, waited. She'd started writing the code only a month ago—two months? How long?—the silence was temporary—she'd get it back. She'd be connected again. But she wasn't, and after so much noise—all the mounting, compacted feelings of her time since moving down here—the silence hurt.

There were too many hours every day, even more hours in the night. How had she spent her time before? She wanted to go for walks, look across the river at the fortress of evil beyond, where Lilith and Sash lived—prisoners, agents? But maybe if she left the abbey for too long, the sorceress might return and find her missing. So she stayed, reading walls she could no longer understand.

In the dark, she chewed on this thought: maybe the sorceress

stopped because Lilith is a good person, and I'm not. I've never
been.

How had grace come to her? She couldn't explain. She woke
up with it, frozen and groaning on her side, midday winter
rain on the far distant roof and spattering through the space
she'd made for sunlight and her plants. She lay there, achy and
dreamy and not wanting to get up, her final encounter with
Lilith again going through her mind. Lilith had asked her what
she'd wanted, and she'd answered by describing the whole great
society she'd build, that the sorceress was showing her. No, the
three of them would build it together. This was what finishing
the game had always meant. But maybe it was the rain, or the
ache, or the smell of old fire, or the season, or just how tired
she'd become. Whatever the cause, she suddenly understood the
solution. Her destiny wasn't to build a great society: it was to
build a small one. And it wasn't three people who'd build it
together. It was one person—no, not even a person. She wasn't
a person. She was a magic wand. The sorceress was holding her
now, had scooped her up from the bottom of the ocean, where
she'd made a deal, then died. Look down and you can see her—
black soft wraps blowing in unseen winds around her, gauze
and flesh, smiling face. Abraxa was only an instrument with one
last job to do. Gratefully, she performed it: she made the connection she was meant to make, she passed on what she had for
so long held. And in that moment, the curse at last broke. The
sorceress disappeared, and so the abbey became useless, another
skin to shed. She'd beaten the game.

She tosses a beach towel over the barbed wire at each property line she violates, moving toward where she's certain she

remembers seeing a creek, maybe where she dreamed a creek. The world is changing—spring is late arriving—the president is insane. Has her thirty-fourth birthday already happened? Which state is she in? No, this knowledge won't change anything. She's excited, traveling the way she always has: it's likely she's going the right way, or she'll intersect a road that is, or she'll meet someone who will bring her there, or someone who will bring her somewhere else. The fire tries to assume a shape, but the shape is always different. She looks forward to it: wild spaces where she can think all day with no walls to stop her. She could steal an axe, cut trees, build a steeple, grow her own food in the highest possible place, a place she knows she will inherit from no one: surely this land belongs to no one. She can make a start here.

Now she descends to the creek bed, still dry: but there will be water in it somewhere, not enough to change her, just enough to keep her alive and climbing. There will be enough to let her wash her sunburned skin, keep it as clean as she can.

The whole time walking away from Northwood—out along the highway, past sulfurous refineries, away from lights until there were only trees—she'd thought she could hear Marcie calling her name. But she knew this moment's apparition had been a gift. She was never going to see Marcie again.

The creek is full of black sacks of garbage: printed coupons, iPhone batteries, keyboards, packing foam. Gasoline skims across its surface, creating a rainbow she disrupts when she kneels and dips her canteen. She drinks: it dissolves as much of what's inside her as she can spare. There's a depression in the dead grass where she kneels; there's animal scat. Others have been drinking here, too.

Above her, last night, she saw the stars. She forgets, when

she's in cities, that the stars are real, distant fires, always present. The trees here wait to receive their light and convert it into power the earth can use, every wild food she finds. She will learn to get closer to them, because spring is late this year. System D will one day burn everything on earth. It will melt the glaciers of Greenland, and the rivers will become first lakes then oceans; the mountains will become islands. So she knows she has to hurry, white knuckles turning red with March cold and full canteen sloshing at her side: she has to find the high land that no one has ever owned. If she finds it fast enough, she can use it to protect everyone. In water will be my end: therefore, as ever, toward fire. Fire is the only way to make a start.

Clarity is what you need. And at least at first, clarity is hard to achieve: the new woman, Marcie, is screaming at you, and also she's driving you away from the scene of what will certainly become a major arson investigation. It took both you and Lilith to convince her to leave the church in the first place; she wanted to stay and look for Abraxa. *What if she's hurt? What if she's in trouble; what if she needs me now?* But the police, you both reminded her, and you were the ones Abraxa chose to email; she must have felt she had to take you along.

In the tunnel—the first time you've been in it, red-smeared restroom-tiles, echo of cars, the river passing overhead, a totally linear dungeon—Marcie seems to lose her nerve, starts to insist on going back. But Lilith's voice is firm, anchoring: *I understand, that's really hard. I understand. But right now we have to drive.* Help her, prove your merit: your phone has a map, use it to help find a place for you to go. Grounding and direction: these are what each of you can provide. You're a team.

You end up at a diner in Brooklyn near the BQE, one whose name delights both Marcie and Lilith as soon as you suggest it. The table has four seats; you occupy three of them. Lilith sits next to Marcie, making sure to stay close: the woman, already upset when you met her earlier, looks ten years older than she had in the dark of the church lawn. Sit across, watching them, your eyes at last on Lilith in the present tense. Dark teal coat—fuchsia earmuffs—tan scarf—blond bangs. Do not stare. You know nothing at all about this person in the present. All you know is what you can see: her giant salad, stacked with olives and grape leaves, her kind eyes as Marcie goes through the story of her and Abraxa and the last months.

Be present and practical. —And you don't know of anywhere else she might have gone, you ask. —Does she have a home city, or a family? Somewhere she could go if she didn't have anywhere.

Marcie looks into the skinned-over surface of the bowl of cream clam chowder you both encouraged her to order. —Brax has lived everywhere, she says. —We met in Florida a long time ago—she was coming from Oregon when she arrived—I think she used to live in California. That about covers the whole country.

Alaska, Lilith suggests. —Hawaii?

Maybe she went back to California, Marcie says. —Maybe that's where we should start to look.

Sip your hibiscus Italian soda to conceal your alarm at the thought of going to search for Abraxa. —I don't know if she wants to be found, you say carefully.

Marcie doesn't respond. Lilith frowns at her salad.

If she wanted to leave me, Marcie says, —Then I wish she would have told me. I wish I could have helped her.

No one speaks—not you, not Lilith—and after some time, Marcie puts her spoon into her soup. She takes it out again, studies the spoonful, lets it slide back into the bowl, untouched.

So how did both of you know Brax, she asks.

We were all in a video game corporation together, you say.

It wasn't like a real corporation, Lilith explains. She's looking at you suddenly—you're being perceived. —I mean, we took it very seriously.

Very seriously, you confirm, looking her in the eye.

Really astoundingly so, she says.

I'm confused, Marcie says. —Did you sell video games or not?

We never had any to sell, Lilith says.

Marcie nods. —What did you all do for your corporation? The not-real one.

I was the head of the not-real corporation, you say. —Also I wrote the script.

And I was the level designer, says Lilith. She dabs salad dressing from her lip: plum stain on white napkin edge.

What did Brax do, Marcie asks.

Find yourself looking at your drink. Find yourself remembering the empty seat—the writing on the walls. Lilith is at last the one to answer: —She did everything else.

The mood doesn't pick up again, though Lilith works hard to draw Marcie out: asks about her work, her life, her favorite games and shows. Excuse yourself to go to the bathroom—sit alone, slumped in a stall, graffiti over your shoulder that lets you know HE ISN'T WORTH IT—then sneak outside, leaving Lilith and Marcie at the table.

Car lights on the BQE, red and white comets: lean against the cold diner wall, watching cabs honk and inch past. You'll go back inside in a minute—it's freezing and awful out here; here is your breath against the full-moon cold—but take this moment to breathe, alone. Lilith is inside. The two of you are engaged in a project: comforting someone, putting together the truth. The two of you remember your corporation. She remembers designing levels for you. You spoke to her and she smiled.

Look at the traffic and will yourself not to be stupid, to have clarity, not to be destructive and foolish and all the things you always are. Will yourself to do things right. You have been given another chance. Will yourself not to waste it.

In this game, watch the lights move on the highway until everything in your body feels okay. Then turn, which is when you see Lilith there watching you, her own breath hanging before her face. You can see it because it's warm: it came from inside her body, a place that is warm.

Is everything okay, you ask, voice even. —Is Marcie okay?

She's fine, Lilith says. —I'm sorry for interrupting you—I can go back inside?

You can interrupt me, you say quickly. —I'm just looking at cars.

She inclines her head. —May I look at cars, too, she asks.

Nod, and now here she is, at your side, both of your backs against the brick. Watch the cars. Every car is worth ten points. After one thousand points, you will know what the right thing is to do.

I have no idea at all how to navigate this situation, Lilith says.

I know what you mean, you say. And then, too late, realize that she's referring to Marcie. Panic, check her expression: she's looking at the cars. Good: she didn't detect anything strange.

Each car that goes by is ten points, you tell her. —After one thousand points, we'll know how to help her.

She smiles; she closes her eyes. —I'm still counting, she says. —I'm counting by sound. Is that okay?

Good, you tell her, and you continue to count by sight.

Six hundred points go by (you think; it is actually very hard to count cars.) —Do you think Abraxa is okay, she asks.

I don't know, you say. —I don't really know her at all. It feels strange to say that.

No, I know, she says, and suddenly her voice is different, coming in a rush. —It's so strange, all of this—I mean, I talked to her in person before, a couple of times? But it's really strange to meet other people she was connected to, to feel like there were all these sides to her—

She falls silent. —Go on, you say.

It's like—you know a lot about someone because you know this one side to them, she says. —But really you don't know very much about them at all.

Look at her. —I feel the same, you say.

Watch her face—watch for danger—but she's nodding.

What do you think is on the disk, she asks.

It could be anything, you say. But both of you know this isn't true.

We should go back inside, she says. —We shouldn't leave Marcie alone.

We should, you echo, feeling a pulse.

Stop at the bathroom again to check your phone. From Tula: *bitch, you're going to be fine.* Read it twice, then hug it to your chest.

Marcie has finished her chowder and Lilith has paid the check. Does she think you can't pay it? Leave three twenties for the tip. Teamwork.

I'm going to go home, Marcie says. —I'm worried Brax may have gone there.

Good idea, Lilith says. Don't add anything.

Thank you both, Marcie says. —I'm sorry about all of this. I know you were good friends to her.

Lilith blushes; you frown at your feet. But Marcie seems not to notice. —Can I drop you off, she asks. —You live around here, right?

And find yourself speaking before you think: —I'm wondering if there's somewhere we can both go, you say. —Somewhere we can look at this package she gave us.

We can go to my apartment, Lilith says immediately. —It's not that far at all.

She looks at you: look back.

On the car ride to Lilith's apartment—which you note is very close to your apartment; you must have been living just blocks from one another for months now, maybe years—the sun starts to come out, and Marcie plays the radio, and Lilith again sits in the front seat. Sit in the back seat, and watch her, and do not speak.

She lives so close to you, in a building you have passed many times, just in from the corner of Franklin Avenue, a brownstone with a stoop, trash cans all in a row, window boxes full of lavish hanging leaves. Her apartment in the blue dawn seems massive, uncluttered: cartoon artwork on the walls, shelves lined with fantasy novels and comic books. The window is full of house-plants; a label-less can on top of the fridge holds dried flowers.

Shit, says Lilith, looking through a door—her bedroom, unmade bed, scattered clothes—look away, not too quickly. —I'm sorry, she says, —it's a disgusting mess in here, I'm not an adult, not really.

Your apartment is beautiful, you say.

I'm really tired, she says. —Like exhausted. Like is it okay if we—

She trails off, looking at you. —It's okay, you say. —Let's look at what Abraxa left us in the morning. Or—when we get up. I don't mind.

She nods, her eyes watching you: meet them. After a moment, she goes to her hall closet. She returns with a blanket.

There are pillows on the couch already, she says. —I'm sorry. Super not adult here.

It's fine, you say.

Watch the ceiling, stretched on her couch. This is the first time in a long time you've slept away from home. How long has it been? Think, and listen out the window as buses start to whisper at the stop just outside, and the traffic starts, and morning voices laugh. Finally, let yourself get up. Her bedroom door is mostly closed. Her sink is full of dishes. Wash them.

The sun is nearly down again when you wake up. Lilith is already moving in the kitchen, texting, boiling water. She hasn't noticed you awake yet: pretend to sleep a little longer, rolled up tightly in her blankets. This is why you haven't stayed away from home for such a long time: you're never sure of the rules for it. What are the rules of normal people's houses? You've never understood. Touch your face under the blanket: rough. Touch your wig, which you've slept in: crushed.

Wait for her to go into the bedroom, then sneak past the open door into the bathroom. She's used it: it smells like steam and fruit. Borrow her razor, put yourself together by touch, a puzzle on automatic. Pretend you belong here. If you pretend you already have the things you want, sometimes you really get them.

Lilith is disentangling cords on the couch. —Do you need help, you ask.

I'll get it, she says. —All this stuff is just super old? She must have been carrying some of this around since the nineties.

A long time to carry something, you say. Fortunately she isn't looking at you.

Go to work in the kitchen, inventorying cupboards, chopping garlic. Sneak glances at her over the kitchen island: her pale shoulders, soft and broad, her hair now in a bun. *Dammit,* she mutters, voice vaguely Texas, as she fails to connect a bent-pinned parallel port.

Proceed cautiously. Construct a vast omelet, using every vegetable, spice, and cheese in her fridge. Cut it in half, then bring two plates to the couch. Sit next to her, leaving some inches. She doesn't get up.

This is delicious, she says. —Thank you!

You're welcome, you say. —Is it working?

It is, she says proudly.

Good girl, you say, keeping your voice very even. —So. Should we begin?

Yes, she says. —Or no, wait!

She tabs to Spotify, quickly scrolls through a playlist. A track begins: from the speakers, synthesized flutes, beats, choirs, a sad and active bass guitar playing countermelody beneath it. *Super Mystic Knights 4*—you know this immediately—the moment you get the second skyship and go searching for your friends in the broken world. Lilith closes her eyes, smiling, nodding to the beat. Watch her. She is almost thirty-five years old, you think. So are you. Then feel embarrassed by that judgment—then close your eyes and listen too, imagining skyships in flight, until the song ends.

Okay, now let's start, she says, and she activates CraftQ.

Something is wrong with the colors, something is wrong with the speed—CraftQ is a DOS program and won't run easily on Lilith's modern laptop, the game data somehow distorted like a fifth-generation videotape—but your fingers still remember the steps you take to start a new game, choose color display rather than monochrome, keyboard rather than the mouse. The file loads in media res, starting a cut scene: a blocky little village, a smiley face gazing at her reflection in a pond. Another smiley face approaches. Feel your skin grow cold with fear; dive for the escape key. But Lilith's hand is in the way.

Please stop it, you say. —Please, I forgot I wrote this part.

She looks legitimately alarmed. —Sure, of course, she says. —Do you need some water?

No: get back in control. Take a very deep breath—now take another. —It's okay, you say. —I just wasn't expecting—it's fine.

She nods. —I know, she says. —We're going to get through it together.

Is this meant to comfort you? Do not display discomfort. Just breathe—just continue to watch the game. The two smiley faces are together by the pond now. They are speaking.

Did anyone see you coming, asks one of the women, who is the sorceress.

The scene continues far longer than you can believe. The two women trade barbs and flirtations; they trade more. You recognize many of them from novels and films you once loved. There is no obvious relationship with human speech or patterns of flirtation as you have come to know them. In the end, the rival sneers: *You think you're better than all of us in this village. Don't you? Well, you're not!* The tiny smiley face that represents her ticks away, one step at a time, all the way off screen. Then, as she disappears, the sorceress speaks again. *But I am*, she says.

I'm truly sorry, you start to say to Lilith, but her eyes are wide: the screen is fading to white. Technically this isn't hard to program in CraftQ—you just have to iterate through all the on-screen objects, changing the color and display character to solid—but then the screen fades out again, and suddenly a comet streaks across, writing big blocky letters in fire: *SAGA OF THE SORCERESS*. It moves precisely, even gracefully, timed with the bleats of PC speaker music that begin to emerge. At last it crashes into the edge of the screen, and for a moment your logo appears, a tiny candle in a crude approximation—

ASCII char 30, char 240: a candle in the air, and then it sputters out like a firework. Around the title, nighttime stars appear, twinkling. Below them white words appear: *copyright and c. MCMXCVIII invocation llc. all rights reserved.*

How did we do that, Lilith asks.

I don't know, you say. —We'd have to ask.

Both of you are silent then, watching the letters of the title smolder on the tiny screen.

The amount of work the three of you completed seems impossible. Room after room in the editor, whole towns full of people and dialogue, battle sequences, magical animations, dramatic

ASCII artwork, mazes, treasures. When did you do all of this? When had you found the time? Who were the people who imagined all of this—every silly, embarrassing line, every ostentatious visual, every accidentally profound thing? It couldn't have been the two of you sitting here reviewing it all, tired and silent.

There's so much of it, Lilith finally says. —I always remembered it as not very much—we only got through a little bit of what we planned. But this would take hours to play.

She had it the whole time, you say. —She kept it with her.

She also worked on it: there are parts of the story you never wrote, that don't fit. These get stranger and hastier as you go— something about a teenager? The planet Saturn?—and by the end, it's almost no longer a game, just static sketches in ASCII, no interaction at all. Go to the end of the file, looking for clues she may have left, but there's nothing. She hadn't had a computer with her, you remember her saying. In the end, whatever she had been thinking must have burned up with the walls.

One of the rooms was called Northwood, you say. —That was going to be one of the most important parts. But we never got that far.

No, says Lilith, her voice strange, small. —The last part we were working on—or I mean, I was working on—it was that wizard tower.

Bell Prix, you say. —After the sewers.

I never finished it, she says. —I never showed it to anyone. The Northwood part was way after that.

Study her, her eyes looking down. You could try to be kind: *I don't remember where we left off.* But you don't want to lie. Instead, look back at the screen: instead, open the room marked Northwood. It's a huge cruciform complex of rooms: black floors, navy walls, a background pattern of dark gray boulders, CraftQ shorthand for *underground*. The rooms are all empty. Abraxa laid it out, but never finished filling them in.

Northwood is what she called the property, Lilith says.

Stare at the empty black floors, imagining Abraxa in the church basement you saw: the shelves of cans, the smells, the dust, the soot on the rocks, the sad and trampled garden. Then close your eyes. When you open them again, take the keyboard—go into the editor—add an object, a blue smiley face.

What are you doing, Lilith squawked. —Don't *change* it!

Why not, you ask. —It's ours, isn't it?

Quickly add some code—astonishing how your fingers remember all of this—then drop into the test mode, to try out the room. The blue smiley takes a step, then speaks. *hello lilith! it's me, sash! i've gone into the COMPUTER*

Lilith smiles, not without fear. —May I, she asks. Relinquish the keyboard: watch her add her own smiley, red.

Hello! I, too, am in the computer! It's weird in here! :/

Continue in this way for some time—pass the laptop back and forth, building a longer conversation, adding body language. One smiley advances, another steps back.

We're dancing, lol! :D, says hers. She is sitting right next to you, turns and smiles.

Do not react: quickly code your smiley. *i don't like dancing.* Then write the code to fire a bullet.

She guffaws, watching the blue smiley shoot her. —Oh, I'll fix you, she says, and she takes the keyboard, opens up her smiley's code. She frowns. —Let's see—let's see—

After a moment, suggest: —The label you want is :shot. That's how you respond to a bullet collision event. Just like how :touch responds to other collisions, right?

Right, she says, taking her hands off the keys. —Duh, I know that. Why was I so slow to remember that? I was always so bad at this.

Study her face. —You'll get it back, you tell her. —I just thought too much about this back then is all. That's the only reason I remembered.

Her face doesn't change. Or no, something is happening to it. What is it? Faces are always so hard to read. You went too far again, you think. You are always going too far.

Should we make one for Abraxa, she asks.

Don't answer her. Look at the empty editor screen, your two avatars standing in the empty church. Her code window is still open: the editor says :shot, and then no response. Think: what is wrong with you.

It's crazy to have this back after all this time, she finally says. —We could pick it up right where we left off, you know? We could finish making the whole thing.

Sit, hands on the keys. She sits beside you, not moving, either. After some time, reach out and close the laptop.

The sun is already down. She offers to order in: have you not eaten since the omelet, how long ago? All your routines and procedures are broken. While you wait for the food, copy the game files to Lilith's PC and secretly email them to yourself, careful to use a burner email. (But no: she already has your real email, doesn't she? You gave it to Abraxa, and Abraxa gave you both away.) Lilith is busy texting someone, face twisted and angry. From the rhythm of her hands, infer that she's typing messages and then deleting them. Think: another point in common.

In the chatroom, you'd said to Abraxa: *I was in love with*

Lilith. This was the first time you'd ever said this to anyone. The thought, here in the moment with Lilith present—her face frown-lined, picking at her eye as she types—feels mortifying, dangerous even to think. Maybe she will feel you thinking it from across the room, skin crawling as if from radiation. You loved a child, decades ago: no, not even that, No, you loved a pattern of words in a chat box, you loved whatever you projected onto it. The woman present is a whole living force about whom you know nothing. And yet something links the two—and yet the large part of your brain that this feeling once colonized is linked as well, and all the feelings are activating again. You have no idea what to do.

Ask yourself: *How do I not hurt her. How do I not hurt her. How do I not hurt her.* Ask it until Lilith finally looks away from her phone: you do not think the message was sent. She holds it in front of her, between two palms.

We should get drunk, she says. —We should get like, really drunk. I don't have to work tomorrow. Maybe I never have to work again.

Yes, you say. —That's a good idea.

She goes beneath her kitchen cupboard and brings out a sticky old bottle of Chambord: *I bought it because it looked like a wizard potion,* she explains. As you work through a sushi boat for two, she fills two glasses. You're not good at drinking; you don't want to get drunk: Should you try to drink less than she does? But that would be an unethical situation. Maybe you should drink more? But neither of you is good at drinking, and after two glasses she takes the bottle away to the kitchen. Returning, she sits down on the floor among the empty plates, and she toasts you, up on the couch, with her empty glass.

To Abraxa, she says.

To Abraxa, you say. —And to the greatest video game company in the world.

Find yourself, from this, talking about the old days online: Do you remember the time—? That person was so weird— Did that game ever come out? Do you know what happened to—?

This is so good, she says. —I haven't thought about any of this stuff in years.

I think about it sometimes, you say. —I haven't talked about it to anyone, though.

Right? —She nods, gets on her hands and knees like a cat. —What do you even say about CraftQ drama? I never told anyone at school, or in Scouts really, or anything. Not like I didn't think it was cool—I just didn't know how to explain it.

I make video games with my teenage friends, you say.

Right, she says. —You'd sound insane.

Both of you sit for a moment. She folds her knees under herself: she moves easily, you think, at home with moving.

Why do you think Abraxa did it, she asks. —I mean, all of this.

Think about how to answer this. —We talked online a lot, you say. —I mean recently, just in the past weeks. It was in the old IRC channel we used to use, the one with the worst name.

What'd she say to you, Lilith asks.

We both said all kinds of things, you say, nervous. —She was convinced she was doing something magical down there? That the sorceress was talking to her—she talked about spells.

Lilith looked at her knees. —I hope she finds help, she says.

She's a brilliant person, you say. —She figured things out about herself before anyone. Living that intensely takes something out of you.

We were all pretty intense back then, she says.

Look at her face. Her expression: What is it saying? An average: her eyes are fond, her mouth is sad. Now is a good moment: you can bring up back then; you can apologize. But before you can find the words, she's looking at you again.

What's your life like now, she asks. —What did you end up doing?

Think: *I'm a whore in a video game.* —I blog and teach, you say. —What about you?

She makes a little farting sound with her tongue. —Well! Up to *yesterday*, I was an assistant loan approvals manager, she says. —Now, I don't know? I probably can't work at a bank anymore. I might be going to jail, even? Who knows! Maybe I'll learn to code.

What are you supposed to say to this? —You could become a level designer, you finally say. —You were good at that.

She smiles, touches her face. —I was terrible, she says.

We just saw all your levels, you say. —They were cleverly designed. They stumped me.

I never understood why you let me be in the company at all, she says. —You and Abraxa, you were both brilliant. You became a teacher—that makes so much sense! I wasn't brilliant. I was just around.

She watches you—her bangs are in her face—her chin is propped in her hand. She is a good person, you think. Now is the moment to be good back to her. Now is the moment to tell her how sorry you are for everything you've done. But again, she speaks first. —I think I need to go to bed, she says, and very easily she draws herself to her feet, and swaying, she goes to her room, leaving you among the ginger and chopsticks. She falls into her bed. She does not close the door.

■ ■ ■

Clean the floor. Extinguish the lights. Then lie on the couch. It's no longer early—it's late, a work day—there are no voices from the street. Lie on the couch, and let your thoughts roll, and then get up. Do not think—do not talk yourself out of it. Her dark apartment already feels familiar—the dark frame of her open bedroom door floats close. Lean on it, old Chambord in your throat—rap on it with your knuckles, twice. Under a duvet with a picture of a great spreading tree, her body stirs.

I can't sleep, you say. —Is it okay if I sleep in here?

A noise, confused, from beneath the sheets.

On the floor, you clarify.

Sure, she says, in a sleepy croak. —Okay.

Glide, swaying only a little, to the side close to where you think she's facing. Hear your knees crack as you lower yourself to the floor—stretch out, back against a wide oval rug. Fold your hands over your solar plexus—look up at the ceiling. Let your eyes unfocus. Let the ceiling blur, then again get crisp, blur, then crisp. There are shelves above her bed: they're lined with dolls, Mystic Knights. A crush of feeling in your heart, as if someone is squeezing out its juice. And the blankets above you shift—she is awake, too.

In this game, you must make everything right again. Here are ways to start:

- I'm sorry.
- I'm so sorry.
- I'm not saying I regret it—I don't—
- I was a different person then. Playing our game, seeing the words I wrote, I wanted to die.

- I must have been so much to deal with.
- I wanted everything a certain way—I was angry and messed up—I didn't know how to be with other people at all—
- I didn't appreciate you, didn't see you, acted like a monster, was one—
- Am I apologizing for the right things? Have I missed anything? I wish I could apologize for all of it, all the time—

I'm sorry: in the end, this is all you manage to say.

Part of you, you can feel, is waiting for her to ask you: *For what?* Go on waiting.

May I ask you a question, comes her voice, at last, from beneath the blankets.

Look at the ceiling. —Go ahead, you say.

Back then, she says. —That night.

Yes, you say.

She asks: —How did you know that I was a girl?

The dolls look down at you: *ushabti*. The court who attends a pharaoh when she's died.

It seemed obvious, you say, turning onto your side. —You acted like one. You had a whole fake wife. And then you pretended to be her, for days.

Silence, and then: —But pretending to be a girl—that was what you told me I should do.

Lie there in the dark—and suddenly find yourself feeling angrier than you can remember being—and suddenly get up.

No, you're remembering it wrong, you say. —Excuse me.

■ ■ ■

Go to her bathroom. Get naked, get into her shower, leave your wig on the sink. Use her fruit body wash—towel off—no, *steal* her fruit body wash. Put it in your bag with all your things. Put your wig back on your head. Go to her cupboard—find her Chambord again—pull a shot of it straight from the bottle, a potion to restore you. Then rap on her door frame again this time loud.

She shifts—she mumbles. She asked you that, and then she fell back asleep.

I'm going home, you say. —Thank you for dinner and conversation.

What? —She sits up, bun half undone from the pillow, tank top twisted around her collarbone. —You don't have to go; you can stay until morning.

I don't want to, you say. —Listen. There's something I want to say to you. (*Do not hesitate or think.*) I'm sorry for everything back then. I was a lot. (*Do not let your voice betray you.*) I was embarrassing. I put you through a lot. And you didn't deserve it. So. I'm sorry. Now that's done.

Hey, she says, her voice strange. What is her expression? In the dark, it is harder still to read—other people are separate—other faces have always been impossible to understand. —Do you want— Her voice trails off. —Do you want a copy of our game, she finally asks.

I'm good, you say. —Goodbye.

Turn, and then turn back.

Listen, you say. —You were always a girl. That's what I saw. She doesn't speak.

In this game, you must escape the apartment as quickly as you can. You must not hesitate anymore. You must leave her sitting in bed—you must walk out of her apartment and onto her street, which is also your street, just thirty minutes apart—you must walk all the way to Eastern Parkway, where the benches are, because some part of you knows you will require one soon. Sit down now—breathe, gasp—and then remember one smiley face shooting the other one—and then start to cry.

The night is cold and clear, and a blue star shines over you in Orion's Belt, one of the few in the city you can see. Abraxa said something to you about stars, signs. She thought the sorceress was using her for some purpose—that there was a spell binding her. Maybe that purpose was finally achieved. A star is a fire—a fire brings destruction. Sit here, crying for yourself, thinking about how there is no other purpose to a fire. And the magic is over—it failed—you will never escape yourself. You will not find what you need.

L.

TO: sashiel@yahoo.com
FROM: lilith83@gmail.com
DATE: (Who knows. Years from now. Never.)
SUBJ: :/

It's been a while, huh?

I sat and thought a long time (uh, obviously :/) about whether I wanted to write this to you. That night at my apartment, I told you I was slow to work, slow to code CraftQ, slow to complete. I still think that's true. Maybe it's just some weird dream that I finished this letter and sent it to you? It would be a fucked-up dream you are having if that is true! But I meant to write you. At least part of me did, at least some of the time.

I'm sitting on the beach. The song about how a man feels himself to be the only real person on a beach—did you ever hear that song? I miss how we used to talk as teenagers, talk through songs, borrowed emotions, borrowed words and eyes. The words were just lying there, common property. We just kind of picked them up. We picked up all kinds of things from one another, whole jokes and beliefs and pieces of our personality.

We did it without thinking, a kind of psychic communism. We had no shame.

I'm writing to you, in part, because I'm really angry with you. I don't like saying that—forgive me for writing you a letter just to say that! Or no, don't forgive me, because actually I really mean it. Why did you leave like that? Why did what I asked you upset you like that? Why do you have to take it so *seriously*, everything I say? (All these are Real Questions, by the way. If that is something you remember.)

You were so sunk into yourself, all that night after Abraxa was gone. It was terrible—I felt like I must be boring you so completely; I had to keep finding ways to fill silence, just to get through. It was so exhausting, you know? And I was going through my own thing—my job was gone! I was breaking up with someone! And I hurt Abraxa I think, I thought I could be helpful to everyone and I just wasn't, and now she's gone, and who knows where. You showing up was the only thing that felt good out of all of it: seeing you after all that time. And what did you do? You walked out and left me alone.

That's the part of this I wrote before, closer to then. (I have maybe been working on this for a while. :/ I'm also doing other things, such as figuring out my apartment, income, and life, but I kinda don't want to get into any of that, so assume I'll turn out okay. Okay?) Today I decided to come write more at the beach, because the sun is coming out for longer and longer each day, and the water is warming up now, and it just felt like something I wanted to do. And I don't know—today other parts of it feel like they stand out. Some days are one way and some days are another; there's no exact accounting. Does that make sense? Probably not? (I was a loan approvals manager; I used to make sense more. :/)

When I met you, long ago now, I was stuck. I didn't even realize then how stuck I was: I was alone, asleep, buried. Back then, all that stuff—CraftQ and #teengoetia and online and all the weirdos we knew—it was a way for me to be alive. You, and Abraxa, and everyone else we knew online, so dramatic and committed and creative and shining and fun. A whole secret world in my heart, no matter where my body was: in Texas, in the Boy Scouts, in the world where I was going to grow up to be a man. Bodies didn't matter there. It was the start of everything, for me, and so much of it flowed from you.

That night—the one just weeks ago, I mean, after Abraxa ran away and we played our old game—you tried to apologize to me for back then. You talked about it like it was this awful thing, everything we'd done then. I won't tell you I never thought about it that way. Maybe I even thought of it that way a lot—maybe that's why I asked you what I did. But there were so many years since then, and I realized you had been eaten up by that for all of them. And suddenly I was seeing it through your eyes all over again: a world where all the power was yours, and all the guilt, too.

Do you really think you're that important? Why do you think that?

For years I thought I was the worst of the three of us. I'd felt so bad when I quit our company—I felt like a failure, like a traitor, like a coward. The electric space of the Internet, our spirits conducted there together by mysterious wizard spells, we could be honest with one another: there where bodies aren't. Why was it so much harder once you introduced me to my body? I don't know. I'm sorry I went away. At the time, it was the best way I could think of to spare you pain. I don't think it worked.

But at the same time, I'm like—not sorry?? I was just a kid; I was facing something too big for me. Now, thinking about how you must have known that—you controlled so much of me, then—sometimes I really do hate you for putting me in a position like that. Sometimes I never want to talk to you again. And then sometimes I remember you were a kid, too. All of us kids, hurting one another. It's ridiculous. Someone should put a stop to all of it.

And sometimes, like that last day at my apartment, I look at you and remember how happy it makes me to see you shine.

Something I once thought about on this beach: all we owe to a friend is to try. I don't know what you'd say about it (and I used to think I knew what you'd say about everything.) I didn't do a very good job of helping Abraxa, did I? And it isn't a great consolation to me that I like, tried, and I'm sure it isn't a great consolation to her, either. But I can't forget that I did it. It meant something that I did it. I think what I'm angriest about is that I think you wanted to apologize for everything because you wanted to make it as if it never happened: wipe out our history like erasing a disk, reset to nothing, and we could start again, be only new and good people now. I hate that! I don't think we get free by settling all our debts to one another. I'm not a debt to settle; neither are you. We get free by something else: by recognizing that what we do to one another is forever. We are what we are to one another. I am what you did to me—you are what I did to you. Despite everything, I like who I am. I hope you do, too.

Back then you made my world feel like magic. What did I give you? (*A limit. Belief. Things I didn't deserve.*) I'll never know. But I hope you keep it; I hope you cherish it. Don't waste it.

Ugh—this letter is so serious! I think this is what made the three of us friends, or coworkers, or just tangled up together, or whatever we were. We were always so *serious*! For years I beat myself up, I really did, for quitting a pretend video game company. Let's not be serious anymore, okay? Let's just not. The tide is up, and I want to go swimming, so I'm going to be done soon. I don't want to settle my debt to you, even if I may not want to see you for a long time.

I tried for so long to see through your eyes, yours and other people's, to call that good, and to live my life according to it. I think you've been trying to do the same thing for me. Is that right? If so, here is maybe what you think I'm thinking: that you hurt me. That you failed me. That you damaged me, that you were a perpetrator and I was your victim. That my life is less now because of you. That I blame you for this.

That's how you might think I see it. Do you want me to tell you what I see? Long ago, you opened a door in me, and I walked through it, and my life became my life at last. You gave me my name. I'm so grateful to you. You did me far more good than you ever did me wrong.

I wish you every good thing in the world, falling down on you like snow for you to make into anything you want. Okay, now I'm done. Remember the principle of Involution? In my beginning is my end. Well I am sorry to report to you, my friend, that this is *ninety-nine percent wrong*. There is all kinds of newness that has nothing to do with where we've been. Look for yourself: it's scattered out there like shells on the beach, ready for you to pick up. It's all free. Please be free.

Yours, Lilith
2016–2024

#endgame

Acknowledgments

The first thanks must go to my former Dungeons and Dragons group circa 2012, on whose emotional adventures the substrate of narrative for the Mystic Knights series of video games is built. Thank you to Philippe, Rosalie, Brecca, Katoki, Ern, Arden, and Susuru, as well as all your earthly anchors. Special thanks go to Caoimhe Harlock, who went above and beyond for this book many times, including translating the complete timeline of Mystic Knights titles into Japanese, lending me the name of her onetime game studio "The Critical Hit" (whose *Spellshard: The Black Crown of Horgoth* is the sort of production Sash and her coworkers would like), and coming up with the gross luxury donut flavors Mr. Swannuken offers Lilith after the 2016 election. I do not even mention the beautiful fan art she made for *Super Mystic Knights 3* on reading a draft of the book. She is a heroine, forever Flame Champion.

CraftQ is a bizarro world rendition of Tim Sweeney's 1991 debut game ZZT (for "Zoo of Zero Tolerance"), whose level editor and the community around it spawned a suspicious number of transsexuals. There's still a ZZT community today, nearly thirty years after I first downloaded it while looking for Calvin and Hobbes video games on AOL's file archive. If curious, the authoritative (and beautiful) book is certainly Anna Anthropy's *ZZT*, published by Boss Fight Books. Much more information is available through the archival work of ZZTer Dr. Dos, custodian of the passion of a thousand burning teenage hearts across now four generations. The long IRC chapter near the start of the book was largely from memory, but for help reconstructing the tone and flow of surreal late-night chat on the #darkdigital IRC channel in 1998, I relied on excerpts ZZTers past had thoughtfully archived at bash.org.

The description of the CraftQ game on page 224 relates to the excellent ZZT game p0p by the mysterious and brilliant tucan, a.k.a. Will Gutierrez. For years it's haunted me, as its fictional equivalent did Sash.

The Mystic Knights games obviously owe a great deal to the real-world *Final Fantasy* games, with some admixture of *Breath of Fire*, *Dragon Quest*, and the *Ultima* series. The staff of The Critical Hit is a dream-logic version of the actual staff of *Final Fantasy*–makers Square in the late 1980s, notably the great Hironobu Sakaguchi, Nobuo Uematsu, Yoshitaka Amano, Nasir Gebelli, Kazuko Shibuya. I must also mention Akitoshi Kawazu: I like to think that if any member of the 1980s Final Fantasy development team had really attempted to blend sigils into the program code, it would have been him. Thank you all for opening a door to something.

Sash's friend Tula is fictional, but her reading series owes much to my memories of the late, lamented Genre Reassignment open mic in Brooklyn, as hosted by Juno Tempest and Dr. Xerxes Verdammt, at which many chapters in this book got their first live audience hearing during the years 2016–2020.

The Hildegard von Bingen quotes Abraxa reads in the Jersey City library are from her *Book of Divine Works*, as translated by Dr. Mark Atherton. The book Lilith reads is John Weir Perry's *The Far Side of Madness*, which I read very late in the process of working on this book but which resonated with it in surprising ways (and is generally recommended). The novel also owes a strong debt to Sascha Altman DuBrul's *Maps to the Other Side* (Microcosm 2013), as well as the Internal Family Systems therapy framework as interpreted by my former therapist Mollie; work we did and wise things she said very deeply inform the underground chapters of the book.

The church Abraxa squats is based on an actual fire-damaged church on Mercer Street in Jersey City, which I think is now just condos; I have no idea what how the real church is constructed or the real history of the fire that damaged it. Some details of the renovation work Abraxa does to its basement owe much to a helpful hand-drawn schematic of "rubble trench" construction by Richard Flatau of Cordwood Construction (cordwoodconstruction.org). Even armed with this schematic, I do not recommend trying to dig through any rubble trench foundation you may encounter.

This is where I must deeply thank my editor, Mark Doten, for intense enthusiasm, as well as for the interest in resolving this problem of how a trans woman in her thirties actually digs into a slab foundation. I really appreciate having an editor who gets and cares about all these things: accurate demolition, video games, these heartfelt teenage queers and thirtysomethings, the suchness of old SNES graphics and sonic crunch—and who is also just a great writer whom I'm fortunate to get to collaborate with. Your line edit comments are a joy: thank you so much for again teaming up on this book.

Also at Soho, thank you to Sarah Rogers for copyedits, including the suggestion for the incredibly sick line "carapaces of scarabs" (replacing "carapaces of death moths," an animal that does not have a carapace). Thank you to managing editor Rachel Kowal for giving me much production assistance on the weird illustrations, plus very clear timelines for delivering all the moving parts—I'm very grateful to be working with you again too! Also to Johnny Nguyen and Lily DeTaeye, who because book publishing is a time warp I've both only just met as I'm approaching the delivery date for these acknowledgments, but whom I already both like, and if you are reading this book, on whose publicity labors you in some way have relied.

Always, always thank you to my agent, Jin Auh, who is willing to keep supporting these strange projects, and who gave invaluable help in shaping the opening chapters.

There are so many people who have given generous time to read and tell me their thoughts on this book. In no particular order: June Facts, Never Angeline North, Carrie O'Hara, Maya Deane, Noah Zazanis, Jackie Ess, Ingrid Vollmond. Also two whole writing groups: our workshop at the Grace Paley Project, Emma Copley Eisenberg, Karen Gu, Rachel Heng, Annie Liontas, and Sarah Marshall, and my Brooklyn Ship of Theseus group: at different eras composed of Megan Milks, Max Zev, Chavisa Woods, Jillian McManemin, Che Gossett, Sam Moore. Special thanks to Rachel Lyon, with whom I hung out many mornings at a sinister barbecue hall in Crown Heights working on the earliest stages of this book, and to Bill Cheng, with whom I traveled evenings after work to Mia's Bakery in Cobble Hill to do the same, and who contributed not just the name "Mr. Papazian" but also many hours talking ZZT community days.

Extra special credit to the aforementioned Caoimhe Harlock, Cat Fitzpatrick, Miracle Jones, Anton Solomonik, and

Kevin Carter (the greatest ZZT composer in the world). As ever, thank you to Wren Hanks for being here for all of this, even through the singularly dark early 2020s years of working on this book; whatever we are building, the foundations endure.

In case he ever reads this, thank you to Sean, the proprietor of the Airbnb I stayed at in Jersey City in the summer of 2022 while finishing revisions on the Abraxa chapters of the book, who didn't bat an eye at me trying to explain the plot to him, who served vast breakfasts of toast, jam, and more hardboiled eggs than anyone could eat, and who told me many strange stories about Jersey City, his political career there, and his family history. I loved every word, and some ghost of these stories surely haunts the book.

Above all the rest, thanks to my dear friend Casey Plett. Without your belief in this book at a time when I had very little belief in it, or really anything I was doing, no one else would be reading this right now. I told you I thought I should cut the ending; I thought it was *ontologically evil*; you told me: "Well, it worked for me." Thank you. <3

I'm very sorry if I've left anyone out! I know it is cold comfort, but let me know and I'll try to get you into the paperback. I honestly forget if I made some form of this joke in the novel you just (presumably??) read, but I remember making the credits pages for teenage ZZT games: one writes a whole list of jobs, *writer designer producer producer's assistant*, and then one lists one's own name for them all. What a rush! But the secret plot of this book is about how we move from that to this, and the above names are its secret protagonists. Thank you; thank you all.